Simplicius Simplicissimus

Simplicius Simplicissimus

Hans Jakob Christoffel von
Grimmelshausen

Translated by Hellmuth Weissenborn
and Lesley Macdonald

ALMA CLASSICS

ALMA CLASSICS
an imprint of

ALMA BOOKS LTD
Thornton House
Thornton Road
Wimbledon Village
London SW19 4NG
United Kingdom
www.almaclassics.com

Simplicius Simplicissimus first published in German in 1669
This translation of *Simplicius Simplicissimus* first published by John
Calder (Publishers) Ltd in 1964
A new edition published by Calder Publications in 2010
This new, revised edition published by Alma Classics in 2023

Translation © Alma Books Ltd

Cover: nathanburtondesign.com

Printed in Great Britain by CPI Group (UK) Ltd, Croydon CR0 4YY

MIX
Paper | Supporting
responsible forestry
FSC
www.fsc.org
FSC® C171272

ISBN: 978-1-84749-878-6

Contents

Introduction

Simplicius Simplicissimus was written over three hundred and fifty years ago. As a novel it is incomparable in its significance – a work of great poetic beauty, satirical strength and a lasting historical document of timeless value. For nearly two centuries its author was unknown to the world, for his name appeared in disguise on the title page of the first editions. The German Romantics Clemens Brentano, Achim von Arnim and Josef von Eichendorff rediscovered the importance of this extraordinary work, and Echtermeyer's research at the beginning of the nineteenth century cast some light on the personality of the writer. Subsequently, the thorough and magnificent research of Hendrik Scholte, the philologist, succeeded in solving the remaining riddles of authorship, and transformed an anonymous soldier-writer into the personality of Hans Jakob Christoffel von Grimmelshausen – the earliest novelist in the German language.

However, only a few details are known about the author. He was born at Gelnhausen in the Spessart near Hanau, probably about 1622 during the horrors of the Thirty Years War. When little older than twelve years he was captured by marauding soldiers, Hessians or Croats, and forced to join the mixed-baggage train of sick soldiers, horse-boys, harlots and hangers-on that followed the armies on their marches. At an early age he joined the Imperial Army as a musketeer and took part in the campaigns through Germany from Westphalia to the Swiss border. Most probably he was involved in the second Siege of Magdeburg in 1636, in the Battle of Wittstock the same year, and also in the fighting around Breisach. From 1643 he was a regimental clerk in Offenburg, and after the war, in 1648, he settled in the Black Forest. In 1667 he was Schultheiss of Renchen under the Bishop of Strasburg, and he died in 1676 at the age of fifty-one as a Catholic. His wanderings definitely took him to Westphalia, Saxony, Bohemia and Switzerland, probably even to parts of Russia, to Amsterdam and Paris.

Apart from a liking for mystification, Grimmelshausen had some reason for disguising his real name behind pseudonyms and anagrams (of which there are about nine altogether): the political atmosphere and the snobbery of high society towards "vulgar" natural writing, which was contrary to the stilted and professional style fashionable at the time.

Grimmelshausen's first satirical book was published in 1666, *Schwarz und Weiss, oder Die Satirische pilgerin* (*Black and White, or The Satirical Pilgrim*), and *Der Abentheuerliche Simplicissimus Teutsch* (*Simplicius Simplicissimus*) appeared in Nuremberg in 1669. In addition to *Simplicius* there are three smaller "Simpliciania" novels extant: *Die Landstörzerin Courage* (*Courage, the Adventuress* – taken up by Bert Brecht); *Der Seltsame Springinsfeld* (*The Strange Jump-into-the-Field*) and *Das Wunderbarliche Vogel-Nest* (*The Magical Bird's Nest*). The convincing and natural strength of his autobiographical narrative gained immediate and astonishing success for *Simplicius*, and a year after first publication a new edition was issued. Indeed so great was its success and popularity among readers that imitations and competitive editions by other publishers urged Grimmelshausen to add a sequel, to which later even more additions and embellishments were made. These have in the end done a disservice to the original concept of the book, which after the author's death took even more grotesque forms, partly caused by a pirating publisher in Frankfurt who made use of the great popularity of *Simplicius* and edited it in a normalized version of German.

The translators, facing at least half a dozen modern German editions, thought the best solution was to use the original edition of Grimmelshausen's *Simplicissimus Teutsch*, a precise reprint of the 1669 *editio princeps* in the original version and language, edited by E. H. Scholte (Tübingen: Max Niemeyer Verlag, 1854), who based his edition on the Berlin University's copy which had belonged to the famous Jacob Grimm. There is a copy of this edition in the British Museum. By using that original version the unity, character and original concept of the book in its true dramatic form are preserved, and the aim was to render the work into English in a style acceptable for modern readers, without expurgation, but retaining the vigour, truthfulness and occasional coarseness of the language – characteristics indivisible from Grimmelshausen as well as from the baroque way of life. Apart from a few repetitive passages which have been shortened, the translators have neither omitted any character nor event, so that this rendering is the first unexpurgated edition in English.

Simplicius Simplicissimus is fascinating to read. The horrors of war in which thousands of villages in Germany were deserted, huge parts of the land completely laid waste and half or more of the population lost through murder, battle, fire and famine, are narrated by an eyewitness, making this book a document of human suffering, folly and courage par excellence. The hero, Simplicius, a child thrown into the abyss of human errors, sees and participates in it all, yet is able to describe the zeitgeist with both satire and wit, and shows how in the end humanity triumphs over brutality. It is remarkable how three hundred and fifty years ago a simple but open-minded man described his fellow soldiers, country people and townsmen with such fidelity and understanding of their social relationship, probing and discovering the problems of the time in their significance for the present and the future. The abyss of human hell was opened: vice, crime, cruelty and hate were let loose; murder, robbery, gambling and whoring were commonplace; soldiers and priests, racketeers and torturers, parvenus and fools, and the sober working man, are images of humanity that could be alive today. Only the frame and the costume have changed, and the machinery of war, but the human element is the same. Comparisons with our own time are obvious, yet there is consolation and hope for mankind – the human soul which turns away from crime and temptation and finds refuge in spiritual values.

Grimmelshausen shows a rare and extraordinary insight and foresight when he describes the secular and Christian utopias in the fantastic superstate revealed through the mouth of the madman, Jupiter, or the quasi-communist Christian society of the Hungarian brethren. His moral philosophy finds its culmination in the visit to Mummelsee, stressing the possibility of salvation for the human race with a chance ultimately to see God face to face. Noteworthy is his visionary image of the tree of social order, on which everyone tries to climb to the upper branches pressing down the people below.

Although his knowledge of natural science and especially military science, chemistry and geography is considerable, he is still entangled in the belief of witchcraft, Walpurgisnacht and superstitions such as invulnerability, soothsaying and prophecy. He certainly believes what he tells of his own religious conversion in Einsiedeln, and although most probably born of Protestant parents, he turned to Catholicism in the end. He shows great understanding and tolerance to most religious beliefs, which is astonishing in a religious war of this magnitude. It was enough for him to be a Christian; he argues that only one of the three Christian confessions – Catholic, Protestant and Reformist – could possibly be the right one, refusing at first to embrace any, thus anticipating a philosophical attitude which more than a century later was taken up by Lessing in his play *Nathan der Weise* (*Nathan the Wise*).

Through the heights and depths of human frailty, sin and foolishness, Simplicius finds his way, as did Parsifal, Eulenspiegel and Dr Faustus. He too succumbs to vice, crime and deceit, but purifies himself and returns to the simplicity of his early youth, thus closing the circle of his life in a magnificent curve. The novel is full of natural strength, born from an unspoilt and open heart.

Grimmelshausen's poetic genius has created a timeless novel in which the adventures of his own life are intermingled with the tragedies of the Thirty Years War. His own experiences combined with events which he witnessed, heard or read, formed the source of his fantasy. *Dichtung* and *wahrheit* both play their part: some pages have even been borrowed from other books (as we now know), yet the strength of his own poetical vision is never disturbed.

– Helmut Weissenborn

Simplicius Simplicissimus

PART ONE

SIMPLICIUS TELLS OF HIS YOUTH

IN OUR CENTURY – and many believe it may be the last – there is a craze, among common people who have saved enough to afford a new-fashioned costume with silk ribbons, of pretending to be lordly masters and noblemen of very old descent. But if you look closer, you will find their forbears were hirelings or carriers; their cousins donkey drivers, their brothers beadles, bum-bailiffs; their sisters whores, and their mothers procuresses or even witches. In short, their whole lineage of all thirty-two forbears is somewhat sullied and besmirched. Indeed these new noblemen are often as black as if they had been born and bred in Guinea.

I do not want to put myself on the same level with such foolish people, although to tell the truth I often imagine that I too have my origin from a great lord, or at least from a lesser nobleman, for by my nature I was always inclined to exercise the craft of a gentleman. Seriously, my descent and education can well be compared with that of a prince. My dad – that is the name given to a father in the Spessart mountains – had his own palace, the like of which no king could build for himself. It was made of loam, and instead of infertile slates, cold lead or red copper, it was thatched with straw grown from the noble corn. The wall surrounding his castle was not built of quarry stones which can be found on the road, even less made with untidy bricks as other lords used, but was of oak wood – that useful, lofty tree bearing sausages and fat hams, and which needs more than a hundred years to reach its maturity. Where is the monarch who can do as well? His rooms and halls and chambers were blackened inside by smoke, for this is the most constant colour in the world, and such painting needs for its completion more time than a painter gives to his most magnificent works of art. The tapestries were of the tenderest tissues in the world, for they were woven by the master spider who once competed with Minerva herself. His windows were dedicated to St No-Glass, for they were covered with linen, which takes for its making more time and labour than the most transparent glass of Murano. Instead of pages, lackeys and stable hands, he had sheep, goats and pigs, everything orderly dressed in its natural livery. Often they offered their service to me in the fields, until I tired of it and chased them homewards. The armoury was sufficiently stocked with ploughs, axes, hoes, shovels, forks for dung and hay, and every day my dad practised in the use of these weapons. Hoeing and ploughing was his military discipline; to yoke the oxen was his duty as a captain. To cart away the dung was his method of fortification, and tilling the land his campaign; chopping wood his daily exercise, clearing the manure from the stables his noble entertainment and his tournament. With all this he held his own in his world and gained at each harvest rich reward. I do not praise myself for all of that, lest anyone should ridicule me as a new nobleman. I do not pretend to be better than my dad. His abode was in a pleasant place, namely in the Spessart mountains, where the wolves bid each other goodnight.

According to the lordly custom of the house, my education developed. When I was ten years of age, I already understood my dad's gentlemanly exercises. In figures, however, I could hardly count up to five, because my dad followed the usage of present times, when noble people do not bother much about studies and school pranks, as they have servants to do this drudgery. Besides, I was an accomplished musician on the bagpipes, with which I could play melodies so pleasant that I almost outdid the famous Orpheus. Concerning theology, I do not think that there was anybody of my age in the whole of Christendom that could be compared with me: I knew neither God nor men, neither Heaven nor Hell, neither angel nor devil, and knew not how to distinguish between good and evil. Thus I lived as our first parents in Paradise, who in their innocence knew just as little of illness, death and dying as of the resurrection. Oh, happy life! You could well say, "life of an ass"! Yes, I was so complete and perfect in my ignorance that it was impossible for me to know that I knew nothing. I say it again: oh, happy life that I led then! But my dad did not want me to enjoy such happiness any longer, and thought it proper that I should live and work to the standards of my noble birth; so he began to guide me to higher things and give me more difficult lessons.

He installed me with the most glorious dignity not only of his own rural court, but of the world – that is, with the profession of a shepherd. Firstly he entrusted me with his sows, secondly with his goats, and lastly with his whole herd of sheep, so that I should care for them, shepherd them and protect them from the wolf through the sound of my bagpipe. Well could I be compared with David, only that he instead of bagpipes had a harp. My investiture was a good omen that I should become in time a world-famous man, if good fortune blessed me, because from the beginning of time great men were often shepherds. We can read in the Holy Scriptures of Abel, Abraham, Isaac, Jacob and his son, and even Moses himself, who shepherded the sheep of his brother-in-law before he became the leader and lawgiver over six hundred thousand men in Israel. Of course you could say that these were holy men of God and no peasant boy from the Spessart who knew nothing of God, but who could blame my innocence? Even among the old heathens we find such examples as we do with God's chosen people. Romulus and Remus were shepherds, and so was Spartacus, before whom the whole Roman might trembled. Shepherds they were all: Paris, King Priam's son, and Anchises, father of the Trojan prince Aeneas, the handsome Endymion, for whom the chaste Diana fretted, and the horrible Polyphemus. Yes, even the gods themselves were not ashamed of this profession; Apollo was cowherd to King Admetus, Mercury, his son Daphnis, Pan and Proteus were arch-shepherds, and are still the shepherds' patrons. The Jew, Philo, rightly speaks about this: "The work of a shepherd is a beginning and a preparation for governing, for as a warlike nature is best trained and exercised through hunting, so should he who is destined to govern be first educated in the pleasant and friendly duties of a shepherd." All this my dad must have had in his mind, and that is why even up to this hour he has given me great hopes of my future glory.

To come back to my herd, however, you should understand that I knew the wolf just as little as I knew my own ignorance. Therefore my dad continued more eagerly with his admonishments: "Boy, work hard! Don't let the sheep run away from each other. Play loudly on your bagpipe so that the wolf doesn't come and do damage, for he is a four-legged rogue and thief, devouring man and beast; if you are lazy I will beat your buttocks!"

I answered with equal charm: "Dad, can you tell me what the wolf looks like? I have never seen a wolf."

"Oh, you clumsy head of an ass," he replied, "you will stay a fool all your life. I wonder what will become of you. You are already such a big dunce and don't know yet what kind of a four-legged rogue the wolf is."

He gave me still more advice and at last became angry so that he went away grumbling. For he thought that my dull brain could not grasp his delicate indoctrination.

But I began to make such a noise with my bagpipe that one could have poisoned the toads in the kitchen-garden, and so I felt safe enough from the wolf who was always in my mind. And because my mum (so the mothers in the Spessart and Vogelsberg are called) told me she was afraid the chickens might die of my singing, so I liked to sing to make my magic against the wolf the stronger. I sang a song which I had learnt from my mum herself:

You peasant-folk, though much despised,
Deserve to be most greatly prized,
No man can set your worth too high
Who looks on you with honest eye.

What kind of world would be revealed
If Adam had not tilled the field?
By hoeing earth the man is fed
From whom a princely line is bred.

The produce of the fruitful soil
Must everywhere await your toil,
The nourishment of all the land
Is first provided by your hand.

The Emperor, whom God ordained
As our Defender, is maintained
By cottars' work, and soldiering bands
Live on the plunder of your lands.

Yours is the meat on which we dine
And yours the hand that prunes the vine;
The earth must feel your ploughman's tread
Before she blesses us with bread.

How desolate the earth would be,
Untended by your husbandry;
What sorrows would beset the place
Uncheered by any country face!

Therefore we rightly honour you
Upon whose nourishment we grew.
Nature bestows her loving praise
And God has blessed your rural ways.

You hear no country-folk complain
Of bitter gout's reproachful pain,
But often enough it must beget
A rich man's death, a lord's regret.

You in your innocence are free
Of our new age's vanity,
And lest you ever fall from grace
God gives you greater griefs to face.

The worst that soldiers can commit
Still works towards your benefit;
Lest pride take hold of you by stealth
They say: We claim your worldly wealth!

Here I ended my song, for I and my whole herd of sheep were surrounded almost in one moment by a troop of cuirassiers who, lost in the great forest, had found their way back through my music.

"Oho!" I thought. "These are the fellows – here are those four-legged rogues and thieves of whom my dad told me!"

For at first I considered horse and man – as once the Mexicans the Spanish cavalry – to be one single creature and did not doubt they must be wolves. Therefore I wanted to frighten these horrible centaurs and drive them away. But as soon as I had blown up my bagpipe to such purpose, one of them grabbed me by the arm and slung me with such vehemence onto a farm-horse which they had just looted, that I tumbled down again on the other side onto my beloved bagpipe. Whereupon the pipe started to wail horribly and to make such a mournful sound as if it wanted to move the whole world to compassion. But it was of no avail: although my pipe did not spare its last breath to mourn my misery, I was forced onto the horse again. God knows what my bagpipe had sung and uttered – but my greatest worry was that the horsemen pretended that I had hurt my bagpipe whilst falling on it, and that was the reason why it had made such an unholy noise. Fantastic ideas then raced through my mind, for while I was sitting on this animal, which I had never before seen, I imagined I would be turned into a man of iron, for I thought those who led me away to be entirely of iron. But as such a change did not happen, I concluded in my stupid mind that these strange creatures had come only for the purpose of helping me to drive my sheep home, inasmuch as no one had devoured a sheep.

We all trotted directly to my dad's farm and I looked out for my dad and my mum expecting them to come out to bid us welcome. But in vain! He and my mum as well as our Ursula, who is my dad's only daughter, had run away through the back-door, not wishing to await these guests.

Although it was not my intention to lead these riders to my dad's farm, truth demands that I leave to posterity the cruelties committed in this our German war, to prove these evils were done to our advantage. Who else would have told me there was a God in Heaven if the warriors had not destroyed my father's house and forced me, through my captivity, to meet other people, for till this moment I had imagined my dad, mum and the rest of our household to be the sole inhabitants of this earth, as no other man nor human dwelling were known to me but the one where I daily went in and out. Soon I had to learn man's origin in this world. I was merely a human in shape and a Christian only in name, otherwise just an animal. Our gracious God looked upon my innocence with pity and wished to bring me both to his and my awareness, and although there were a thousand ways of doing this, he used the one by which my dad and mum were punished as an example to others for their careless education of me.

The first thing that the riders did was to stable their horses. After that each one started his own business which indicated nothing but ruin and destruction. While some started to slaughter, cook and fry, so that it looked as though they wished to prepare a gay feast, others stormed through the house from top to bottom as if the golden fleece of Colchis were hidden there. Others again took linen, clothing and other goods, making them into bundles as if they intended going to market; what they did not want was broken up and destroyed. Some stabbed their swords through hay and straw as if they had not enough pigs to stab. Some shook the feathers out of the beds and filled the ticks with ham and dried meat as if they could sleep more comfortably on these. Others smashed the ovens and windows as if to announce an eternal summer. They beat copper and pewter vessels into lumps and packed the mangled pieces away. Bedsteads, tables, chairs and benches were burnt although many stacks of dried wood stood in the yard. Earthenware pots and pans were all broken, perhaps because our guests preferred roasted meats, or perhaps they intended to eat only one meal with us. Our maid had been treated in the stable in such a way that she could not leave it any more – a shameful thing to tell! They bound the farm-hand and laid him on the earth, put a clamp of wood in his mouth, and emptied a milking churn full of horrid dung water into his belly. This they called the Swedish drink, and they forced him to lead a party of soldiers to another place, where they looted men and cattle and brought them back to our yard. Among them were my dad, my mum and Ursula.

The soldiers now started to take the flints out of their pistols and in their stead screwed the thumbs of the peasants, and they tortured the poor wretches as if they were burning witches. They put one of the captive peasants into the baking-oven and put fire on him, although he had confessed nothing. Then they tied a rope round the head of another one, and twisted it with the help of a stick so tightly that blood gushed out through his mouth, nose and ears. In short, everybody had his own invention to torture the peasants and each peasant suffered his own martyrdom. My dad alone appeared to me the most fortunate, for he confessed with laughter what others were forced to say under pains and miserable lament, and such honour was done to him without doubt because he was the master of the house. They put him next to a fire, tied him so that he could move neither hands nor feet, and rubbed the soles of his feet with wet salt, which our old goat had to lick off. This tickled him so much that he almost wanted to burst with laughter, and it seemed to me so gentle and pleasant – for I had never seen nor heard my dad making such long-lasting laughter – that I half in companionship and half in ignorance joined heartily with him. In such merriment he confessed his guilt and revealed the hidden treasure, which was richer in gold, pearls and jewels than might have been expected of a peasant. What happened to the captive women, maids and daughters I do not know, as the soldiers would not let me watch how they dealt with them. I only very well remember that I heard them miserably crying in corners here and there, and I believe my mum and our Ursula had no better fate than the others.

In the midst of this misery I turned the spit and did not worry, as I hardly understood what all this meant. In the afternoon I helped to water the horses and so found our maid in the stable looking amazingly dishevelled. I did not recognize her but she spoke to me with pitiful voice:

"Oh, run away, boy, or the soldiers will take you with them. Look out, escape! Can't you see how evil…"

More she could not say.

Escape, but where to? My mind was much too weak to find a plan but towards evening I succeeded in escaping into the woods. Where to now? The roads and the woods were to me as little known as the straits through the frozen sea beyond Nova Zembla* which lead to China. Although the deep black night enveloped me, it seemed to my frightened mind not dark enough. So I hid myself in some dense bushes where I still could hear the cries of the tortured peasants and the song of the nightingale. Thus I laid myself carelessly down and fell asleep.

When the morning star in the East started to flicker I saw my dad's house in flames but nobody to quench them. I crawled out hoping to find some of my people but was soon seen by five horsemen who shouted:

"Boy, come over here, or the devil take you! We will shoot you so that you belch smoke!"

I remained standing still and stiff with my mouth open as I did not know what the horsemen wanted, and I looked at them as a cat at a new stable-door. As they were unable to cross to me because a swamp lay between, this made them angry and one of them emptied his carabine at me. The sudden fire and unexpected bang, which the echo made even more terrifying, frightened me to such an extent that I at once fell down to the earth with all four limbs stretched out. I did not move a vein from fear and although the riders went their way, without doubt leaving me for dead, the whole day I did not find the courage to get up nor to look around.

Only when night fell again I rose and wandered a long time in the forest, until I saw a rotting tree, its phosphorescence shimmering in the distance, which terrified me anew. At once I turned back and walked along until again I saw another rotting tree, from which again I ran away. In this way I spent the night approaching and fleeing from one decaying tree to another.

At last sweet daylight came to my help urging the trees to cease plaguing me, but this was not much help, for my heart was full of fear and fright, my legs full of tiredness, my empty stomach full of hunger, my mouth full of thirst, my mind full of foolish imagination, and my eyes full of sleep. I still went on, but did not know where to; the farther I went, the deeper I came into the forest away from my people. An unintelligent animal in my stead would have better known what to do for its preservation. Yet I was clever enough, when again darkness fell, to crawl into a hollow tree, and thus to shelter myself for the night.

2

SIMPLICIUS MEETS THE HERMIT

SCARCELY HAD I SETTLED DOWN to sleep when I heard a voice:

> "Oh, Great Love for us ungrateful men!
> Oh, my only Consolation: my Hope,
> My Treasure, oh my God!"

And more, which I could neither remember nor understand. These were words which in my straits could have consoled and gladdened a Christian's heart. But, oh, simplicity and ignorance! To me they were alien sounds and an incomprehensible language from which I could grasp nothing but that which frightened me by its strangeness.

But hearing that the hunger and thirst of him who spoke thus should be stilled, my unbearable hunger and empty stomach urged me to invite myself as a guest. Therefore I took courage to leave my hollow tree and to approach the voice I had heard. I became aware of a tall man with grey-black hair hanging down raggedly on his shoulders. He had a wild beard almost shaped like a Swiss cheese. His face, though pale yellow and haggard, was yet refined and his long robe was stitched and patched out of more than a thousand pieces of cloth. Round his neck and his body he had wound a heavy iron chain like St Wilhelmus, and altogether appeared to my eyes so horrible and frightening that I started to tremble like a wet dog. My fear increased even more when he took a crucifix about six feet long and pressed it against his breast, and not knowing what to make of him I could only think that this old man must be the wolf of whom my dad had spoken.

In an agony of fear I reached for my bagpipe which I had saved as my only treasure from the horsemen. I blew, tuned up and made a terrific noise to drive this horrid wolf away. Such sudden and strange music in this wild place shocked the hermit at first, doubtless believing a devilish monster had come as had happened once to the great Antonius, to frighten and disturb his prayers. But as soon as he recovered, he mocked me as his tempter in the hollow tree into which I had taken refuge again. Indeed he was so courageous that he advanced towards me to jeer the enemy of mankind:

"Oho," he said, "you are the right fellow to disturb saintly men..."

More I could not understand as his approach caused in me such shuddering and horror that I lost my senses and swooned away. I do not remember how I came to myself again. I only know that I found myself outside the hollow tree and the old man was holding my head on his lap and had opened my jerkin. When I saw the hermit so close to me I started such a gruesome crying in fear that he might tear the heart out of my body. But he said:

"My son, be quiet! I will not harm you. Be calm."

But the more he tried to console me and caress me, the more I cried.

"Oh, you will devour me! You are the wolf and you will eat me up!"

"Oh, no, my son," he said. "Be calm. I won't eat you."

This struggle I continued for a long while until at last I was persuaded to follow him into his hut. Here Poverty was housekeeper, Hunger was cook and Scarcity was kitchen maid. My belly was refreshed with some vegetables and a drink of water, and my mind which was completely confused was consoled through the old man's friendliness. Thereafter I easily followed the temptations of sweet sleep and paid my tribute to nature. The hermit understood my need and left me alone in his hut as there was room for one only. About midnight I woke up again and heard him singing this song, which I later learnt myself:

Come, nightingale, console the night!
Allow your voice's smooth delight
To fill the air with ringing;
Come, magnify your Maker's name
And put all sleeping birds to shame
That will not join your singing:
Pour from your throat
Your crystal call: you can for all
The earth recite
God's praises in the heavenly height.

Although the light has died away
And now we must in darkness stay,
Yet we in jubilation
Sing of God's goodness and His power
Because no night can hinder our

Unending acclamation.
Pour from your throat
Your crystal call: you can for all
The earth recite
God's praises in the heavenly height.

Echo, wild and wandering noise,
Seeks out the clamour of your joys,
All descants far excelling:
No lurking weariness can be
Our master while his melody
All slumber is dispelling.
Pour from your throat
Your crystal call: you can for all
The earth recite
God's praises in the heavenly height.

The stars which ornament the sky
Reveal themselves to glorify
And honour God's creation.
The owl as well, who cannot sing,
Is hooting that she too may bring
To God her adoration.
Pour from your throat
Your crystal call: you can for all
The earth recite
God's praises in the heavenly height.

Come, songbird closest to my heart,
We will not play the sluggards' part
And waste the night with slumbers:
But rather till the blushing day
Has made these gloomy forests gay
Praise God in tuneful numbers.
Pour from your throat
Your crystal call: you can for all
The earth recite
God's praises in the heavenly height.

During this song I really believed that nightingale and owl and echo had joined in, and if I had known the melody I would have rushed out of the hut to get my bagpipe, so enchanted was I with the harmony of the song. But I fell asleep again and did not wake up until well into the day, when the hermit stood before me and said:

"Get up, my little one. I will give you food and then show you the path through the forest that you may reach your people and get to the next village before nightfall."

I asked him:

"What do you mean by 'people' and 'village'?"

"Have you never been in a village," he said, "and do you not know what people or men are?"

"No," I replied, "Nowhere have I been but here. But tell me, what are people, men and village?"

"God bless me," answered the hermit, "are you a fool or sane?"

"No," said I, "my mum's and my dad's boy am I, and not a fool or sane."

The hermit was amazed and crossed himself, sighing deeply.

"Well, dear child, for God's sake, I am obliged to enlighten you."

And then our questions and answers went on as follows:

"What is your name?"

"I am called Boy."

"I can well see that you are not a little girl. What did your father and mother call you?"

"I had no father nor mother."

"Who then gave you your shirt?"

"Oh, my mum."

"What did your mum call you?"

"She called me boy, even rascal, long-eared ass, clumsy dunce, gallows-bird."

"Who was your mum's husband?"

"Nobody."

"With whom did your mum sleep at night?"

"With my dad."

"What did your dad call you?"

"He, too, called me Boy."

"But what was the name of your dad?"

"He's called Dad."

"What did your mum call him?"

"Dad, and even Master."

"Did she never call him something else?"

"Oh yes, she did."

"What, then?"

"Bully, rough bumpkin, old pig, and many more names when she was cross."

"You are a poor, ignorant wretch, for you know neither your parents' nor your own name."

"Oho, but neither do you!"

"Do you know how to pray?"

"No, my dad told me only wolves prey."

"That's not what I mean, but whether you know the Lord's prayer. 'Our Father…'"

"Yes, I know it."

"Then, repeat it."

"Our dear Father, chart in Heaven, hollow they name, kingdom come, woe-be-gone on earth and Heaven, give us trespass as we give trespass, not in temptation but deliver us from kingdom, power and glory for ever and ever Ama."

"Have you ever been to church?"

"Tell me, what is a church?"

"Oh, God bless me, don't you know anything about our Lord?"

"Yes, I do. He hangs at our chamber door where my mum glued him when she brought him back from the church festival."

"Oh, merciful God, now I see what a blessing and grace it is when you bestow your knowledge upon us. Oh, Lord, make me worthy to honour your holy name and to thank you for your grace which you have amply given to me. Hear, now. Simplicius – for I can't call you by any other name – when you say the Lord's prayer you must say it like this: 'Our Father which art in Heaven, hallowed be thy name. Thy kingdom come, Thy will be done on earth as it is in heaven. Give us this day our daily bread and…'"

"And cheese as well."

"Dear child, be quiet and learn; that is more important to you than cheese. A lad such as you should not interrupt an old man in his speech, but be silent, listen and learn. If only I knew where your parents live I would like to take you back and teach them as well how to bring up their children."

"I don't know where to go. Our house is burnt down and my mum has run away, and my dad too; and our maid was ill in the stable."

"Who has burnt down your house?"

"Oh, iron men came. They were sitting on things as big as oxen but without horns. They stabbed sheep, cows and pigs, and so I ran away, and then the house was burnt."

"Where was your dad, then?"

"Oh, the iron men bound him up and our old goat licked his feet, and so my dad had to laugh and gave the iron men many silver coins, big ones and small ones, also pretty yellow ones and lovely glittering things, and a pretty string with white beads."

"And when did that happen?"

"Oh, when I was shepherding the sheep. They even wanted to take my bagpipe."

"When were you looking after the sheep?"

"Oh, didn't you hear, when the iron men came, and then our Ann told me to run away, or the soldiers would take me with them; she meant the iron men, so I ran away, and came here."

"And where do you want to go now?"

"I don't know. I will stay with you."

"To keep you here is neither good for you nor me; eat now and afterwards I will take you back to your people."

"Oh, tell me, what do you mean by 'people'?"

"People are men like you and I. Your dad, your mum, and your Ann are humans, and when there are many together we call them people. Now go and eat."

This was our conversation during which the hermit looked at me often with the deepest of sighs, and I do not know whether it was because he pitied my very great simplicity and ignorance, or because of a reason about which I heard many years later.

I started to eat and stopped chattering, and when I had eaten enough the old man told me to go away. So I used the tenderest words which my peasant rudeness allowed to persuade him to keep me with him, and although he found it difficult he at last consented to let me stay, more perhaps to teach me the Christian religion than to make use of my help in his old age. His greatest worry was that my tender youth would not be able to endure for long the rigours of such a hard life.

My proving time lasted about three weeks. I behaved so well that the hermit developed a strange liking for me, not so much because of the work I did for him but because I was so eager to listen to his teachings and the smooth waxlike tablet of my heart was able to accept them. For these reasons he became more and more enthused to lead me to godliness.

He started his lessons with the fall of Lucifer. From there we came to Paradise from which we and our forbears were dispelled. We touched on the law of Moses, and he taught me with the help of God's ten commandments and their interpretation – of which he said they are the true guide to learn God's will – to distinguish virtue from vice and to do good and avoid evil. At last he came to the Gospels and he told me of Christ's birth, suffering, death and resurrection. Finally he concluded with the Last Judgment, and evoked heaven and earth before my eyes. All this he did without diffuseness, as in this way he believed I would better understand it. When he had finished with one subject, he started another, and was able to answer my questions so kindly that he could not have instructed me better. His life and his lessons were to me a continuous sermon which I absorbed through God's grace fruitfully, for my mind was not at all so stupid and wooden. So in three weeks' time I had not only grasped all that which a Christian should know but I developed such a love for his teachings, that I could scarcely sleep at night.

Since then I have thought very often of these events and have found that Aristotle in the third book of his writings, *De anima*, concluded rightly in comparing the human soul with an empty, unmarked tablet of wax. The reason why I comprehended everything that the pious hermit taught me so quickly was that he found the tablet of my soul completely empty and lacking impressed pictures on it which could prevent acceptance of his teaching. In spite of all that, my naive simplicity towards other people remained unchanged, and that is why the hermit – as he did not know my real name – continued to call me Simplicius. I learnt even to pray, and when he at last had given in to my persistent intention to stay with him, we built a hut similar to his own for me. It was of wood, twigs and earth, shaped almost like the tents of the musketeers in the field, or even more like the dug-outs which peasants make for their turnips, and so low that I could hardly sit in it. My bed was made of dry leaves and grass, and was just as long as the hut itself so that I do not know whether I should call such an abode or hole, a covered bed or a hut.

The first time I saw the hermit reading the Bible, I was unable to imagine with whom he could be having such a secret yet solemn conversation. I perceived very well the movement of his lips and even heard him murmur, but I saw and heard nobody who talked to him, although I did not know anything of reading and writing, I realized through his eyes that it had something to do with the book.

I watched the book carefully and when he had put it aside I took and opened it by chance at the first chapter of Job, and a beautifully illuminated woodcut appeared before my eyes. I asked the pictures odd questions, but as I got no answers, I became impatient and said, just when the hermit unnoticed stood behind me:

"You little bunglers, have you no tongues any more? Haven't you just spoken to my father?" (That is what I called the hermit.) "I see well that you drive my poor dad's sheep away, and burn his house – stop! I will quench this fire."

With that I got up to fetch water as I thought it was needed.

"Where to, Simplicius?" asked the hermit behind my back.

"Oh, father," I answered, "There are soldiers. They have sheep and want to drive them away. They have taken them from the poor man with whom you have spoken; his house is in full flame and will soon burn down if I don't put it out."

With these words I pointed with my finger at what I saw.

"Keep still," said the hermit, "There is no danger here."

I answered, according to my idea of politeness: "But are you blind? Stop them from driving the sheep away whilst I fetch water!"

"Oho," said the hermit, "These pictures are not alive. They are only made to bring old stories before our eyes."

I answered: "But you yourself have talked to them just now. Why should they not be alive?"

The hermit was forced to laugh, quite against his will and habit, and said: "Dear child, these pictures cannot talk. But what their meaning and character is I can see from these small black lines. This is called reading, and when I read you think I am talking with the pictures but that is not so."

I replied: "If I am a human as you are I should be able to see from the black lines what you can see. How can I understand your words, dear father? Do explain it to me."

Thereupon he said: "Well, my son, I will teach you so that you can talk to these pictures just as well as I can, and so that you will understand what they mean. However it will take time in which I must have patience and you perseverance."

He then wrote me an alphabet on birch bark which was shaped like the printed letters and when I knew the letters I learnt to spell, and later to read, and at last to write even better than the hermit himself as I always copied the printed type.

I remained about two years in this forest until the hermit died, and after that perhaps still a little longer than half a year. Therefore I think it as well to describe to the curious reader what he might care to know of our work, doings and how we spent our life.

Our food consisted of all sorts of vegetables from our garden, carrots, cabbage, beans, peas. We did not refuse beech nuts, wild apples, pears and cherries, even acorns when we were hungry. The bread, or better cake, we baked in hot ashes from ground maize. In winter we caught birds with traps and nets; in spring and summer God presented us with young ones from the nests. Often we had nothing but snails and frogs. And we did not dislike fishing with nets and hook, for not far from our hut there flowed a stream rich in fish and crayfish. Once we caught a young wild pigling which we put into a sty and reared and fattened it with acorns and beech-nuts, which in the end we ate. My hermit knew that it could not be a sin if one enjoys what God has created for such purpose. We used very little salt, and no spice at all, to avoid arousing the lust for drinking as we had no cellar. Our supply of salt we obtained from a parson who lived about ten miles away from us and of whom I still have much to say.

As for utensils, we were sufficiently stocked. We had a shovel, a hoe, an axe, a chopper, and an iron pot for cooking, which however was not our property but was borrowed from the parson. Each of us had a much-used worn knife. These were our possessions – nothing else. We did not need bowls, plates, spoons, forks, cauldrons, frying pans, roasting spits, nor salt cellar nor other table and kitchen ware, for our pot served us as bowl, and our hands were our forks and spoons. If we wanted to drink we used a pipe at the well, or put our mouths into the water. We had no clothing, no wool, no silk, no cotton, nor linen, for bed, table and tapestries, but that which we carried on our bodies, and we thought we had enough when we were able to protect ourselves from rain and frost.

We kept no special rule or order in our household except on Sundays and Holy Days, when we started to depart about midnight in order to reach the parson's church early without being observed by anyone, for it was a little away from the village. There we climbed onto the broken organ from where we could see the altar and pulpit. When I saw the priest for the first time entering the pulpit I asked the hermit what he wanted to do in this big tub. After the service was over we went home in the same way unobserved as we arrived; with tired feet and body we reached our abode and with good teeth ate bad fare. The rest of the time the hermit spent in praying and instructing me in godly things.

On working days we did what was most urgent and that which time and circumstance made necessary. Sometimes we worked in the garden, another time we collected rich soil instead of dung from shady places and from hollow trees to improve our kitchen-garden. Sometimes we wove baskets or fish-traps, or prepared firewood, went fishing, or occupied ourselves with other tasks against idleness.

Under all these occupations the hermit never ceased to teach me faithfully in all good faculties. In the mean time, I learnt by this hard life to endure hunger, heat, cold and heavy labour – indeed, to overcome every hardship and, above all, to recognize God and serve him truthfully. This was the noblest task of all.

My loyal hermit wished me to know only as much as he believed a Christian should know to reach best his goal, to pray and work hard. So it happened that I became well acquainted with Christian knowledge, and could speak the German language most beautifully as if it were spoken by Orthographia herself, but nevertheless I remained a simpleton. So much so that when I eventually left the forest, I was such a miserable fool in the ways of the world that not even a dog would leave his place by the stove to answer my call.

I spent almost two years in this manner, and was scarcely accustomed to the strenuous life of a hermit when my best friend on earth took his hoe, gave me the shovel and led me, as it was his daily habit, to our garden, where we used to say our prayers.

"Now, Simplicius, dear child," he said, "God be praised! The time has come that I must quit this world and leave you behind. As I can foresee vaguely that you will not stay in this wilderness for long, I want to strengthen you on the road of virtue and give you some advice which may guide your life to salvation, so that you may be blessed to stand with all the holy chosen ones in the presence of God."

His words filled my eyes with tears. They appeared to me unbearable, and I said: "My most beloved father, will you leave me alone in this wild forest? Will you…"

I could not utter more as the passionate love for my faithful father overwhelmed my tortured heart so much that I fell as though dead at his feet. But he lifted me up again, consoled me and admonished me, almost questioning my error, whether I would like to oppose the will of the Almighty.

"Don't you know," he continued, "that neither Heaven nor Hell can do this? Not like this, my son. With what do you want to burden my poor body which is longing for peace? Do you want to urge me to remain longer in this valley of lament? Oh no, my son, let me go, as God's explicit will calls me thither. With all joy I prepare myself to follow His godly command. Instead of uselessly crying, follow my last words which are: Know thyself. Even if you grow as old as Methuselah, keep this maxim in your heart. For most men are condemned because they do not know what they have been and what they could and should have become. Further: beware of bad company for its perniciousness is unspeakable."

He gave me an example, and said: "If you put a drop of Malvoisier in a vessel with vinegar, it will turn at once into vinegar. Dearest son, stand firm and don't be diverted from the praiseworthy work which you have begun, for he who perseveres will be blessed. But should you, in your human weakness, fall, do not cling spitefully to your sins but lift yourself up through penitence."

The pious man admonished me because of my youth with only these few words, for few words can be better kept in mind than a long sermon which may soon be forgotten. These three ideas: to know yourself, to avoid bad company, and to remain constant, the holy man found good and essential as he had proved them himself and had not failed in them. For after he had known himself, he fled not only bad company but even the whole world, and remained constant in that condition to his very end.

After speaking, he began to dig his own grave with a hoe and I helped as well as I could and, as he ordered me, without guessing what his intention was. And then he said to me:

"My dear, true and only son, for I have created no other being than you to the honour of our Lord, when my soul has gone to its appointed place, give my body your duty and last rites. Cover me with the earth which we have dug from this grave!"

Then he took me into his arms, pressed me and kissed me much harder to his breast than I believed it was possible for him.

"Dear child," he said, "I recommend you into God's protection, and I will die the happier in the hope that he will protect you."

I, however, could do nothing but lament and wail. I clung to his chain which he carried round his neck and hoped to keep him so that he should not escape me. But he said:

"My son, leave me, that I can see whether my grave is long enough."

Therewith he took his chain and his gown off, climbed down into the grave like somebody who wished to lie down and sleep, and said:

"Oh, great God, take again the soul which thou has given me. Lord, into thy hands I commend my spirit..."

SIMPLICIUS SIMPLICISSIMUS

He closed his lips and eyes gently; but I stood there stiff like a stock-fish and did not know that his dear soul had already left his body, as I had seen him often in such ecstasies.

I remained, as it was my habit in such events, several hours beside the grave in prayer. When my most beloved hermit did not rise I went down to him in the grave and started to shake him, to kiss and caress him. But there was no more life. Grim unrelenting Death had robbed poor Simplicius of his gentle companion. I wept and showered the soulless body with my tears, and ran with miserable crying hither and thither. At last I began with more sighs than shovels to cover him with earth, and when I had almost covered his face, I went down again and uncovered it so that I could see and kiss it once again. This I went on doing the whole day until I was finished and the funeral ceremonies had come to an end – for neither hearse, coffin, pall, candles, sexton nor clergy were present to mourn the dead.

3

SIMPLICIUS ALONE AND DREAMING

A FEW DAYS AFTER THE HERMIT'S DEATH, I made my way to the vicar and told him of my master's fate and begged his counsel on what I should do now. Although he very strongly dissuaded me from remaining longer in the forest, I insisted bravely in following my predecessor and for the whole summer I performed the duties of a pious monk.

But as time changes all things, so gradually my sorrow for the hermit waned, and the winter's frost quenched the ardour of my intentions. The more I wavered the lazier I became in my prayers, and instead of dwelling on divine thoughts I became more and more overwhelmed by a desire to see the world. Realizing that it was neither good nor useful for me to stay longer there, I concluded that I would visit the vicar again to hear whether he still advised me to leave the forest.

So I made my way to the village, but when I arrived found it in full flame; a troop of horsemen had just looted it and put it on fire. They had killed some of the peasants, driven away many and captured a few, amongst whom was the vicar. Oh, God, how human life is full of pain and misery! Scarcely one misfortune has ended when we are overcome by another. The riders were ready to go and were leading the vicar on a rope. Some shouted: "Shoot the rascal down!", and others demanded money from him. He raised his hands and asked for the sake of the Last Judgment for pardon and Christian charity. But in vain. One of them rode towards him giving him a blow over the head so that he fell to the ground and recommended his soul to God. Nor had the other captive peasants any better fate.

While the horsemen in their tyrannic cruelty appeared completely mad, a troop of armed peasants emerged from the forest as if from a disturbed wasp's nest. They started to shout horribly, and to attack and shoot so fiercely that all my hairs stood on end, for never had I participated in such a harvest festival; the peasants of the Spessart and Vogelsberg, just like the peasants of Hessen, The Sauerland and Black Forest, do not like to be insulted on their own dung heaps. With that the horsemen ran away abandoning not only the looted cattle but throwing away sack and pack with all their stolen booty in order to escape, but some of them fell into the hands of the peasants.

This entertainment almost spoilt my desire to see the world: I thought if that's how it goes, then the wilderness is far more comforting. But I wanted to hear what the vicar advised and though he was weak and powerless from wounds and bruises, he told me he could neither give advice nor help, as he himself would soon have to find his bread with the beggar's staff, for I could see that his church and vicarage were on fire. Dejected I returned to my abode in the forest, and as this journey had consoled me very little but had made me much more devoted, so I made the decision never to leave the wilderness again but to conclude my life in the meditation of divine things as the hermit had done. Indeed I even considered whether it would be possible to live without salt (which previously the vicar had provided) and so forgo the company of all humans.

To fulfil this decision and to become a real forest brother I dressed myself in my hermit's hair shirt and girdled it with his chain; not that I needed it to mortify my lustful flesh, but to imitate my predecessor, and as such clothing was better to protect me from the rough cold of the winter.

The day following the burning of the village, as I was sitting in my hut saying my prayers and cooking carrots for sustenance, about forty to fifty musketeers surrounded me. These, although astonished at my unusual appearance, stormed through my hut seeking that which was not to be found, for I had nothing but books which they threw about as they were of no value to them. Finally, looking at me more carefully and seeing what a poor bird they had trapped, they realized that there was no good booty to be gained from me. My hard life amazed them and they had great pity for my tender youth, especially the officer who was in command. Indeed he honoured me and politely requested me to show him and his men the way out of the wood in which they had been lost for a long time. I did not refuse but led them by the nearest path towards the village where the vicar had been so badly treated, as I knew no other way. Before we left the wood we saw about ten peasants partly armed with blunderbusses and others occupied in burying something. The musketeers went up to them shouting: "Halt! Halt!" The peasants answered with their guns but when they saw they were overpowered by the soldiers, they dispersed so that the tired musketeers could not follow them. The latter however dug up what the peasants had buried and this progressed the quicker as their hoes and shovels had been left behind. Hardly a few thrusts had been made when they heard a voice from below which called: "Oh, you reckless villains! You arch sinners, do you think Heaven will leave unpunished your unchristian wickedness? No, there is still many an honest fellow alive who will revenge your inhumanity, so that none of your fellow men will ever again lick your arses!"

The soldiers looked at each other as they did not know what to do. Some believed they had heard a ghost; I thought I was dreaming. The officer ordered them to go on digging. Soon they reached a barrel, broke it open and found a man in there who had neither ears or nose but still lived. As soon as he had recovered a little and recognized some of the troop, he told how on the previous day some of their regiment had gone out to forage and the peasants had taken six of them prisoner. Of these they had shot five dead hardly an hour ago; they had to stand one behind the other, and as the bullet after piercing through five bodies did not reach him, the sixth one, they had cut off his nose and ears, after forcing him to lick the behinds of the five dead peasants. Finding himself thus insulted by these God-forsaken villains, he shouted at them in the rudest terms, and although they promised to spare his life, he called them by their right names, hoping some might lose patience and grant him a bullet; but in vain. After he had angered them so much, they put him in the barrel and buried him alive, saying that as he so eagerly desired death, out of spite they would not kill him.

As he was bemoaning his misery, another troop of soldiers entered the wood on foot who had come across these peasants, made five prisoner and shot dead the rest. Among the prisoners were four to whom the mutilated horseman a short while ago had had to pay his shameful homage, and only the fifth one had opposed the burying of him alive. When the two troops recognized from their shouting that they were from the same regiment, they assembled and heard again from the rider himself what had happened to him and his comrades.

Now one should have seen the spectacle of how the peasants were tortured and tormented. Some wanted to shoot them in their first rage but others said: "No, let us torture these reckless beasts thoroughly and give them what they deserve." And so the peasants received such hard thrashings with the muskets that they had to vomit blood.

At last one soldier stepped forward and said: "Gentlemen, as it is a shame on the whole soldiery that this villain (and he pointed to the rider) has been tortured so horribly by five peasants, so it is fair that we wipe away this blemish by making these rascals lick the horseman a hundred times."

However another said: "This fellow is not worthy of such honour, for had he not been such a clumsy fool then he would not have done this shameful thing to the disgrace of all honest soldiers, but would have a thousand times preferred to die."

Finally all agreed that each of the peasants who had cleaned the rider should make it good on ten soldiers and should say each time: "Herewith I wipe out the shame done to the soldiers when one of them licked our bottoms!" They concluded what further to do with the peasants when the purifying work was over, and forthwith went to the heart of the matter. But the peasants were so stiff-necked that they could not be forced to lick, neither by promises to let them off with their lives nor through tortures of any kind. One led the fifth peasant (who had not been licked) aside and said to him:

"If you will disavow God and all his saints, I will let you run off wherever you wish."

Hereupon the peasant answered that all the days of his life he had not believed in saints and so far had very little acquaintance with God himself. Then he even solemnly swore that he did not know God and did not wish to participate in his kingdom. Whereupon the soldier shot a bullet at his forehead but it had so little effect as if it had bounced against a mountain of steel. So he drew his cutlass and cried: "Holla, are you such a one? I have promised to let you run wherever you wish; so I send you now to the hellish kingdom as you do not wish to go to Heaven."

And he split his head down to the teeth. As he fell the soldier said: "That's the way to take revenge and to punish these vicious fellows, now and forever."

In the mean time, the other soldiers had taken hold of the four peasants who had been licked, bound their hands and feet over a fallen tree-trunk so that their buttocks were stretched upwards. After they had stripped off their trousers they took several yards of slow match, knotted it, and treated the peasants until the red juice ran. "That is the way," they said, "in which to dry up your purified bottoms, you villains!" The peasants screamed miserably, but it was only a pastime for the soldiers as they did not leave off sawing until skin and flesh had disappeared from the bone. The soldiers now allowed me to return to my hut so that I did not see what happened finally to the peasants.

When I arrived back I discovered that my flint box and all my belongings, including my whole store of miserable victuals, which I had grown all through the summer in my garden and saved up for the winter, had disappeared. Whither now, I thought. Need taught me to pray the more.

I exercised all my poor wit to find out what to do and what not to do – but with my small experience I could not come to any real decision. The best was to recommend myself to God and put all my trust in him, otherwise I would have despaired and perished. My mind was still full of that which I had seen and heard that very day. I did not think so much about food and my own preservation as about the hatred between soldiers and peasants, and in my foolishness there seemed no other explanation than that there must undoubtedly be two kinds of men in the world, not one single stock derived from Adam, but as different as wild and tame animals, for they persecute each other so cruelly.

With such thoughts I fell asleep ill-humouredly, cold and with a hungry belly. I imagined, as in a dream, that all trees around my dwelling suddenly changed their shape and appearance. On each treetop sat a cavalier, and the branches were decked with all sorts of fellows instead of leaves; some of these fellows had long spears, others muskets, short guns, halberds, pennants, even drums and pipes. This was a gay picture as everything branched off in a regular and orderly pattern. The root however was formed of people of poor esteem, artisans, labourers, peasants and the like, who nevertheless gave their strength to the tree and replaced the fallen leaves out of their own ranks at their own peril. Thereby they complained of those who were sitting on the tree and this with justification, for the whole weight of the tree laid upon them and pressed them so much that their money rolled out of their purses and even out of the seven-times locked treasure chests. If the flow of money stopped, the commissioners treated them roughly with brooms (called by one "punitive expeditions'), so that sighs escaped from their hearts, tears from their eyes, blood from under their nails, and the marrow from their bones. Nevertheless there were still people among them called jesters who cared very little, took everything easily, and tried to console themselves in their misery through all sorts of scoffing. Thus the roots of the trees had patiently to carry on in sheer hardship and misery, and those on the lower branches in even greater labour, toil and discomfort, although these were gayer but spiteful, tyrannical, often godless and always a heavy unbearable burden on the roots. Around them was the following rhyme:

Hunger and thirst and heat and chill,
Labour and want, as Fortune will,
Bloody act and lawless deed
Are all the life we soldiers lead.

This rhyme moreover was no lie, as was confirmed by their deeds. For gluttony and boozing, hunger and thirst, whoring and harlotry, raging and gaming, murder and being murdered, killing and being killed, tormenting and being tormented, hunting and being hunted, looting and being looted, in short ruin and destruction, and in return to be ruined and destroyed, was their fate. In these activities they were hindered neither by winter nor summer, snow nor ice, heat nor cold, neither by rain nor wind, hill nor dale, fields nor swamps, neither by moats, passes, seas, walls, fire, water nor ramparts, neither by father nor mother, brothers nor sisters, neither by peril to their own bodies, souls and conscience, indeed neither by loss of life nor of heaven, nor any other thing that can be named. But eagerly they continued in these actions until at last one by one they perished in battles, lost their lives in sieges and assaults, died in campaigns and miserably decayed in their billets (the soldiers' earthly paradise, especially so when peasants are well off). Only very few escaped, who in their old age, if they had not stolen and looted enough, became the finest of beggars and vagabonds.

Next to these suppressed people sat some older soldiers who had spent several years in great danger on the lower branches and had been fortunate enough to escape death so far. These looked somewhat more serious and reputable than those on the lowest branches, for they had climbed one grade higher. But above them there were still some higher ones who had greater ambitions because they commanded the lower ones. These were called provost-sergeants and they groomed the soldiers' backs and heads with their truncheons. Above these, the trunk of the tree showed a gap; it was a smooth piece of the branches which was rubbed in with the soap of envy so that no fellow except the nobility was able to climb up with either fortitude, cleverness or cunning, however well he could climb, as it was polished more smoothly than a column of marble or mirror of steel. Above sat the commissioned officers, some young and some older ones. The young ones had been pulled up by their cousins, and the older ones had climbed partly unaided and partly by a silver ladder called Bribery, or by some other style which Fortune had placed there. Above these were still higher ones who, too, had their toil, worries and privations, but they enjoyed the advantage that they were able to cut the fat bacon from the roots for their own pockets with a knife called Requisition. And they succeeded most fortunately when a commissioner with plenipotentiary powers arrived to empty a tub of gold over the tree to revive it. Then those above caught the best and left those below hardly anything. Thus among the lowest, more died of hunger than perished before the enemy, and such danger did not exist for the high ones. There was an incessant crawling and climbing around the tree as everyone wanted to sit in the highest blissful places.

The lower ones, who were very ambitious, hoped that those above might fall, so that they could sit in their places, and if among ten thousand one succeeded in reaching so far, it mostly happened at an ill-humoured age when he was better suited to sit behind the oven to fry apples than to be in the battlefield before the enemy. And if he fulfilled his duties well, he was envied by the others and might by unfortunate treachery be robbed of his commission and his life: nowhere was life harder than here. Nobody liked to lose a good sergeant by making him an ensign. Instead of old soldiers they preferred flatterers, footmen, grown-up pages, poor noble-men, all sorts of cousins and parasites, thus taking away the bread from those who deserved a commission. This angered an old sergeant-major so much that he started to curse violently, but a nobleman from above, called Adelhold, answered him:

"Don't you know that everywhere and always the official positions in war are occupied by noble persons as they are most suited to them. Greybeards alone would not beat the enemy, or otherwise one could hire a herd of goats to do it. We say:

A bullock in the herd may be
More wise than all the others
And braving elder rivalry
Command his wandering brothers;

The cowherd too can give him trust,
His youthful years forgetting,
Only by wicked custom must
Old age be virtue's setting.

Tell me, you old crank, whether nobly born officers are not more respected by the soldiery than those who were once commoners? And what will happen to discipline where there is no true respect? Should not a com-mander trust a cavalier more than a peasant boy who has run away from his father's plough and wasn't good enough to work for his parents? An honest nobleman would rather die than bring shame to his family name through unfaithfulness or desertion. Preference belongs to nobility eve-rywhere: such is the usage in all lands and is confirmed in the Scriptures.

SIMPLICIUS SIMPLICISSIMUS

Even if one of you may be a good soldier capable of smelling gunpowder, he may not be able to command others, which virtue is innate to nobility being accustomed to it from youth. Besides, nobility have more means to support their subjects with money than a peasant. According to the old proverb, it would not be wise to put a peasant above the nobility and the peasants would become much too conceited if one would make them so easily into masters. As one says:

> There is no sword which cuts sharper
> Than when the peasant becomes master

If you peasants, through long and praiseworthy traditions were in posses-sion of the high posts of war as are now the nobility, soon no nobleman would ever be admitted to them. And finally, you soldiers of fortune, as you are called, if one thinks you worthy of higher honours you are mostly so worn out that one has doubts to advance you further; a young dog is more prepared for hunting than an old lion!"

The sergeant answered: "What fool would then like to serve if he has no hope of promotion or of reward for his faithful service? May the Devil take such a war! In this way it doesn't matter whether somebody is brave or not. I have heard from our old colonel often that he wanted no soldier in his regiment who did not firmly believe that he might become a general through his good conduct."

To this Adelhold replied: "If a brave man's true qualities are observed, he will indeed not be overlooked and we find today many who have exchanged the plough, the needle, the cobbler's last, the shepherd's crook, for the sword, and through their fortitude have surpassed the lower nobility and have gained a viscountcy. Who was the Imperial Johann von Werth? Who was the Swedish Stallhans? Who the Hessian Little Jacob and St Andreas?* Many more of them are well known who, in short, I cannot mention. It is in the present times that lowly but honest men reach high honours through war."

"This sounds all very well," replied the sergeant, "However I see that the gates to higher dignity are closed to us by the nobility. A nobleman as soon as he has crawled out of his eggshell is put in such a position as we can never hope to reach. And as under the peasant many an intelligent man perishes having no chance to study, so many a brave soldier becomes old under his musket who deserved to lead a regiment and be of great service to his commander-in-chief."

I had no desire to listen to this old ass any longer, but begrudged him not the fate of which he complained as he had often whipped poor soldiers like dogs. I turned again round to the trees and saw how they swayed and crashed together. Thus these fellows fell down in masses, crash and fall were one, in one moment alive and dead, in a flash one lost an arm, another a leg, and a third even a head. And when I looked further, it appeared to me that all the trees were one single tree and on its peak was sitting the war god Mars, and he covered with the branches of the tree the whole of Europe. And as I thought this tree could have soon overshadowed the whole world, a horrible north wind caused by envy, jealousy, hatred and conceit, rose up and filled the air. From the gigantic howling of this destructive wind and the shattering of the tree itself I was awakened out of my sleep and found myself alone in my hut.

Again I considered in my mind what I should do. It was impossible to remain in the forest as everything had been taken away. Nothing was left except a few books which lay scattered and thrown about. When I picked them up with weeping eyes and prayed fervently to God to lead and guide me to where I should go, I found by chance a little letter which my hermit had written whilst he was still alive, and it read as follows:

DEAR SIMPLICIUS,

When you find this letter, leave the forest as soon as you can and save yourself and the vicar from the present calamities as he has done much good to me. Keep God always in your mind and pray often. He will bring you to a place which is good for you. Serve God continuously as if you were still in my presence in the forest. Remember and act without ceasing on these my last words, so you will succeed. Farewell!

I kissed this little letter, and the hermit's grave, many thousand times, and went on my way without further delay to look for people. So I walked two days in a straight direction and at night I looked for shelter in a hollow tree. My food was nothing but beech nuts which I picked up from the ground. The third day I came, not far from Gelnhausen, to a rather flat field. There I enjoyed almost a wedding feast because the whole field was everywhere covered with sheaves which the peasants, to my good fortune, were not able to harvest as they had been chased away after the Battle of Nördlingen.* In one of these sheaves I made my bed for the night as it was terribly cold, and I satisfied myself with rubbed wheat which appeared to me a most delicate food as I had not tasted it for a long time.

4

SIMPLICIUS COMES TO HANAU AND
BECOMES A PAGE

AT DAWN I FILLED MYSELF UP AGAIN with wheat and went directly to
Gelnhausen where I found the gates open but partly burnt and still partly
fortified with dung. I entered the town but could see no living soul; the
streets were strewn here and there with dead people, of whom some had
been completely stripped of clothing whilst others were left only with a
shirt. To me this was a horrible spectacle. My innocence could find no
reason for the tribulations that had come to this place. I heard soon that the
Imperial Armies had taken a Weimar detachment by surprise and mauled
them miserably. I went only two stone throws into the town before I had
seen enough, so I turned back, and found a good country road which led
me to the magnificent fortress of Hanau. When I perceived the first guards
I tried to run away but at once two musketeers pounced upon me, took
hold of me and led me to the guardroom.

My clothes and appearance were most unusual, astonishing and repulsive,
so that later the governor had a picture painted of me. My hair had not
been trimmed for one-and-a-half years, neither cut, curled nor crimped in
the Greek, German nor French fashion, but stood in its natural confusion
covered with dust instead of powder. As I always used to go bareheaded
and my hair was naturally curly it looked as if I wore a Turkish headdress, and my pale yellow face looked out from under it like a tawny owl
waiting for a mouse. The rest of my outfit was in conformity with the
appearance of my head. I was wearing my hermit's gown, if it still could
be called that, as its original had completely disappeared and nothing
was left except its shape, which was composed of a thousand different
coloured patches. Over that I wore the hair shirt instead of a shoulder
cape, from which I had cut off the sleeves to use as stockings. My whole
body was girded back and front with the iron chains of St Wilhelmus.
My shoes were carved from wood and my laces were made from the bast
of a lime tree; my feet looked like lobsters, as if I wore stockings of the
Spanish national colours.

Although any reasonable man should have at once realized from my meagre, starved appearance and neglected apparel that I had not run away from an eating-house, neither from a lady's chamber, nor even from a grand gentleman's residence, I was severely examined in the guardroom. And just as the soldiers were amazed at me, so in my turn I admired the magnificent dress of the officer who questioned me. I did not know whether he was a "he" or a "she" as he wore his beard and moustache in the French fashion; on both sides he had long plaits hanging down like horse-tails and his moustache was cut so miserably short and mutilated that between his nose and mouth were only a few hairs left so short that they were hardly visible. Nonetheless his white breeches gave me much doubt concerning his sex as they appeared to me more a woman's skirt than a pair of men's trousers. I thought: if this is a man then he should have an honest beard, for this dandy is not as young as he pretends to be. If however it is a woman, why has this old whore so much stubble round her mouth? Certainly it is a woman, I thought, for no honest man would maltreat his beard so horribly – even a billy-goat out of shame would not join a strange herd with its beard trimmed like this. And as I was so much in doubt, and not knowing the present fashion, I considered him both man and woman in one.

This manly woman or this womanly man ordered me to be searched everywhere but found nothing on me except a little book made of birch bark in which I had written my daily prayers and in which was the little note left to me as a farewell by my pious hermit. This he took but as I did not want to lose it I fell down before him, embraced both his knees and begged: "Oh, my dear Hermaphrodite, pray leave me my prayerbook!"

"You fool!" he answered, "Which devil has told you that my name is Hermann?"

Thereupon he ordered two soldiers to lead me to the governor, handing over my prayerbook to them, as I soon noticed the braggart could neither read nor write. So I was taken into the town, and every man came running along as if a sea-monster was to be put on show. As everyone wanted to see me and inspect my astonishing appearance, so everyone had his own idea about my character; some believed me to be a spy, others a lunatic, others a wild man or some even a ghost, a spirit or some other miracle. Most considered me a fool, and indeed they were nearest to the truth, had I not knowledge of our dear Lord.

When I was brought before the governor he asked me from where I came. But I answered that I did not know. He asked me further: "Where do you want to go?" And again I answered: "I do not know."

"What the devil *do* you know?" He asked again. "What is your profession?"

I answered as before that I knew not.

He asked: "Where is your home?"

And as again I answered that I did not know, he changed his expression – I know not whether from rage or astonishment. But as everyone suspected evil, especially with the enemy nearby who had stormed Gelnhausen the previous night and had routed a regiment of dragoons, so he agreed with those who believed me to be a traitor or a spy, and ordered them to search me. When he heard from the soldiers of the guard that this had been done and nothing was found on me but the little book, which they then handed over to him, he read a few lines in it and then asked me who had given it to me. I answered it had been mine from the beginning as I had made it myself and written it. He asked:

"Why on birch bark?"

I answered: "Because the bark of other trees is not suited for it."

"You boor!" he said, "I asked why you have not written on paper?"

"Oh," I answered, "We never had any in the forest."

The governor asked: "Where? In which forest?"

I answered in my old tune that I did not know.

With that the governor turned to some of his officers who were just paying him a visit, and said: "Either this man is an arch villain or a fool! But he can't be a fool when he writes like that." Whilst he spoke he turned the leaves of my little book violently to show them my beautiful handwriting, thus the hermit's letter fell out. He had it picked up but I at once changed colour as I considered this my greatest treasure and sacred relic. The governor, realizing that, became even more suspicious concerning treason, especially as he had read the letter, and said:

"I recognize this handwriting and know that it comes from an officer well-known to me! But I do not remember from whom!"

Even the contents appeared to him unusual and incomprehensible, so that he said:

"This is without doubt a pre-arranged language which no one else understands but he with whom it is planned."

Then he asked me what my name was and when I answered, "Simplicius", he said:

"Indeed, you are made of the same wood! Away with him, away! At once lock him hand and foot in irons!"

So the two soldiers took me to the new billet destined for me, the prison, and handed me over to the warder, who according to his orders, decorated my hands and feet with even more iron fetters and chains as if I had not already enough of these to carry round my body.

But this welcome was not enough. There came hangmen and knaves of the rack with horrid instruments of torture, and although I consoled myself in my innocence, they made my wretched condition still more miserable. Oh, God, I said to myself, how I deserve this because I have deserted God's service. That is the reward which I reap for my wantonness. Oh, you unfortunate Simplicius, where does your ingratitude lead you? As soon as God has brought you to his knowledge and to his service you run away and turn your back on him. Could you not have eaten more acorns and beans as before to serve your Creator unhindered? Did you not know that your faithful hermit and teacher fled the world and has chosen the wilderness? Oh, you blind block! You have abandoned it in the hope of satisfying your shameful lust to see the world, but look now! You poor Simplicius, now go on and receive the reward for your worldly thoughts and presumptuous foolishness. Thus I accused myself, prayed God for forgiveness and recommended my soul to him.

So we approached the thieves' tower and when the need was greatest, God's help was nearest. As I was surrounded by catchpoles together with a big crowd and was waiting in front of the prison for it to be opened and to enter, my vicar who recently lost his village through loot and fire, was there also as prisoner. When he looked out through the window and recognized me, he called with loud voice, "Oh, Simplicius, is that you?" As I heard and saw him I could do nothing else but stretch both my hands towards him and called:

"Oh, Father, Father, Father!"

He asked me what I had done. I answered that I did not know but probably because I had run away from the forest. As he heard from some of the people around him that I was held as a traitor he asked them to wait with me until he had reported to the governor, as such would lead to his and my release and prevent him from doing injustice to us, for he knew me better than anyone.

The vicar obtained permission to go to the governor and about half an hour later I too was fetched and placed in the servants' room. There already two tailors, a shoemaker with shoes, a merchant with hats and stockings, and another one with various cloths were assembled to clothe me as soon as possible. They took off my gown as well as the chain and my hairshirt, so that the tailor could take measurements. Soon followed a regimental barber with a strong caustic lather and perfumed soap, and just when he started to exercise his art on me, another order came through which dismally frightened me, which was that I should at once be put back into my old clothes.

But this was not of such bad intent as I had feared; for soon came a painter with his tools. He brought cinnabar and vermilion for my eyelids, with lacquer, indigo and ultramarine for coral-red lips, with yellow sulphide, Dutch gold and yellow-lead for my white teeth, which I ground in hunger. He had pine soot, carbon black and umber for my blond hair, and white lead for my gruesome eyes, and still many other tints for my weather-stained gown. With his hands full of brushes, he started to look at me and to make a sketch, putting on the underpaint, and leant his head over the side to compare his work carefully with my features. Soon he changed the eyes or the hair, quickly my nostrils, in short everything which he had not painted correctly at the beginning, until at last he had painted a natural portrait of Simplicius as he was.

Only now was the barber allowed to tackle me. He pinched my head and toiled for an hour and a half with my hair and cut it in the prevailing fashion. Then he put me into a little bath and cleaned the three or four year old grime from my starved emaciated body. As soon as he was finished they brought me a white shirt, shoes and stockings, a collar, a hat with feathers, and trousers beautifully lined and braided. Only the jacket was still missing which in the mean time the tailors were working on with haste.

The cook appeared with a strong broth and the cellar maid with a drink. There sat my gentleman, Simplicius, like a young count, equipped with the best. I ate heartily, although not knowing what they intended to do with me; fortunately I had no knowledge of such things as a hangman's meal. That is why this delicious meal went down so smoothly that I cannot praise it enough. Indeed, I hardly believe that I enjoyed all my life long one single meal with more pleasure than at that time.

When my jacket was ready I put it on and presented in this new garment such a clumsy figure that I looked like a trophy or a decorated gatepost. The tailors were ordered to make my garments wide in the hope that I would soon put on weight, which indeed happened as a result of the excellent food. My forest clothing, including the chain, was put into the art museum with other rare things and antiquities, and my portrait in life-size was put next to them.

After the evening meal my gentleman was put into a bed which had never happened to me before, neither with my dad nor with my hermit. But my belly rumbled and grumbled the whole night long so that I could not sleep, perhaps for no other reason than that it did not know what was good or that it was amazed by these pleasant new dishes which had been offered to it. In spite of that I remained in bed until the dear sun shone again (for it was cold), and I contemplated how remarkably my fate had changed in the last few days and how dear God had faithfully helped me and led me to such a good place.

This same morning the governor's marshal of the household ordered me to go to my vicar and hear what his master had told him of me. He allotted me a bodyguard to take me to him, and the vicar led me into his study, sat down, bade me to do the same, and said:

"Dear Simplicius, the hermit with whom you stayed in the forest was not only this governor's brother-in-law but was his superior in war and his dearest friend. The governor deigned to tell me that he possessed from his early youth the fortitude of a heroic soldier and a divine devotion which normally only a man of God would have – both virtues rarely found together. His religious mind and unfortunate events at last stopped the course of his worldly happiness so that he forsook his nobility and considerable estates in Scotland, where he was born, as all worldly deeds appeared to him vain and detestable. In short he hoped to exchange his high position for a better future glory, for his spirit felt disgusted with worldly splendour, and all his thoughts and efforts were concentrated on the miserable life in which you found him in the forest and kept him company until his death. I believe that he was influenced through the reading of many papish books on the lives of the old hermits, and I will not conceal from you how he came to the Spessart and according to his wishes took up the life of a hermit, that you in future may tell others of it.

"The second night after the bloody battle near Höchst was lost, he came quite alone to my vicarage. I had just fallen asleep with my wife and children towards morning, as we had been awake the whole night before and half this night because of the noise in the country which the fleeing armies and the pursuers made. He knocked first modestly, but later on violently until he woke me and my drowsy household, and I opened the door after a plea from him and a few simple words between us. I saw a cavalier dismounting from his horse and his costly garment was covered as much with the enemy's blood as it was braided with gold and silver. As he still held a naked sword in his fist I was overcome by fear and fright but when he sheathed it and uttered nothing but polite words, I had reason to be astonished that such a brave gentleman should ask a humble village vicar so kindly for shelter. I took him for General Mansfeld* himself because of his fine character and his magnificent appearance. He said that he was in great distress as he had to bemoan three things: firstly his lost wife who was about to give birth to a child, secondly, the lost battle, and lastly, that he had not, like other honest soldiers, been fortunate to give his life for the Gospels.

"I wanted to console him but I soon realized that his greatness of spirit did not need sympathy. So I gave him what my house could afford, had a soldier's bed made for him of fresh straw as he did not wish to lay in any other, although he needed rest urgently. The first thing he did the next morning was to make me a present of his horse and his money – for he had gold in no small amount – including some precious rings which he distributed between my wife, children and servants. I did not know what to think of him as soldiers are used to taking rather than giving, and I therefore hesitated to accept such valuable gifts. I objected that I did not deserve them nor ever would be able to deserve them; besides if such wealth especially the magnificent horse, which I could not hide, should be discovered at my place, people might conclude that I had helped to rob or even to murder him. But he said I should not be anxious on that score. He would protect me from such danger with his own handwriting. Indeed he did not want to take away his shirt, nor his clothing, from my vicarage, and he confessed to me his intention to become a hermit. I protested with all my powers as I thought his intention had too much flavour of papacy and I reminded him that he could serve the Gospels better with his sword. But in vain. He persuaded me so long and so strongly that I agreed to everything and supplied him with those books, pictures and household necessities which you found with him. He only asked for the woollen blanket under which he had slept that very night on the straw, for all that which he had given to me. From this he had his gown made. I had to exchange my wagon-chain (he wore this always) for his golden one on which he kept his sweetheart's miniature, so that he neither kept money nor money's worth.

"My servant boy led him to the most deserted part of the forest and helped him there to build a hut. How he now spent his life and how I occasionally assisted him you know partly better than I.

"When I was completely looted and miserably injured at the time the Battle of Nördlingen was lost, as you know I fled here for safety for my best possessions were here. Becoming short of money I took three rings from the hermit's gift, among them his signet ring, and the gold chain with the miniature, and carried them to the Jew to turn into money. He however, because of the precious and beautiful workmanship, offered them for sale to the governor, who at once recognizing the coat of arms and the portrait, sent for me and asked from where these came. I told him the truth, showed him the hermit's handwriting and letter of bequest, and recounted the whole story, even how he had lived in the forest and died there. But he did not want to believe me and ordered my arrest until he learnt the truth precisely; he was just going to send a patrol away to inspect the abode of the hermit when I saw you being led into the tower.

"Now the governor can no longer doubt my explanations, for I can prove the place where the hermit lived and can rely upon you and other living witnesses, especially the verger who so often let you both into the church before dawn. Above all, this little letter which the governor found in your prayerbook will not only prove the truth but even the holiness of the departed hermit. So he will reward both of us because of his beloved brother-in-law and will provide richly for us. You need only decide what you wish to do and he will grant it. Would you like to study, for he will pay the expenses; are you inclined to a handicraft, for he will let you learn; if, however, you want to stay with him, he will keep you as his own child, for he said that even if only a mongrel would come from his beloved brother-in-law he would receive him."

I answered him that whatever the honourable governor would do with me I would be pleased.

The vicar kept me in his room until ten o'clock before he went with me to the governor to tell him my position and to be his luncheon guest, for an open table was kept. In these days Hanau was blockaded and it was a meagre time for the common people, particularly for the refugees in the fortress, so that even such people who imagined themselves to be somebody did not despise picking up frozen turnip peelings in the street. The vicar succeeded in sitting next to the governor and I had to wait at table with a plate in my hand as the marshal of the household had instructed me. To this I was suited as a donkey at the chessboard, but the vicar excused with his words where the awkwardness of my limbs failed. He told them that I was educated in the wilderness and had never been among people, therefore I had to be excused as I had no experience of how to behave. The faithfulness which I had shown to the hermit and the hard life I had endured with him were admirable and alone deserving of patience for my clumsiness, even being preferable to the best of pages. Further he told that the hermit had found all his pleasure in me as he had often said that my face resembled his dear wife, that he was frequently amazed at my constancy and unchangeable will to stay with him. In short he could not emphasize enough with what serious devotion the hermit, just before his death, recommended me to the vicar and confessed that he loved me as his own child.

These words rang so sweetly in my ears that I thought I had already received enough pleasure for all that which I had suffered with the hermit. The governor asked whether his blessed brother-in-law had not known that he was in command in Hanau.

"Indeed!" answered the parson, "I myself told him, but with friendly face and gentle smile he listened so indifferently as though he had never known a Ramsay.* Still today I am astonished over the firmness of this man as he succeeded not only in forsaking the world but even in dismissing from his mind his best friend who was so near."

The governor who really had not the soft-hearted soul of a woman, but on the contrary was a brave soldier, had eyes full of tears. He said:

"If I had known that he was still alive and where he was to be found, I would have fetched him even against his will to me to reward him for his good deeds. But as Fortune has refused this to me, so I will in his stead care for his Simplicius. Oh!" he continued, "This honest cavalier had good reason to lament his pregnant wife, for she was taken prisoner by a troop of Imperial riders who were in pursuit, and that too happened in the Spessart. When I received news of this and knew only that my brother-in-law had been killed near Hæchst, I at once sent a trumpeter to the enemy to enquire after my sister and to offer ransom. But I did not succeed except to learn that this troop of riders had been dispersed in the Spessart by several peasants and in such a skirmish my sister was lost to them again, so that to this hour I do not know what has become of her."

This and suchlike was the conversation at table between the governor and the vicar, about my hermit and his sweet wife, and the couple were pitied the more as they had been married only one year. I now became the governor's page, and such a dandy that the people, especially the peasants when I had to announce them to my master, addressed me as "Young Gentleman", although one seldom sees a boy who is first a gentleman, but there are gentlemen who have been boys first!

5

SIMPLICIUS IS CRITICAL OF HIS NEW LIFE

AT THIS TIME I TREASURED a clean conscience and a truly pious mind, invested with noble innocence and simplicity. I was ignorant of all vices except the ones that I had heard and read about. When I saw a sin committed it was horrifying and extraordinary to me because I was brought up in such a way as to keep God's presence in constant observance and to live according to His Holy Will. I felt nothing but sheer horror when I compared the teachings of God with the actions of men. Oh, God! How amazed I was when I looked at the earnest warnings of the Holy Gospel and Christ's Commandments, and then at the deeds of those who pretend to be his followers! Instead of true belief which every devout Christian should have, I found hypocrisy and immeasurable folly, so that I doubted whether I was living in a world of Christians. I noticed that everybody was familiar with God's will but nobody made any effort to obey it.

Thousands of fantasies and strange ideas came into my mind that I was tormented with doubts, remembering Christ's command: "Judge not, and ye shall not be judged." Nevertheless I remembered the words of Paul the Apostle to the Galatians: "Now the works of the flesh are manifest, which are these: adultery, fornication, uncleanness, lasciviousness, idolatry, witchcraft, hatred, variance, emulations, wrath, strife, seditions, heresies, envyings, murders, drunkenness, revellings, and such like, of the which I tell you before, as I have also told you in times past, that they which do such things shall not inherit the kingdom of God." I thought as almost everyone openly commits these sins I must conclude that only a few can enter heaven.

After vanity and greed, gluttony, drunkenness, whoring and villainy were the habits of the rich. What astounded me most of all was that many, especially young soldiers, made fun of their godlessness, and God's Holy Will. For example, I once heard an adulterer utter these boastful words: "It serves the cuckold right that he should wear his horns: I did it more to hurt him than to please her for I sought to wreak my vengeance upon him."

"What senseless revenge," answered an honest soul, who stood nearby, "to besmirch your conscience and bestow upon yourself the shameful title of marriage-breaker."

"What! Marriage-breaker?" answered the soldier mockingly, "I'm no marriage-breaker as I have only bent the marriage. Only God is the marriage-breaker as he separates man and wife through death."

The soldier used many such words, so that I was horrified at his devil's catechism, and thought "Oh, you blasphemous sinner, calling yourself a marriage-bender and God a marriage-breaker."

"Don't you think," I approached him with contempt in my voice, although he was an officer, "that you commit an even greater sin with these words than by your adultery."

"Hold your tongue, you mouse-head," retorted the soldier, "or I will box your ears."

And I am sure he would have hit me at least a dozen times had he not been afraid of my master. I kept quiet and realized that it was not rare that the unwedded lusted for the wedded and wedded for unwedded.

When I was studying the road to eternal life with the hermit, I had wondered why God had forbidden his people idolatry with such severe penalty. I imagined to myself that it was because when one had come to know the true and eternal God, one could honour and worship no other. Due to my foolish reasoning I concluded that this Commandment was both futile and unnecessary. But, Oh, fool that I was, I was mistaken, for almost as soon as I was brought into the world I noticed that all worldly men have an idol as well as a God. Indeed, some possess even more idols than the ancients. Some have them in their money-chests upon which they put all their consolation and hope. Some have their idols in the court, upon which they place their trust, even though they be merely favourites and lazy good-for-nothings depending on the whims of the Prince. Others have their idols in their reputation and imagine if they receive recognition they would be demi-gods themselves. Some have their idols in their heads which God had blessed with cleverness to grasp the arts and science, so that they put God aside and rely on their gifts to give them prosperity. There were many whose god was their own belly, to whom they made daily offerings as the heathens made offerings to Bacchus and Ceres. And if the belly became weak and other human ailments announced themselves, these miserable men turned their doctors into gods and sought salvation in the apothecaries, from whom however they more often received death instead of life. Other fools turned their smooth-skinned prostitutes into goddesses, gave them tender names, worshipped them by day and night with a thousand sighs, composed sonnets praising their charms and pleaded with them for sympathy and compassion.

On the other hand there were the womenfolk who proclaimed their beauty as their god; this they thought would protect them well, may God in Heaven say what he pleases. This false god was kept and honoured with creams, ointments, scented waters and powders.

I saw people who made gods of well-situated houses, who claimed that as long as they lived within, good fortune and money would pass down the chimney. I even knew a man who had given his heart, body and soul to his tobacco business, instead of devoting them to God! And this fool, upon death, faded away as does tobacco smoke.

I once accompanied a noble gentleman to inspect his art collection, which housed many beautiful and rare antiquities. Among the paintings nothing pleased me more than an "Ecce Homo" because of its pitiful representation which drew sympathy from the spectator. Next to it hung a Chinese scroll painting; the picture portrayed Chinese gods attired in all their majesty, some having the features of devils. The nobleman asked me which piece in his collection pleased me the most. I pointed to the "Ecce Homo"; but he said that I erred, the Chinese painting was rarer and therefore more valuable and he would not exchange it for ten "Ecce Homos".

I answered: "Sir, do your lips express the true feelings of your heart?"

He replied that he had meant what he said, whereupon I exclaimed:

"Then the god of your heart must be as true as the gods on the painting you treasure."

"Dreamer," he jeered, "I treasure the rarity!"

And I answered, "What can be rarer and more deserving of admiration than the Passion of Christ as portrayed by your painting?"

As much as these and other false gods were worshipped was the true and holy God despised. Christ said: "Love thine enemy, do good to them which hate you, bless them that curse you and pray for them which despitefully use you, and unto him that smiteth thee on the one cheek, offer also the other." But I saw no one who wanted to obey the words of Christ and I saw many who were opposed and worked against them. It is said: "Blood is thicker than water!" Yet nowhere have I found more envy, hate, ill will, brawling, quarrelling than among brothers, sisters and kinsmen, especially when there was a legacy to be shared.

The trade guilds regarded each other with such hate that I concluded the publicans and tax collectors of long ago (so despised because of their sinfulness) would appear to us Christians today superior in brotherly love. And I thought: if we can have no reward for not loving our enemies, what terrible penalty can we expect for hating our friends. Where there should have been love and friendship, I found only hate and enmity. Many lords mistreated their servants and subjects, whilst as many servants betrayed their virtuous masters. I noticed much wrangling between married couples; tyrant husbands treated their honest wives like dogs, whilst vicious shrews regarded their husbands as fools and asses. Many shameless lords and masters cheated their industrious servants of their compensation and grudged them meat and drink besides; on the other hand, I also saw many treacherous servants who took advantage of their masters by thievery, or who dragged their masters into ruin through carelessness. The tradesmen and craftsmen competed with the moneylenders to cheat and deceive the peasants by sucking sour sweat from their brows. On the other hand, many of the peasants were such godless knaves that they sought, as if their evilness were not enough, to abuse and slander their neighbours under the pretext of simplicity. I saw once a soldier give a comrade a blow on the mouth, and I imagined, never having witnessed a brawl before, that he would turn the other cheek. But I was wrong for the insulted soldier drew his sword and wounded the culprit on the head. I shrieked with trembling voice: "Oh, Friend! What are you doing?"

"I would be a coward," he answered, "and would rather die, by Satan, than not take revenge. Zounds! One would be a sorry scoundrel if he let himself be bullied."

As the uproar between the two fighters increased, their companions and interested bystanders joined the brawling. I heard them cursing God and their souls, so light-heartedly, that I could not believe they respected them as their most sacred treasures. But that was only child's play, for they did not stop at infant's curses, but followed up with: "May God strike me with thunder and with lightning and with hail! May the Devil come to me, and let Satan carry me to Hell." The Holy Sacraments were abused in their curses not seven times, but a hundred thousand times, so that they would have filled the holds of a galley and so that my very hair stood on end. I thought: Are these Christians? Where are the words of Christ that say: "Thou shalt not curse. Swear not at all: neither by heaven, for it is God's Throne, nor by the earth, for it is His footstool; neither by Jerusalem, for it is the city of the Great King. Neither shalt thou swear by thy head, because thou canst not make one hair white or black. But let your speech be "Yea, yea – nay, nay" – for whatsoever is more than these cometh of evil."

I considered all that I had seen and heard, and, concluding that these ruffians were no Christians, I looked for other companionship. What horrified me most of all was when I heard a braggart boasting of his wickedness, sin, infamy and viciousness; and almost daily I could hear: "By the holy blood! How we boozed yesterday! That very day I got drunk three times and vomited just as often! By God! How we tormented those rascally peasants! By the Devil! What booty we plundered yesterday. By a Hundred Poisons, what fun we had with the women and maidens." Such and similar unchristian boastings filled my ears all day, and I heard and saw many sins committed in God's name so that it was pitiful. These crimes were mostly practised by the soldiers, who said: "In God's name we enjoy going on expeditions to plunder, loot, murder, trample, attack, take prisoners and burn down" – and whatever more horrible deeds and actions existed.

The usurers also practised their trade of money lending in the name of God, and never failed to satisfy their devilish greed by cheating and exploitation. I once saw two wretched fools being hanged; they wanted to rob a house in the name of God, but as one was on the ladder the watchful owner threw him down in the name of the Devil, so that he broke a leg, and was captured and hanged with his companion a few days later.

When I heard and saw such behaviour I criticized it and quoted the Holy Scriptures, as was my way, so that the people considered me to be a fool; indeed, my good intentions were met with scorn and laughter so that I became impatient and would have stopped my preachings but for my love of Christian charity. I wished that everybody had been educated by my hermit, so that they would have seen the world as I, Simplicius, saw it. I was too naive at that time to realize that if the world was populated only by Simpliciuses there would not be many vices. It is well known that a worldly man accustomed to indulging in foolery and wickedness, is the last to realize that he walks with his companions on a dangerous road.

As I had reason to doubt whether I lived amongst Christians, I visited the vicar and told him all I had seen and heard, namely, that I considered the people not to be Christians but mockers of Christ and his Word. I beseeched him: "Help me out of my dream, show me how to understand my fellow men." The priest answered:

"Indeed, they are all Christians, and I would not advise you to call them otherwise."

"My God!" I said, "How can that be? If I admonish one or the other because of his crimes against God, I am mocked and ridiculed."

"Don't be astonished at this," answered the priest, "I believe if the pious Christians who lived at the time of Our Lord, yes, even the Apostles themselves, would now stand up in their graves and re-enter the world, they would ask the same questions as you have asked, and would likewise be ridiculed and scorned by everyone. This, which you have seen up to the present, is common and mere child's play compared to that which otherwise openly and violently happens against God and mankind. However, do not let this disturb you, for you will find few Christians like your hermit, the blessed Samuel."

As we were conversing together, several prisoners were led across the square thus ending our discourse, and I now encountered such foolishness as I had never dreamt possible. It was the new fashion to welcome and greet one another and a member of our garrison, who had served in the Imperial Army, recognized one of the prisoners and shook hands with him. Displaying much friendship and sincerity he said:

"May the hail kill you! Do you still live, brother? A thousand curses! How the devil has brought us together again! May thunder strike me – I thought you had been hanged long ago!"

Whereupon the prisoner answered: "Damn the lightning! Brother, is it really you! May the Devil take you! How did you get here? I never in my life thought that I would see you again, thinking the Devil had led you astray." When they parted, instead of saying "God be with you." the other said "By the hangman's knot, tomorrow we will meet, get drunk together and make merry!"

"Is that not a blessed welcome?" I said to the vicar, "are these noble Christian desires? Have these two godly intentions for the morrow? Who could mistake them for Christians or listen to them without astonishment? If they speak thus out of Christian love, how will it sound when they quarrel? Oh, Father! if these be Christ's flock, and you their appointed shepherd, I implore you to lead them to better pastures."

"Yes," replied the vicar, "My good child, thus it is with these godless soldiers. God have mercy on us! But if I spoke to them it would be as if I spoke to the deaf who hear not, and I would only gain the dangerous hatred of these godless men."

I wondered at this, yet stayed awhile longer with the priest, and then went to pay my respects to the governor. I had his permission at certain hours to see the town and speak with the vicar, the governor having my simplicity in mind and hoping that it would be overcome if I roamed about town seeing and hearing, letting others teach me, or as it is said, allowing myself to be smoothed and polished.

6

SIMPLICIUS MISBEHAVES

MY MASTER'S FAVOUR TOWARDS ME increased daily the longer I stayed because my resemblance to him and his sister (the hermit's wife) became more evident as the good food and leisure made my skin smooth and my appearance pleasant. I was favoured by everyone, for all in the service of the governor showed me kindness, and the secretary was especially amiable. Whilst he had to teach me counting, he found much entertainment in my simplicity and ignorance. He had just come from his studies at the University and was still full of school pranks, which gave him at times the appearance of having too many screws in his head, or perhaps too few. He often tried to persuade me that black was white and white black, and it happened that while I had first believed everything he said, I now believed nothing. I once criticized his filthy inkpot, but he answered that it was the most precious item in the entire chancellery as he could extract from it whatever he desired: precious ducats, beautiful clothes, and in short everything that he possessed had been fished out of the inkpot. I could not believe that such a small contemptible object could produce such magnificent gifts. However he said: "Such is the power of the *spiritus papyri*," as he named the ink, "that the inkwell is called a well because it is so deep that it contains these wondrous things."

I asked him how it was possible to get anything out at all, if one could hardly put two fingers inside it. He answered that there was an arm in his head able to execute such work. He soon hoped to fish out a rich and beautiful virgin and if successful, eventually his own property and servants. I was astonished at such cunning and asked whether other people were familiar with these crafty arts.

"Indeed," he answered, "all chancellors, doctors, secretaries, procurators, solicitors, commissioners, lawyers, merchants and innumerably more, if they only fish patiently, soon become rich gentlemen."

I said: "So the peasants and other hard-working people are fools that they eat their bread with the sweat of their brows and do not learn this art."

He replied: "Some are not familiar with it and do not wish to learn; others would like to learn but lack the magic arm in their heads. Others again are familiar with this art, and have sufficient magic arms, but are not acquainted with the proper manipulations that this art requires to become rich. Others still are very familiar with the art and possess all that is required, but unlike myself live in the wrong place and lack the opportunities to exercise it in the proper way."

As we were discussing the inkwell, which reminded me of the purse of Fortunatus, I came by coincidence across the Book of Titles. Therein I found more foolishness than ever my eyes had encountered before.

I said to the secretary: "All these are only children of Adam and of one breed, and made of dust and ashes! From where do they derive such great distinctions? Most Holy! Most Invincible! His Most Serene Highness! Are these not divine properties? Here one is Most Merciful and there he is Most Gracious. Why do we always mention one's noble birth? We know quite well that no one falls from heaven, or is formed from the water, or grows out of the earth like a cabbage. Why do we have Sirs, Lords, Your Worships, and well-born gentlemen? What a foolish world, are we not all well-born? Who has eyes at the back of his head?"

The secretary laughed, and took the trouble to explain the various titles to me, but I persisted that the titles were not deserved. It would be more praiseworthy to call a man Friendly instead of Serene. In the same way, if the word "noble" refers to only praiseworthiness and virtues, why then is it put before such princely titles as Count and Duke, if it only minimises their importance? The words "well born" are a complete lie! as any baron's mother will confirm when asked what she had to undergo at her son's birth.

Whilst I was thus ridiculing, quite without warning there escaped from me such a gruesome fart that both the secretary and I were horrified. Its stench filled our noses as well as the study – as if we had not already been aware of it!

"Get away, you swine!", he said to me, "to the pigs in the sty where such clots as you are better suited than to converse with honest people!" But he too had to leave the room abandoning the study to that dreadful stench, and through this I lost favour with the secretary.

I fell innocently into this misfortune because the unaccustomed food and medicines that were daily given to me were restoring my shrunken stomach and dried up bowels back to normal, thereby causing much stormy weather and strong winds which disturbed me constantly by their violent eruptions. As I did not imagine it to be wrong to let nature take its course, it being impossible to resist such internal pressure for long, and as even my hermit – such stomach disorders were unknown by us due to our meagre diet – never taught me to behave correctly under such circumstances, nor had my dad ever forbidden it: I merely permitted the gusts to escape and let pass what wanted to pass, until I lost credit with the secretary. Well could I have done without his favour had I not tumbled into even greater misfortune.

My master had a hard-boiled rascal as a page in addition to me, who had been with him for several years. I gave my heart to him as he was of the same age and I said to myself: "He is Jonathan, and you are David." But he envied me because the favour which my master showed me increased daily. He feared that I would someday fill his shoes, and therefore secretly spied on me with distrust and jealous eyes, and sought means to get rid of me through an accident. But I had the eyes of a dove and was of a different character than he. Yes, I trusted him with all my secrets, which consisted of nothing but childish innocence and religious thoughts, so that he never had a chance to trap me. One night we were long conversing in bed before we fell asleep, and talking of soothsaying he promised to teach me such arts free of charge. Thereupon he bade me put my head under the covers, as that was essential to learning this art. I obeyed willingly and expected the arrival of the Spirit of Soothsaying. By all Fortunes! This very spirit took possession of my nose so violently that I had to remove my head from under the bedsheets.

"What is the matter?" asked my instructor.

I replied: "You let go a fart."

"And you," he answered, "have spoken the truth and know now the art of foretelling the future."

This I did not consider to be an insult as I did not yet know hatred, but I wanted only to know from him in what manner I could loose these winds quietly.

My comrade answered: "This trick is simple; you must only raise your left leg as a dog that stands at a corner, say quietly to yourself "*Je péte, je péte, je péte*" and contract your body as hard as you can so that your winds will pass from your body as silently as thieves."

"That's fine," I thought, "and if it stinks afterwards everyone will think that the dogs have polluted the air, especially as I have raised my left leg. If only I had known this art in the Chancellery this afternoon!"

The next day my master arranged a princely feast for his officers and close friends, as he had received pleasant news: his troops had taken the castle of Braunfels without the loss of a single man. It was my duty, as my office warranted, to help the other table servants to carry the dishes, pour the wine, and to wait with a plate in my hand. The first day a huge fat calf's head – of which they used to say that it is no dish for the poor – was given to me to serve. As the calf's head was boiled very tender, one of the eyeballs with the substance behind it protruded which appeared to me very pleasant and tempting. The fresh odour of the broth with its ginger seasoning tempted me so much and I felt such craving that my mouth began to water. The calf's eye laughed at my eyes, my nose and my mouth, and bade me devour it. I did not wait long to satisfy my hunger. On the way I scooped out the eyeball skilfully with my spoon which I had only received that very day and sent it quickly without delay to its proper place, so that nobody realized what had happened until the dish reached the table and betrayed us both. As the calf's head was about to be cut with one of the choice parts missing, my master realized why the carver hesitated. The master did not relish the insult that one dared to bring him a one-eyed calf's head. The cook was brought to the table, and all who had helped to serve were examined with him. Finally it came to light that the calf's-head with both eyes had been given to poor Simplicius to serve; but no one knew what happened afterwards. My lord asked, with what appeared to me to be a terrible temper, what had happened to the missing eyeball. I did not allow myself to become frightened at his sour face, but quickly I pulled my spoon out of my pocket, gave the calf's head a second scoop, and – Hey Presto – showed them what they wanted to know, swallowing the second eyeball as quickly as I had the first.

"Par Dieu!" exclaimed my master, "this prank tastes better than ten calves' heads!"

The assembled gentlemen praised these words and called my deed, which I had done out of simplicity, a wondrously clever act, indicating my future fortitude and fearless determination. This time I escaped my just punishment by repeating the original crime. I was even praised by the jesters and entertainers for putting both eyes together again as nature had originally intended. My lord warned me however that I should not repeat such mischief again.

At this banquet – and I assume at others too – the guests approached the table solemnly in the Christian way. They said their prayers silently, and to all appearances with great devotion. Such piety lasted through the soup and the first course, as if they were eating in a refectory of Capuchin monks. But hardly had they uttered three or four "God Bless Us" when everything became much noisier. I cannot describe how by-and-by every voice sounded longer and louder. I compared the entire company with an orator, whose voice starts gently and finishes like thunder. Dishes were brought in called "entrées", because they are spiced and supposed to be eaten before the drinking, so as to stimulate the thirst. Then followed a course to accompany the wine, not to mention French terrines and Spanish olla podridas, which by a thousand artistic preparations and numerous spices were peppered, mixed and camouflaged to excite the thirst, and so that the natural ingredients were hardly recognizable. I thought: why should this food and drink destroy the senses of a man and change him, and turn him into a beast? Who knows, whether Circe used other means than these when she changed the companions of Ulysses into swine? I now saw how the guests gulped down their food like sows, gurgled like cows, behaved themselves like donkeys and finally vomited like dogs. The noble vintages of Hochheim, Bacherach and Klingenberg they poured down into their bellies in barrellike glasses, and the effects showed in their heads. I saw to my amazement how everything changed; reasonable men who shortly before had possessed their five senses and could lead an intelligent conversation, all of a sudden became foolish and uttered the most stupid things in the world. These senseless follies that they committed, and the heavy drinks that they offered one another, became with time larger and larger, so that foolishness and drinking competed to see which was greater. At last this contest turned into an obscene piggery. I did not know from whence their giddiness resulted, because the effect of wine, nay drunkenness itself, was unknown to me. This gave me strange thoughts and fantastic ideas as I encountered their eccentric behaviour, for I did not know the origin of it. Up to now each one had emptied his plate with good appetite, but when the stomachs were filled they found it hard going, like a wagon driver who with his rested horses gets along well on a level road, has to stop at the foot of a hill. When the head became also filled, the impossibility to drink further was overcome by one through his courage found in the wine; by the other it was overcome by his faithfulness to his friend whom he could not let drink alone, and by the third it was overcome by his desire to respond with Teutonic honesty. But as such endeavours could not last for ever, they beseeched one to the other in the name of great lords, of dear friends, of sweethearts, to pour more wine by the gallon into their bellies until their eyes watered and the sweat of fear appeared on their brows. But the drinking must continue! At last they made noise with drums, pipes and stringed instruments, and shot into the air with muskets, as if the wine must storm the stomach. I wondered where they could put such great quantities of wine, as I did not know that wine before it was yet warmed inside, was surrendered with great pain from the very place into which it had been poured, amidst considerable danger to their health.

The vicar was present at this banquet. He too being human like others had to leave the room for he had participated, though against his will, in the drinking. I followed him and said:

"My dear vicar, why do people act so strangely? Why is it that they weave hither and thither? It appears to me that they have lost their wits. They have eaten and drunk themselves full, yet they swear by the Devil that they cannot drink another drop, but still they do not stop filling their bellies. Must they act thus or do they waste voluntarily to spite God?"

"Dear child!" replied the parson, "Wine in, wit out! This is nothing to what will follow. Hardly will they break up before dawn, for while their bellies are as tight as drums, they are not yet gay enough."

"Do their bellies not burst if they force their stomachs so violently?" I asked. "Can their souls, which are the images of God, remain in such fattened swine carcasses that are like dark dungeons and vermin infested towers? Their noble souls, why are they thus tortured? Are not their senses, which should serve their souls, buried in the intestines of irrational beasts?"

"Keep your mouth shut!" retorted the parson, "or you will get a sound thrashing. This is no time to preach, and besides I can do that better than you."

As I heard this I could see on turning round how food and drink was still being cheerfully wasted, without notice being taken of poor Lazarus, who in the shape of hundreds of refugees from the Wetterau, was starving in front of our doorstep, hunger looking out of his eyes.

My mind was tormented by all sorts of scruples as I waited at table with a plate in my hand; my inside too gave me no peace. My belly gnawed and snarled incessantly, and let me know that there were some winds inside which wanted to escape into the open. I thought to rid myself of these unwelcome fellows and let them pass, using the art which only last night I had learnt from my comrade. According to the instructions I lifted my left leg high into the air, pressed with all my might and prepared to utter quietly "*Je péte*" three times. But when one terrifying fellow escaped from me, there was such an explosion contrary to my intentions, that I was at a loss what to do for fear. I suddenly became so frightened as if I were standing on the ladder leading to the gallows and the hangman was about to place the noose over my neck and I became so confused with terror that

I could not command my own limbs. My mouth too became rebellious and what was intended to be whispered quietly (as if to spite my behind) was shouted as if somebody wanted to strangle me; the louder the lower wind roared, the louder my throat bellowed: "*Je pète!*" as if the exit and entrance to my stomach were competing to see which could produce the loudest thunder. I thus gained relief in my intestines but lost favour with my lord the governor. His guests became as a result of this explosion and roar of trumpets, almost entirely sober. But as I could not stop the winds, despite all my efforts, I was bound hand and foot and bent over a feeding trough, whereupon I received such a thrashing that I still remember it to this very hour. This was my first whipping since I breathed air, and I received it because I had fouled that very air in which we live. Then they brought frankincense and perfumed candles, and the gentlemen sought their musk-balls and boxes of balsam and took out their snuff boxes, but even the best of perfumes seemed of no avail. So there resulted from this act, which I played better than the best comedian in the world, peace in my stomach, sound blows on my back, a stench in the noses of the guests and much trouble on the part of the servants to restore fresh air into the hall.

When this was over I continued to wait at table as before. The vicar was still at the banquet and like the others was urged to drink. However he was reluctant, and said he did not care to swill like an animal. But another boon companion declared that the parson drank like a beast and he and his companions swilled like men. "For an animal," said he, "drinks only as long as he enjoys it and until its thirst is quenched, for it knows not what is good and cares not for wine; we men, however, enjoy the juice of grapes and make the most out of drinking it as did our forefathers."

"Very well," replied the parson, "It is my duty to observe moderation."

"Well, an honest man keeps his word," said the other, having his goblet filled and toasting the parson. Whereupon the parson departed and left the drunkard alone with his bucket.

When he had gone, everything went topsy-turvy so that it appeared as if the banquet was the only time and opportunity where guests could take revenge by getting drunk and shaming each other or by playing pranks. And when one reached the stage where he could neither walk, stand nor sit, it was said: "Now we are quits. You have cooked a stew for me before and now I offer you one in return." And he who could stand the longest and drink the most, boasted and thought himself a grand fellow. Finally all began to sway as if they had eaten henbane seeds. It was a miraculous carnival to behold but nobody, except myself, appeared astonished. One sang, the other cried, one laughed, the other was sorrowful, one cursed, the other prayed, one shouted "Courage!" the other could not talk, one was quiet and peaceful, the other wanted to fight with the Devil, one slept and was silent, the other talked so much that no one else could say a word, one discussed his amorous adventures, the other related his terrible deeds of war, some talked of the Church and spiritual matters, others of politics and affairs of state, some rushed hither and thither and could not remain still, others lay down and were unable to move even their little fingers, some devoured their food like threshers who had starved for eight days, others vomited all they had eaten that day. In short, all their doings and actions were so droll, foolish, strange and thereby so sinful and godless that my evil smell, for which I had been punished so gruesomely, was only a minor joke in comparison. Finally some serious quarrels rose up at the end of the table: they threw glasses, beakers, dishes and bowls at each other's heads. They fought not just with their fists but with the legs of stools and with swords, as well as with all other sorts of objects, so that on some red juice trickled down their ears; however my master soon quenched the quarrel.

As soon as peace was restored the master-drinkers, all the musicians and the womenfolk made their way to another house, where a hall was prepared for a new folly. My master however sat on his couch as he felt ill with rage or from overeating. I let him be where he lay, so that he could rest and sleep. I was hardly out of the door when he tried to whistle for me, but could not do it. He called me, but managed nothing more than "Simples". I ran towards him and found him squinting his eyes like cattle do when about to be slaughtered. I stood before him like a dried cod and did not know what to do. He pointed to the wine table and stammered: "Br... bring the, the, you rascal, the la... lavatory bowl. I mus... must sh... shoot a f... f... fox." I hurried to bring a basin and when I returned he had a pair of cheeks like a trumpeter. He grabbed my arm and ordered me to stand holding the basin in front of his mouth. His stomach erupted with painful revulsions so that I almost fainted because of the insufferable stench, and especially because some of it sprayed into my face. I almost joined him in the vomiting but stopped when I saw how pale he looked because I feared he had vomited his soul out as the cold sweat appeared on his forehead and his face looked as if he were dying. But he soon recovered and bade me bring fresh water so that he could rinse out his wine-filled belly.

He then ordered me to carry the fox away, but it appeared not contemptible as it lay in the silver bowl, but more like a dish for four men which should not be wasted. I well knew that my master had not collected anything bad in his stomach, but delicate and savoury meat pies, all sorts of bakeries, poultry, game and milk-fed veal, which one could still distinguish and recognize. I took it away but did not know what to do with it or where to go, and I could not enquire of my master. I sent to the chamberlain and asked him what to do with this pleasant treat that my master called a fox.

He answered: "You fool! Go and take it to the furrier that he may prepare the pelt."

I asked where the furrier was.

"No," he answered, seeing my simplicity, "take it to the court physician that he may see in what condition our master is."

I would gladly have gone on this fool's errand if the chamberlain had not been afraid of the consequences. He then bade me bring the trash to the kitchen and have the kitchen-maids keep it and strew it with pepper. This mission I duly fulfilled and was therefore much ridiculed by the girls.

My master was just leaving the house when I had rid myself of the basin. I followed him on foot to a large building where in the great hall men and women were whirling about like swarming ants. There was such trampling and shouting that I thought they had all become mad, as I could not imagine what reason there was behind this rage and fury. Indeed, this spectacle appeared to me so gruesome and horrible that all my hair stood up on end and I could only believe that they had lost their senses. As I approached I recognized them to be our guests who this morning were still in command of their wits.

"My God!" thought I, "What are these poor people doing? Oh, surely they have been overcome by madness!" It soon came to me that they must be devilish spirits who, in this accepted manner, were making sport of the human race by their pranks and monkey-play. For I reasoned: had they only human souls or God's image within them, they would not act in this inhuman manner. As my master entered the room from the entrance hall, the uproar ceased, but now they curtseyed and bowed with their heads and scraped with their feet, as if they wanted to erase from the floor what they hitherto had stamped in their rage. From the sweat on their faces and their heavy breathing I could see that they had laboured hard, but their happy faces made it appear that such efforts were not without enjoyment.

I had a great desire to know what the meaning of these foolish doings was. I therefore asked my comrade, confidant and trustworthy friend, who had so recently instructed me in the art of soothsaying, what these ragings and stampings meant. He told me as the honest truth that the people present had conspired to stamp the floor out of the great hall.

"Why else do you think they jump so violently about?" said he. "Have you not seen that for amusement they have already knocked the windows out and the same will soon happen with this floor."

"My God!" I answered, "So must we all perish and while falling break our necks and bones?"

"Yes," said my comrade, "that is their intention, and the devil they care. You will see that as soon as danger of death approaches each of the men will take hold of a pretty woman or girl, and this because it is said that a couple falling in this manner will escape harm."

As I believed all this I was overcome by such fear of death that I did not know where to run. Suddenly the musicians, whom I had not previously noticed, made themselves heard and all the menfolk ran towards the ladies as soldiers run to their muskets when the drums roar the alarm, and took the ladies by the hand so that it appeared to me as if the floor was already falling and would break the necks of both myself and of many others. As they started to jump about to a popular melody, so the whole building trembled and I thought: "Now your life is ended!" for I really believed that the whole building would collapse.

In my great terror I suddenly grabbed hold of a lady of high nobility and great virtue, with whom my lord was having a conversation. I hugged her like a bear and stuck to her like a burdock. As she drew back in fear, not knowing what foolish notions were in my head, I became panicky and screamed with despair as if I were being murdered. And as though that were not enough, there escaped by chance something into my trousers which emitted a most horrible smell, such as my nose had not experienced for a long time. At this moment the musicians became still, the dancers stopped and the virtuous lady on whose arm I clung thought herself highly insulted, imagining that my master had chosen to play a joke on her. Thereupon my master ordered me to be beaten and then locked up, as I had played enough pranks for that day. The soldiers of the Quartermaster, who were to carry out his orders, not only had pity on me but they could not stay near me because of my stench. They omitted the beating and locked me in a goose-pen under a stairway. Since then I have often thought of that day and have come to the conclusion excrements caused by fear and horror emit an odour far worse than if they had resulted from a strong purge.

PART TWO

7

SIMPLICIUS BECOMES A JESTER

DURING MY TIME IN THE GOOSE-PEN I thought of events related to dancing and drinking. But I cannot conceal that I was still in doubt as to whether the dancers raged in earnest to break through the floor or whether I had been deceived. Three whole hours, until the *Praeludium Veneris* or I should have said the honourable dance had ended, I remained sitting in my own filth, until someone crept stealthily to the door and started to fiddle with the lock. I listened like a sow that pisses in a puddle. This fellow however not only opened the door but slipped in as quickly as I wanted to slip out, and he even dragged a wench in after him holding her by the hand as I had seen men do at the dance. I had no idea what was about to follow. As my foolish mind had that day encountered and become accustomed to so many strange adventures, it was now resigned to accept whatever fate prescribed with patience and silence. Trembling with fear I pressed myself against the door and waited for the end. There soon came a murmuring from between the two which I could not understand, except that she complained of the evil smell while he tried to console her.

"Indeed fair lady!" said he, "it troubles my heart that envious fortune does not grant us a more honourable place to enjoy the fruits of love. But I assure you that your lovely presence will transform this horrible corner into a place more pleasant than Paradise itself."

I heard them kissing and noticed strange postures; however, as I did not know what this was nor what it meant, I remained as quiet as a mouse. A ludicrous noise came forth and the goose-pen, which was made simply of wooden boards underneath a staircase, started to shake and creak. The maiden behaved as if she were in pain, so that I thought here are two of those enraged people who attempted to stamp through the floor and now they have come here to take my life. As soon as these thoughts took hold of me I pushed open the door to escape death and rushed through with the same murderous shriek that had caused my confinement. But I was clever enough to bolt the door behind me, and then looked for a way out of the house. This was the first wedding that I had attended, though I was uninvited; I did not need give a present but the groom later charged me a heavy bill for it, which I paid honourably. Dear Reader! I do not tell this story to make you laugh but only to complete my tale and demonstrate what honest fruits are to be expected from dancing, for I know that bargains are made at a dance of which we can well be ashamed later on.

Although I had made a lucky escape from the goose-pen, only now I became fully aware of my misfortune, because my trousers were full and I did not know what to do. In my master's house all was silent and everybody asleep and I could not approach the sentry who stood before it. In the guard-room they would not allow me to stay because my stench was too evil, and it was much too cold and impossible to remain in the street so I did not know which way to turn. It was already past midnight when I remembered I could take refuge with the vicar. I knocked at the door with such impertinence that at last the maid unwillingly allowed me to enter, but as soon as she smelt what I brought with me – her long nose at once guessed my secret – she became angry and started to abuse me so that her master, who by now had almost finished his sleep, could hear. He called both of us to his bedside and as soon as he realized what the mischief was, he looked down his nose at me and said:

"In such condition one should take a bath even though it be not due by the calendar."

He ordered his maid to wash my trousers before dawn and to hang them by the stove, and to put me to bed as he saw that I was almost stiff with frost. I was hardly warm when day broke and the parson stood by my bed to hear what had happened to me and how my affairs were going, for my shirt and trousers still being wet I could not go to him. I told him everything and started to tell of the art which my comrade had taught me and how badly I had fared. Then I told him that the guests, after he had left, had become quite mad, and as my friend had told me, wanted to stamp down the floor, and through this I became terribly frightened and wished to save myself from destruction. Wherefore I was locked in the goose-pen and how finally I had seen and heard the couple who were the means of my release from there, and how I had locked them in instead of me.

"Simplicius," said the vicar, and scratched himself behind the ears, "Your affairs stand lousily. You had a good chance but I fear you have lost it forever. Get quickly out of bed, and away from my house so that I do not come into disfavour with your master should they find you with me."

So I had to take myself off in wet clothes, and experienced for the first time how well a man is if he still possesses his master's favour, and how evil it goes with him when the favour is in bad repair.

I went into my master's quarters where everyone still slept like logs, save the cook and a few maids. These were cleaning the room in which the night before the drinking feast had taken place, and the cook prepared breakfast from the remnants. When I approached the maids, the floor was covered with broken drinking vessels and window-glass and all that which the drinkers had let go either upwards or downwards, as well as big pools of spilled beer and wine, so that the floor resembled a geographical map with seas, islands and continents. The stench everywhere in the room was far worse than that in my goose-pen. Therefore I did not stay long but soon hurried away to the kitchen and let my clothes dry on my body by the fire. I expected with fear and trembling what fortune would further have in store for me when my master should have finished his sleep. I also contemplated on the world's folly and senselessness and thought over everything which had happened to me during this last day and night, and all that I had seen and heard and experienced. And I lauded my previous meagre and miserable life with the hermit and wished I were back with him in the forest.

When my lord arose he sent his valet to fetch me from the goose-pen, who brought news to him that he had found the door open and behind the bolt a hole cut with a knife, so that the prisoner had freed himself; but my master had already heard that I was in the kitchen. In the mean time, the servants rushed hither and thither to invite yesterday's guests for breakfast, among them the vicar who had to come earlier than the others as my lord wished to talk with him about me before the meal. He asked him first if he considered me sane or a fool, whether I were simple or wicked, and told him exactly how obscenely I had behaved the previous day and evening. Many of his guests had objected thinking this insult had been done on purpose. He had ordered me to be locked in the goose-pen as a safeguard against further fooleries, but now I had escaped and walked about in the kitchen as a young lord who need not serve him any more. In his whole life never had such a prank been played on him in front of so many honourable guests. He knew not what else to do with me but to have me flogged and because of my stupidity to chase me to the devil.

While my lord so complained about me, the guests were assembling, and when he had finished speaking my parson answered that if it would please his lordship to listen with patience, he would tell him a few amusing facts regarding Simplicius, through which not only his innocence would be proved, but even those who had taken objection to his behaviour would be relieved of their mistrust towards him.

Meanwhile the wild ensign whom I had imprisoned in my stead came up to me in the kitchen. Through threats and a thaler which he thrust upon me, he forced me to promise to keep my mouth shut as to his adventures.

The tables were laid again as on the day before, covered with food and attended by guests: wormwood and sage wines, with elecampane, quince and lemon wines, with hippocras, were offered to reconcile the heads and stomachs of the drunkards, as almost all of them were the Devil's martyrs. At first they started to talk about themselves, mainly how bravely they had filled their bellies last night, and there was no one among them who would admit he had been drunk, though the night before they had sworn they could hold no more. When they were tired of talking of their own follies, poor Simplicius became the object of their discussion. The governor himself reminded the parson to recount according to his promise the amusing stories.

First the vicar asked to be pardoned if he had to use words which were not appropriate to a member of the clergy. Then he started to talk, firstly by which natural causes I was tortured by winds in my belly, and that through such causes I had insulted the secretary in his chancellery, and how I had learnt the art of soothsaying and how this had been my downfall. Then further how strange the dancing had appeared to me as I had never seen this before and how my comrade had enlightened me and how I had grabbed the distinguished lady. The parson explained all this with such well-chosen words that almost the entire company burst into laughter, and he apologized so politely for my simplicity and ignorance that I regained my lord's favour and was allowed to wait once more at his table. Nothing did he tell of my adventures in the goose-pen and of how I was freed from there, as he thought some ill-humoured old men might be annoyed believing the clergy should tell only sour stories.

And now my lord asked me, to amuse his guests, what reward I had given to my comrade who taught me such refined arts. And when I answered "Nothing", he said, "Then I will pay the apprentice fee for you." Whereupon he had my companion page bound over a feeding trough and whipped in the same way that I had experienced the day before when I practised the arts and failed.

The governor realized now the extent of my simplicity and wanted to persuade me to amuse his guests even more. He saw that the musicians were of no value while I was present as everybody preferred my foolish caprices to seventeen lutes. So my lord asked me why I had cut the door of the goose-pen and I answered: "Someone else may have done that." He asked: "Who then?" and I said, "Perhaps he who came to me."

"Who came to you?"

"That I am not allowed to tell." I answered.

My lord was quick-witted and saw well how I had to be deloused. He therefore asked me suddenly who forbade this, and I answered at once: "The wild ensign."

Through the general laughter I realized that I had been fooled, and the wild ensign who was sitting at table became as red as a hot cinder. I did not want to talk any more unless he gave me permission, but it only needed a sign from my master to him, and I was allowed to tell all I knew. Thereupon my lord asked me what business brought the wild ensign to me in the goose-pen, to which I answered:

"He brought a young maiden to me."

"What else did he do?"

"I think he wanted to let his water."

My lord asked, "But what did the lady do? Was she not ashamed?"

"Oh no, my lord," said I, "she lifted her skirts and wanted – my honourable readers who love decency, honour and virtue, forgive my rude pen, that it writes so crudely – she wanted to shit."

At this the whole assembly burst into such laughter that my master could neither hear me nor could he ask any more questions, and it was not even necessary or that honest and pious virgin would have been brought into disgrace as well.

The chamberlain now told the whole company that I had said some time before, after returning from the ramparts, that I knew where thunder and lightning came from and had seen big tree trunks on carts which were hollow, into which had been stuffed onion-seeds and iron-white turnips, off which the tails had been cut. After which the tree-trunks had been tickled with a spiky stick behind and at once steam, thunder and hellish fire escaped in front. They recounted many more such follies so that through the whole breakfast, they only talked and laughed about me. All this brought about my final downfall, which was that all believed in time I would make a rare table entertainer, meaning a jester, by whom even the greatest potentates of the world might be honoured, and dying people made to laugh.

While the guests were indulging in food and drink as on the previous day, the guard announced that a Commissary was waiting at the gates, ordered by the War Council of the Crown of Sweden, to inspect the garrison and investigate the fortress. This salted all pleasure away, and the gay feast shrivelled like a bagpipe when the wind is out. The musicians and guests disappeared like the smoke of tobacco of which only the smell remains. My lord trotted along with his aide-de-camp who carried the keys, together with a detachment of the guards and many lanterns towards the gate, in order to admit the Inkslinger, as he called him, personally. He wished the Devil might break his neck into a thousand pieces before he stepped inside the fortress, but when he admitted him and offered him his welcome on the inner drawbridge, he showed so much devotion that he almost held his stirrups, and the compliments from both sides were so overwhelming that the Commissary dismounted and accompanied my lord on foot, wherewith each of them pressed to walk on the other's left. I thought: "Oh, what a hypocritical spirit reigns over man as each is fooled by the other."

As we approached the main guard, the sentry called out: "Who goes there!" although he saw it was my master, who did not want to answer but wished to leave the honour to the other. Therefore the sentry became more obstinate and repeated his call. Finally the Commissary answered the last "Who goes there!" by the words: "He who brings the money."

When we had passed the sentry, I followed slowly and I heard the very same sentry – he was a newly enlisted soldier and had been before a young well-to-do peasant from the Vogelsberg mountains – mumble the following words: "You lying rogue! He who brings the money! A torturer who takes the money, that's what you are! So much money you have pressed out of me that I wish hailstones would kill you before you leave the town!"

From this moment I had the idea that this strange gentleman with his velvet hat must be a holy man, as not only did no curse have effect upon him but even all those who hated him showed him honour, love and reverence. That very night he was treated like a prince, made blind drunk and put into a magnificent bed.

The next day when the inspection took place everything went topsy-turvy. Even I, simple wretch, was clever enough to deceive the astute Commissary (to which appointment truly no innocent children were taken). I hardly needed an hour to learn this deception as the whole trick consisted in beating the five and the nine on the drum, being still too small to appear as a musketeer. They gave me to this end some borrowed uniform and a borrowed drum (my short page breeches did not suit such an occasion) and I passed the inspection without mishap. But as they did not trust my simplicity to remember a strange name to answer and step forward at roll call, I had to remain Simplicius, and the surname the governor invented himself and had me entered in the roll as Simplicius Simplicissimus. So he made me the first of my clan, as if I were the son of a whore, although according to his own opinion I looked like his sister.

And ever after I kept this name and surname until I heard my right one, and I played my role fairly well under this name to the advantage of the governor and with little detriment to the Crown of Sweden. This was all the war service I ever gave to the Swedish Crown and her enemies have no reason to be jealous of me on this account.

As soon as the Commissary had gone, the vicar called me secretly to his dwelling, and said:

"Simplicius, I feel pity for your youth and your future miseries. Listen, my child, and believe me. Your master is determined to deprive you of all your reason in order to make you into a jester – already the fool's costume has been ordered for you. Tomorrow you shall receive your lessons which will make you lose your reason. Undoubtedly they will cruelly torture you so that if God will not prevent it, you will become mad. For the sake of your hermit's piety and your own innocence, in true Christian love I will help you with advice and I will give you this medicine. Take this powder which will strengthen your brain and memory so that you will easily overcome everything without damage to your mind. And here, take this ointment and smear it on your temples, on the nape of your neck, and on the nostrils. Do this as soon as you go to bed, as at no hour will you be safe lest they fetch you from your bed. But beware, and look out that nobody hears of my warning and sees your medicine, or it may go ill both for you and me. And if they give you this cursed maltreatment, do not believe all that they want to persuade you to believe, but pretend that you believe. Talk but little that they do not guess they are beating empty straw or they will prolong your torments. I do not know in which manner they will treat you, but as soon as you are dressed in your feather cap and fool's costume, come back to me so that I can give you further advice. Meantime I will pray to God that He may preserve your mind and health."

With that he gave me powder and ointment and I went back home. As the parson said, so it happened. When I was still in my first sleep, four fellows dressed up in horrifying devils' masks came to my bedside. They jumped around like buffoons and carnival jesters. One had a red-hot hook, another a torch in his hands. The other two fell upon me, dragged me out of bed, and danced with me hither and thither and forced my new clothes on my body. I pretended to take them for real, live devils and screamed terribly, behaving as if in great fear. They told me that I must go away with them and bound my head with a towel so that I could neither see, hear nor shout. So they led me, poor wretch, trembling like an aspen, making many detours, up steps and down steps, and at last into a cellar in which a huge fire was burning. After they had undone the towel, they started to treat me with Spanish wine and Malvoisier. They had easy play to make me believe that I had died and was now in the abyss of hell as I readily pretended to believe all their lies.

"Drink bravely!" they told me, "as you have to stay with us in all eternity, but if you refuse to be a good companion, sharing in everything, then you shall be thrown into this very fire!"

These poor devils tried to disguise their voices so that I should not recognize them, but I noticed at once they were my master's riflemen. I let no one suspect this but laughed to myself that these who wanted to make me a fool were tools to me. I drank my share of the Spanish wine but they drank even more than I, as such heavenly nectar rarely comes to such fellows, and I can swear they were sooner drunk than I.

I now thought it was time to start to sway hither and thither as I had seen my master's guests behave, and at last I drank no more but only slept. However, they chased and pushed me with their hooks, which they kept putting into the fire, to all the corners in the cellars so that it appeared as if they had gone mad themselves. They did that to make me drink more or at least that I should not sleep. And if I fell in the chase, which I often did on purpose, they dragged me up again and pretended to throw me into the fire. So it happened to me like a falcon which they want to keep awake, and this was a great torment to me. I could have overcome them in drunkenness and sleep but they were not always together but relieved each other, so that at last I had to succumb. Three days and two nights did I spend in that smoky cellar which had no other light but that which came from the fire.

My head started to swirl and to rage as if it were bursting so that at last I had to invent a trick to get rid of my pain and my tormentors. I acted like the fox who pisses in the dog's face if he thinks he can no longer escape, and as my nature just forced me to obey my need I also put my finger into my throat to make myself vomit. In such manner all at once I paid my bill with such unspeakable stench that my devils could no longer stay near me. Enraged with this they laid me in a sheet and flogged me mercilessly that all my innards and my soul wanted to flee my body. Through this I lost consciousness and lay as dead, so that I knew not what else they did to me.

When I came to myself again I was no longer in the gruesome cellar with the devils, but in a splendid hall in the hands of three of the most ugly old hags that ever the earth has borne. In the beginning when I opened my eyes only a little I took them for real hellish spirits. If however I had already studied the old pagan poets I should have thought them to be the Eumenides or one of them to be Tisiphone from hell to rob me, like Athamas, of my senses, for I knew in advance that I was there to be made a fool. This old witch had a pair of eyes like will-o'-the wisps and between them a long skinny hawk nose, the end of which easily touched her lower lip. I saw only two teeth in her mouth, long and yellow, and her face looked like Spanish leather, while her white hair hung unkempt around her head as though she had just been taken from her bed. Her long breasts were comparable with two flabby cow's udders from the ends of which hung a brownish-black nipple half a finger long. Indeed a horrifying sight, good for nothing else but an excellent medicine to counteract the mad love of amorous billy-goats. The other two were not at all more handsome, only that they had blunt monkey noses and were dressed more tidily. As soon as I had recovered a little I recognized one of them to be our dish-washer and the others as the wives of the riflemen.

I pretended I was unable to move – and truly I did not feel like dancing – when these old grandmothers undressed me to the skin, and as if I were a little child, washed all the dirt off me. This comforted me and these three showed so much patience and compassion that I almost revealed to them how well I still was. However, I thought: "No, Simplicius, do not trust any old women, but remember that you will have a wonderful triumph if you in your youth can deceive three such old cunning hags with whom one could verily catch the Devil in open field. From this occasion you may take hope that with growing years you may achieve even more!"

When they had finished with me they put me into a sumptuous bed in which I fell asleep without being rocked. They went away and took their basins and other things with which they had washed me, and my clothes and all the filth. I believe I slept without break for more than twenty-four hours.

On waking, two handsome boys with wings stood before my bed. They had white shirts, sashes of taffeta, and were preciously decked with pearls, jewels, golden chains and other glittering objects. One boy carried a gilded bowl full of wafers, sugar-bread, marzipan and various confections, while the other had a gilded beaker in his hands. Pretending to be angels, these boys wanted to make me believe that I had now arrived in heaven, having successfully endured the fire of hell and escaped the Devil and his mother. Thus I should ask whatever my heart desired inasmuch what I wished would be available or easily procured. Being tortured by thirst and seeing the beaker before me I asked for a drink, which was given more than willingly. This was no wine but a soothing sleeping draught which I drank in one gulp, and as soon as I felt it becoming warm within me, I fell asleep again.

The following day I woke anew and found myself no longer in bed nor in that hall nor with the angels, much less in heaven, but in the old dungeon, the goose-pen. There as in the cellar was gruesome darkness and I was dressed in a garment of calfskins with the fur turned outwards. The trousers were cut in the Polish or Swabian fashion and the coat made in a still more foolish manner. Above, at my neck, was a hood sewn on like a monk's cowl which was pulled over my head and decorated with a beautiful pair of large donkey's ears. I had to laugh at myself in my misfortune as I at once realized by nest and feathers what kind of a bird I was meant to be. Only then I began to search my heart and consider what was best for me. I decided to behave as foolishly as possible and await with patience how my fate might turn out.

With the help of the hole which the wild ensign had cut in the door of the goose-pen, I could easily have escaped, but as I had to be a fool, I wanted to play the part. I not only acted like one who has not wit enough to walk out but I even behaved like a hungry calf that longs for its mother. My bleating was soon heard by those who were ordered to watch and so two soldiers approached the pen and asked who was in it. I answered: "You fools, can't you hear that a calf has arrived?" They opened the pen, took me outside, and were amazed that a calf could speak; they behaved like two newly-hired clumsy comedians unable to play their roles properly so that I felt I ought to help them in their pranks. They discussed together what they should do with me and agreed to make a present of me to the governor, who, because I could speak, would give them a better price than the butcher would do.

They asked me how I was and I answered: "Rotten enough!" They continued: "Why?" I replied: "Because of the custom here to lock decent calves in a goose-pen. You rascals should know if you want me to become a proper ox, you must rear me as an honourable bull deserves."

After this short conversation they led me across the street to the governor's quarters. A huge crowd of boys followed us and as they, imitating me, shouted like bleating calves, a blind man would have thought according to the noise that a herd of calves was being driven along, but in fact it only looked like a crowd of old and young fools.

The two soldiers presented me to the governor as if they had taken me as booty on one of their patrols. He gave them some reward and promised me I should be treated well by him. I answered: "Indeed, my lord, but no one should lock me in a goose-pen as we calves cannot stand such treatment if we are to grow into good cattle!" The governor promised me a better state and thought how clever he was to have turned me into such a laughable jester. I thought however: "You only wait, my dear lord, I have passed the trial of fire and I have been hardened in it. Now let us try which of us will fool the other best."

At this moment a refugee peasant was watering his cattle and as soon as I saw this I ran bleating like a calf after the cows as if I wanted to suck. The cows were more frightened of me than of a wolf, even though I wore their kind of pelt. Indeed they became so enraged and rushed wildly away from each other as if a swarm of hornets in August had been let loose upon them, so that their master was unable to herd them together again, which caused great amusement. At once a crowd of people rushed hither to gaze at the buffoonery. My lord laughed as if he must burst and said at last: "Verily one fool makes a hundred." But I thought to myself: "Indeed, and you are the first among them."

From now on everybody called me "The Calf", and I too gave everyone else a mocking name, which in the opinion of all and especially of my master were wittily chosen, as I christened every man according to his qualities. In short, everybody thought me to be a witless fool, and I knew them to be fools with their wits. This seems to be the usage of the world that everybody is satisfied with his own wit and imagines himself to be the cleverest among them all.

As it was mid-winter, the pranks I played with the peasants' cattle shortened for us the already short morning. At the midday meal I waited at table as I did before but also launched some tomfooleries, such as when I had to eat I refused to swallow human food or drink; I only wanted grass which at that time was impossible to procure. So my lord had a pair of fresh calves' skins fetched from the butcher and had them pulled over the heads of two little boys. These he placed by me at table and treated us for the first course with winter salad and told us to eat heartily: he even ordered a live calf to be brought and enticed it with salt to eat the salad. I stared at this as if I were greatly amazed but those standing around persuaded me to play my part.

"Truly," they said, when they found me so reluctant, "it is nothing new for calves to eat meat, fish, cheese and butter, and such like. They even get drunk occasionally. These beasts know nowadays quite well what is tasty, and the difference between us and them is no longer great. Why should you alone not participate?"

I was gladly persuaded for I was hungry, and after all I had seen before that men could be more piggish than pigs, more ferocious than lions, more lecherous than goats, more envious than dogs, more wayward than horses, coarser than donkeys, more insatiable for drink than cattle, more cunning than foxes, greedier than wolves, more foolish than apes, and more poisonous than snakes and toads. Yet they all ate human food and differed from the brutes only through their shape, and could not at all be compared for innocence with the calf. So I feasted with my calf companions according to my appetite, and if a stranger had seen us at table doubtless he would have believed that the ancient Circe had come to life again to turn humans into beasts – the art which now my lord had practised.

In the same way as at midday I was treated at the evening meal, and similarly as my companions at table or parasites had eaten with me so that I would eat, they had to go to bed with me, for my master would not permit me to spend the night in the cowshed. Thus I fooled those who took me for a fool and came to the conclusion that the most gracious God gives every human so much reason as he needs for self-preservation. Many mistakenly imagine that they alone possess wit and have their fingers in every pie, whether they be learned men or not, but beyond the mountains there, too, people are dwelling.

When I woke up in the morning my two becalfed bed companions had already gone. I arose and when the adjutant fetched the keys to open the town gates, I stole out of the house to my parson to whom I told everything that had happened to me in heaven and in hell. When he realized that my conscience was disturbed by deceiving so many people and especially my lord, by pretending to be foolish, he said:

"Do not worry about that. This foolish world wants to be deceived. As they have still left you your reason, so you should use it to your advantage. Imagine yourself to be like the Phoenix which is born again through fire from folly to wisdom, and thus to a new human life. Consider that you have not jumped over the ditch yet, but you have slipped into the fool's cap by risking your reason, and times are so strange that nobody knows whether you can escape without losing your life. You can quickly run into hell, but to get out of it you need much struggling and snorting. You are far from being grown-up or man enough to face the future danger, as you can well imagine. You will have to take more care and use more wit than ever before when you knew not the difference between wit and folly. Remain humble and await in patience for things to change."

His words were intentionally severe because he was able to read from my brow that I was boastful for having slipped through the whole ordeal with masterly deception and such clever tricks. I could see from his expression that he was tired and weary of me. And of what use was I to him? Therefore I changed my tone of speech as well and paid him many thanks for the magnificent drugs which he had given to me for the preservation of my reason. Indeed I made all sorts of impossible promises, as my duty demanded, to repay him gratefully. This tickled him and brought him back into a better mood. He praised his medicine as being of great excellence and told me Simonides Melicus had invented an art which Metrodorus Skeptius had perfected with great efforts, with the help of which he taught men to repeat anything to the word that they had ever heard or read. Yet such a feat, he told me, could not have happened without this brain-stimulating medicine which he had given to me.

"Yes," I thought, "my dear parson, when with my hermit, I read in your very own books quite different things about Skeptius's secret art of memorizing!"

But I was cunning enough not to say a word, for to tell the truth, since they forced me to become a fool, I acted more craftily and formed my words more carefully. The parson went on to tell me how Cyrus knew every one of his thirty thousand soldiers by his right name, and Lucius Scipio all the citizens of Rome by name, and Cineas, ambassador of Pyrrhus, could call out the names of all the senators and noblemen by heart on the second day after his arrival in Rome. Mithridates, king of Pontus and Bithynia, he said, had peoples of twenty-two different tongues in his kingdom, to whom he could give judgment each in their own language, and even speak personally with them. The learned Greek, Charmides, could quote from memory what anybody wanted to know from the books which he had in his library, even though he had only read them once. Lucius Seneca could repeat two thousand names as they were spoken to him, and as Ravisius reports, could repeat two hundred verses spoken by two hundred students from the last to the first. Esdras, as Eusebius tells us, knew the five books of Moses by heart and could dictate them word by word to the scribes. Themistocles learnt the Persian language in one year, and Crassus mastered five different dialects of Greek in Asia Minor, and administered the law to his subjects. Julius Caesar could read, dictate and give audience all at the same time. Apart from the Romans, Aelius, Hadrianus or Portius Latro and others, the Holy Jerome understood Hebrew, Chaldaic, Greek, Persian, Median, Arabic and Latin, while the hermit Antonius knew the whole Bible by heart only from hearing.

The parson continued: "In view of all this you should not think it impossible that the human memory can be truly strengthened and preserved through certain medicines, just as it can be weakened in many ways or even annihilated. For, as Plinius writes, nothing is so fragile in human nature as memory, which through illness, horror, fear, worry or grief, could fade away altogether or lose great parts of its strength. We read of a scholar at Athens that after a stone had fallen on his head he forgot everything he had studied, even his alphabet. Another through illness, forgot his servant's name, and Messala Corvinus did not remember his own name any more though before he had a very good memory. And Schramhans writes of a priest who drank blood from his own veins and forgot how to write and read, but otherwise retained his memory undamaged. When a year later at the same place and time he again sucked his own blood, he was able to write and read again. More credible is what Johannes Wierus tells us in his third book of hellish miracles that if man eats of the brain of a bear he will fall into such a heavy trance and delusion as if he had become a bear himself as proved by the example of a Spanish nobleman, who, after having eaten such brains ran into the wilderness and imagined nothing else save that he was a bear. My dear Simplicius, if your lord would have mastered this art you could have been changed sooner into a bear like Callisto than into a bull like Jupiter."

The parson told me many similar things, gave me again some of his medicine, and instructed me regarding my future behaviour. With that I went home again, and with me more than a hundred boys, who followed all bleating like calves. My lord, who had just risen, ran to the window, and seeing so many fools at once, condescended to laugh heartily.

As soon as I entered the house I was called into the chamber, as my lord was in the company of some noble ladies who were eager to see and hear his new jester. I appeared and stood there as though dumb, so that the lady whom I had grabbed earlier at the dance at last said that she had heard this calf could speak but now she realized this was not true. I replied:

"And I have heard monkeys cannot talk, but I hear now that this too is not true!"

"What!" said my lord, "Do you perhaps mean these ladies are monkeys?"

"If they are not already," I answered, "they soon will be. I did not want to become a calf, and yet I am one."

My lord asked me how I could see that these ladies would turn into monkeys. I answered:

"Our monkey carries his bottom naked but these ladies reveal their bosoms which other maidens keep covered."

"You wicked bird," cried my lord, "You are a foolish calf, and as you are, so you talk! The monkey goes naked for want of clothes, but these ladies show on purpose what is worthy to be seen. Quickly atone for your impertinence or you will be whipped and the dogs will chase you into the goose-pen as is the custom for calves which know not how to behave. Let us hear whether you know how to praise a lady as is her due."

Whereupon I looked at the lady from head to foot and again from foot to head, and I stared straight and lovingly at her as if I wanted to marry her. At last I said:

"My lord, I can well see where the mistake lies: the thievish tailor is wholly to blame, for he has put that cloth which should cover the neck and the bosom at the hem; that's why the skirt trails behind so much. The bungler should have his hands cut off if he cannot tailor better than this. And, my lady," I told her, "send him away so that he will not disfigure you any more, and try to get hold of my dad's tailor! His name was Master Paulkin and he could cut beautifully plaited skirts for my mum, our Ann and our Ursula, which were quite even and round at the hem so that they did not trail along in the dirt as yours. Yes, you can't believe what beautiful clothes he could make for the pretty whores."

My lord asked whether my dad's Ann and Ursula were more beautiful than this lady.

"Oh no, my lord," I replied. "This lady has hair as yellow as a little babe's shit, and her locks so prettily rolled that they look as if on each side a few dozen sausages are hanging. Look only at her lovely smooth forehead. Is it not curved more finely than a fat ham, and whiter than a dead man's skull which has hung in the weather for many years? The pity only is that her tender skin is spoilt from hair-powder so that people who do not know much about this would think our lady has inherited the scab which throws off scurf. More's the pity because of her sparkling eyes whose blackness shines clearer than the soot of my dad's oven which our Ann lit with a bunch of straw to heat the room, indeed her eyes are fiery as if they would kindle the whole world. Her cheeks are beautifully rosy; however, the bright red which she has put on her lips surpasses far such colour. If she laughs or

75

speaks – please, my lord, take note of this – you will see two rows of teeth in her mouth so perfectly even and sugar-like as if they had been chipped from white turnips. Oh, miraculous beauty, I cannot imagine that it can hurt to be bitten by these teeth. Furthermore her neck is sheer white as curdled milk and her bosom beneath of similar hue, and without doubt as hard to feel as the goat's nipple which is overflowing with milk and not as flabby as those of the old women who cleaned my behind the other day when I arrived in heaven. Oh, my lord, look only at her hands and fingers; they are so supple, so long, so tender and clever as those of Gypsy women when they go fishing in other people's pockets. But how does this compare with her whole body which I, alas, cannot see. Is it not as tender, slim and pretty as though for eight whole weeks she had suffered from dysentery?"

Whereupon such a burst of laughter broke out that nobody could hear me any more, nor could I talk, and with that I left quietly like a Dutchman so that I ended the scoffing at my pleasure. The midday meal followed at which I bravely pursued my profession, for I had made up my mind to denounce all follies and to punish all vanities, which my position as a fool gave me the freedom to do. No companion at table was too grand for me to reproach and ridicule and if there were some who did not like this, the others laughed at him or my lord reminded him that no wise man is infuriated by a fool. I attacked especially the wild ensign, my worst enemy, and quickly made an ass of him. The first who, at a wink from my lord, argued reasonably with me was the secretary. I had called him a title-forger and ridiculed him because of his silly titles, asking him what title would be given to the first father of all mankind.

"You are talking like an unreasonable calf," he replied, "as you do not know that after our first parents, diverse people have lived who, through rare virtues such as wisdom, manly, heroic deeds and through invention of fine arts, have ennobled themselves and their descendants to such an extent that they have been raised by others above all earthly things, indeed above the stars to divine personalities. If you were human or at least if you had as a human read history, you would understand that there is a difference between men and you would not envy everybody his title of honour. But as you are only a calf, incapable and unworthy of any human honour, so you are talking of this like a foolish calf and grudge the noble human race the honour which they rightly enjoy."

I answered: "I was human once, just as you, and have read a good deal too, and can therefore judge that you do not clearly understand the whole affair, or that your personal interests prevent you from saying what you know. Tell me what glorious deeds have been done and what praiseworthy arts have been invented which are sufficient to ennoble a whole family for several hundred years after the death of the hero or the artist himself? Has not the hero's strength and the artist's wisdom and craft died with them? If you do not believe this and if the parents' qualities are inherited by the children, then I am convinced your father was a stock fish and your mother a flat fish."

"Ho!" the secretary cried: "If we are going to compete by insulting each other, I could remind you that your father was a rude peasant from the Spessart and though in your homeland and in your family there are notorious bull-heads, you have lowered yourself even more by turning into an unreasonable calf."

"Very well," I answered. "Now I've caught you out even more; that's what I wanted to prove, that indeed the virtues of the parents are not always bequeathed to the children and therefore the children do not always deserve the virtuous titles of their parents. It is no disgrace to have turned into a calf as I have the honour to follow the mighty king Nebuchadnezzar, and who knows if it will not please God that I like him turn again into a human, and become even greater than my dad has ever been? Once and for all, I praise only those who become noble through their own virtues."

"Well, suppose for argument's sake," the secretary said, "that the children should not always inherit their parents' title of honour, but you have to admit that they are praiseworthy who make themselves noble through good behaviour, and if that is so, it follows that we have to honour the children for the sake of the parents, for the apple never falls far from the trunk. Who would not praise the descendants of the great Alexander, if there were any left, for their ancient ancestor's fortitude in war? He proved already in his youth, before he could carry arms, his fighting spirit, by fearing that his father might conquer everything and leave him nothing to vanquish. Did he not subdue the world before he reached the age of thirty, and yet wished to conquer another one? Did he not when fighting a battle with the Indians, abandoned by his men, sweat blood in his anger? Did he not appear as if surrounded by sheer flames of fire, so that even the barbarians fled from him in fear? Here I could mention even Julius Caesar and Pompeius, one of whom besides the glorious victories in the civil wars, fought fifty times in open battles and has slain 1,152,000 men; whilst the other besides taking nine hundred and forty ships from the pirates, has taken and conquered eight hundred and seventy-six towns and villages from the Alps to the farthest corners of Spain. Moreover, let us not omit Hercules the Strong and Theseus and others, whose immortal praise it is impossible to describe. Should they not be honoured in their descendants?

"But let me now leave arms and weapons and turn to the arts which though they seem to be of less esteem, nevertheless bring glory to their masters. What skill can we find in Zeuxis who through his genius and dexterous hand could deceive even the birds in the air? And equally in Apelles, who could paint a Venus so natural, so beautiful, so perfect, and with all her features so neat and tender that even bachelors fell in love with her. Who would not praise the man who first invented letters and the noble art of book-printing? Indeed, who would not raise above all artists the man who invented agriculture and the corn mill? Why should it not be just that others be praised in honour according to their deeds. It matters little whether you, clumsy calf, can grasp this with your unreasonable bullock's brain or not. You are behaving like the dog who, lying on a heap of hay, grudged this to the oxen only because he could not eat it himself. You are unworthy of any honour and for this reason you begrudge those who deserve honour."

As I saw myself so cornered, I replied: "These glorious and heroic deeds were indeed praiseworthy if they had not caused the detriment and destruction of so many people. But what glory is that which is besmirched with the blood of so many innocents? And what nobility is that achieved by the annihilation of so many human lives? Concerning the arts, what else are they but sheer follies and vanities! Indeed, they are just as vain, empty and useless as the titles themselves with which they are rewarded, for they only serve greed, lust, gluttony and the ruin of others, just like those horrible cannons which I recently saw on the gun carriages. Indeed, we could easily do without printing and writing, according to the sayings of that holy man who believed that the whole wide world was enough of a book in which to observe the miracles of his Creator and recognize the divine supremacy."

Now my lord, too, wanted to make a joke with me and remarked:

"I see very well that as you cannot ever hope to become noble, you therefore disdain the honoured titles of nobility."

"My lord," I replied, "and if I in this very hour should replace you in your dignified position, I would refuse."

The governor laughed and said: "This I believe very well – the ox's due is straw of oats. If you possessed an elevated mind as noble spirits should have then you would eagerly strive to achieve honours and dignities. For my part I consider it no mean thing that fate makes me superior to others."

I sighed and answered: "Oh wearisome happiness! My lord, I assure you that you are the most miserable man in the whole of Hanau."

"Why so, calf?" my lord asked, "Tell me why for I do not feel so."

I answered him: "If you as governor of Hanau do not realize with how many sorrows and worries you are laden, for this very reason, you are either blinded by too great an ambition for honour or you are made of iron and altogether without feeling. Certainly you have the power to command and whoever comes under your eyes has to obey you. But are they doing that for nothing? Are you not the servant of them all? Must you not care for each of them? Look, you are surrounded by enemies everywhere and the preservation of this fortress hangs alone upon your neck. Your aim is to cause damage to the enemy and to look out that your plans are not betrayed. Is it not often necessary that you stand on guard like a common soldier? As well you have to watch that there is no lack in money, munitions, provisions and reserves, and for this reason you have to keep the whole country in continuous extortion by tribulation and confiscation. Whenever you send your soldiers out to such purpose, robbing and looting, stealing, burning and murder is their best work. Only lately your men have looted Orb, taken Braunfels and burnt Staden to ashes, from which they gained some loot but you have gained a heavy responsibility before God. It may well be that besides the honour, you reap some advantage which pleases you, but do you know who will finally enjoy the treasures you have acquired? Even if your wealth remains with you (which nobody can foresee), in the end you must leave it in this world and can take nothing with you but your sin through which you acquired it. And if you are fortunate enough to make use of your loot, you are only wasting the sweat and blood of the poor, who now suffer in misery or even perish and die of hunger. Oh, how often do I see that because of the magnitude of your office your thoughts are going astray while I and other calves can quietly sleep without sorrows. And if you do not so, and neglect something which is essential to the preservation of your garrison and fortress, it will cost you your head. Look, such cares do not touch me! And as I know that nature once will claim my death, so I do not worry that somebody may attack my stable or that I have to battle grimly for my life. Should I die young, I am spared the miseries of an ox under the yoke. But you are pursued in a thousand ways, that is why your whole life is nothing but continuous worry and interruption of sleep. You must fear friends and enemies alike as they are trying to rob you of your life or your money or reputation or your command, or something else, in the same way that you intend to do to them. The enemy attacks you openly and your pretended friends secretly envy your fortune – and even among your subjects you are in no way secure.

"I will not mention how you are tortured daily by your ardent cravings which drive you hither and thither to make your reputation even greater and to climb higher in rank and collect greater wealth, to trick the enemy or to take this or that place by surprise. In short: to do almost everything that tortures other people and is detrimental to your soul and displeases God's majesty. But the worst is that you are so much spoilt and poisoned by your flatterers that you do not know any more your true self and you do not see the dangerous road on which you walk. For all that you do they will say is right, and all your vices are turned into sheer virtues and are praised. Your ferocity they call justice, and if you allow land and people to perish, they call you a brave soldier and incite you to do harm to others, in order that they may remain in your favour and fill their own pockets."

"Foolish babbler!" said my master, "who taught you to preach like that?"

I answered: "My dearest lord, did I not tell the truth that you have been ruined by your cajolers and fawners, and beyond help? But others will soon find out your faults and will criticise you not only in big and important matters but even in small things. You know enough examples of high persons who lived in former times? The Athenians grumbled at Simonides because he talked too loudly. The Lacedemonians sneered at Lycurgus because he stooped. The Romans jeered at Scipio because he snored loudly, and they mocked Julius Caesar because he did not wear his belt properly. Do you think, my dear lord, I would like to change with someone who, besides twelve or thirteen table companions, adulators and parasites, has more than a hundred or perhaps more than ten thousand secret and open enemies, slanderers and evil-minded enviers. What happiness, what pleasure and gladness can such a master enjoy under whose care and protection so many people live? Is it not essential that you have to watch for all of them, to care for them and listen to their every grievance and complaint? Is such a thing not worry enough in itself without having enemies and enviers? I can well see how bitter is your lot and how many miseries you have to bear. Oh, my dearest lord, what in the end will be your reward? Tell me, what will you gain? If you do not know, so learn it from the Greek Demosthenes, who after he had served the community of the Athenians, bravely and faithfully, against all law and justice, was exiled and chased into misery. Socrates was rewarded with poison, and Hannibal was so badly recompensed by his people that he had to wander miserably through the world. Likewise the Greeks paid off Lycurgus and Solon, one being stoned to death and the other blinded and driven away from his country as a murderer. Therefore, keep your command as well as the reward which you will gain from it. You do not need to share it with me. If everything goes well you will reap a bad conscience; but if you take care of your conscience, you will be considered a failure and pushed out of your command as if you had turned like me into a stupid calf."

While I talked like that, everybody looked at me and were amazed that I could utter such words which, as they said, a reasonable man would not have been ashamed to improvise.

I concluded my sermon by saying: "My dear lord, I do not want to change places with you, for the wells give me a healthy drink instead of your precious wines, and He whom it pleased to turn me into a calf will also bless the plants of the soil in such way that they serve me to the preservation of my life. So has nature already given me a good fur, whilst you however often enough abhor the best things and the wine splits your head and throws you into this or that disease."

My master answered: "I do not know what I actually have in you. As a calf you seem to be much too intelligent. I almost believe that under your calf-skin you have the skin of a roguish rascal."

I pretended to be enraged and said: "Do you humans believe that we animals are all fools? Do not imagine that. I believe if older animals could talk as I can, they would tell you even more. If you think that we are so stupid, tell me who has taught the wild doves, the jays, the blackbirds and the partridges how to purge themselves with bay leaves. Who taught dogs and cats to eat the dewy grass if they want to cleanse their full belly? Who taught the stag when he has been shot to take refuge in the dictamnus or the wild fleabane? Who let the wild boar recognize the ivy and the bear the mandrake, and told them that it is good for medicine? Who advised the eagle to look for the eagle-stone and to use it if he has trouble laying his eggs, and who makes the swallows understand how to heal the weak eyes of their young ones with celandine? And who has taught the snake to eat fennel if she wishes to slough off her skin and to heal her dim eyes? Who taught the stork to purge himself, and the pelican to let blood, and the bear to use bees as scarifiers? I would rather say that you humans learnt your arts and science from us animals. You eat and drink yourselves to disease and death such as we animals never do. A lion or wolf, if he becomes too fat, will fast until he is thin, fresh and healthy again. Who acts more wisely now? And moreover, look at the birds in the heavens! Look at the different artifices of their tender nests, and as nobody can imitate their work you must confess that they are more intelligent and skilful than humans themselves. Who tells the migrating birds when to come to us in the spring and hatch their young ones, and in the autumn when to go away to warm lands? Who teaches them to find a meeting place at this end? Who leads them or shews them the way? Or do you, men, lend them perhaps your ship's compass that they might not go astray? No, my dear people, they know the way without your help and know how long they need and when to depart from one place or the other. They need neither your compass nor your calendar.

"Furthermore, watch the industrious spider, whose web is almost a work of wonder; see if you can find a single knot in all his work. Which huntsman or fisherman has taught him how to spread his net, and to lay in wait for his prey, sitting either in the farthermost corner or even in the middle of his web. You men marvel at the raven of whom Plutarch writes that he threw so many stones into a vessel which was only half full of water until the water rose high enough for him to drink thereof easily. What would you do if you would live near and amongst the beasts and would watch their actions, their doings and their undoings? Then you would realize that all beasts possess their own natural powers and virtues in all their emotions, in their foresight, strength and mildness, timidity and ferociousness, teaching and learning. Each one knows the other; they differ from each other; they pursue that which is useful to them, and flee from that which is harmful, avoid danger, collect what is necessary for their nourishment, and even deceive human beings. Therefore many old philosophers have pondered earnestly and were not ashamed to ask whether the unreasonable beasts had not reason also. But I do not wish to continue to talk of these things; go to the bees and behold how they make wax and honey, and then tell me what you think."

My lord's guests at the table all gave different judgments of me. The secretary declared me a fool as I considered myself to be a reasoning beast, and therefore proved that he who has some bats in the belfry and yet believed himself to be wise, is actually the most perfect fool. Some others said if my fancy that I were a calf could be taken away or if I could be persuaded that I had again turned into a human, I could be considered sane and reasonable. But my lord himself said: "I believe him to be a fool as he has told everybody the truth unashamedly. Yet his speech is such that it does not fit a fool!"

And all this they spoke in Latin that I should not understand.

My master asked me whether I had studies when still a human being. My answer was that I did not know what study was. "But my dear sir," I went on, "tell me what things are these studs with which men study? Do you perhaps mean the ninepins with which men play bowls?" Upon this the wild ensign cried out:

"What is the matter with this fellow? He has the Devil in his body. He is possessed, and the Devil is speaking through him."

Whereupon my lord took the opportunity to ask me since I had been turned into a calf, whether I still had the habit to pray like other humans and whether I believed I would go to heaven.

"Indeed," I answered, "I still have my immortal human soul, which as you well can imagine does not wish to go to hell, especially as I fared so badly there once before. I have only changed as once did Nebuchadnezzar and in time I might become a man again."

"This I wish for you," replied my master, with something of a sigh, from which I could easily guess that he felt a certain regret that he had dared to turn me into a fool. "But let us hear," he continued, "How do you pray?"

Thereupon I knelt down and lifted eyes and hands to heaven, like a good hermit, and as my lord's repentance consoled my heart exceedingly, I could not keep back my tears. So to all appearance, after saying the paternoster, I prayed with great devotion for all Christendom, for friends and foes, and even that God would grant me that I might live my life in this time and that I might become worthy to praise Him in all eternity, as my hermit had taught me such a prayer with piously conceived words. Here some tender-hearted spectators almost started to weep for they had deep compassion for me; even my master's eyes were filled with tears.

After the meal my lord sent for the parson, to whom he told everything that I had said, and let him understand that he feared all was not right with me and perhaps the Devil was in league with me, because before I had shewn myself quite simple and ignorant but now I knew how to talk of things which were amazing. The parson who knew my condition best answered that one should have thought of that before daring to turn me into a fool, for human beings were images of God with whom and especially with such tender youth, nobody should fool about as with beasts. Yet in no way he believed that the evil spirit had been allowed to take part in the play, as I had at all times commended myself to God through ardent prayer. Should this however have happened against all hope, the governor had taken a heavy responsibility before God as there was almost no greater sin than to deprive a human being of his reason and so deprive him from praising and serving God for which he chiefly was created.

"I found before," the parson went on, "enough proof of his reason but that he could not adjust himself to the world because he was brought up by his father, a coarse peasant, and later with your brother-in-law in the wilderness in all simplicity. If people had shown a little patience with him at the beginning, in time he would have behaved better as he was a pious simple child who did not know yet the evil world. However, I do not doubt that he may be brought to reason again if we can rid him of his fancy that he has been turned into a calf. I have heard of a man who firmly believed that he had changed into an earthenware jug and therefore asked his people to place him high up on a shelf that he might not be broken. Another imagined nothing less than that he were a cock, and crowed in his illness day and night. Still another imagined he had already died and was wandering about as a ghost, so he refused medicine and food and drink until at last a wise doctor employed two fellows who pretended to be ghosts as well, and bravely filled themselves up and persuaded him that nowadays all ghosts ate and drank. Thus he was brought to reason. And I have heard of another madman who believed his nose was so long that it reached down to the ground; they hung a sausage to it which little by little they cut off until they reached his nose and when he felt the knife at it, cried out that his nose was now in its right shape again. In the same way as these people were cured, our good Simplicius could be helped."

"All this I very well believe," answered my lord, "but what I cannot explain is that before he was so ignorant, and now he knows how to talk about everything and discusses things so perfectly which is rarely found among older, more experienced and better read people than he. He talked so much of the qualities of animals and described my own person so pointedly as if he had lived his whole life among people, that I was astonished and had to consider his speech almost as an oracle or a warning of God."

"My lord," said the parson, "this may well be quite natural. I know that he is well read as he and the hermit studied all my books, and there were not a few of them. And as the boy has a good memory but his mind is now latent and forgetting his own person, he can quickly produce whatever his mind had previously absorbed. I firmly hope that in time he will become normal again."

So the parson kept the governor in suspense between fear and hope. He defended my case to his very best ability and achieved good days for me and for himself with access to my lord. Their final decision was to bide their time with me and this the parson did more for his own sake than for mine, because by going in and out to the governor and pretending to be caring for me he came into the governor's favour. Consequently he was taken into his service and made chaplain of the garrison, which was no small thing in these hard times. But in my heart I grudged him not this.

8

SIMPLICIUS TAKEN PRISONER BY THE CROATS AND SEES THE WITCHES' SABBATH

FROM THIS TIME ON I enjoyed my lord's grace, favour and love fully, of which I can truthfully boast. My good fortune was only hampered by having too much calf-skin and too little experience in years, though I was scarcely aware of this. The parson himself did not wish me to be considered sane again, as it seemed to him not yet time and advantageous for his own interest.

My lord, realizing my love for music, had me taught and made me the pupil of an excellent player of the lute, whose art I soon mastered and soon surpassed him, for I could sing to the lute better than he. So I served my lord to his entertainment, pleasure, delight and amazement. The officers showed me their favourable intentions, the richest citizens honoured me, and servants as well as soldiers were friendly when they saw how much my master favoured me. One presented me with this, the other with something else, as they knew that jesters have often more influence with their masters than honesty should allow, and that was the meaning of their gifts; some made presents to me so that I would not slander them, and others for the very reason that I should slander their adversaries. In this way I accumulated quite a heap of money which I mostly gave to the parson as I did not yet know its value. No one dared to sneer at me and from this time on I suffered no opposition, worry or care. All my thoughts were centred on music and on how to criticise politely the shortcomings of this or that man. So I grew like a maggot in cheese, and my physical strength increased visibly. It was evident that I did not mortify myself as in the forest with water, acorns, beechnuts, roots and herbs, but that good food, Rhine wine and Hanau double-beer suited me well. This was a great favour of God in these miserable times, for then the whole of Germany was kindled in bright flames of war, and hunger and pestilence raged everywhere; Hanau itself was surrounded by enemies, but all this did not trouble me. My lord's intention was, if the siege were raised, to send me as a present to the Cardinal Richelieu or to the Duke Bernhard of Weimar;* he hoped in this way to earn much gratitude and he further pretended that it was impossible for him to endure seeing me daily in the costume of a fool, as I became more and more alike to his lost sister. From this intention the parson however dissuaded him as he thought the time had come to perform a miracle and turn me into a reasonable man again. He therefore advised the governor to prepare a few calf-hides and to have them put on two other boys, and afterwards to order a third fellow, disguised as a doctor, prophet or wayfaring quack, who should under a mysterious ceremonial undress me and the other two boys, pretending to change animals into humans and humans into animals. In such a way I could very well be brought back to reason when I would see how others like me were transformed from calves into men. As soon as the governor agreed to this proposal the parson told me what they had planned and easily persuaded me to give my consent.

But jealous Fortune did not wish me to abandon my fool's costume so easily, nor to enjoy longer a pleasant life of comfort. While tanners and tailors already prepared our costumes, which belonged to the comedy, I and several other boys were strolling outside the fortress on the ice when suddenly a party of Croats pushed us altogether onto several riderless peasant horses which they had just stolen, and kidnapped us. At first they were doubtful whether to take me or not until at last one of them said in Bohemian, "Let's take this fool with us and bring him to the colonel." To whom another answered: "By God, yes, put him on the horse; the colonel understands German – he will have fun with him!" So I was forced to mount the horse and realized how one single unfortunate little hour can deprive us of all happiness and welfare, so that we feel it for the rest of our days.

Although the people in Hanau at once raised the alarm, sent out riders, who held up the Croats for a while, harrying them through skirmish, they could not regain the loot. And so these speedy riders successfully escaped and pressed on to Büdingen, where they fed their horses and made the burghers there pay ransom for the rich captive sons of Hanau, and sold their stolen horses and other booty.

From there they moved on again almost before it was night, and long before daybreak, riding quickly through the forest of Büdingen towards the monastery of Fulda, and looted on the way whatever they could carry. Looting and plundering did not hinder them in their hasty journey, like the Devil, who, as one used to say, can woo as he flies without losing time. That same evening we arrived at the Abbey of Hirschfeld where they were quartered, carrying much loot. Everything was divided and I was given to Colonel Corpes as his share.

With this master all appeared to me repulsive and strange. The delicacies of Hanau had changed into coarse black bread and skinny beef and occasionally a piece of stolen bacon. Wine and beer had turned for me into water and in place of a bed I had to be content to lie in the horses' straw. Instead of playing the lute by which I had before entertained everyone, I had to crawl like other boys under the table and to howl like a dog and be jabbed with the spurs, which was no joke for me. Instead of my pleasant strolls in Hanau, I had to ride out foraging, to groom horses, and dung out their stables. This foraging was nothing else than swooping down on villages, with great hardship and often not without danger to life and limb, and there to thresh, to mill, to bake and to loot whatever could be found; to harass and despoil the peasants and even to rape their maids, wives and daughters. And when the wretched peasants objected or even dared to hit back at one or the other of the foraging soldiers engaged on such work, they were hacked down when they got hold of them or at least their houses went up in smoke to heaven.

My master had no wife, as altogether these kinds of warrior were not used to take their womenfolk along; he had no page, no chamberlain, no cook, but a crowd of horse grooms and boys, who looked after both him and the horses. He was not ashamed to saddle his horse himself nor to feed it, and he always slept on straw or on the naked ground, covering himself with a coat of fur. On account of this, mill fleas* could often be seen crawling about on his clothes, of which he was not in the least ashamed and he would laugh if somebody picked one off. He wore his hair short and his beard was wide in the Swiss style. This served him well as he used to disguise himself in peasant clothes to reconnoitre. Although he did not entertain princely dignitaries, nevertheless he was honoured, beloved and feared by his own folk and by all who knew him.

We were never at rest, sometimes here, sometimes there. At times we assaulted and in turn were assailed ourselves; there was no respite from damaging the might of the Hessians but on the other hand Melander, the Hessian general,* did not remain idle either and took many riders prisoner and sent them to Cassel. I did not like this restless life at all and often wished in vain to be back in Hanau. My heaviest cross was that I could not converse with the fellows, and had to endure to be pushed, tormented, beaten and chased by almost everyone. The greatest amusement that I could give my colonel was to sing to him in German and like the other grooms to pipe for his pastime, which happened rarely, yet brought me so many heavy blows making the red blood flow that I had more than enough of it for a long time.

Eventually I busied myself with some cooking and kept my master's firearms in order, of which he was very fond, for I was of no use yet to ride out foraging. All this was very much to my advantage as I at last gained my master's favour so that he had made for me a new coat of calf's skin with even bigger donkey's ears than I had ever worn before. My master's taste was not particular, so I needed less skill in my art of cooking, but as I often had neither salt, lard nor spice, I grew tired of this handiwork and contemplated day and night how I could successfully run away, especially as spring had arrived. To bring this about I pretended to remove the guts of sheep and cows which lay in heaps around our quarters, so that they should not any longer cause such an evil stench; to this the colonel agreed, and when I was engaged on this and it became dark I did not return but escaped into the nearest forest.

My fate became worse, indeed so bad that I believed I was born only for misfortune. I was but a few hours away from the Croats when I was seized by some marauders. Doubtlessly they believed they had made a good catch in me, and as in the dark night they could not see my fool's dress, two of them took me to a certain place deep in the forest. On the way one of the fellows abruptly demanded money from me; he put his gauntlets and blunderbuss down and started to search me in the pitch dark and said: "Who are you? Have you money?" But when he touched my hairy coat and felt the long donkey's ears on my cap, which he mistook for horns, and saw the bright sparks which emanate from animal skins if stroked in the dark, he was so frightened that he shuddered. At once I realized this, and stroked my coat zealously with both hands, so that it sparkled as if I were filled with burning sulphur, and before he could recover and regain his senses, I answered him with gruesome voice:

"The Devil am I, and I will twist your neck and your comrade's too!"

That terrified them so much that they ran off through the undergrowth so quickly as if chased by hellish fire; although in the darkness they bruised themselves against stumps, stones and trunks, and more often fell, they got up again as quickly as they could, until I could hear them no longer, while I laughed horridly that the whole forest resounded, which in the dark solitude was ghastly to hear.

When I was about to withdraw into the bushes, I stumbled over the blunderbuss, so I took it as I had learnt from the Croat how to handle a fire-arm. Going on, I knocked against a knapsack which was made of calf skin just like my coat. This too I picked up and found that a cartridge pouch, with powder, shot and all necessities was attached. I hung this on me, took the fire-arm on my shoulder like a soldier and hid myself not far away among thick bushes to sleep there for a while.

At daybreak, the whole band came to the place searching for the lost fire-arm and the knapsack. I pricked my ears fox-like and kept quiet like a mouse. As they could not find anything, they jeered at the two who had fled from me: "Shame! You cowardly fools!" they cried, "Shame upon your soul that a single fellow could frighten, chase you away and take your arms!"

One of the robbers swore the Devil might fetch him if it were not the Devil himself, as he had touched the rough skin and the horns with his own hands. The other became violent and said: "Let it be the Devil or his mother, if only I could get back my knapsack." One of the band, whom I took to be the leader, answered him: "What do you think the Devil would do with your knapsack and your musket? I would bet my neck that the fellow whom you have so disgracefully allowed to escape took both with him." Another argued that some peasants could have arrived, found the things and taken them away. At last all agreed to this so that the whole band firmly believed that they had had the Devil under their noses, especially as that fellow who had wanted to search me in the darkness confirmed it with the most horrifying oath, and described so clearly the rough sparkling skin and the horns as devilish attributes. I believe if I had suddenly shown myself at this moment the whole band would have run away.

When at last they had searched long enough and found nothing, they again went on their way. But I opened the knapsack to have some breakfast and with the first fistful found a purse in which were three hundred and some sixty odd ducats. No question that I was glad at that, but the reader may be assured I was still more pleased with the provisions with which the knapsack was filled. Concerning the money, I am sure that no common soldier would have taken such a big sum with him on a raid, but must have stolen it secretly on the way and quickly pushed it into his knapsack in order not to divide it with the rest.

Gaily I had some breakfast and soon found a pretty little spring at which I refreshed myself and counted my beautiful ducats. Even for the price of my life I could not have said in which district I roamed. I stayed in the forest for as long as my provisions lasted, with which I economized sparingly; but when my bag became empty, hunger drove me to the cottages of the peasants. There I crawled by night into cellars and kitchens and took what food I could find and carry; this I dragged with me into that part of the forest where it was wildest. Here again I led the life of a hermit as before, only that I stole very much and prayed very little; I had no constant dwelling but wandered about, sometimes here, sometimes there. It was fortunate for me that the summer had begun, although I was able to kindle a fire with my musket whenever I wished.

On my roamings in the woods I met peasants here and there but they always fled from me, maybe because the war had frightened them or that the marauders had spread the story of the adventure which they had had with me, that all who met me believed the Devil himself was wandering about in person in the neighbourhood. Therefore I feared my victuals would disappear and bring me into the utmost misery or I would have to eat roots and herbs again, to which I was no longer accustomed. Reflecting on this, I heard two wood-cutters at work, which pleased me greatly. I followed the sound and when I saw them, took a handful of ducats from my purse, stalked up to them, shewed them the tempting gold and said: "Gentlemen, if you will only help me I will make you a present of this gold !" But they, perceiving me and my money, ran away at once, leaving behind their mallet and wedges and also their cheese and sack of bread. From this I filled again my knapsack, turned back into the wood and almost despaired of ever meeting human beings in my life again.

After long thought I came to the conclusion: "Who knows what will happen to you? If you have money and bring it to good people in safety you can live from it for a fair while." I therefore decided to stitch it up, and out of my donkey ears which chased people to flight, I made two armlets, and put all my ducats which I had received from Hanau and from the robbers therein and tied them round my arms just above the elbow. After safeguarding my treasure, I again visited the peasants and took from their stores what I needed and could pilfer. Although I was still simple, I was clever enough never to return to a place where I had thieved before, and so was fortunate with stealing and was never caught.

Once at the end of May when I again in my usual although forbidden way crept into a farmyard to fetch my food, I found myself in the kitchen, but soon realized that the folk were still awake (where dogs hung about I wisely never went). I kept the kitchen door leading into the courtyard wide open so that if danger came I should be able to run away, and there I remained quiet as a mouse, waiting until the people would go to bed. In the mean time, I noticed a slit in the kitchen-hatch leading to the living room. There I stealthily crept to see whether the peasants would not soon go to sleep. But my hopes came to nothing, as they had just dressed themselves, and instead of a candle a sulphurous blue flame stood on a bench, near which they smeared grease on sticks, brooms, forks, stools and benches, and rode out on these through the windows. At this I was terribly amazed and felt great horror, but as I had been accustomed to still more horrible things and had all my life neither read nor heard of witches, I did not take it too seriously, mostly because everything happened so quietly.

After all had flown away, I went into the room and here I considered what I could take with me and where to look for it. With such thoughts, I sat down astride a bench, but as soon as I did so I flew with the bench out through the window, leaving behind knapsack and blunderbuss, which I had put down almost as a reward for witches' ointment. My sitting down, flying off and descent happened in one moment, for I arrived as it seemed to me instantly amongst a great mass of people; possibly because of fear I did not realize the length of my journey. These people were dancing a remarkable dance such as I had never seen in my life. They held hands and turned their backs inwards as one has seen the Three Graces painted, so that their faces turned outwards, forming many rings one within the other. The innermost ring consisted of seven or eight persons; the next one of double this number; the third had more than both, and so on, so that in the outer circle were more than two hundred. And as always one circle danced to the left and the other to the right, I could not see how many rings they had formed nor what stood in the middle around which they danced. It looked strange and horrid as all bobbed their heads ludicrously, and just as strange was the music. Everyone, it appeared to me, sang as he danced which gave an amazing harmony. My bench which carried me there came to rest near the musicians who stood about outside the rings of the dancers. Some of the musicians had instead of flutes, bagpipes and shawms, nothing but adders, vipers and blindworms, on which they whistled merrily. Some had cats into whose behinds they blew and fingered on the tail, which sounded similar to bagpipes. Others bowed on the skulls of horses as on the best fiddles, and others played the harp upon cow skeletons like those which lie in the flayer's pit. One held a bitch under his arm whose tail he turned and fingered her teats. In between devils trumpeted through their noses that the whole forest echoed, and when the dance came to an end, the whole hellish crowd started to rage, shriek, rustle, roar, howl and storm as if they were all mad and senseless. And so one can imagine how I was struck by horror and fear.

In this turmoil a fellow approached me with a gigantic toad under his arm, easily as big as a kettledrum. Its guts had been pulled out through the arse and pushed into its mouth, which looked so revolting that I had to vomit.

"Look here, Simplicius," he said, "I know that you are a good lute player. Let's hear a fine tune!"

I was so terrified that I almost fell down on hearing the fellow call me by name; out of fear I became completely speechless and imagined I lay in a deep dream and prayed fervently in my heart that I might wake up. The fellow with the toad however, at whom I stared, pushed his nose forwards and backwards like a Calcutta cock, and at last he knocked me with it on the breast so that I nearly choked. At this I started to cry loudly to God and there upon the whole host disappeared, and in a flash it was pitch dark and my heart felt so fearful that I fell to the ground, making the sign of the cross well-nigh a hundred times.

As there are many people and among them well-esteemed scholars, who do not believe that there are witches and wicked spirits, and still less that they can fly hither and thither through the air, I do not doubt some will say, "Simplicius, do not tell tall stories!" With these I will not argue as tall storytelling is today no longer an art, but almost the commonest of crafts: I cannot deny that I too understand it, otherwise I would be a miserable liar. But those who deny the flying of witches should only remember Simon the Sorcerer who was lifted up by the evil spirit into the air and came back to earth at the prayer of St Peter.

Nicolas Remigius, a brave, learned and reasonable man, who had burnt more than half a dozen witches in the dukedom of Lorraine, relates of Johann of Hembach how his mother, who was a witch, took him in his sixteenth year to one of her meetings to play the pipe, as he had learnt it, for the dancing. For this he climbed up a tree, and piped and looked eagerly at the dance, which appeared to him strange. At last he said: "O beware, dear God, from where come such foolish and mad crowds?" As soon as he had spoken these words, he fell from the tree, sprained one shoulder, and called for help. But there was no one there, save himself. When he later talked of this, most people believed it to be a fable, until shortly afterwards, Catherine Prevotia was caught because of witchcraft, having been present at the very same dance. She confessed everything as it had happened, except that she knew nothing of the cry which Hembach had made.

Majolus has two examples, one of a servant who clung closely to his wife, and the other of an adulterer who had used the ointment of the adulteress and had anointed himself with it, and so they had both come to the witches' sabbath. So goes the story of a farm-hand who got up early and greased his cart, but as in the darkness he took the wrong pot, the cart flew up into the air and had to be pulled down again. It is more than well known how maidens and wives in Bohemia allowed their lovers to be fetched by night from far away on the backs of goats. How Doctor Faustus with others, who were no sorcerers, flew through the air from place to place, is well known in history. I myself knew a woman and a maid. This maid was greasing her lady's shoes by the fire and when she had finished with the first one and put it aside to grease the other, suddenly the greased one flew out through the chimney. But this story has been suppressed.

All this I only mention that people may in principle be convinced that witches and sorcerers really do at times fly to their meetings, and not that people should believe me that I myself flew there as well. It is the same to me whether I am believed or not, and he who will not believe may invent a different way by which I could have marched from the monastery of Hirschfeld or Fulda into the Archbishop's Cloister in Magdeburg in so short a time.

9

WITH THE IMPERIAL ARMY, SIMPLICIUS
MEETS HERZBRUDER, FATHER AND SON

I CONTINUE MY NARRATIVE and assure the reader that I lay on my belly until it was bright daylight, for I could not find the heart to rise. I still doubted whether all these events were dreams or not but in spite of my fears, I dared to fall asleep for I thought I was lying in no worse place than in a wild wood to which I was accustomed since I had left my dad.

It was about nine o'clock in the morning when some foraging soldiers came and woke me up. Only then I realized that it was in the middle of a wide field that I was lying. They took me along to some windmills and after they had milled their corn, led me to their camp in front of Magdeburg.* There I was taken to a colonel of infantry who questioned me from where I came and to which master I belonged. I told him everything in detail, and as I could not name the Croats I described their costume and gave examples of their language, and how I escaped from them. I kept quiet about my ducats and what I told of my ride through the air and the witches' sabbath they took to be imagination and foolery inasmuch as I mixed up the thousands with the hundreds in my description.

Meanwhile a great crowd gathered round me, as one fool makes a thousand. Amongst them was one who had been a prisoner in Hanau last year and had served there, but later had returned to the Imperial Army. He recognized me at once and said:

"Ho, ho! There is the governor of Hanau's calf." The colonel asked him further questions about me, but the fellow knew no more than that I could play the lute well and that the Croats of the regiment of Colonel Corpes had abducted me outside the fortress of Hanau, and also that the governor of Hanau had been very sorry to lose me as I had been such an amazing jester. Hereupon the wife of the colonel sent to another colonel's wife who played well upon the lute, and therefore carried one with her, asking for the loan of it. The lute arrived and it was handed to me with the order that I should let them hear something. But it was my opinion they should offer me first something to eat, as an empty belly and a fat one such as the lute had, would not harmonise well. And so it happened, and after I had gulped considerably and had swallowed a good draught of Zerbst beer, I let them hear the best I could do with lute and voice. In between I uttered all sorts of fantasies that came into my head, so with little effort the people were soon convinced I was that which my costume promised.

The colonel asked where I wished to go, and as I answered I did not mind, he soon agreed that I should stay with him and become his page. He even wanted to know what had happened to my donkey's ears.

"Indeed," I answered, "if you should know where they are they would fit you well!" But wisely I kept quiet as to their present task, as all my wealth lay within them.

In a short time I was well known to most of the high officers in the Imperial camp and also in the Elector of Saxony's camp, but especially with the ladies, who decorated my cap, sleeves and clipped ears everywhere with silken ribbons of many colours, so that I believe the fops have copied their present fashion from me. But the money which the officers gave to me I lavishly wasted and spent to the last penny drinking the Hamburg and Zerbst beer with good fellows; I liked these brews immensely and was treated to beer wherever I went.

When the colonel had acquired for me a lute of my own, as he intended I should always stay with him, I was no longer allowed to roam between the two camps but he put me under the care of a marshal who had to keep an eye on me and to whom I had to be obedient. He was a man after my own heart, quiet, reasonable, learned, of good but not superfluous speech, and most important, he was thoroughly God-fearing, well read, and in science and the arts well trained. I slept in his tent at night, and was not allowed from his sight by day. He was once a counsellor and official to a distinguished prince, and had been very rich, but the Swedes had ruined him completely, his wife had died and his only son who could no longer study because of poverty, served in the Electoral Army as a clerk of the Roll. This marshal stayed with the colonel and was also in charge of his stables, awaiting the time when the dangerous events of war on the Elbe should change, and the sun of his earlier fortune would shine on him again.

My marshal, being more old than young, could not sleep the whole night through. For this reason he discovered my deceit in the first week and learnt with certainty that I was not the fool I pretended to be. He had been suspicious and had guessed from my face my true nature, for he understood physiognomy well. Once at midnight I awoke, and, reviewing in thought my own life and its remarkable adventures, I stood up and told in a prayer of thanks all the blessings which God had bestowed on me and all the dangers from which He had saved me. Then I lay down with deep sighs and fell asleep. My master heard everything though he pretended to be fast asleep, and that happened several nights in succession, so that he became quite certain that I had more reason than many elder men with much conceit. But he never spoke to me of it in our tent as the walls were too thin, and for some reason he did not wish other people should know of my secret before he was completely convinced of my innocence.

Once I went for a walk behind the camp, which he gladly allowed as he so found the chance to follow me and talk with me alone. As he wished, he found me in a lonely spot, just as I was about to voice my thoughts, and he said to me:

"Dear good friend, as I have your well-being in mind, I am glad to be able to talk alone here with you. I know that you are no fool as you pretend, and you do not wish to live in this wretched and despised rank. If you value your own welfare and you will trust me as an honest man, tell me all your troubles, and I for my part will as far as possible help you with advice and action to rid yourself of your fool's dress."

Overwhelmed with joy I embraced him as if he were a prophet come to free me from my fool's cap. We sat down on the ground and I told him my life story. He peered at my hands and was amazed at the curious signs of my past and future. However he dissuaded me fervently not to dispose of my fool's costume too soon, as he could see with the help of chiromancy that my future was threatened with imprisonment, including danger to life and limb. I thanked him for his sympathy and advice and prayed to God that he might reward his loyalty, and as I had been forsaken by all the world I implored him to be and remain my loyal friend and father.

We then arose and went over to the gambling place, where tournaments were held with dice and everyone cursed in their hundreds and thousands, gave away galley loads and moats' full of curses. The place was almost as big as the old market square in Cologne, covered everywhere with cloaks and equipped with tables each surrounded by gamblers. Every party had three four-cornered "rascal-bones" (dice) to which they entrusted their fortunes – thus they shared their money, giving it to one and taking it from the other. At every cloak or table, one acted as dice-master (who might better be called a vice-master), and he was the adjudicator who had to see that no wrong was done. He supplied cloaks, tables and dice, and kept back from each winning a fee so that he commonly snapped up most of the money. But even to them the money did no great service, as they lost it again in gambling or spent it at the sutler, if not at the surgeon who often enough had to stitch up their heads.

These foolish gamblers all hoped to win, which could only have been possible if they would have played with money from another's pocket. And though they all had this one hope, it could be said "Many heads, many arguments' as each longed for his own good luck. Some hit, some missed, some gained, some lost. Some cursed and others thundered; some cheated, others were deceived. The winners laughed and the losers ground their teeth; some sold their clothes and everything they treasured, and others gained them. Some asked for honest dice but others wanted loaded ones, smuggling them secretly into the game, until their opponents threw them out, smashed them, bit them with their teeth and tore the play-masters' cloaks into tatters. Some of the loaded dice were Netherlander, which had to be thrown with a slide; they had sharp edges where they carried the fives and sixes, as sharp as the wooden donkeys on which the soldiers had to sit for punishment. Others, called "Highlanders", needed a special twist called "the Bavarian Height" to be thrown effectively. Some were made of stag's horn, light above and heavy underneath; some were lined with quicksilver or lead, and others with chopped hair, tinder, chaff and charcoal. Some had sharp corners; on others the corners were completely ground off; some were long like rifle butts and others broad like turtles. And all these species were solely made for cheating: they fulfilled that for which they were made, whether they were thrown violently or shuffled gently, and no amount of shaking could help, not to speak of those which had two fives and sixes, or on the contrary, two aces and two deuces. With these rascal-bones they snatched, lured and stole each other's money, which in turn they had robbed or looted or gained with bitter trouble and toil, endangering body and life.

As I stood there looking at the gambling place and the gamblers in their folly, my master asked me how I liked these goings-on. I answered: "I dislike that they blaspheme God so horribly but otherwise I cannot judge their merits or faults as something unknown to me and of which I have no experience."

The marshal answered: "You should know that this is the most evil and most despicable place in the whole camp, because here a man tries to gain the other's money and loses, by doing so, his own. And he who only puts a foot down here in order to play, has already broken the tenth commandment – "thou shalt not covet thy neighbour's goods". If one gambles and wins by fraud and loaded dice, one has broken also the seventh and eighth commandments. Indeed, one can even become a murderer if he who is robbed of his money falls into poverty, utmost misery, despair or takes to disgusting vices. No excuse can help even if one says: "I risked my share and have won honestly". They are villains who go to the gambling place meaning to become rich through the loss of another. If they lose, their loss is not sufficient penitence but they have, like the rich man in the Gospels, to answer painfully to God that they have in futility squandered the goods which He has given them for the livelihood of themselves and their families. He who gambles not only endangers his money but his body and his life: indeed, most fearful of all, he may even lose his soul's eternal life. This I tell you for your enlightenment, dear Simplicius, as you say gambling is unknown to you, so that your whole life you may beware of it."

"Dearest sir," I answered, "If gambling is such a horrid and dangerous thing, why do the officers permit it?"

"I do not just want to pretend that it is because the officers participate in it," he replied, "but it happens because the soldiers will not, indeed cannot, stay away, for whoever has surrendered to gambling, or of whom habit, or better, the gambling devil, has taken possession, he will in time, whether he wins or loses, become so addicted to it that he can be less without it than without his natural sleep. We can often see them gambling the whole night through, and forgoing the best food and drink, go on playing even if they depart without shirt in the end. Gambling has several times been forbidden by penalty of life and body, and was prevented by order of the generals through provost-marshals, hangmen, or catchpoles, publicly and with force. But all that led to nothing, for the gamblers assembled elsewhere in secret corners and behind hedges, took each other's money away, quarrelled and broke each other's necks over it, so that to avoid murder and manslaughter, and also to prevent that some might not gamble away their weapons, horses and daily rations, gambling is not only again publicly allowed but they have even allotted this special ground so that the main guard is always at hand to forestall disaster, although they cannot always prevent that one or the other is left lying dead on the ground.

"As gambling is the shameful Devil's own invention and brings him much profit, he has commanded special gambling-devils who wander about in the world and have nothing else to do but induce men to play. To these, various light-hearted fellows surrender through special agreements and pacts, that he may let them win. And yet among ten thousand players, you will rarely find one rich one, but on the contrary, they are generally poor and miserable as their gains are little valued, and therefore at once gambled away or else squandered wickedly. Hence arose the unfortunately too true but pitiful proverb: "the Devil never leaves the gambler but leaves him miserably poor". For he robs them of wealth, courage and honour and will not leave them until they finally (unless God's unbounded mercy may not save them) have been deprived of their soul's eternity. And if there is a gambler of gay nature and humour and so high-spirited that no misfortune or loss can bring him to melancholy sorrow and despair, and all vices are caused through these, the treacherous, evil fiend lets him win bravely, so that he may bring him finally into his net through squandering, pride, gluttony, drinking and whoring."

I made the sign of the cross and blessed myself at the thought that in a Christian army such evil could be practised which the Devil had invented, and from which obviously resulted much harm and detriment for this life and for eternity. But my marshal said all that which he had told me was nothing and it would be impossible to describe all the misery which resulted from gambling. "When one says," he continued, "that if the dice that has left the hand belongs to the Devil, I should imagine that with each dice that falls upon the cloak or table a little devil is let loose beside it, who reigns over it and makes it fall as the advantage of its hellish principle demands. Also I believe that the Devil never takes care of the gambler for nothing but certainly knows how to safeguard his own splendid profit.

"And remember further that next to the gambling place usurers and Jews take up their stand, buying cheaply from the gamblers what they have won in rings, clothing and jewels, or exchanging into silver to gamble away again: that even here some devils are on guard to provoke thoughts in the gamblers detrimental to their souls, whether they have won or lost. And so the devils build for the winners horrifying castles in the air, and for those who have lost with minds already quite disturbed and easily accessible to damaging ideas, they insinuate thoughts and intentions which have no other aim than their final destruction. I assure you, Simplicius, that I have in mind to write a whole book on this theme. As soon as I shall be living in peace again among my own people I will describe the wastage of precious time that is squandered futilely by gambling. No less will I describe the gruesome curses with which man blasphemes God by their play. I will report the insults with which men taunt one another, and will bring in many horrible examples and stories which occur during the play, not forgetting the duels and manslaughter caused by gambling. Indeed, I will paint in the most lively colours, setting before men's eyes avarice, rage, envy, jealousy, falsehood, deceit, selfishness, thievery, and in a word all the senseless fooleries of dice and card players. So that they who will read this book but once, shall have such distaste for gambling as if they had drunk milk from the sow, which is given to gamblers without their knowledge to cure this disease. Thus to the whole of Christendom I will show that our dear God is more blasphemed by a single company of gamblers than by a whole army."

I praised his good intention and wished him opportunity to fulfil this task.

The marshal became ever more dear to me and I to him, but we kept our intimacy very secret. I still played the fool but no longer used obscene language nor played the buffoon so that my behaviour and speech, although still simple, became more sensible than foolish. My colonel who found great pleasure in hunting, once took me along with him when he went to catch partridges with a net. I liked this invention very much but the retriever dog was too eager that he jumped among the birds before we were able to close the net and for this reason we caught only a very few. I therefore gave the colonel the advice to mate the bitch with a falcon or golden eagle, as it is done with horses and donkeys to create mules, so that the young dogs would grow wings and could then easily catch the birds in the air. On another occasion, as the conquest of Magdeburg which we were besieging went on rather sleepily, I proposed that he should make a gigantic long rope as thick as a wine-barrel of half a tun to surround the whole town and harness all men and animals in both camps to it, thus razing the fortress to the ground in one day. Such foolish pranks I invented daily in abundance as it was my calling, so that my workshop was never empty. To this end my master's clerk, who was a vile fellow and a hardened joker, incited me so that I kept on walking the road of the fools, because whatever that mocking-bird told me, I not only believed myself but gossiped with it to others when I found the opportunity.

When I asked him once what kind of a man our regimental chaplain was, as his dress differed from the others, he answered:

"That is Master DICIS ET NON FACIS, which means in German a fellow who gives wives to other men, but never takes one himself. He is the arch-enemy of thieves as they do not tell what they do, and he on the other hand tells what he does not do. And so the thieves do not like him because they are commonly hanged when they are his best clients."

When I later addressed the good honest father by that title, he was laughed at, but I was judged to be an evil and mischievous jester and because of this I was thoroughly whipped. Furthermore, the clerk persuaded me that in

Prague the brothels behind the walls had been pulled down and burnt, and from there the sparks and dust were dispersed in all the world like seeds of pernicious weeds. He even would have me believe that of soldiers no brave heroes nor courageous fellows would enter heaven, but simpletons, cowards and dastards, and such like, who are satisfied with their soldier's pay. And likewise no cavaliers à la mode and no gallant ladies, but only patient Jobs, sneaking hypocrites, boring monks, melancholy priests, saintly sisters, poor, begging whores, and all sorts of outcasts who in this world are neither good to boil nor fry, and young children who wet the benches everywhere, would go to Heaven.

About warfare he told me that people would shoot sometimes with golden bullets and the more precious they were the greater damage they would do.

"Yes," he told me, "sometimes whole armies including artillery, munitions and baggage were led away as prisoners on golden chains."

Finally he lied to me concerning women that more than half of them wore trousers, although you could not see them, and that many, though they could not make magic and were no goddesses like Diana, yet could conjure greater horns on their husbands' heads than those carried by Actaeon. All that I easily believed as I was such a simple fool.

My marshal however entertained me with quite different discussions when we were alone. He even made me acquainted with his son who, as I mentioned before, was muster clerk in the Elector of Saxony's Army and possessed far better qualities than my colonel's clerk. For this reason the colonel was not only very fond of him but intended to barter him away from his captain and make him his regimental secretary, but his own clerk hoped for this job as well.

I entered into a pact of friendship with the muster clerk, who, like his father, bore the name Ulrich Herzbruder, vowing eternal brotherhood by which we would never forsake each other in fortune or in disaster, in love or in sorrow, and as this happened with his father's consent, we kept our pact the more resolute and close. We wished most earnestly that I could escape honourably from my fool's robes so that we could serve each other more loyally, but to that the old Herzbruder, whom I honoured as my father, did not agree, and he emphatically stressed if I would change my position so soon this would entail me in hard imprisonment and danger to life and limb. Predicting for himself and his son in the near future a great humiliation, he thought he had reason enough to live very carefully and cautiously, and so the less he wished to mix in my affairs in which he foresaw great danger. Moreover he feared he might be dragged into my future misfortuncs if I revealed my true nature, as he had known my secret in every aspect, without disclosing it to the colonel.

Shortly afterwards I realized more clearly how the colonel's clerk became violently jealous of my new brother as he feared he might be promoted in his place to the post of secretary. I could see very well how morose he was, how envy gnawed at him, and it did not escape me that he sighed in deep thought whenever he encountered the old and the young Herzbruder. From this I judged with certainty that he planned to trip him and make him fall. So I told my brother in loyal affection and duty my suspicion that he might beware of this brother Judas. But he took it light-heartedly because he was more than superior to the clerk with his pen as with his sword and in addition held the colonel's great favour and affection.

As it is customary in war to promote old experienced soldiers to provost, so we too had such a man in our regiment, and he was such a hardened arch-scoundrel and villain that one could justly say of him that he was more experienced than was necessary. He was a true necromancer, sorcerer and inciter of devils, and he himself was invulnerable as steel, and could make others invulnerable too and could conjure into battle whole squadrons of horsemen. His features exactly resembled those of Saturn, as painters and poets represent him, except that this scoundrel carried neither stilts nor scythe. Although the poor captive soldiers who fell into his unmerciful hands were very unhappy under him, yet there were people who liked to associate with this unholy bird, and especially our clerk, Olivier. The more his jealousy grew against the young Herzbruder, who was of friendly humour, the closer grew the intimacy between him and the provost. So I could easily foresee that the conspiracy of Saturnus and Mercurius would augur no good to my honest Herzbruder.

At this time the wife of my colonel was gladdened by the birth of a young son, and the christening celebration was given in an almost princely style. The young Herzbruder had been asked to serve at table and out of politeness he gladly appeared, which gave Olivier the long-desired opportunity to bring forth his act of villainy with which he had been pregnant for a long while. When all was finished the colonel's large gilded goblet was missing, and he could not easily believe that he had lost it, as it was still there when the guests from afar had already departed. Although the page said that he had seen it last in Olivier's hands, Olivier himself denied this. Whereupon the provost was called to give advice, and he was ordered through his art to recover the theft and proceed in such a way that the thief should be known to nobody but the colonel, for there had been officers present from his regiment whom, even if one of them should have fallen into temptation, he would not care to bring into dishonour.

As everybody knew himself to be innocent, we all came gaily into the colonel's tent where the magician took command of the case. Everyone looked at the other and wanted to know what would happen and from where the lost goblet would appear. After the provost had murmured some words, one, two, three and more young puppies sprang here and there out of each man's pockets, sleeves, boots, and cod-pieces, and where else their dress slit. These little dogs jumped nimbly hither and thither in the tent, very prettily, being of many colours and each with special markings so that it was a gay and pleasant spectacle. My own tight-fitting Croat breeches of calf-skin were conjured full of so many young puppies that I had to pull them off and as my shirt had rotted away on my body already long ago in the forest, I had to stand there naked.

Finally one puppy jumped out from the slit of young Herzbruder, which was the quickest of them all, wearing a collar of gold. This one swallowed up all the other puppies of which there were so many crawling about in the tent that one could hardly put a foot down. When it finished with all of them, it became smaller and smaller and the collar larger until at last it changed into the colonel's goblet.

Then not alone the colonel, but all the others present had to believe that nobody else but the young Herzbruder had stolen the goblet. So the colonel said to him:

"Look here, you ungrateful guest, have I through my kindness deserved this villainous theft, which I would never have expected of you? See, tomorrow I wanted to make you my secretary, but now you deserve that I should let you hang this very day, which unfailingly would happen if I would not spare you for the sake of your honest old father. Hurry away from my camp, and do not come before my eyes again as long as you live!"

Herzbruder wanted to vindicate himself, but none listened, as his deed was plain as daylight, and when he departed his good old father fainted so that they had sufficient trouble to restore him, and the colonel himself had to console him, saying that a pious father should not be punished for his wicked child. Thus Olivier obtained, with the help of the Devil, that for which he had long struggled, but could not attain by honest means.

As soon as young Herzbruder's captain heard this story he deprived him of his post as muster clerk, gave him a pike and made him a common soldier. From this time on he was so despised by everybody that any dog might have pissed on him, and he therefore often longed to die. Moreover his father grieved himself so much over this that he fell into a serious illness and prepared himself for death. As he had foreseen already that the twenty-sixth of July, which was close at hand, would bring him danger to life and body, he obtained from the colonel permission for his son to visit him once again as he had to talk with him about his heritage and disclose his last will. I was not excluded from this meeting but was the third companion of their sorrows. There I could see that the son needed no apology towards the father who knew his character and good upbringing too well, and therefore was convinced of his innocence. As a wise, reasonable and philosophical man he judged easily from the circumstances that Olivier had brought him into this predicament through the provost. But what power had he against a magician, from whom he could expect still worse if he wished to take revenge? Moreover he expected death but could not die peacefully as he had to leave his son in such infamy, and the son on the other hand had no desire to live either, but wished to die before his father. The laments of the two made such a miserable spectacle that I wept from my heart. At last they agreed together to put their case patiently in the hands of God, but the son should find ways and means to free himself from his regiment and look for his good fortune elsewhere. However when considered clearly, they realized they had no money with which he could buy his freedom from the captain. Among all these lamentations of their poverty which deprived them of all hope to improve their present misery, I suddenly remembered my ducats which I still carried stitched into my donkey's ears. I therefore asked them how much money they needed in their adversity.

Young Herzbruder answered: "If someone came and brought us a hundred silver thalers, I could dare to get away from all my miseries."

I replied: "Brother, if that will serve you, take heart, as I will give you a hundred golden ducats."

"Oh, brother!" he cried, "What is that? Are you truly a fool or so light-hearted that you can joke in our grave distress?"

"No, no!" I said, "I will count out the money."

So I tore off my coat and took one of the donkey's ears from my arm, opened it, and let him count out and take a hundred ducats. The rest I kept and said: "With these I will succour your sick father if he is in need."

They then both embraced me, kissed me and in rejoicing did not know what to do. They wanted to give me a letter assuring me therein that I should share the inheritance of the old Herzbruder with his son, and to pay back the sum to me with interest and thanks when God should return their possessions. All this I did not accept, but I asked them only for their everlasting friendship. Hereupon the young Herzbruder swore to take revenge on Olivier or else to die, but his father forbade him and foretold that whoever would kill Olivier would in the end be killed by Simplicius.

"However," he said, "I am assured that you two will not kill each other, as neither of you shall perish by arms."

Afterwards he urged us to swear on oath to love one another until death and to help each other in all dangers.

The young Herzbruder bought himself out of the regiment for thirty thalers, for which his captain gave him an honourable discharge. With the remaining money, having an opportune chance to travel, he set off for Hamburg, where he furnished himself with two horses and joined the Swedish Army as a volunteer cavalryman. In the mean time, he commended his father to my care.

TWO PROPHECIES FULFILLED

NONE OF MY COLONEL'S MEN was more capable of caring for the old Herzbruder in his illness than I, and as the patient was well satisfied with me, this duty was deputed to me by the colonel's wife, who rendered him many favours. With such good nursing, and being consoled as regards his son's fate, his condition improved day by day so that even before the twenty-sixth of July, he had regained almost perfect health. Notwithstanding he wanted to stay indoors and to pretend to be ill until the aforesaid day had past, of which he was obviously terrified. In the mean time, all sorts of officers from both armies visited him in order to hear of their future fortune or misfortune, as he was a good mathematician and teller of horoscopes besides being an excellent physiognomist and chiromantist: his predictions went seldom awry. Indeed he foretold the day on which the Battle of Wittstock* later took place, for many came to him who at the very same time were threatened by violent death.

He foretold to my colonel's wife that she would complete her pregnancy while still in the camp, as Magdeburg would not surrender to us before the end of six weeks. He predicted definitely to the false-hearted Olivier, who made himself a nuisance, that he would die a violent death and that I, when it happened, would avenge him and then slay his murderer; for which reason thereafter Olivier respected me highly. To me however he prophesied the whole course of my life in such detail as if it had already been completed, and he had been present all the time. I took little notice of this but later remembered many events which he had foretold, after they had happened and had become true. Above all he warned me against water as he feared I might perish therein.

Now when the twenty-sixth of July arrived, he admonished me and the sentry whom at his plea the colonel had given him to assist me for this day, most earnestly to admit no one into his tent. There he lay alone, and prayed unceasingly. But when the afternoon approached a lieutenant from the cavalry camp came riding up and asked for the colonel's marshal. He was sent to us but we refused him straight away; he would not be refused and pressed the sentry under all kinds of promises to let him see the marshal, with whom he wished to talk urgently that very evening. As this was of no avail, he started to curse and rage like hail and thunder, saying that so many times he had ridden for the marshal's sake and never found him at home, and now he was here, why should he not have the honour to speak only one little word with him. With that he dismounted and we could not hinder him from unfastening the tent himself, and when I bit into his hands he slapped my face sharply.

As soon as he had entered and saw the old man, he said:

"Forgive me, Honourable Sir, that I had to be impertinent to procure a word with you."

"Well," answered the Marshal, "and what may be the desires of the gentleman?"

"Nothing more," replied the lieutenant, "than that I would like to ask your honour for the favour of telling me my horoscope."

The marshal answered: "I hope the respected gentleman will forgive me that on account of my illness I cannot today oblige. This work needs many calculations which my silly head could never fulfil now, but if he will be patient until tomorrow I hope then to be able to satisfy him."

"Sir," he replied, "will he only read from my hand in the mean time?"

"Dear Sir," said old Herzbruder, "this art is very doubtful and treacherous and I therefore ask the gentleman to excuse me. Tomorrow however I will gladly do anything that the gentleman desires."

But under no circumstances did the lieutenant wish to be denied, and he stepped up to the bed of my father, stretched out his hand to him and said: "Sir, I only ask for a few words concerning the end of my life, and I assure you if it should contain some evil, then I will accept the words as a warning from God to take better care of myself; I ask you therefore for God's sake, to speak straightforwardly and not withhold the truth."

The honest old man answered him thereupon with few words and said:

"Well then, the gentleman should take care not to be hanged in this very hour."

"What, you old villain!" cried the lieutenant, who was drunk like a dog, "How dare you address a cavalier with such words?"

With that he drew his sword and stabbed my dear old Herzbruder to death in his bed. I and the sentry shouted and cried "Murder", so that everyone ran to their weapons. But the lieutenant ran straight to his swift horse and would doubtlessly have ridden away and escaped if the Elector of Saxony in person, with many horsemen, had not happened to pass, and had him caught. When he heard of the affair, he turned to von Hatzfeldt,* our general, and said only this: "It would be bad discipline if in an Imperial camp a sick man in bed were not safe from murderers."

That was a sharp verdict and sufficient to bring the lieutenant's life to an end, for our general had him hanged straight away by his very fine neck.

We can learn from this true story that not all prophecies are to be rejected, as many a fop would do who cannot believe in anything. And from this we may expect that man cannot escape his foretold fate whether his destiny has been predicted to him a long or a short while ago. If I were asked whether it is essential, useful or beneficial for anyone to have his fortune told and the horoscope cast, I would like to answer that the old Herzbruder has told me so much that I have often wished and still wish he had kept silent. For I have never been able to escape the prophesied disasters, and those which are still in store for me make only my hair grey in vain, as these disasters will happen to me willy-nilly, whether or not I take precautions.

But in regard to good fortunes that are prophesied I think they are more often deceptive, and serve man less well than prophecies of misfortune. What use was it to me that the old Herzbruder swore emphatically that I was born and bred of noble parentage, and yet I knew of none save my dad and mum who were coarse peasants in the Spessart? What use was it to von Wallenstein, Duke of Friedland,* that it was foretold to him he would be crowned king to the music of stringed instruments? Do we not all know how they sang him to sleep at Eger? Others may break their heads over this question – I return to my story.

After I had lost both my Herzbruders, the whole camp at Magdeburg became loathsome to me, which anyhow I used to call merely a town of canvas and straw with walls of mud. Now I was tired and sick of my position and jester's clothes, as if I had gulped them down with nothing but iron cooking spoons; in a word, I decided no more to be fooled by everyone but to rid myself of my fool's costume, even should I lose body and life through it. This I put into effect in the following way, very carelessly, as I could find no better opportunity.

Olivier, the secretary, who had become my marshal after old Herzbruder's death, allowed me to ride out often foraging with the soldiers. Once we entered a large village in which a part of the personnel and baggage belonging to our cavalry were billeted, and everyone went back and forth into the houses in search of what he could loot. I, too, sneaked away to see if perhaps I could find an old peasant's garment to exchange for my fool's cap. However I could not find what I wanted but had to satisfy myself with a woman's dress. This I put on as I found myself alone, and cast my own clothing into a cesspool, believing I was now saved from all my miseries.

In this costume I crossed the street and approached some officers' wives, making such small steps as perhaps Achilles may have done when his mother disguised him and put him among the daughters of Lycomedes. But as soon as I came out into the open some foragers perceived me, and taught me to jump better than ever before. As they shouted: "Stop! Stop!" I only ran faster and so reached the officers' wives before them. I fell on my knees and prayed for the sake of all women's honour and virtue to protect my virginity from these lustful villains. My plea was not only well received but I was accepted by the wife of a cavalry captain as a maid. With her I stayed until Magdeburg and the fortifications at Werben and Havelberg and Perleberg were all taken by our troops.*

This captain's wife was no longer a child, though still young, and fell so foolishly in love with my smooth skin and slim body that at last after long efforts and frustrated roundabout ways, she let me know in all too plain German where her shoe pinched most. But I was then still much too conscientious, pretended not to understand and behaved steadfastly so that no one could suspect anything in me but a pious virgin. The captain and his servant were ill together in hospital; therefore he ordered his wife to have me better dressed so that she need not be ashamed of my filthy peasant's tunic. She did more than was ordered and spruced me up like a French doll, which stirred the fire more in all three of them. Indeed, it became finally so big that master and servant most eagerly demanded from me that which I could not give them, and which I even had to refuse courteously to the lady. At last the captain became resolved to take the opportunity to get from me by force that which was in fact impossible to get from me. Such efforts his wife soon noticed and being hopeful of still gaining me in the end, she obstructed all his efforts and frustrated all his tricks, so that he believed he would become crazy with his mad desire.

Once when master and wife were asleep, the servant stood before the wagon in which I had to sleep at night, lamenting his love for me with hot tears, and prayed devotedly for my favour and compassion. But I showed myself harder than stone and let him understand that I wished to preserve my chastity until marriage. As he now offered me marriage well-nigh a thousand times, and heard on the other hand nothing but my assurance that it was impossible for me to wed him, he at last despaired completely, or at least pretended to despair, and drew his sword from the scabbard, put the point to his breast and the hilt to the cart, behaving as if he would stab himself. I thought to myself the Devil is a rascal, and therefore talked kindly to the man, consoling him that I would give my final answer in the morning. With that he was content and went to sleep, but I, considering the predicament in which I now was, remained awake longer. I knew well that my strange position in the long run would do no good. The captain's wife became more and more violent with her temptations; the captain more and more audacious with his insinuations; and the servant more desperate in his continuous love. And I could find no way out of this labyrinth. Often I had to catch fleas on my lady in plain daylight, only to see her alabaster white breasts and to fondle fully her tender body, and this became more unbearable as time went on as I too was of flesh and blood. If the lady let me in peace, then the captain tormented me; and if by night, both should leave me in tranquillity, the servant tortured me, so that my woman's clothing appeared to me more troublesome to wear than my fool's cap.

Although much too late, at this time I seriously remembered Herzbruder's prophecy and warning, and imagined the time of imprisonment and dangers to body and life had arrived which he had foretold. The womanly dress kept me captive as I could not run away in it, and the captain would have done me ill if he would have recognized me and would have discovered me catching fleas with his beautiful wife. What should I do? At last I decided that same night to reveal myself to the servant as soon as the day would break as I thought to myself: "his amorous desires will soon quieten if you present him with some of your ducats and he will help you to gain a man's dress and so help you out of all your troubles." The plan was well designed if only fortune would have agreed, but this was against me.

My Hans let the day start shortly past midnight to collect my promised consent, and started to rattle at the wagon when I was in deepest sleep. Somewhat too loudly he called:

"Sabina, Sabina, Oh my sweetheart, arise and keep your promise!" so that he woke up the captain sooner than me, for his tent stood close by the wagon. The captain saw green and yellow before his eyes as jealousy had taken possession of him. But he did not come out to interrupt, merely standing up to watch what course the affair would take.

At last the servant woke me up with his insistence and urged me either to come out of the wagon to him or let him come in to me, but I scolded him and asked him whether he took me for a common whore. My yesterday's promise was based on marriage and without it he could never have me. He answered that I should get up anyhow as day was dawning and I should prepare the meal in time for the household, whilst he would fetch me wood and water and kindle the fire. I replied: "If you want to do that, then I can sleep longer. Go along and I will follow soon."

But as the fool would not desist I arose, more for the sake of my work than to please him, because it seemed to me that his desperate madness of yesterday had left him again. I could easily be taken for a maid in the camp as I had learnt from the Croats how to cook, bake and wash, and soldiers' wives anyhow do not spin in the field. What other womanly work I did not understand, as brushing, combing and braiding her plaits, my captain's wife willingly overlooked, for she knew only too well I had never learnt it.

As I now descended from the wagon, with my sleeves rolled back, Hans became so violently inflamed by my white arms that he could not resist kissing me, and as I did not particularly object, the captain, before whose eyes all this happened, could not restrain himself any longer but jumped out from his tent with brandished sword to give my poor sweetheart a blow. Hans however ran away and forgot to return. The captain said to me: "You bloody whore! I will teach you…"

More he could not utter from rage, but slashed at me as if he were mad. I started to shout so that he had to stop in order not to cause an alarm, for both armies, the Saxon and the Imperial, lay at this time close together as the Swedish Army was approaching under Banér.

When daylight came my master handed me over to the stable lads, just as both armies were preparing their departure. These were a horde of the lowest rabble which made the harassing which I had to suffer only the greater and more horrid. They rushed with me to a little copse to satisfy their animal lusts more easily, as is the habit among these Devil's brats when a female is handed over to them in this way. Many other youths followed to look at this miserable jest and among them was also my Hans. He did not let me out of his sight and when he realized they were after me he wanted to save me by force, even at the cost of his head. He found supporters because he said that I was his betrothed bride and they pitied me and him and wished to give help. But this was very unwelcome to the boys who believed they had a better right to me and did not want to let such a good prize slip through their fingers, and therefore intended to combat force with force. On both sides they started to deal out blows; the tumult and the noise grew greater as time went on and it appeared almost like a tournament in which everybody does his best for a fair lady. Their horrible clamour brought the provost to the place, who arrived just when they had torn my clothes from me and seen that I was no womanly creature. His presence brought dead silence as he was dreaded more than the Devil himself, and those who had laid hands on each other suddenly disappeared. Quickly he had himself informed of the affair and whilst I hoped he would free me from all my distress, he made me prisoner as it was an extraordinary and indeed a suspicious thing to find a man disguised in woman's clothes in an army. So he and his men took me over to the regiments (which stood in the field ready to march) intending to hand me over to the judge-advocate, or to the quartermaster-general. As we passed my colonel's regiment, I was recognized, spoken to and clothed by my colonel suitably to my sex, and again delivered to our old master provost as a prisoner, who locked my hands and feet in irons.

It was very bitter for me to march thus in chains and fetters, and hunger would have tormented me greatly had not Olivier, the secretary, helped with some money; for my ducats, which so far I had saved, could not be brought to light for I might lose them altogether and land myself in greater peril. That same evening Olivier told me why I was kept in such strict imprisonment, and our regimental sheriff had orders to cross-examine me so that my testimony could be quickly put before the judge-advocate. For they believed that not only was I a reconnoitrer and spy but that I was one who practised black magic, as soon after my disappearance from the colonel some witches had been burnt, confessing before their death that they had seen me at their Witches' Sabbath when they had come together to dry out the river Elbe so that Magdeburg could be more quickly taken. The questions on which I had to give answers were the following:

Firstly, whether I had studied or at least had experience in writing and reading.

Secondly, why I had approached the camp before Magdeburg disguised as a jester, although I had shown in the captain's service and afterwards that I was of clear mind.

Thirdly, for what reasons I had disguised myself in women's clothing.

Fourthly, whether I had been with other fiendish monsters at the witches' dance.

Fifthly, where was my fatherland and who were my parents.

Sixthly, where I had been before reaching the camp of Magdeburg.

Seventhly, where and for what purpose had I learnt women's work, such as washing, baking, cooking and the like, as well as playing the lute.

Whereupon I wanted to tell the story of my whole life and to explain clearly to all present my rare adventures, so that they could compare these questions reasonably with the truth. The regimental sheriff however was not so curious but tired and ill-humoured from marching, so he only wished for a short and simple answer on that which I was asked. Thus I answered in the following way, from which no one could grasp what actually had happened:

To the first question: I had not studied, however I could read and write German.

To the second question: as I had no other clothes, I had to appear in a fool's garb.

To the third: as I had become tired of the fool's costume and could not find a man's clothes, I dressed as a woman.

To the fourth: yes, I had been present but against my will, but all the same I had no knowledge of witchcraft.

To the fifth: my home is the Spessart and my parents peasants.

To the sixth: at the governor of Hanau, and with a colonel of the Croats called Corpes.

To the seventh question: against my will I learnt washing, baking and cooking with the Croats; but lute-playing I learnt at Hanau because I found pleasure therein.

As my statement was being written down, the Sheriff said to me:

"How can you deny and say that you did not study? When they took you for a fool, during a mass you answered a priest in Latin, to his words "Domine non sum dignus" which means "O Lord, I am not worthy", that he need not say so as everybody knew it already?"

"Sir," I answered, "Other people have taught me that and assured me it was a prayer that one has to say at Mass when our chaplain celebrates the service."

"Indeed," replied the sheriff, "I think you are the right one whose tongue should be loosened on the rack."

I thought to myself: "so help me God if it should go according to your foolish mind!"

Next morning early, the order came from the judge-advocate to our provost to watch me most carefully as he intended as soon as the armies came to rest, to interrogate me himself, in which case, I would undoubtedly have come to the rack, if God had not otherwise ordained. In this captivity I continuously thought of the parson in Hanau, and of the deceased old Herzbruder, as both had prophesied what would happen to me if I were to abandon my fool's costume.

The same evening when we had scarcely finished encamping, I was led to the judge-advocate. He had in front of him my statement and also some writing utensils, and he started to examine me more thoroughly. I told him my adventures truly as they were, but they were not believed; and the judge-advocate could not find out whether he had a fool or a hard-boiled villain before him, as question and answer followed so swiftly and the whole story was in itself so strange. He ordered me to take a quill and to write, to see what I could do, and to see if my handwriting was known, or of such quality as to reveal my character. I took quill and paper as nimbly as someone who daily practises it, and asked what I should write. The judge-advocate, who perhaps was annoyed that my cross-examination dragged on deep into the night, answered me:

"Ho! Write "Your mother the whore"."

I put down these words and when they were read, they made my case only worse because the judge-advocate said he could now well see what kind of a gallows-bird I was.

He asked the provost whether they had searched me and whether any written documents had been found on me. The provost answered:

"No. Why should he have been searched as he was brought to us almost naked?"

But unfortunately that did not help. In the presence of everyone, the provost had to search me, and whilst he did that with all care and attention, he found, Oh, misfortune, both my donkey's ears with the ducats tied round my arms.

So they called: "What further evidence do we need? This traitor undoubtedly intended to commit some piece of great roguery, for why should a reasonable man disguise himself as a fool or why should a man camouflage himself in woman's clothes? Why do you think and for what purpose should he have been supplied with such a considerable sum of money, unless he wanted to commit some big crime? Did he not admit himself that he had learnt to play the lute with the governor of Hanau, who is the most cunning of all soldiers in the world? Gentlemen, what other cunning tricks may he have learnt with those sharp-nosed foxes to set against us? The quickest way with him is to put him on the rack tomorrow, and then as he deserves into the fire, for he has anyhow been at the witches' meeting and is worth nothing better."

Anyone can easily imagine in what mood I now was. I knew I was innocent and had strong confidence in God; however, I saw my peril and lamented the loss of my lovely ducats which the judge-advocate had put into his own pocket.

But before this painful procedure could be launched against me the Swedish troops under Banér came to grips with ours. In the beginning both armies were fighting for the advantage of the better position, and later on for the possession of the heavy guns which our men lost straight away. Our provost stayed with his henchmen and prisoners rather far behind the battle line, yet we were close enough to our brigade to recognize everybody from behind by his uniform. And when a Swedish squadron encountered our own, we were in danger of death just as much as the people fighting, for suddenly the air above us was full of singing bullets that it seemed the salvoes were fired to please us. The fearful ducked down as if to hide within themselves, but those who had courage and were accustomed to such amusement let the bullets fly over their heads without blenching. In the battle itself each one tried to prevent his own death by slaughtering his nearest enemy. The horrible shooting, the rattling of harness, the crashing of pikes, and the shouts of wounded and aggressors made with trumpets, drums and pipes, a gruesome music. One could see nothing but thick smoke and dust, which seemed to veil the fearful view of the wounded and dead, and in it one heard the lamentations of the dying and the gay shouting of those still full of courage. Even the horses seemed to grow more and more invigorated in the defence of their masters and showed such ardour in the fulfilment of the duty forced upon them. Some were seen falling down dead under their masters, covered with wounds which they had innocently received in payment for loyal service. Others fell for the same cause upon their riders, and gained thus in their death the honour to be carried by those whom they had had to carry during life. Still others, having lost their stout-hearted burden which had dominated them, abandoned humans in their fury and rage, and ran away seeking their first freedom in the open fields.

The earth, whose habit it is to cover the dead, was there itself strewn with bodies which were marked each in its own manner. Heads lay there which had lost their natural masters, whereas there were bodies with heads missing. Some had their guts hanging out, horribly and pitifully, and others had their heads smashed and the brains spattered. There could be seen lifeless bodies despoiled of their own blood and the living covered with the blood of others. There lay arms shot off, on which the fingers still moved as if willing to return to battle, and on the other hand, fellows ran away who had not spilt a drop of blood. There lay legs torn off which although relieved of the burden of their body had become much heavier than they had been before. Mutilated soldiers begged for their coup de grâce although certain death was close enough and others prayed for pardon and the sparing of their lives. In short, there was nothing else but a miserable and pitiful spectacle.

The Swedish victors chased our defeated army from their positions, which they had so unfortunately defended, and dispersed them by their quick pursuit completely. In these circumstances, my provost also took to flight with his prisoners, although we had to expect no enmity from the conqueror as non-combatants. And while the provost threatened us with death and forced us to flee with him, young Herzbruder rushed up with five other riders, and greeted him with a pistol:

"Look here, you old dog," he said, "Is it still time to conjure up young puppies? I will pay you for your troubles."

But the shot harmed the provost so little as if he were an anvil of steel.

"Oho! Are you of this kind?" said Herzbruder, "I will not have come in vain to please you! You must die, even if your soul has grown onto your bones."

Herewith he forced a musketeer of the guard which the provost had around him, if his life should be spared, to strike him down with an axe. So the provost received his deserved reward; but I was recognized by Herzbruder who at once ordered them to take my chains and fetters away, had me mounted on a horse, and instructed his servant to lead me to safety.

Now while the servant of my rescuer led me away from further danger, his master in sheer lust for honour and booty was driven deeper into it; and lost himself in the heat of the battle that he himself was taken prisoner. After the victors had divided the loot and buried their dead, I was given, in Herzbruder's absence, to his cavalry captain, together with servant and horses. I had to serve as a horse-boy for which I got no reward but the promise that if I would behave myself well and outgrow my youth, he would mount me, which meant that he wanted to make me a rider, and with that I had to be content.

Soon afterwards my captain was made a lieutenant-colonel, and I held with him the office which in olden times David held for King Saul: in quarters I played the lute and on the march I had to carry his cuirass which indeed was a troublesome task. Although armour was invented to protect the wearer against hostile assaults, I experienced the contrary, as my own brood of lice which I hatched persecuted me under such protection more safely. Under it they had free passes, amusement and tilting ground, so that it seemed as if I wore the cuirass for their sake and not for mine, inasmuch that I could not put my arms inside and combat them. I thought of all sorts of tricks of war, how to exterminate this invincible Armada, but I had neither time nor chance to expel them through fire (as it is done in the baking-ovens) nor through water nor poison – though I knew well what effects quicksilver had. Much less had I the means to discard them through another garment or a white shirt, but had to drag myself on and on with them, giving them my body and blood as their prey. When they tormented me so under the breastplate and gnawed at me, I took out a pistol as if to exchange bullets with them, but only used the ramrod to push them away from their feast. At last I invented the art of winding a scrap of fur round the gun stick and so prepared an artful decoy for them, and when I thus pushed with this louse-hook under the breastplate, I fished them out by the dozen from their comfortable hiding-places and broke their necks; but all this had little effect.

It happened that my lieutenant-colonel commanded a strong squadron on a patrol into Westphalia, and if he had been as strong in riders as I was in lice, he could have frightened the whole world, but as that was not the case he had to advance carefully and for this reason concealed himself in the Gemmer March, a forest between Hamm and Soest. That was the time when the agony with my lice had reached its height; they tormented me so wickedly with their digging that I was afraid they might take up lodgings between my pelt and flesh. It is no wonder that the Brazilians guzzle their lice in rage and revenge. In short I could not bear my pain any longer, and when some of the riders were feeding, others sleeping or standing sentry, I stole aside under a tree to fight a battle with my enemies. To such end I took off my cuirass (contrary to others who put it on to fight), and started such strangling and murdering that soon the two swords on my thumbs were dripping with blood and were covered with dead bodies, or better empty carcasses. All those however which I could not slaughter I sent into misery and left them in exile under the tree.

As often as this battle comes back to memory my skin itches me everywhere as if I were still in the heat of the fight. Though I thought to myself that I should not rage thus against my own brood, and especially against such faithful servants who would cling to me whether I am hanged or put on the wheel, and with whom I had slept so often in the open fields on hard ground. But in spite of it I continued in my tyranny without pity that I did not notice how the Imperial forces attacked my lieutenant-colonel, and at last came upon me, relieved the poor lice, and made me a prisoner.

These fellows had no fear of my manhood whatsoever, through which I had just shortly before killed so many thousands, having even surpassed the exploits of the tailor who slew "seven at one blow". I became the booty of a dragoon and the best spoil he gained from me was my master's cuirass, which he sold in Soest where he was quartered for good money to the commandant. And so in this war the dragoon became my sixth master and I had to be his stable lad.

SIMPLICIUS DELOUSED, ENTERS PARADISE

OUR HOSTESS WHERE WE LODGED had no desire that I and my armies of lice should occupy her whole house, so she had to liberate me from them. And this she executed quickly and well by putting my rags into the baking-oven and burning them out as clean as an old tobacco-pipe, and when I was rid of these vermin I lived again as if in a rose garden. Indeed nobody can believe how happy I felt in escaping this torture which had been like sitting in an ant heap for several months. On the other hand I now had quite another burden on my neck. My master was one of those soldiers who hoped to gain admission to heaven. He modestly contented himself with his soldier's pay and furthermore never made a child cry. His whole fortune consisted in that which he earned as sentry and what he could scrape from his weekly pay. Although it was little enough, he treasured it more than others would treasure their oriental pearls. Every penny he stitched into his clothes, and to increase this hoard, I and his horse had to help him in his thrift. So it happened that I had to chew dry Pumpernickel and to content myself with water – or, when lucky, with thin beer; this was indeed a distasteful affair for me and my throat became rough from dry black bread and my whole body extremely skinny. If I wanted to guzzle something better I had to steal but with the special condition that he knew nothing of it. For him there was no need in the world for gallows, the wooden-horse, the hangman and pikemen, nor army-surgeons, not even sutlers and drummers to recall him back to camp, because all his doings were far from gluttony and drunkenness, gaming and duelling. And whenever he was commanded somewhere on convoy, patrol or ambush, he staggered along like an old hag on a stick. I am convinced if this good dragoon had not possessed such heroic soldierly virtues, he would never have taken me prisoner – he would have ignored me, a lousy boy, and instead pursued my lieutenant-colonel. I could not hope to receive any garments from him as he himself walked about patched and mended all over, like my hermit. His saddle and harness were hardly worth three pennies and his horse was so shaky from hunger that neither Swede nor Hessian need fear his pursuit.

All these reasons determined his captain to send him on guard duty to Paradise, a convent of that name, not that he was of much use for such purpose but that he might graze himself into good condition and re-equip himself anew, and also because the nuns had asked for a pious, conscientious and quiet man. And so he rode along, I walking as alas he had only one horse.

"Our luck is in, Simbrecht!" he told me on the way (he could not keep the name "Simplicius" in his mind). "When we come to Paradise, how we shall guzzle!"

"The name is a good omen." I answered him, "May God grant that the place will fulfil its promise!"

"Indeed," he said, for he did not well understand the meaning of my words, "if we can only gulp down every day an ohmen* of the best beer, it will do us good. Be only brave. I will soon have a new greatcoat made for myself and you shall have my old one, which will still make a fine garment for you."

He called it rightly the "old one' for I believe it could still remember the Battle of Pavia, so weathered and worn it looked: little did he please me with such a promise.

We found Paradise as we had wished, and even better. Instead of angels there were beautiful virgins who filled us up with food and drink that I in a short time regained my smooth skin, for there we enjoyed the strongest beer, the best Westphalian hams, smoked sausages, tasty and tender beef, boiled in salt water and eaten cold. Here I learnt to spread black bread finger high with salted butter and to cover it with cheese so that it slipped down the better, and whenever I got hold of a leg of lamb larded with garlic, and a good tankard of beer beside it, then I refreshed body and soul and forgot all previous misery. In short, this Paradise suited me so well as if it had been the real one, and therewith I had no other worries save that I knew it would not last for ever, and that I had to walk about in rags and tatters.

But just as misfortune had struck me down heavily whenever it had chased me before, so it seemed to me now as if good fortune would make up for it, for when my master had sent me to Soest to fetch the rest of his baggage, I found on the way a bundle with several ells of scarlet cloth for a coat including red velvet for the lining. This I took with me, and exchanged it in Soest at a cloth merchant for common green woollen material for my attire, including accessories, with the condition that he should have such clothes made and in addition provide a new hat. As I now only needed a pair of new shoes and a shirt, I gave the mercer the silver buttons and braid which belonged to the coat and he provided me with everything that I needed. So I emerged newly decked out. I returned to Paradise and my master, who raged violently that I had not brought the find to him; indeed, he even spoke to me of whipping and almost made me undress in order to wear the clothes himself but for shame and the fact that the garment would not fit him. I however imagined I had done the right thing.

But now the niggard miser was abashed that his boy was better clothed than he himself. Therefore he rode to Soest, borrowed money from his captain and equipped himself in the very best, promising to repay the money from his weekly sentry pay, which he did conscientiously. He had sufficient means of his own but was much too cunning to dip into his own pocket, for had he done so he would have lost the comforts on which he could rest this winter in Paradise and another naked fellow would have been put in his place. By this method the captain had to let him stay there if ever he were to regain his loan.

From this time on we led the laziest life of any in the world, where a game of ninepins was our heaviest labour. When I had groomed, fed and watered my dragoon's nag, I practised the craft of a nobleman and strolled for pleasure. Our enemies too, the Hessians from Lippstadt, had billeted a musketeer as a guard in the convent, who was by trade a furrier, and also an accomplished singer and a master-fencer. In order not to forget his art he practised daily with me on all sorts of weapons to combat boredom. Through this I became so sure and skilled that I did not fear to take up his challenge whenever he wished. My dragoon however would play skittles with him instead of fencing and for no other wager than who should gulp down most beer at table. Thus each man's loss was borne by the convent.

This convent possessed its own hunting ground and kept its own huntsman, and as I too was dressed in green, I attached myself to him, and that same autumn and winter learnt from him all his crafts, in particular the hunting of small game. For this reason and because the name Simplicius was somewhat strange, easily forgotten or difficult to pronounce for the common man, everyone there called me "the little huntsman". I learnt to know all highways and byways, which later on was greatly to my advantage, and if through bad weather I could not roam in forest and field, I read all sorts of books which the administrator of the convent lent me. When the noble ladies of the convent became aware that as well as having a good voice, I could play the lute and strum the keyboard a little, they took more notice of me than before, and stimulated by my rather well-proportioned body and handsome face, they all considered me, by my manner and conduct, to be of noble origin. Therefore I was now surprisingly esteemed a very amiable young gentleman, and they were all astonished that I was attached to such a ragged dragoon.

When I had spent the winter in this delightful comfort, my master was relieved of his post. After such a good life this appeared to him so horrible that he fell ill, and a raging fever together with his old ailments caught during his lifetime in the war made things worse, so that he cut it short and within three weeks I had something to bury. I composed the following epitaph for him:

> A miser lies here, a soldier brave and good
> Who never all his life has shed a drop of blood.

According to law and usage the captain could have taken and inherited the horse and arms and the corporal the rest of his belongings. But as I was already a fresh, well-grown youth, and gave promise that in time I would fear no man, everything was offered to me if I would enlist in place of my late master. This I accepted the more willingly as I knew that my master had left a considerable amount of ducats stitched into his trousers, which he had scrimped together during his lifetime.

When I gave my name as Simplicius Simplicissimus to the roll clerk who was called Cyriacus, he could not spell it correctly and exclaimed:

"There's no devil in hell called that!"

I quickly asked him whether there was someone in hell called Cyriacus, for which he had no answer, clever though he thought himself, and my wit pleased the captain so much that right from the beginning he thought well of me and had high hopes for me.

As the commandant in Soest needed a stable-boy of the kind I appeared to be, he was displeased that I had been made a soldier. He tried to get hold of me, using as pretext my youth, not wanting to let me pass as a man. And when he brought this before my master, he sent for me and said:

"Listen, little huntsman, you shall become my servant."

I asked what kind of service I had to do. He answered:

"You shall help to serve my horses."

"Sir," I said, "We are not made for each other: I prefer a master in whose service the horses serve me. But as I cannot find such, I would rather remain a soldier."

He replied: "Your beard is still much too small!"

"Oh no, sir," I said, "I dare to fight a man of eighty years. A beard defeats no man, otherwise billy-goats would be highly honoured."

He replied: "If your courage is as good as your quick tongue, I will let you pass."

To which I answered: "That can be proved at the next opportunity."

And with that I let him know that I did not want to be used as a stable-boy. So he let me stay where I was, saying the work would praise the master.

Whereupon I got hold of my dragoon's old trousers and, having examined their anatomy, cut them to pieces, and purchased from their intestines a good cavalry horse and the best musket I could find, and all that was made to shine for me like a mirror. I had myself dressed anew in green as the name of "Huntsman" pleased me well. My old dress I gave to my boy as it had become too small for me. I rode about like a young nobleman and thought myself a fine fellow. So audacious was I that I decked my hat with a big bunch of feathers like an officer and in this way soon found enviers and grudgers. Angry words between them and me arose and at last even blows. But as soon as I had shown one or two of them what I had learnt in Paradise from the furrier, not only did everyone leave me in peace, but even sought my friendship.

Besides all that I often participated in patrols either on horse or on foot; for I was a good horseman and as quick on my feet as anyone could be, and if we had to skirmish with the enemy I pushed myself forward as chaff before the wind and wished always to be in front. Through that I was in a short time well-known by friend and enemy, indeed so famous that both sides kept me in high esteem, so that the most dangerous assaults and even the command of a whole expedition was entrusted to me. I started to loot like a Bohemian, and if I snatched up something of value, I gave my officers such a generous share of it, that they allowed me to exercise such craft even on forbidden ground, for everywhere I found support in this.

The general, Count von Götz, had left behind in Westphalia three enemy garrisons, one in Dorsten, one in Lippstadt, and one in Kosfeld, to which I became a great menace. With small parties I appeared before their gates, now here, now there, almost daily, and snatched much good booty; and as I escaped everywhere with good fortune, the people believed I could make myself invisible and that I was invulnerable as iron and steel. Therefore I was feared like the plague and thirty of the enemy were not ashamed to run away from me if they only knew that I was with fifteen men in the neighbourhood.

In the end it happened thus: wherever a place had to pay a war levy I had to see that this was done. From this my purse became as big as my reputation. My officers and comrades loved their Huntsman, and the most distinguished partisans of the enemy went in fear, and the peasants I kept through terror and love on my side. For I knew how to punish my opponents and how to reward generously those who rendered me even the smallest service. Altogether I squandered almost half of my booty and paid well for spying. This was the reason that neither patrol nor convoy nor transport could leave the enemy lines without my knowledge, and anticipating their intentions I made my plans accordingly – and, with the assistance of good fortune, succeeded mostly so well that everybody was amazed, especially on account of my youth, so that many officers and brave soldiers of the enemy wished to see me. What's more, I showed great consideration to my prisoners, so that they often cost me more than my whole booty was worth. Whenever I could render a courtesy to one of my enemies, especially the officers, even if I did not know them, without infringing my duty, I did so.

With such conduct I would soon have been promoted to an officer if my youth did not prevent it, but whoever at my age wished to be an ensign had to be of noble birth. Also, my captain could not promote me, as no vacancies in his company could be found, and he begrudged giving me to someone else, as he would have lost in me more than a milking cow. But at least I became a corporal, and this honour, preferring me above old soldiers, although it was only a little thing, together with the praise I gained daily, were almost like spurs which goaded me to higher ambitions. Day and night I considered what to do to appear greater, more renowned and amazing. Indeed I often could not sleep because of such foolish thoughts. And by seeing that I had no chance to prove through my deeds the courage I possessed, I was worried that I did not daily find opportunity to cross swords with the enemy. I often wished to live in the time of the Trojan War or during the Siege of Ostend, and fool that I was I did not think that a jug goes to the well until it breaks. But so it happens if a young, rash soldier has money, good fortune and courage. Then arrogance and pride follow, and in such haughtiness I kept instead of one boy, two servants whom I equipped superbly and put on horseback, so burdening myself with the envy of all the officers.

12

THE DEVIL STEALS THE PARSON'S HAM

I WOULD LIKE TO RELATE a few adventures that happened to me before I left the Dragoons, and though these are of no great importance yet they may be amusing to hear, because I had not only big ideas in mind and did not despise the small ones too if thereby I could hope to gain glory and admiration among the people.

My captain was ordered with some fifty men by foot to the fortress of Recklinghausen to effect an ambush, and as we thought before carrying it out we ought to hide ourselves for a few days in the woods, everybody took a week's provisions along. But as the rich caravan which we awaited did not arrive at the expected time, our bread gave out, and we could not go plundering for fear of giving ourselves away and frustrating our purpose. So hunger vexed us violently, especially as at this place I had no acquaintances as elsewhere who could supply me and my men secretly. Therefore we had to think of other means to find food if we were not to go home empty-handed.

My comrade, a student in Latin, who had recently run away from school and joined the colours, sighed vainly for the barley soup which his parents had provided but which he had despised and abandoned. Recollecting thus his former fleshpots, he remembered his school satchel, in whose company he had enjoyed those meals.

"Oh, Brother," he said to me, "Isn't it a shame that I have not studied the arts sufficiently to know how to feed myself now? Brother, I know indeed if only I could go to the parson in that village, there we would find an excellent feast."

I considered these words and quickly judged our position, and as those who knew the district well could not leave our hiding place for fear of being recognized, and those who were unknown had no chance to steal or buy anything secretly, so I took the student into account and proposed the matter to the captain. Although the undertaking involved danger, the captain had confidence in me, and as our position was so wretched, he finally agreed.

I exchanged my clothes with those of another and trotted off with the student towards the village, making a wide detour, although it was only half an hour away. There we soon recognized the house next to the church as that belonging to the parson as it was built in town fashion and stood by the wall which surrounded his vicarage. I had already informed my comrade what he should say as he still wore his shabby student's cloak. I pretended to be a journeyman painter, hoping that I should not have to practise this art in the village, as peasants rarely have painted houses. The holy man was very polite, and when my friend greeted him in Latin, and told him a heap of lies as to how the soldiers had plundered him on his journey, robbing him of all his provisions, the priest offered him butter and bread and a mug of beer. I myself behaved as if I did not belong to him and said I would eat at the inn, calling for him afterwards so that we could go on our way a little further the same day. So I went to the inn, more to spy out what to loot during the night than to satisfy my hunger, and was fortunate on the way to find a peasant mortaring up his baking-oven in which lay huge pumpernickel which had to rest and bake there for twenty-four hours.

I did not stay long with the innkeeper as I already knew where to get bread; but I bought some small white loaves to take back to my captain, and when I returned to the vicarage to remind my comrade to leave, he had his belly already full and told the parson that I was a painter and intended to travel to Holland to perfect my craft there. The parson welcomed me heartily and asked me to go with him into the church to see some painting which needed retouching. Not to spoil the play, I had to follow. He led us through the kitchen and when opening the night lock on the strong oaken door leading to the churchyard, oh, miracle, here I saw that the black sky was full with lutes, flutes and fiddles – I mean of course, hams, sausages and sides of bacon hanging in the chimney. I looked at them sympathetically as they seemed to smile at me, and I wished in vain that they were with my comrades in the woods, but so obstinate were they that to spite me they remained hanging there.

I thought of means by which I could make them join company with the loaves from the baking-oven, but it was not easy to find a way as the parson's yard was walled and all the vicarage windows heavily guarded with iron grilles. Moreover two gigantic dogs lay in the courtyard which I feared would certainly not sleep at night if anyone tried to steal that which was part of their own reward for faithful watch.

As we now entered the church, we discussed together the paintings, and the parson wanted to commission me to retouch several panels, but I tried to find all sorts of excuses, especially under the pretext of my journey. The sexton or bellringer remarked:

"You, fellow, appear to me more like a runaway soldier-boy than a journeyman painter."

I was not any more accustomed to such talk, yet had to tolerate it. However I shook my head a little and answered:

"Oh, you rascal. Give me quickly brush and paints, and in a flash I will paint the fool that you are."

The parson laughed and said to both of us that it was unseemly to tell each other home truths in such a holy place. With that he let us know that he believed us both, and after he had given us another drink, he let us depart. But I left my heart behind with the smoked sausages.

Still before nightfall, we reached our comrades where I changed back into my own clothes and took my musket, reported to the captain, and chose six brave fellows to help me to carry home the loaves. We arrived at midnight in the village and lifted the bread from the oven in complete silence, as we had someone with us who was able to cast a spell upon the dogs. But when we reached the vicarage I could not persuade my heart to pass by without the bacon. I stood still and pondered how to get into the parson's kitchen; but I could see no other entrance except the chimney which therefore this time had to be my door.

We carried the loaves and our weapons into the charnel house in the graveyard, and procured a ladder and a rope from a barn. As I could climb up and down chimneys as well as any sweep, which I had learnt from hollow trees in my youth, I climbed onto the roof which was covered with double rows of hollow tiles and built convenient for my purpose. I twisted my long hair above my head into a tuft and let myself down on the rope to my beloved bacon, tying one ham after the other and one side of bacon after the other on to the rope, which he on the roof fished most carefully out through the chimney, passing it on to the others who carried it into the charnel house.

But, oh misfortune. Just as I had completed my work and wanted to climb up again, a rafter broke beneath me, and poor Simplicius fell down and the wretched Huntsman found himself caught as in a mouse-trap. My comrades on the roof let down the rope to pull me up again, but it broke before they lifted me from the ground. I thought: "Now, Huntsman, you have to endure a chase whereby your hide will be torn violently as it once happened to Actaeon." The parson was awakened by my fall and ordered his cook to kindle a light. She entered the kitchen in her shift and had her skirt hanging over her shoulders; she stood so close to me that she touched me with it. She reached for an ember, put a candle to it and started to blow. But I blew as well and much stronger than she. Thereupon this good woman was so frightened that she trembled and dropped both fire and candle and fled to her master.

So I gained some air to think by what means I could escape but nothing came into my mind. My comrades let me know through the chimney that they wanted to break open the house by force and take me out; but I did not allow it, ordering them to take care of their arms, leaving only my fellow Harum-Scarum on the roof by the chimney to wait to see whether I could escape without noise and rumpus, so that our plan should not be foiled; only if that should not succeed, then they should do their best.

In the mean time, the parson himself kindled a light while his cook told him that she had seen in the kitchen a horrible ghost with two heads, perhaps she had seen my tuft of hair on my head and taken it for another head. All this I heard and so with my dirty hands in which I rubbed ash, soot and coal, made my face and hands so horrid that without doubt I no longer resembled an angel in Paradise as the noble nuns had called me, and if the sexton had he seen me now, he would have passed me for a clever painter. And now I started to clatter noisily in the kitchen and made a violent uproar by throwing pots and pans about. The kettle-ring came into my fingers and this I hung round my neck; however I kept the firehook in my hand to defend myself in emergency.

The God-fearing parson was not to be frightened by this but advanced with his cook as in a procession; she carried two wax candles in her hands and a vessel with holy water on her arm; he fortified himself with a cope and stole, carrying the holy sprinkler and a book in the other, from which he started to exorcize me by asking me who I was and what I was doing there. As he took me for the Devil, I thought it was proper for me to behave like the Devil and took refuge in lies. Therefore I answered:

"I am the Devil and I will twist the necks of you and your cook!"

He continued with his exorcism, reproaching me that I had nothing to do with him nor with his cook and constrained me in the most solemn formulas to depart whence I had come. I answered in a most horrible voice that this was impossible even if I wished it. In the mean time, my Harum-Scarum continued with his fantastic pranks on the roof, and although he did not understand Latin, he knew what was going on in the kitchen and that I played the Devil to deceive the parson. He shrieked like an owl, barked like a dog, whinnied like a horse, bleated like a billy-goat, brayed like a donkey, and soon could be heard down the chimney now like a rabble of cats mating in February and then like a cackling hen wanting to lay an egg; for this fellow could imitate all animal noises and could howl if he wished as naturally as if a whole pack of wolves were assembled. All this frightened the parson and his cook to the uttermost and it depressed my conscience that I was exorcized as the Devil, which he believed me to be, as he had read or heard that the Devil likes to be seen in green garb.

In the midst of these anxieties in which we both were entangled, I discovered to my great fortune that the night-lock on the door leading to the churchyard was not locked but only bolted. Quickly I pushed it back and rushed out through the doorway into the churchyard where I found my comrades standing there with fingers on their triggers, and left the parson behind to exorcize the Devil as long as he wished. After Harum-Scarum had brought my hat down from the roof and we had picked up our provisions, we returned to our comrades, as we had nothing more to do in the village but to put back the borrowed ladder and rope in their place.

The whole detachment enjoyed that which we had stolen and not one got hiccups, such blessed people we were! All laughed at my adventure, and only the student was displeased that I had robbed the parson who had so generously stuffed his mouth. Indeed he swore strongly and solemnly that he would gladly pay him for his bacon if only he had some money at hand, yet nevertheless he gobbled it up heartily with us as if he had paid for it.

We stayed two more days at this place expecting the convoy for which we had already waited so long. In the ambush we lost not a single man, and yet took more than thirty prisoners and such a magnificent booty as I had ever helped to share out. Because of my courage and as I had done the best, I received a double share. This was three beautiful Friesian stallions laden as heavily with merchandise as they could carry in our haste. If we had had more time to sort out the loot thoroughly and bring it all to safety, each would have been rich with his share, but we were forced to leave more behind than we could carry away as we had to escape in all haste. So we withdrew for safety's sake to Rehnen where we fed the horses and divided the loot, as there lay part of our army.

Here I remembered the parson from whom I had stolen the hams and the reader may think what a foolhardy, wicked and ambitious character I had been that I was not satisfied to have robbed and frightened the parson, but that I even wished to gain honour therefrom. So I therefore took a sapphire set in a golden ring which I had snatched on this ambush and sent it with the following letter from Rehnen through a reliable messenger to the parson:

MOST REVEREND SIR,

If I had had food in the woods, I would have had no cause to steal Your Reverence's ham, by which you most likely were terrified. I testify before the Highest that I caused you such fright against my will and therefore hope the sooner for your pardon. Concerning the ham itself, it is only proper that it should be paid by those for whose sake the loot was taken, with the plea that Your Reverence will be content therewith. I assure that Your Reverence will find an obedient and faithful servant in him whom your sexton believed to be no painter and who is otherwise called...

THE HUNTSMAN

To the peasant whose baking oven they had emptied, our patrol sent sixteen thaler out of the communal loot, for I had taught them that in this way they could bring the peasants on their side, who can often help a party of soldiers out of their miseries or on the other hand can betray them, sell them and make them lose their lives. From Rehnen we went to Münster and from there to Ham, and so home to our quarters in Soest, where a few days later I received an answer from the parson which read as follows:

NOBLE HUNTSMAN,

If he from whom you stole the ham would have known that you would appear to him in devilish disguise, he would not have wished so often to see the Huntsman, so well-known throughout the land. As the borrowed meat and bread had been paid for much too highly, so the fright was the easier to overcome as it had been inflicted by such a well-known person against his wish, who is herewith pardoned absolutely, with the plea to visit without hesitation him who is not afraid to exorcize the Devil. Vale!

So I behaved everywhere and gained great reputation. The more I gave away and spent, the more the loot flowed in and I considered that I had well invested that ring, even though it was worth a hundred thalers.

PART THREE

13

SIMPLICIUS PUNISHES THE HUNTER OF WERL
AND ACQUIRES THE GREAT GOD* JUPITER

THE SYMPATHETIC READER will have learnt from the previous part how ambitious I had become in Soest, where I sought and found honour, glory and favour in actions for which others would have been punished. Now I will tell how my foolishness misguided me even further, so that I lived in continuous danger to body and life. I was so eager to chase after honour and glory that I could hardly sleep and when I fostered such caprices and lay awake many a night to invent new feints and tricks, I had fantastic ideas. So I invented a type of shoe which one could wear back to front so that the heel came under the toes; at my own expense I had thirty different pairs made. When I distributed them among my men and went on a raiding excursion, it was impossible to trace us, because sometimes we wore these and sometimes our ordinary boots, with the others in our kitbags. It appeared, if somebody reached a spot where I had ordered a change of shoes that according to our tracks two parties had met, and thereafter had disappeared altogether. If however I kept these new shoes on all the time, it looked as if I were approaching a place where I had already been, or as if I had left a place to which I was going! So my sorties, if they left any tracks, were more confusing than a maze, so that those who pursued me by my tracks found it impossible to catch up with me or to bring me into their nets. Often I was quite close to the enemy who searched for me far away, and more often I was some miles away from the copse which they would surround and search in trying to capture me.

In the same way as I arranged it with the patrols on foot, so I tricked the enemy when I was out on horseback. For it was not unusual for me to dismount at cross-roads and have the horseshoes set back to front. The common advantages that a soldier takes if he is weak on patrol and yet from his footprints appears strong, or if he is strong and would like to be considered weak, all these appeared to me such common tricks that I think them unworthy of description.

133

Besides that I invented an instrument with which I could hear at night, if there was no wind, a trumpet blow three hours' walking distance away, a horse's neigh or a dog's bark at two hours' distance, and hear men's talk at one hour's distance. This art I kept very secret and gained much fame thereby, for it appeared to everyone unimaginable. During the day however this instrument, which I kept together with a telescope in my pocket, was of little use except in a lonely, quiet place, for with it I could hear everything, from horses or cattle to the smallest bird in the air, or the frog in the water, or whatever in the whole district moved or uttered a noise. And all this sounded as if I were in the middle of a market among men and beasts where each makes itself heard and because of the shouting of one you cannot understand the other. I know very well that up to this hour there are still people who will not believe what I have just told; however, whether they believe it or not it is the truth. With such an instrument I can hear a man's voice at night when he speaks in ordinary tones, even if he be as far away from me that I could just distinguish his clothes through a good telescope by daylight. However I blame nobody for not believing what I am now writing, because none of those believed who saw with their own eyes when I used this instrument and told them: "I hear horsemen riding, for the horses are shod! I hear peasants coming for the horses go unshod! I hear cartmen, but they are only peasants, for I recognize their dialect! Musketeers are coming, about so many, as I hear the clattering of their shoulder-belts! In this or that direction there is a village, for I hear the cocks crowing and the dogs barking! There goes a herd of cattle for I hear sheep bleating, cows lowing and pigs grunting!"

My comrades in the beginning thought these words were jokes, fooleries and boasts. Later when indeed they found I always foretold the truth, all was explained by black magic and that which I had told them was revealed to me by the Devil and his mother. So I assume the sympathetic reader will think likewise. Nevertheless through all that, I often miraculously and cleverly escaped the enemy if he by chance had news of me and came to seize me. I am convinced that if I had revealed my knowledge to someone it would have come into common use, as it would have been extremely useful to men in war, especially at sieges. But now back to my story.

If I was not on patrol, I went out looting and neither horses, cows, pigs nor sheep were safe from me in their stalls, which I stole from miles around. To avoid being trailed I knew how to put boots or shoes on cattle and horses until I brought them to a much used highway. Besides I shod the iron on the horses back to front, or if they were cows and oxen I put shoes on them which I had ordered to be made specially and brought them thus to safety. The huge, fat swine-fellows who in their laziness do not like to travel by night, I knew how to move on in a masterly way, however they might grunt and decline. I made a well-salted porridge with meal and water and soaked a sponge therein, to which I had tied a strong rope and let those that I wanted to keep, swallow the sponge full of porridge, keeping the rope in my hand, whereupon they followed patiently without further dispute, and paid the bill with hams and sausages.

What I brought home in this way I divided faithfully with the officers and my comrades. Thus I was allowed out at other times and if ever my thieving was discovered or denounced, they helped me handsomely. Altogether I considered myself much too good to thieve from the poor, or to catch chickens or to pinch such small fry.

So I began by and by with eating and drinking to lead an epicurean life, as in time I forgot the teachings of my hermit and had no one to guide my youth nor to whom I could turn. My officers participated in everything, sponging off me, and those who could have punished or admonished me, enticed me the more in all these vices. Through this in the end I became so godless and evil that there was no knavery which I would not have dared to commit. Eventually I was secretly envied, especially by my comrades, for having a more fortunate hand for stealing than anybody else, and on the other hand, by my officers because I considered myself so audacious, acted so successfully on patrols and achieved a greater name and reputation than they had themselves. I am quite convinced that one or the other would have sacrificed me in time if I had not bribed them so lavishly.

In this manner I continued and was just going to make myself some devil-masks and horrifying costumes with horse and ox hoofs to match, by which to frighten the enemy and go out looting unrecognized even by my friends. The idea for this came to me through the stealing of the hams. At this time I heard that there was a fellow at Werl, a clever partisan who dressed himself like me in green, who under my name committed many cruelties by raping women and looting, especially in our neighbourhood. The most horrid accusations were made against me, and I would have fared badly if I had not been able to prove expressly that I was elsewhere when he had committed this or that evil in my name. I was not willing to let him get away with this nor to tolerate that he used my name any longer nor that he should loot in my disguise, thus bringing me into disgrace.

With the knowledge of the commandant in Soest, I invited him to duel with swords or pistols in the open field, but as he had not the courage to appear I declared that I would take revenge on him, even if it should happen in his own commandant's fortress in Werl, who himself was not willing to punish him. Indeed I said publicly that if I should get hold of him on patrol I would treat him as an enemy. This not only caused me to leave untouched my masks, with which I intended to do great things, but I also chopped all my green huntsman's clothing into pieces and burnt them publicly in front of my house in Soest, ignoring that my costume alone, without plumes and riding gear, was worth more than a hundred ducats. In my rage I even swore that the next one who again called me "the Huntsman" should either kill me or die by my hand, might it cost me my neck! Nor did I want to lead a foraging patrol again, which anyway was not my duty, for I was no officer, until I had taken revenge on my counterpart in Werl.

So I kept myself in seclusion and made no soldierly excursions, except for sentry duty and if I was especially ordered somewhere, which I fulfilled sleepily as any dullard would. News of this soon spread through the whole neighbourhood and the enemy patrols became so daring and assured, that almost daily they lingered before our toll gates, which in the end I could not tolerate. But what annoyed me most was that the "Huntsman" of Werl continued to impersonate me and to collect considerable loot in my name.

While everybody believed I had fallen asleep on a bearskin from which I would not rise so soon, I spied upon the doings of my adversary in Werl and heard that he not only imitated me by name and costume, but even went out by night to steal secretly whenever he could. So I soon woke up again and made my plans accordingly. I had gradually trained my two servants like retriever dogs and they were so faithful that each of them if need be would have gone through fire for me as they had good food and drink and much booty through me. I sent one of them to Werl to my counterpart, to pretend that as I, his former master, was living now as a common scoundrel and had forsworn ever to go on patrol again, so he did not wish to stay longer with me but had come to serve him, who had now adopted the green hunting costume in place of his old master and he wished to serve him as an honest soldier; he knew all the roads and foot-paths in the country and could give much advice how to take good booty. The fine fool of a man believed my servant and was persuaded to accept him and to follow him with his comrade on a certain night to a sheep farm to steal some fat lambs. I and Harum-Scarum and another servant were there waiting. We had bribed the shepherd to tie up his dogs and let the on-comers enter the barn unhindered as I wanted to give my blessing to their mutton. As soon as they had made a hole in the wall, the hunter of Werl asked my servant to crawl in first. But he answered:

"Oh, no! Somebody may be watching in there and hit me on the head: I see very well that you don't understand much about stealing; one must first examine the matter."

So he drew his sword from the scabbard, hung his hat on the tip and thrust it several times through the hole, saying: "This is the way you have to inspect whether the old fellow is at home or not."

When this was done, the hunter of Werl was the first to crawl through. But Harum-Scarum at once caught him by the arm with which he carried his sword and demanded if he asked for mercy. His companion on hearing this, tried to run away, but I, not knowing which one was the hunter ran after him and being swifter on my legs than he, got hold of him after a few springs. I asked him: "Which side?"

He answered: "Imperial."

I asked further: "Which regiment? I too am Imperial; he is a scoundrel who denies his master!"

Replied he: "We are dragoons from Soest and are here to get a few sheep. Brother, I hope if you are Imperial too, you will let us pass."

I enquired further: "Who are you then – from Soest?"

And he answered: "My comrade in the barn is the Huntsman."

"Knaves, you are!" I shouted, "Why do you loot your own quarters? The 'Huntsman of Soest' is not such a fool to be caught in a sheep pen!"

"No, from Werl, I meant to say," he rejoined.

While we disputed, my servant and Harum-Scarum came along with my counterpart.

"Look here, you honest bird!" I told him, "Thus we meet at last! If I did not honour the Imperial arms that you carry against the enemy, I would fire a bullet through your head. So far I have been the 'Huntsman of Soest' and I consider you a knave if you don't take one of these swords and fight it out with me as a soldier."

In the mean time, my servant who was dressed, like Harum-Scarum, in a fearsome devil's disguise with goat's horns, laid down at our feet a pair of swords which I had brought from Soest, and gave the hunter of Werl the choice of one of them. Hereupon the poor hunter was frightened so much that it happened to him as it happened to me at Hanau when I ruined the dance: for he filled his trousers to the brim so that nobody could stand near him. He and his comrade trembled like wet curs, fell upon their knees and prayed for clemency. But Harum-Scarum bellowed as if from the inside of a hollow vessel and said to the hunter: "No, you must fight, or I will break your neck!"

He answered: "Oh, highly honoured Master Devil, I did not come for the sake of fighting. Save me from this, and I will do whatever you wish!"

Whilst he was talking confusedly, my servant pressed one sword into his hand and one into mine, but he trembled so much that he could not hold it.

The moon shone so brightly that the shepherd and his fellows could see and hear everything from their cottage. I called him to us, to have a witness of the spectacle; he came, pretending that he did not see the two men disguised as devils and asked what lengthy quarrel I had with these fellows in his sheep fold; whatever I had to do with them I should settle in another place, for our affairs did not concern him; he paid his war levy every month regularly and hoped to live in peace on his sheep farm. To the two men he asked why they had allowed themselves to be beaten by me without knocking me down.

I replied: "You clot, they wanted to steal your sheep!"

The peasant answered: "To hell with them, let them lick my behind and my sheep's behinds!" With that, he departed.

Hereupon I pressed again to take up the fight, but my poor hunter could hardly stand upon his legs from sheer fright so that I pitied him. Indeed, he and his comrade prayed so piteously that in the end I forgave and pardoned everything. But Harum-Scarum was not satisfied with this and forced the hunter to kiss three sheep – so many as they had intended to steal – on their bottoms, who besides had scratched his face so abominably that he looked as though he had eaten with the cats. With that poor revenge I was content.

The hunter however, far too ashamed, soon disappeared from Werl, for his comrade spread the story everywhere, assuring with strong oaths that I possessed two real living devils who were in my service. For this I was feared even more but loved the less.

This I soon realized. Therefore I ceased to pursue my previous godless life completely and devoted myself to virtue and piety. Although I went out again on foraging patrols, I behaved to friend and foe so politely and considerately that all who came in touch with me thought better of me than they had heard. I even stopped the senseless extravagance and saved many pretty ducats and jewels which I hid in hollow trees in the plains round Soest; this was the advice of the well-known fortune-teller of Soest, who assured me that I had more enemies in the town and in my regiment than outside and in the garrison's of the enemy, and they were after me and my money. While the rumour went round that the Huntsman had disappeared, I suddenly struck upon those who rejoiced, and before a village had heard fully that I had damaged another, it soon had to realize that I was still very much in action. I rushed about like the wind, now here, now there, so that they talked more about me than before when that other one pretended to be the huntsman.

Once I lay in ambush with five and twenty muskets not far from Dorsten, waiting for a convoy with several wagoners who were expected there. As was my habit, being near the enemy, I myself stood sentry. A solitary man approached, distinguished in dress, who talked to himself, waving strangely with his cane, as if fighting a strange duel. I could understand nothing else but that he said:

"I will punish the world if men do not submit to me as their supreme God!"

From this I assumed he was perhaps a powerful prince, who thus disguised wished to discover the lives and morals of his subjects, and as he did not find them to his liking was now resolved to punish them accordingly. I thought to myself: "If this man is from the enemy, I will get a good ransom; if not, I will treat him so politely and so conquer his heart that I will profit from him for the rest of my life."

I sprang forward, presented my musket, trigger at the ready, and said: "Would the gentleman be kind enough to advance before me to that copse if he does not wish to be treated as an enemy."

He replied most seriously: "Men of my rank are not accustomed to such treatment."

But I pressed him politely on, saying: "Will the gentleman for once not object and adapt himself to the times."

When I had brought him to my people in the wood and had sent out sentries, I asked who he was. He answered with dignity that I would well care little if I knew that he was a great god. I thought he might perhaps know me and be a nobleman of Soest, speaking thus to anger me, because so the burghers of Soest used to be teased about their great god and his golden kerchief. I soon realized that instead of a prince I had caught a dreamer of fantasies who had studied too much and lost his way in the heights of poetry, for as soon as he had warmed up a little in my company he gave himself out to be the God Jupiter himself.

Although I wished I had not made this catch, since I had the crank I had to keep him with me until we moved on again. As the time was tedious I intended to keep him in good spirits and make use of his gifts. Therefore

I told him: "Now, my dear Jupiter, how does it happen that your high divinity quits his heavenly throne and descends to us on earth? Forgive, O Jupiter, this my question which you may consider inquisitive, but we too are related to the heavenly gods, for we are proud spirits of the woods, born of fauns and nymphs, to whom this secret should rightly be revealed."

"I swear to you by Styx," answered Jupiter, "that you should hear nothing of it did you not resemble my cup-bearer Ganymede, even though you were the very son of Pan. But for Ganymede's sake, I will reveal to you that great clamour over the world's wickedness has reached me through the clouds, and in the council of all the gods it has been decided that I should in justice annihilate the earth with floods as in the time of Lycaon. But as I with strange benevolence favour the human race and always preferred kindness to severe actions, I stroll and wander round to explore the deeds and misdeeds of men. And though I find everything worse than I imagined, I do not intend to exterminate all men without discrimination, but I wish to punish only those who deserve to be punished, and thereafter to guide the rest to my will."

I wanted to laugh but suppressed it as well as I could, and said: "O, Jupiter! Your toil and labour will be entirely in vain unless you will chastise the world again as once before with water, or even with fire. If you send war, all evil and audacious rascals will eagerly follow and will torture peace-loving and pious men. If you send famine, this will please the money-lenders as the price for corn is high. If you send plague, the misers and the rest of mankind have easy game as they will inherit much. You must exterminate the whole world, lock, stock and barrel, if you want to punish at all."

Jupiter answered: "You speak of the matter as a mere mortal, as if you did not know that we gods have the power to punish only the wicked and preserve the good. I will awaken a German hero who will consummate all this through the strength of his sword; he will slay all wicked men and protect and exalt the good."

"Then this hero," said I, "must also have soldiers and where there are soldiers, there is war, and where there is war, the innocent have to suffer with the guilty."

"Are you earthly gods as foolish as earthly men?" Jupiter questioned, "that you cannot comprehend anything? I will send such a hero who needs no soldiers and yet will reform the whole world. In his hour of birth I will bestow upon him a more beautiful and stronger body than Hercules, endowed in abundance with vigilance, wisdom and prudence. To this,

Venus shall give him a handsome appearance that he shall surpass even Narcissus, Adonis and even my Ganymede himself, and to all his virtues she shall give him special charm and grace to make him beloved by every man, for I will be smiling kindly upon Venus at the hour of his birth. Mercury shall endow him with incomparable intellect, and the changeable moon shall not harm him, but benefit him by giving incredible swiftness to him. Pallas Athene shall educate him on Mount Parnassus and Vulcan in the hour of Mars shall forge his weapons, especially a sword with which he shall vanquish the whole world, and without the aid of a single man helping him as a soldier, he shall exterminate all the godless. He shall need no support. Every great city shall tremble before his presence, and every fortress otherwise unconquerable, shall be obedient to him in the first quarter hour. He shall in the end command the mightiest rulers of the world and shall reign over earth and sea so praiseworthily that both gods and men shall rejoice."

I replied: "How can the killing of all the godless without bloodshed, and the command over the whole, wide world, be achieved without great force and a strong arm? Oh, Jupiter, I frankly confess that I can understand these things less than any mortal."

Jupiter answered: "This does not astonish me as you do not know what strange power my hero's sword shall possess. Vulcan shall forge it of the same elements from which my thunderbolts are made. He shall make its power so that if my hero only draws the sword and flourishes it but once in the air, he can behead a whole armada, though they be standing a mile away behind a mountain, thus the poor devils shall lie there without heads before they even know what has happened. When my hero shall start his conquest and approach a town or fortress, he will follow Tamerlan's example, and as proof that he comes for the sake of peace and for the promotion of the welfare of all, he will display a white standard. If they come before him and surrender, all is well. If not then he will draw his sword and through its might he will cut off the heads of all magicians and witches in the whole town, and thereafter show a red standard. If in spite of that they still do not surrender, he will destroy in the same way all murderers, moneylenders, thieves, villains, adulterers, whores and profligates, and thereafter show a black standard. If now, not all who remain in the town surrender to him in humility, he will extermi- nate the whole town and its inhabitants as a stubborn and disobedient crowd. However, he will only destroy those who oppose the others and prevented them from surrendering earlier. So he will advance from one town to the other, giving to each its surrounding country to govern in peace. And from each town in the whole of Germany he will take two of the wisest and most learned men to form with them a parliament. He will unite the towns with each other forever. He will put an end to slavery, tolls, excises, interest, dues and taxes throughout Germany and make such laws which prevent forced labour, sentry-duties, contributions, taxes, wars or any other burdens for the people, and men will live more happily than in the Elysian fields.

"Thereafter," Jupiter continued, "I will take the whole assembly of the gods and descend to Germany and enjoy their vines and fig-trees. I will set up Helicon within their frontiers and create new Muses thereon. I will bless Germany with abundance, more than happy Arabia, Mesopotamia and the land around Damascus. I will forswear the Greek language and only speak German. In one word, I will show myself to be so good a German that I will grant them, as I did before to the Romans, domination over the whole world."

"Almighty Jupiter," I answered, "What will kings and princes say if the hero of the future dares to take their rights so unlawfully and surrender them to the towns? Will they not resist with strength, or at least protest before gods and men?"

Jupiter replied: "This will trouble our hero little. He will divide all the mighty into three groups and will punish those who do not live exemplarily but lead an evil life like ordinary people, for no earthly power can resist his sword. To the others he will give the choice to remain in the country or not. They who stay and love their fatherland will have to live like other commoners, but the civic and private life of the Germans will thereafter be more contented and blissful than is today the life of a king. This will be the second group. The third group however who wish to remain lords and want to reign for ever, he will lead through Hungary and Italy into Moldavia, Wallachia, to Macedonia, Thrace and Greece, even over the Hellespont into Asia. He will conquer these countries for them, giving them mercenaries from the breadth of Germany, and then turn them into kings. Thereafter he will conquer Constantinople in one day and put the heads of all the Turks who will not be converted and render obedience in front of their behinds. And there he will reinstate the Roman Empire and withdraw to Germany with his Parliament where he will build a city in the middle of Germany greater than Manoah in America and richer in gold than Jerusalem in the time of Solomon. Its walls shall be compared with the mountains of Tyrol and its moats the width of the sea between

Spain and Africa. He will build a temple therein from sheer diamonds, rubies, emeralds and sapphires, and in the art chambers which he will build the treasures of the whole world shall be assembled, from the rich presents sent to him by the kings in China and Persia, the Great Mogul in the Oriental India, the great Kahn of the Tartars, the Arch Priest John in Africa, and the great Tsar in Moscow. Indeed, the Turkish Emperor would more eagerly contribute if my hero would not have taken his empire and given it to the Roman Emperor as fief."

I asked Jupiter how the Christian Kings would act in this affair. He answered:

"The kings of England, Sweden and Denmark, being of German blood and origin, and those in Spain, France and Portugal, because the old Germans once conquered and governed them, would receive their crowns, kingdoms and countries as fiefs of the German nation, and then there will be, as in the time of Augustus, an eternal peace among all nations in the whole world."

Harum-Scarum who was listening too, enraged Jupiter and almost ruined the whole farce when he said:

"Then it will be like Schlaraffenland* in Germany, where it rains pure muscatel wine and meat pies grow overnight like mushrooms, and I shall have to stuff both cheeks full at the same time like a thresher and drink Malmsey till I cry."

"Indeed," answered Jupiter, "Especially as I will punish you with the eternal hunger of Erysichthon, for you it seems mock my dignity."

But to me he said: "I thought myself to be among genuine spirits of the wood but now I see I have come upon Momus, the envious god of mockery. Should I reveal to such traitors what Olympus has decided? Should I throw such noble pearls before swine? Shit on the hunchback for the sake of a necktie!"

I thought to myself, here is a remarkable god who besides highflown words utters such coarse language. I saw clearly that he did not like to be laughed at, so I suppressed my laughter as well as I could and said to him: "Most great-hearted Jupiter, because of this ill-mannered faun's impertinence, do not prevent your other Ganymede from learning what else will come to pass in Germany."

"Oh no!" he answered, "First command this blasphemer to hold his tongue before I turn him into a stone, but you yourself, confess to me that you are really my Ganymede and that my jealous Juno in my absence has chased you out of the heavenly realm."

I promised to tell him everything when I had first heard what I wanted to know. So he said:

"Dear Ganymede, deny no longer, for I see very well you are he a time will come in Germany when gold-making will be so well known and common as making pots, so that every stable lad will have the philosopher's stone in his pocket."

I asked him: "But how will Germany have such lasting peace with such different religions? Will not the hostile clergy incite their followers to unloose another war?"

"Oh no," said Jupiter, "my hero will anticipate this disaster with wisdom and once and for ever will unite all Christian religions in the whole world."

"Oh, miracle!" I exclaimed, "that would be a great, rare and magnificent work! How will it happen?"

"I will gladly reveal that to you," Jupiter answered. "After my hero has given universal peace to the whole world, he will address the spiritual and temporal princes of Christian nations in a most moving sermon, emphasizing the detrimental gulfs in matters of faith, and will convince them through intelligible and indisputable reasons and arguments that they themselves shall desire a universal alliance, and delegate to his high wisdom the leadership of this work. He, then, will assemble the wisest, most learned and pious theologians of all religions in a beautiful but quiet retreat, giving them the task first to settle the strifes between their religions as soon as possible, yet with careful thought, and then to make a written declaration with the full consent of all of the right, true, holy Christian religion according to Holy Writ.

"At this time Pluto will scratch himself violently behind his ears as he will fear the lessening of his kingdom. Indeed he will invent all sorts of wiles and tricks to push in a clause or, if not able to prevent the whole scheme altogether, to postpone it indefinitely. He will attempt to show to each theologian his own interest, his own profit, position and pleasant life with wife and child, in order to sway them to his cause. But my brave hero will not be idle. As long as the council sits he will ring the bells in the whole of Christendom, continuously urging the Christian people to pray to the highest God and entreating for the descent of the Spirit of Truth.

"But if he should suspect that one or the other will be persuaded by Pluto, he will torment the whole assembly with hunger, and if they still hesitate to speed up such noble work, he will threaten them with the gallows, and brandish his miraculous sword. Thus he will first in kindness, and afterwards in earnestness and with threats, force them to accomplish his task, and not to mock the world with their stiff-necked false opinions as of old. When unity has been achieved, then will he prepare a great festival of jubilation and announce the purified religion to the whole world. And he who still will not believe shall be put on the stake with pitch and sulphur, or such a heretic barbed with box twigs should be presented to Pluto as a New Year's gift.

"Now, my dear Ganymede, you know all that you wished to know. Tell me now, why you have left heaven where once you offered me so many delicious drinks of nectar."

I thought: "This fellow is perhaps not such a fool as he pretends to be, but will fool me as I fooled others at Hanau, the more easily to escape." Therefore I tried to enrage him as one can best recognize a fool then, saying:

"The reason why I came down from heaven is that I missed you there, so I took the wings of Daedalus and flew down to earth to seek you. But wherever I asked for you, I found only ill reports. Zoilus and Momus denounced you and all the other gods in the whole wide world as debased and lewd and stinking that you have lost all credit with mankind. You, they say, are a crab-lousy adulterous fornicator; what then gives you the right to punish the world for its wickedness? Vulcan, they say, is a patient cuckold who condoned the adultery of Mars without noticeable revenge. What kind of weapons could such a limping gawk forge? Venus herself because of her unchastity is the most hated whore in the world; what kind of grace and favour could she dispense? Mars is a murderer and a robber; Apollo an impertinent lecher; Mercury a useless gossip, thief and procurer; Priapus a lewd fellow; Hercules an empty-headed savage. In short, the whole crowd of gods is so infamous and debased that they should be kept nowhere else but in the Augean stables which anyhow stink throughout the whole world."

"Oh!" Jupiter said, "Would it be strange if I should lose my temper and persecute these incurable slanderers and blasphemous libellers with thunder and lightning? What do you think, my faithful and dearest Ganymede, shall I torment these gossips with eternal thirst like Tantalus, or hang them up next to that malicious tattler Daphitas on Mount Therax, or grind them with Anaxarchus in a mortar, or stuff them into the red-hot bull of Phalaris at Agrigentum? No, no, Ganymede. These punishments and plagues are much too petty. I will fill up Pandora's box anew and empty it over the incurable heads of these rascals. Nemesis shall wake up Alecto, Megaera and Tisiphone to harry them, and Hercules shall borrow Cerberus from Pluto and hunt these wicked villains like wolves. When I have chased, tormented and tortured them sufficiently, I will bind them to a column close to Hesiod and Homer in the house of Hell, and have them punished mercilessly in eternity by the Furies."

While Jupiter threatened in this way, he let down his trousers in front of the whole company without shame and chased the fleas which from his speckled skin one could see had caused him horrid tribulation. I could not imagine what was to come until he said:

"Away with you, you little flayers. I swear to you by Styx in eternity you shall not get what you so eagerly desire!"

I asked him what he meant by these words. He replied that the nation of fleas, once they heard that he had descended to Earth, had sent their ambassadors to greet him.

"Although I allotted them living quarters," he continued, "in the skins of the dogs, they told me that some fleas occasionally go astray, and because of some qualities possessed by females, intrude on them and lodge in their furs. Such poor lost ninnies were cruelly treated by the women, not only caught and murdered but first miserably tortured and ground between their fingers, so that even stones could feel pity."

"Indeed," continued Jupiter, "they presented to me their petition so movingly that I felt compassion for them and promised help. However, on condition that I first should listen to the women. The fleas however protested that if the women were permitted to put their case forward in opposition, they knew very well with their poisonous tongues they would stupefy both my honesty and kindness, and outvote the fleas, or through their charming words and beauty would enchant me and seduce me to a false, and for them detrimental, judgment. So I allowed them to lodge with me and make my body their home in order to understand their ways of life and form my own opinion and issue a judgment. But the ragamuffins began to torment me so that I, as you have seen, have had to rid myself of them. I will put a privilege upon their noses that the women may crush and grind them as much as they like, and if I myself get hold of such a wicked rascal I will serve him no better."

We dared not laugh heartily but kept quiet to please the fantastic fool, although Harum-Scarum almost wanted to burst. At this moment our lookout, whom we had posted in a tree, announced that he saw something coming in the distance. I climbed up and saw through my telescope that these must be the wagoners for whom we were waiting. They had no one on foot but some thirty horsemen as an escort, therefore I could easily imagine that they would not pass through the wood in which we lay but would remain in the open field, where we could gain nothing from them. There was, however, a stretch of difficult road which led through the plain about six hundred paces from us and about three hundred paces from the end of the wood or hill. It angered me to have waited here so long in vain, and only to have captured a fool, so I quickly made another plot which in the end went well.

A brooklet ran down from our camping place through a crevice along which it was easy to ride down to the plain, and I occupied the end of it with twenty men. But I left Harum-Scarum in hiding in the old place. I ordered my men to aim each at his man when the convoy should come, and instructed who should shoot and who should hold their fire in reserve. Some old campaigners asked what I had in mind and whether I believed that the convoy would come to this place where they had no business and where for over a hundred years no peasant had set foot. Others however who thought that I had magic powers (for which I had the reputation at this time) believed that I would bewitch the enemy to fall into our hands. But I did not use any devilish magic, but only my crafty and cunning Harum-Scarum.

When the convoy which was heavily protected wanted to pass by just opposite us, Harum-Scarum began on my order to bellow so horribly like an ox and to neigh like a horse, so that the whole copse echoed and one would have sworn there were horses and cattle. As soon as the escort heard it they hoped to make booty and to grab something from this place although the whole district was empty and laid to waste.

They rode in such haste and without order into our trap, as if everybody wanted to be the first to be knocked out. And the defeat followed so swiftly that with the first welcome that we gave them, thirteen saddles were emptied and others were heavily bruised. Whereupon Harum-Scarum ran towards them into the crevice and shouted: "Huntsman! Here!"

Through this these fellows became even more frightened and confused as they could ride neither forward, backward, nor beside each other. They dismounted and tried to escape on foot; but I took the lot prisoner, all seventeen, including the lieutenant who had commanded them, and approached the wagons, unharnessed twenty-four horses, but otherwise found only a few bales of silk and Holland cloth. I dared not waste my time plundering the dead nor searching the wagons thoroughly, for the wagon drivers on horseback had quickly ridden off when the skirmish started, through which I might have been denounced in Dorsten and caught on my way back.

As soon as we had packed up everything, Jupiter too came running from the copse, shouting whether Ganymede wanted to leave him behind. I answered:

"Indeed, if you do not wish to grant the privilege for which the fleas have asked."

He replied: "I would rather see them drowned in the Cocythus."

Upon which I had to laugh and, as we had enough empty horses, I allowed him to mount, but as he could ride no better than a walnut, I had to tie him to the horse, whereupon he said the scrimmage had reminded him of the battle between the Lapithae and the Centaurs.

When all was over and we galloped away with our prisoners as if pursued, the captive lieutenant started to worry at the clumsy mistake he had made in delivering such a handsome troop of horsemen carelessly into the hands of the enemy, and with thirteen brave soldiers butchered. He became quite desperate, refuted the pardon which I had given him myself, indeed he seriously wanted to force me to shoot him dead. His mistake was not only a shame for him but would prevent his further promotion, if that misfortune would not demand his head. But I consoled him that fickle fortune had played her tricks on many a brave soldier without making them lose their courage or despair; his behaviour was cowardly and a brave soldier would make up for the damage the next time, and he could never make me rescind my pardon, or to commit such a shameful deed against the code of honour and the praiseworthy usage of soldiers.

When he saw that I would not consent, he started to insult me to arouse my anger, saying that I had not fought with him frankly and honestly but that I had acted like a criminal and a highwayman, and like a thief had stolen the lives of his soldiers. Upon this his own soldiers whom we had taken prisoner became mightily frightened, and my own men in the same degree became enraged, so that they would have holed him like a sieve had I not prevented them with all my power.

I took no notice of his ravings and made friend and enemy witness to the scene, and had the lieutenant bound and guarded as a madman. I promised him that as soon as we reached my regiment, and my officers permitting – I'd supply him from my own horses and armour, to his own choice, and to prove to him publicly with pistol and sword that in war it is a soldier's right to practise deceit upon his enemy. Why did he not stay with the wagons which it was his duty to guard? Or, if he wanted to know what was going on in the copse, why did he not first reconnoitre properly? That would have stood him better than to start playing the fool, for which no one cares.

To this, both friend and foe agreed, saying that among a hundred partisans they had not found one who would have, after such insults, not only shot the lieutenant dead but would have sent all the other prisoners with him to the devil.

Happily next morning I brought booty and prisoners to Soest and gained more honour and praise from this foray than ever before. All said: "He will become another young Johann von Werth" – which tickled me pleasantly. But the commander would not allow me to exchange bullets or to fight with the lieutenant as he said I had vanquished him twice already. The more my fame increased in this way, the more grew the envy of all those who grudged me my good fortune.

14

SIMPLICIUS FIGHTS A DUEL

I COULD NOT GET RID OF JUPITER – the commandant did not wish to keep him as he was not worth the plucking, and he made a present of him to me. Now I had my own jester and did not need to buy one – while only a year ago I myself had played the fool. So miraculous is fortune and so changeable is time! Shortly before the lice had tortured me, and now I had the god of fleas in my power; half a year ago I served a common dragoon as a stable boy and now I kept two servants who called me master. Not quite a year had passed since hooligans ran whoring after me, and now the girls were starting to make fools of themselves by falling in love with me. And so I became aware that there is nothing in this world so constant as inconstancy. I feared that Fortune in her fickleness might take heavy revenge for my present well-being.

At this time Count von der Wahl,* as governor in command of the Westphalian province, was assembling troops from all garrisons to make a cavalry patrol through the bishopric of Münster towards Vecht, Meppen, Lingen and other places. Especially however he wanted to rout out two companies of Hessian cavalry in the monastery of Paderborn two miles outside this town, which had done our people much harm. I too was ordered out with the dragoons, and after assembling at Hamm we departed swiftly to attack their quarters which was a poorly defended little town. The enemy broke through trying to escape but we chased them back into their nest, offering them release if they would leave their horses and armament, retaining only that which they carried in their belts. But to this they did not agree and wanted to defend themselves with their carbines like musketeers. So it came to pass that I had to prove the very same night my good fortune in storming the place, for our dragoons now attacked.

Together with Harum-Scarum, I succeeded to be among the first to enter the little town unharmed. We soon emptied the streets, killing everyone in armour; the inhabitants had no wish to defend themselves and so we went into the houses. Harum-Scarum suggested we should tackle a house with the biggest heap of manure in front, as there the most wealthy fellows dwelt and where usually officers were quartered. Such a house we tackled, Harum-Scarum to search the stable and I the house, each agreeing to divide his booty with the other. We both lit our wax tapers and I called the master of the house, but got no answer as everyone was in hiding. Now I reached a chamber wherein I found nothing but an empty bed and a chest which was locked. This I hammered open hoping to find some treasure, but when I lifted the lid a coal-black thing raised itself against me, which I thought was Lucifer himself. I swear that never in my life was I so frightened as when I suddenly perceived this black devil.

"May the Devil strike you down!" I cried out in spite of my terror, and lifted my little axe with which I had broken open the chest. Yet I had not the heart to smite his skull. He knelt down, raised his hands and cried: "Mah dear lord, Ah pray to God, spar mah life!" As he spoke of God and prayed for mercy, I knew that he was no devil. I ordered him out of his chest and he came with me naked as God had created him. I cut a piece from my taper and gave it to him to light me. This he did obediently and led me to a small closet in which I found the master of the house, who with all his household, witnessed this ludicrous spectacle and trembling, begged for mercy.

I gladly pardoned him, as we were anyhow not allowed to harm the townspeople, and he gave me the cavalry captain's baggage, among which was a knapsack well filled and locked. He told me that the captain and his men, except one servant and this Moor, had gone to their positions to defend themselves.

In the mean time, Harum-Scarum had caught the servant with six fine saddlehorses in the stable. These we brought into the house and bolted the doors, told the Moor to clothe himself, and ordered the master of the house to lay the table with all that which he had prepared for the captain.

However, when the town gates were opened, and the sentry posts occupied, the master-general of artillery, Count von der Wahl, entered the town and took up his quarters in the very same house in which we lodged, therefore in the dark night we had to look for other quarters. These we found with our comrades who had stormed the town with us. There we made merry and spent the rest of the night in eating and drinking after I and Harum-Scarum had divided our loot. I for my part got the Moor and the two best horses, one of which was of Spanish breed, and on which any soldier could show himself to the enemy, and on which I later paraded splendidly. In the knapsack I found several precious rings and a golden locket set with rubies in which was a miniature of the Prince of Orange. The rest I left to Harum-Scarum. Altogether if I had sold my loot, including the horse, I would have gained about 200 ducats; regarding the Moor, the sourest portion, I presented him to the major-general of ordnance, who gave me two dozen thaler for him.

From there we marched hastily towards the river Ems with very little achievement, and as it happened that we were approaching Recklinghausen, I took leave, with Harum-Scarum, to visit the parson from whom I had stolen the ham. We made merry together and I told him that the Moor had paid me back the terror which he and his cook had lately experienced. I gave him a fine repeating watch to wear round his neck as a farewell gift, which I had taken from the captain's knapsack. Thus I tried to make friends with all those who otherwise had reason only to hate me.

My arrogance grew apace with my good fortune and nothing else could result from it but my final downfall. We were camping about half an hour from Rehnen and I with my best comrade were granted permission to enter this little town to have our arms patched up. As we wanted to make merry together we entered the best tavern and called for musicians to fiddle wine and beer down our throats. There was great feasting and no money was spared. Indeed I asked fellows from other regiments to be my guests and threw money about like a young prince who owns land and people with much money to spend yearly. Therefore we were better served than a company of horsemen who were also dining there but who spent less madly than we. That made them angry and they started to taunt us.

"How is it that these stay-at-homes," they said to each other, "boast so with their ha'pennies?" They thought we were musketeers, for no beast in the world looks more like a musketeer than a dragoon, for when a dragoon falls from his horse a musketeer will rise.

"This breast-sucker," another one answered, "is certainly a mock-squire whose mother has sent him a few milk-pennies with which he treats his comrades so that they may sometime carry him out of the mud or through the ditch."

Thus they taunted me as they took me for a young nobleman.

All this was whispered to me by the serving-maid but as I had not heard it myself, I could do nought but have a huge tankard filled with wine, letting it go round to the health of all honest musketeers; and each time round there was such a noise that no one could hear his own voice.

This made them angrier still and they cried out loudly:

"What an easy life, in the Devil's name, these stay-at-homes have!"

At this Harum-Scarum answered: "And what concern is it of the boot-blackers?" This they let pass as he looked so horrifying and made such a grim face that nobody dared to quarrel with him.

But soon they were roused again and a strong fellow, believing we were stationed there, as our clothing was not so weathered as that of musketeers who lay day and night in the open field, said:

"Where else should these wall-pissers boast but on their own manure heap? Everyone knows that in battle we shall get hold of them as the falcon seizes the dove."

"We have to storm towns and fortresses and know how to defend them," I answered him, "but in front of the most miserable rat's nest you horsemen are unable to entice a dog from the hearth. Why, then may we not make merry in this town which anyway is more ours than yours?"

The trooper answered: "The fortresses will fall to him who is master in the field – to prove we're the winners of battles I will take three such children as you, including muskets, stick two of you on my hat and ask the third if there are any more! If I would be sitting at your table," he mocked, "I would give that young lord a few slaps on his cheek to prove it!"

I answered him: "I have as good a pair of pistols as you have, and although I am no horseman, but only a bastard between that and a musketeer, look out! I, the child, have heart enough with my musket alone to challenge such a boaster on horseback as you to combat on foot in the open field."

"Ah, scoundrel!" the fellow retorted, "I declare you to be a villain if you do not immediately as an honest man of nobility prove your words."

Hereupon I threw my glove at him and said: "Look out! If I will not retrieve this glove on foot in open field from you through my musket, you can call me that which you in your boastfulness have already called me."

So we paid the inn-keeper, and the trooper as my antagonist prepared his carabines and pistols and I my musket, and when he with his comrades rode to our special meeting place, he told Harum-Scarum to prepare my grave in the mean time. Harum-Scarum answered that he had better give the same order to his own comrades, but he reproached me with my foolhardiness and said bluntly that he feared I should soon have whistled my last tune. I laughed over this, as I had long before made up my mind how I had to meet a well-armed horseman if ever I should be attacked alone in the open field, on foot and only armed with my musket.

On reaching the spot where this beggar's dance should take place, I had already loaded my musket with two bullets, freshly primed, and had smeared the cover of the touch-pan with tallow, as careful musketeers do, to protect touch-hole and powder in rainy weather.

Before we began, both our comrades arranged that we should attack in open field, one from the East, the other from the West, should enter a fenced plot, and each should do his best as a soldier, facing his enemy, and neither before nor during nor after the battle should either of the parties dare to help their comrade or revenge his death or wounding. When these promises were given with hand and mouth, I and my adversary shook hands and each forgave the other's death.

And with such most foolish stupidity which any reasonable human can commit, each hoped to prove the superiority of his arms as if their honour and reputation depended on the result of our devilish action.

When I now entered the field from my end, with a double-burning match-cord and saw my enemy before my eyes, I pretended as if I were shaking off the old priming as I walked. But I did not do so, but put only priming powder on the cover of my pan and blew off, putting two fingers on the tinder pan as is usual. Before I could see the white in the eyes of my enemy, who kept me sharply in his vision, I aimed at him, and burned my false priming powder on the lid of the pan. My mad adversary, believing my musket had misfired and that the touch-hole was blocked, galloped now pistol in hand straight towards me, meaning to pay me back for my impudence and finish me off. But before he was aware, I opened the pan, aimed again and gave him such a welcome that crash and smash were one.

Upon this I retired to my comrades who almost received me with kisses; his comrades however disentangled him from his stirrups, treating him and us as honest soldiers, and returned to me my glove with great praise. But when I thought my honour had reached its height, twenty-five musketeers came from Rehnen, and took me and my friends prisoner. I was at once put in chains and fetters, and sent to the general's quarters, as all duels were forbidden on penalty of death.

As our general in command of Artillery used to keep strict discipline, I feared to lose my head. However I still had some hope to get off safely, for I in my lusty youth had always stood courageously against the enemy and had earned great name and fame for bravery. But this hope was doubtful as such duels happened daily and it had become a necessity to set an example. Our troops had recently stormed a fortified rats' nest of a town and asked for surrender, but were refused as the enemy knew we had no heavy guns. Therefore Count von der Wahl moved with his whole corps to this place, asked again through a trumpeter for surrender and threatened to attack, but he achieved nothing more than the following letter:—

HIGH AND WELL-BORN COUNT, etc.,

From your Excellency's report to me I have heard what your Excellency in the name of his Roman Imperial Majesty expects. But your Excellency will know well, in your great wisdom, how a soldier would be called irresponsible and a coward if he would surrender a place like this to the enemy without special need. Your Excellency will not blame me, I hope, if I intend to await until the armour of your Excellency is appropriate. If however in my modest way I shall have the opportunity to do you any favour outside my loyalty, I shall be your Excellency's most obedient servant,

N. N.

There was much talk about this in our camp, for to leave the fortification untouched was not advisable, but to storm it without a breach would have cost much blood and it would still remain doubtful whether we would overcome it or not. But to fetch first our heavy guns and appurtenances from Münster or Hamm, much labour, time and costs would have been lost. While now the great and the small debated, it occurred to me to make use of this situation to find my freedom. I put all my wits and five senses together and considered, as only the guns were missing, how to deceive the enemy. And as I soon had an idea how to help our cause, I informed my lieutenant-colonel that I had plans through which the place could be taken without trouble and cost, if I could have my pardon and be set free. Some old and experienced soldiers laughed and said, "Drowning men catch at straws, and this good fellow only wants to talk himself out of prison."

But the lieutenant-colonel and others who knew me well took my talk like an article of faith. Indeed, he went himself to the general in command of Artillery with my proposal, and told him many stories about me. As the Count had previously heard of the Hunstman, he ordered me to come before him and for the time being my fetters were removed. The Count was at table and my colonel told him how the previous spring, when standing my first hour as sentry at St Jacob's Gate at Soest, a heavy downfall of rain with great thunder and gale occurred. All those in the fields and gardens rushed towards the town. As the crowds on foot and on horse had grown into a turmoil, I had already at that time shown so much intelligence as to call out the guard, as in such turmoil a town can best be taken, which many an old soldier would not have thought of.

"Finally," the lieutenant-colonel continued, "an old woman approached dripping wet, and as she passed the Huntsman, she said: 'Indeed, I have had this storm hidden in my back for the last fortnight!' The Huntsman, hearing this, struck her with a stick which he happened to have in his hand over her hunchback, crying, 'Could you not have let it out before instead of waiting until I was on guard!' And when his officer intervened, he answered: 'It serves her right. The old carcass knew four weeks ago that everyone was crying out for rain. Why did she withhold the rain from honest people, and barley and hops would have grown better?'"

Over this the general laughed heartily although he was usually of serious mind, but I thought to myself, if the colonel tells him such trifles and tomfooleries, to be sure he will not have left out what else I had done. And so I was admitted. When the general asked me what my petition was, I answered,

"Gracious sir, although my crime and your Excellency's rightful order and command forfeit my life, my most obedient loyalty (which I owe his Roman Imperial Majesty, my most gracious Lord, unto death) shows me a way to damage the enemy and to foster His Majesty's advantage and arms."

The Count interrupted me and said: "Did you not lately bring me that Moor?"

I answered: "Indeed, gracious sir."

To this he said: "Your endeavours and loyalty may perhaps deserve your pardon, but what is your plan to oust the enemy from this place without much loss in time and men?"

I answered: "As the fortress cannot withstand heavy guns, I humbly believe that the enemy will soon negotiate if only he were convinced that we have heavy armament."

"That a fool could also have told me," the Count answered, "but who will persuade them to believe it?"

I replied: "Their own eyes! I have observed their guard on the watchtower through my telescope; they can be deceived. If we fix a few tree-trunks shaped like conduit-pipes on wagons, and have them drawn with a strong span of horses into the field, they will soon believe they are heavy guns; especially if your Excellency will order a battery to be built somewhere in the open as if guns were to be brought there into position."

"My dear little boy!" replied the Count, "They are not children in that town, and they will not be taken in by this hocus-pocus, but will want to hear the guns, and if your hoax does not succeed," he addressed the surrounding officers, "we shall be ridiculed by the whole world."

"Gracious sir," I said, "I will make the guns roar in their ears if you will let me have a pair of double muskets and a fairly big barrel, as there will be no effect without the bang. But should against all hope my experiment not succeed but bring only mockery, then I, the inventor, as I have to die anyhow, will take such shame upon me with my life."

Although the Count still hesitated, my lieutenant-colonel persuaded him, saying that I was most fortunate in such undertakings and he had not the slightest doubt this trick would succeed. Therefore the Count gave orders to arrange the matter as he thought fit and told him jokingly: the honour which he would gain should belong to him alone.

So three such tree-trunks were prepared and twenty-four horses were harnessed before each one, although two of them would have been enough. Towards evening we moved these into the view of the enemy. In the mean time, I procured three double muskets, and a huge barrel from a manor house, and prepared them all to my needs; these were brought at night to our mock artillery. I gave the double muskets a two-fold charge and discharged them through the barrel from which I had removed the bottom, as if they were three warning shots. These thundered so much that everyone would have sworn, by stone and bone, they were siege guns or cannons-royal. Our general laughed heartily at this fool's performance, and sent another proposal to the enemy, with the addition that if they could not come to terms that evening they would fare less leniently in the morning. Thus hostages were soon exchanged on both sides, agreement concluded, and we were that same night admitted into the town through one of the gates. This was greatly to my advantage, for the Count not only pardoned my life, which I had forfeited through his order, but freed me the same night and ordered the lieutenant-colonel in my presence to give me the command of the first company of soldiers which should become vacant. This did not really please the colonel, for he had so many cousins and brothers-in-law who were eager that I should not be promoted before them.

Nothing further of interest happened on the march that was extraordinary, but when we re-entered Soest the Hessians from Lippstadt had snatched my servant, whom I had left behind with the baggage in my quarters, together with a horse which was grazing. From him the enemy enquired about my comings and goings and they esteemed me from now on even higher than before, as through general rumour they had been convinced that I used black magic. My servant even told them that he himself had played one of the devils who had frightened the hunter from Werl in the sheep-fold, and the hunter was so ashamed that he ran away from Lippstadt to the Hollanders. But it was my greatest good luck that this servant of mine had been taken prisoner, as you will hear from the rest of my story.

I began now to behave myself more seemly than before as I had the ambitious hope soon to become an ensign, and gradually I joined the company of officers and young noblemen who also were after that which I hoped to achieve. These were therefore my bitterest enemies, though pretending to be my best friends. The lieutenant-colonel no longer favoured me as he had orders to promote me before his kin. My captain, too, bore me ill will because I showed more splendour in horses, accoutrements and weapons than he, for I did not spend so much on the old miser as before. He would have rather seen my head chopped off the other day than an ensigncy promised to me, for he had hoped to inherit my beautiful horses.

Even my lieutenant hated me for one single word only, which once unintentionally had slipped my tongue. It happened like this. On our last expedition we were both ordered to hold a lonely outpost, and when the watch fell to me, which had to be done laying down – in spite of the pitch dark night – the lieutenant crawled on his belly to me like a snake, saying: "Sentry, have you observed anything?"

I answered, "Indeed, Sir!"

"What is it? What is it?" he exlaimed.

"I observe that your honour is frightened!"

From this time on, my favour with him had gone, and wherever it was most dangerous, I was commanded and had to be there first. Indeed everywhere he found a chance and cause to harass me prior to my becoming ensign, for I was not allowed to defend myself against him. No less, all the sergeants showed enmity towards me for I was preferred above them all. As for the common soldiers, they too started to waver in their love and friendship as it seemed as if I despised them, for I no longer sought company with them but with the big-heads who however loved me neither.

The worst was that not one soul told how everyone felt towards me, and I myself was unable to discover it, for many spoke fair words to my face who would rather see me dead. So I lived like a blind man in all security and became more and more conceited, although I knew that many were angered that I surpassed in splendour the nobility and high officers; yet I did not desist. After being made lance-corporal, I did not hesitate to wear a collar worth sixty thalers, scarlet-red trousers and white satin sleeves trimmed all over with gold and silver, which then was the fashion amongst the highest officers, thus dazzling every man's eyes.

I was a monstrous young fool to sport like that; if I had acted otherwise than to hang my wealth uselessly and conceitedly on my body but had bribed in the right places, not only would I soon have had my ensigncy but would have made less enemies. Yet I did not stop here, but decorated my best horse, which Harum-Scarum had taken from the Hessian captain, with saddle, harness and armour to such an extent, that when I was mounted thereon, people might well have taken me for a second Knight St George. Nothing irked me more than to know I was no nobleman and therefore could not dress my servant and my stable-lad in my livery. I thought to myself, all things have their beginning: if you have a coat of arms, you have your own livery, and as soon as you become an ensign, you must have your own seal though you are not a nobleman.

I had not been pregnant long with such ideas when, through a Count Palatine* I acquired a coat of arms. This consisted of three red masks in a white field, and as a crest on the helmet, the head and shoulders of a young jester dressed in calfskin with a couple of hare's ears and decorated with little bells. For that I thought would suit my name best as I was called Simplicius. Thus I would make use of the fool to remind me in my future high position continuously of what kind of a fellow I had been in Hanau, in order not to become too arrogant, although I had now already no swinish opinion of myself.

In this way I became truly the first of my name, of my lineage and coat of arms, and if anyone had ridiculed me, doubtlessly I would have challenged him with the sword or a pair of pistols.

Although I had as yet no interest in womenfolk, I accompanied the young noblemen when they visited pretty maidens, in order to show off and boast with my beautiful hair, clothing and plumes. There were many young ladies in town and I must confess that I was preferred because of my fine figure, and yet I had to hear that these spoilt hussies compared me to a handsome and well-formed but wooden image, in which except for beauty there was neither strength nor sap; for there was nothing else in me that pleased them. Except for playing the lute I could give them no pleasure, for as yet I knew nothing of how to make love.

When those who knew how to charm womenfolk jeered at me because of my wooden ways and clumsiness, in order to find more favour and boast with fluent phrases, I only answered that it was sufficient for me to find pleasure in a bright sword and a good musket. As the womenfolk agreed with me, the men became so angry that they secretly conspired my death, though there was none among them who had the courage to challenge me, or give me cause that I could challenge him, for which a couple of slaps or any rude word would have sufficed, and for which I gave plenty of opportunity. From this the womenfolk concluded I must be a resolute youth and they said quite frankly that my appearance alone and praiseworthy courage made more impression on a lady than all the compliments and pleasantries that Cupid ever invented. This however embittered the assembly even more.

15

SIMPLICIUS FINDS TREASURE

I POSSESSED TWO SPLENDID HORSES which at that time were the only pleasure I enjoyed. Every day I rode them to the riding school or for a short trot if I had nothing else to do. Not that the horses needed to learn more, but I did it so the people should see that these fine creatures belonged to me. When I boastfully rode down a street, or rather my horse pranced beneath me, the foolish throng gaped, saying to each other: "Look, that's the Hunstman! Oh, what a beautiful horse! What lovely plumes!" Or: "My god, what a brave fellow that must be!" I pricked up my ears eagerly and enjoyed it as much as if the Queen of Sheba had compared me with Solomon presiding in his highest majesty.

But I, fool, did not hear what perhaps reasonable and experienced men thought nor what my enviers were saying; the latter doubtlessly wished that I might break neck and bones since they could not compete with me. Others certainly considered that if everybody had his due means, I would not be so magnificently equipped. In short, the wisest without doubt held me to be a young fop, whose arrogance would necessarily not last long for it was based on a bad foundation and was only supported from unstable loot. And if I myself confess the truth I must admit that these latter did not judge wrongly, though at the time I was not aware of it. I was good for nothing else but to make man or enemy, whoever had to deal with me, sweat and so I could have passed for a simple, good soldier although I was really nothing more than a child. Only this fact brought me fame: that in this time the lowest stable-lad can kill the bravest hero in the world – if gunpowder had not yet been invented I would have had to pipe a different tune.

When I rode about it was my habit to reconnoitre and to memorize all roads, lanes, ditches, swamps, copses, hills and brooks, so as to make use of the place whenever I should meet the enemy in a skirmish for attack or defence. With this purpose in mind I once rode not far from the town, passing old ruined walls where once a castle had stood. At the first glimpse I thought: this is just the right place to lay an ambush or for retreat, especially for us dragoons if ever we should be overpowered and pursued by

161

cavalry. I entered the courtyard, the walls of which had fallen down, and tried to find out whether in a case of emergency one could retreat there on horseback, and how one could defend it on foot. In order to inspect everything carefully, I approached the cellar, where the walls were still standing and desiring to ride past, I could not persuade my horse, which normally showed no fear, neither with love nor force, to go where I wished. I spurred it till I felt pity but I could not move it one whit. To be prepared for another time I dismounted and led it by hand down the broken cellar steps, at which it shied. It jumped back as far as it could. At last with kind words and caresses I got it down and while I stroked and fondled it I realized that it was sweating in fear and kept its eyes continuously fixed towards one corner of the cellar where it refused to go but where I myself could see nothing to frighten even the most temperamental horse.

As I stood there and looked in astonishment at my trembling horse, I too was attacked by such horror that I felt as if I were pulled up by my hair and a tub of cold water poured over me, and yet I could see nothing. But the horse behaved even more strangely so that I could only imagine I and the horse had been bewitched and would find our death in that very cellar. Therefore I wanted to go back but my horse would not obey; I became still more frightened and finally so confused that I hardly knew what I did. At last I took my pistol in my hand and tied the horse to a strong elderberry tree which had grown in the cellar, intending to leave the place and look for people in the neighbourhood to help me to get my horse out. While I was about to do so, it occurred to me that perhaps in this old ruin a treasure may be hidden and thus the place was haunted. Following this idea I looked more carefully into that corner where my horse would not go and saw a part of the wall about the size of a common window-shutter which was different in colour from the rest of the old wall. When I tried to approach closer I experienced as before that all my hair stood on end. This confirmed even more my belief that a treasure must be hidden here.

Ten times, indeed a hundred times, rather would I have exchanged bullets than find myself in such horror. I was tormented and knew not by whom, for I could see and hear nothing. I took the second pistol also from my horse and wanted to run away and leave the horse behind. However I could not clamber up the steps as it seemed to me a strong wind kept me back. Now my fear crept even higher up my spine! At last I thought to fire my pistols, so that the peasants working in the fields nearby would come to me and bring help. This I did as I had no other means, ideas nor hope to escape from this bewitched place of horror.

I was so enraged, or better, desperate – I hardly knew any more exactly how I felt – that I fired my pistols at the very place where I believed the cause of my strange adventure lay; I hit that piece of wall described above with the two bullets so hard that a hole appeared in which two fists could be put. When the shot was fired my horse neighed and pricked up his ears. This pleased me heartily and I still do not know whether the monster or ghost had disappeared or the poor beast rejoiced at my shots.

In a word, I took fresh courage and went unhindered and without fear to the hole which my shot had opened. I started to break into the wall and found of silver, gold and jewels such rich treasure, which I might still be enjoying to this very hour if I had only known how to preserve and invest it well. There were six dozen antique table beakers of silver, a great gold goblet, several double beakers, one gold and four silver salt-cellars, an antique golden chain, various diamonds, rubies, sapphires and emeralds, either set in rings or other jewellery. There was also a little chest full of large pearls but they were ruined and stained; in a mouldy leather sack there were eighty of the oldest Joachim thalers of fine silver, and further, 893 gold pieces with the French coat of arms and an eagle, which coin nobody knew as none could read the writing any more. These coins, the rings and other jewels I put into my pockets, boots, breeches and holsters, and as I had no sack with me, having ridden out for only a short outing, I cut the caparison from the saddle and packed into it – as it was lined – the rest of the silver tableware, hung the gold chain round my neck, gaily mounted my horse, and trotted back towards my quarters.

As I left the courtyard I perceived two peasants who tried to run away as soon as they saw me. I easily caught up with them, having six feet in an even field, and asked them why they had run away and why they were so terrified. They told me that they believed I was the ghost who haunts this deserted mansion and miserably torments all folk who come too close to him. When I asked them further about his character, they answered that for fear of the monster not a single man had come to this place for many years, only a stranger losing his way perhaps came there by accident. It was said in the neighbourhood that an iron trough full of gold lay there guarded by a black dog and a virgin with a spell upon her. As the old saga told, and this they had heard from their grandparents, a strange nobleman who neither knew his father nor mother would come into the land and deliver the virgin, open the iron trough with a fiery key and take away the hidden gold. And many more such foolish stories they told me, saying they had never heard of anybody who had escaped unharmed, or without experiencing horrible fear caused by the gruesome monster.

I asked the peasants what they had in mind to do as they would not dare to enter the ruins, and they said they had heard a shot and a loud cry, so they had run close to see what was to be done. When I told them that I had shot in the hope that people would come to the ruin as I too was frightened, but I could not recall any cry, they replied: "There might be many shots heard in this castle before anyone from our neighbourhood would run there: for truly, things there are so mysterious that we would not believe that the gentleman had been there if we had not seen him riding from it."

Hereupon they wanted to know many things from me, especially what it looked like in the ruin and whether I had seen the virgin and the black dog sitting on the iron trough. If I had wished to boast, I could have told them some tall stories, but I said not a word, not even that I had lifted out the treasure, but I rode on my way back to my quarters and there inspected my find, which gave me much joy.

Those who know the value of gold and make it their god have reason to do so, for if anybody in the world has experienced the power of wealth and its almost divine virtues, I am the one. I know how a man feels who has plenty, though on the other hand I have experienced more than once what a man feels who does not own a single penny. Indeed I dare to prove that gold has more virtue, might and magic than all precious stones. For it expels melancholy like the diamond; it induces desire and love for learning like the emerald, for usually more children of rich people than of poor become students. It takes away timidity and makes man gay and happy as the ruby does. It often hinders sleep like the garnet, but it also has great power to promote tranquillity and sleep as the jacinth does. It fortifies the heart and makes men glad, virtuous, lively and well-disposed like the sapphire and amethyst. It drives away bad dreams, brings joy, sharpens your wit. It quenches lewd and unchaste desires, for beautiful women can be achieved easily for gold. In short, what that dear gold can do, can hardly be expressed, if one only knows how to use it well.

My own wealth, which I had then acquired through loot and the discovery of this treasure, was of a rare character; firstly it made me more arrogant than I ever was before, so much that I grieved in my heart that I was only called Simplicius. It prevented sleep and many a night I lay awake thinking what to do to gain even more. It turned me into a perfect computer for I reckoned what my uncoined silver and gold was worth, added this to what I had now and then loaned, and what I still had in my satchel, and found it amounted (without the precious stones) to a considerable sum. It encouraged me to emulate its own inborn craftiness and evil nature by following truly the proverb – he who has much wants more – and made me so miserly that anyone could have felt enmity against me.

My money gave me foolish ideas and put queer caprices into my head, and yet I followed none of the fancies I conceived. Once it came into my mind to quit the war, settle down somewhere and gaze out of the window with a well-filled belly. But I soon dropped this idea considering what a free life I was leading and what hopes I had to become a big-wig. I thought to myself: "Ho, Simplicius, have yourself made a nobleman, and from your pocket raise your own company of dragoons for the Emperor! Then you will be a perfect young gentleman who will rise high in time."

But as soon as I considered that My Highness could be killed through a single unfortunate skirmish or the war could find a speedy and lasting peace, I no longer liked this plan. So I wished to attain my full manly age, for if you had that, I told myself, you would take a young beautiful and rich wife, and buy somewhere a noble residence and lead a comfortable life. I wanted to turn to cattle breeding and earn an honest income. But as I knew I was far too young, I had to abandon this plan too.

I had many such ideas, until at last I decided to give my best assets to a wealthy man for safe-keeping in some well-defended town, and to await what Fortune had in store. At that time Jupiter was still with me, for I could not rid myself of him. Sometimes he talked most wisely and for several weeks was quite sane. He loved me excessively for I did him many favours, and when he saw me walking about in deep thought, he said:

"Dear Son, give your blood money away, gold and silver alike."

"But why, Jupiter?"

"For one reason, that you acquire friends and banish your futile cares."

"I still prefer more money!"

"Then try to find more but I tell you that in this way all your life you will find neither peace nor friends. Let old misers be mean, but you behave as a young brave fellow should. Indeed, you will soon experience the lack of good friends rather than money."

I ruminated on this and concluded that Jupiter judged the matter truly; but avarice had taken possession of me to such an extent that I did not dream of giving anything away. However I finally presented a pair of silver gilt double beakers to the commandant, and to my captain a pair of silver salt-cellars, with no other result, these being rare antiquities, than to make their mouths water for the rest. To my most faithful comrade, Harum-Scarum, I gave twelve thalers, who nevertheless advised me to get rid of my wealth or I must expect to fall into trouble, for officers dislike a common soldier possessing more money that they do themselves. He himself once had seen that a comrade had secretly murdered another for money's sake. Until now, he went on, I had been able to keep secret what I had snatched and saved, as everyone believed I had spent everything again on clothing, horses and arms, but now I could conceal nothing nor pretend that I had no abundance of wealth. Everyone believed my treasure to be far greater than it was and as I spent now less than before, he often heard what rumours circulated among the young folk. If he were in my place he would let war be war, would put himself somewhere in safety and let our dear God do His Will.

I answered: "Listen, brother, how can I throw the hope of attaining an ensigncy so easily to the winds?"

"Yes, yes," said Harum-Scarum, "May the Devil take me if you ever get your ensigncy. Others who have the same hopes would rather break your neck a thousand times than see you fill the next vacancy. Don't tell me what a carp looks like, for my father was a fisherman! Forgive me, brother, but I have seen longer than you what happens in war. Can't you see how many a sergeant with his short sword becomes grey who deserved above many others to lead a company? Don't you think these brave fellows, too, are entitled to hope? And by right such promotion is more due to them than to you, as you must realize."

To this I had to be silent as Harum-Scarum in his honest German heart spoke only the truth without hypocrisy. Yet secretly I gnashed my teeth, as I had still great ambitions. Meanwhile I pondered over this and Jupiter's words thoroughly and concluded that I had not one single inborn friend who would take care of me in need or would revenge my death, be that by murder or in battle. I, too, could easily see how matters stood with me, and yet I neither abandoned my craving for honour nor my avarice for money, and even less my hopes to rise high, to quit the war and live in peace, but I stuck to my first intention. An opportunity occurred for me to go to Cologne with a hundred dragoons, some merchants, and goods wagons, which I had to convoy from Münster. I bundled up my treasure, took it with me and handed it over to one of the most worthy merchants in Cologne for safekeeping, for which I got a hand-written inventory as receipt. It was seventy-four marks of uncoined fine silver, fifteen marks of gold, eight Joachim thalers, and in a sealed box various rings and jewels, which with gold and precious stones, weighed altogether eight and a half pounds; in addition to that were 893 old coined gold-pieces which had the weight of one-and-a-half gold guilders.

I took Jupiter with me to Cologne, for he had reputable kinsfolk there and wished to visit them. He praised the favours he had received from me and arranged with them that they should show me much honour. But he continued to advise me to invest my money in a better way and buy friends for it, which would help me more than gold in boxes.

SIMPLICIUS TAKEN PRISONER
BY THE SWEDES

ON THE WAY BACK all sorts of ideas chased through my head of how in future I could gain the favour of every man. Harum-Scarum had opened my ears to suspicion and had finally convinced me that I was envied by all, and this was indeed the truth. I remembered too what that famous soothsayer in Soest had once said and I worried even more. With such thoughts in my mind I came to the conclusion that a man who lives his life without worries is practically nothing but an animal. I was amazed how humans could be so false, speaking pleasant words to me whilst they hated me. And so I made up my mind to behave in future like them, talking to please everyone, and to meet everybody respectfully even if it were contrary to my heart.

Particularly I realized that my own conceit had burdened me with most of my enemies and so I considered it essential to play humble (although I did not feel so), be on good terms with the lower fellows, flatter the upper class, and dress myself in a less bombastic way until my position changed.

I had borrowed a hundred thalers from the merchant in Cologne, of which I wanted to spend half among the convoy as I knew that greed does not make friends. Such were my intentions of changing my ways immediately, but my plans were in vain and came to nothing.

As we were passing through the Bergish Land, eighty musketeers and fifty riders lay in ambush for us, just when I had been sent ahead with a corporal and five men to reconnoitre the road. The enemy kept silent when we reached their position and let us pass in order not to warn the convoy until they came into the trap, at the same time sending a cornet with eight riders to keep us under surveillance. When the attack on our convoy started and we turned to help our wagons, they then approached us and asked whether we would surrender.

I personally was well mounted on my best horse; in spite of that I did not want to run away but turned around to a small mound to see whether I could fight with honour. However when I heard the salvoes directed on our convoy I realized the hour had struck, and I tried to flee. The cornet had already anticipated this and blocked my escape and as I tried to cut my way through he again offered me quarter for he took me for an officer. I thought it is better to save my life than risk it hazardously and asked if he would grant me pardon as an honest soldier. He answered: "Indeed, honestly."

So I presented him with my sword and became his prisoner. He at once asked who I was, thinking me to be a nobleman and an officer. When I told him I was called the "Huntsman of Soest", he replied:

"Then you are lucky that you did not come into my hands four weeks ago because at that time I could neither have kept my promise nor my pardon to you, for everyone believed you to be a notorious black magician."

The cornet was a brave young cavalier, not more than two years older than I, and he was obviously delighted to have the honour of capturing the famous "Huntsman". He kept his promise of pardon most honestly, even in accordance with the Dutchmen whose custom it is not to take anything from their Spanish enemies which is covered by the belt. Indeed he did not even search me personally. But I was courteous enough to take the money from my pockets and handed it to them when they started to divide the loot; moreover I told the cornet secretly that he should see that he got hold of my horse, saddle and harness, as in the saddle he would find thirty ducats, and the horse itself was incomparable.

Because of all this the cornet became so affectionate to me as if I were his real brother, and he at once mounted my horse and had me ride his own. The convoy lost only six men dead, and thirteen were taken prisoner, among them eight wounded. The rest escaped but did not have the courage to recapture the loaded wagons in the open field, and this they could easily have done as they were all mounted.

After booty and prisoners were divided, the Swedes and Hessians parted that same evening for they came from different garrisons.

Myself, the corporal and the dragoons were handed over to the cornet as he had captured us and we were led to a fortress (Lippstadt) which was not quite two miles away from my own garrison, Soest. As I had done much mischief to that place before, my name was well known there and I myself more feared than loved. When we were in sight of the town the cornet sent a rider ahead to announce his arrival to the commandant and report the outcome of the skirmish and whom he held prisoner. This news caused an indescribable hullaballoo in the town for everyone wished to see the Huntsman. One said this, another that about me, and it was as if a great potentate had arrived.

We prisoners were at once taken to the commandant who was amazed at my youth. He asked me if I had served on the Swedish side and what was my native land. When I told him the truth, he wanted to know if I were not inclined to serve again with them. I answered that I would not mind; however as I had sworn an oath to the Roman Emperor I considered it my duty to keep it. Thereupon he ordered us to be taken to the Regimental Advocate, but allowed the cornet's plea to treat us to a banquet as I had treated my prisoners (among them his own brother) in the same way. When the evening came, various officers as well as soldiers of fortune and nobleman assembled there. I was treated most courteously; I behaved so gaily as if I had lost nothing and let myself be questioned frankly and openly as if I were not captive with an enemy but among my very best friends. I showed as much modesty as was possible, for I imagined the commandant would be informed of my behaviour, which indeed happened as I later heard.

The next day we prisoners, one after the other, were taken to the Regimental Advocate, who interrogated us. The corporal was the first, and I the second. As soon as I entered the hall, he was struck by my youth and to emphasize this he said to me:

"My child, what has the Swede done to you that you make war against him?"

This angered me, especially as I had seen just as young soldiers among them, and I retorted: "The Swedish soldiers have pinched my marbles and I want to get them back!"

As I paid him back in his own coin, his supporting fellow officers felt embarrassed, and one spoke to him in Latin saying that he should question me in a serious way as it was apparent there was nothing of the child about me. Thus I learnt his name was Eusebius, as the officer had addressed him so. Thereupon he asked me my name and after I had told him he replied:

"There is no devil in hell called Simplicissimus!"

To which I answered: "There is most probably none in hell called Eusebius."

So I paid him back handsomely but the officers did not take it well, admonishing me to remember I was their prisoner and not called here to make jokes. I neither blushed nor apologized over this reprimand, but answered: that as they had taken me prisoner as a soldier and would not let me run away as a child, I did not expect to be teased like a child. I had answered as they had questioned and I hoped by doing so I had done nothing wrong. So they asked me about my country, my origin and my birth, and especially if I had ever served on the Swedish side; item – how things stood in Soest; how strong the garrison, and similar queries. I answered cleverly, briefly and well. Concerning Soest and its garrison, only so much as I dared to give away. But I kept silent that I had meddled in the profession of a jester as I was ashamed of it.

In the mean time, in Soest they learnt what had happened to the convoy and that I together with the corporal and others had been made prisoners and where we had been taken. Already the next day a drummer came to collect us; the corporal and the three others were handed over to him. He also took back a letter from the commandant which first I had to read, having the following content:

DEAR SIR, ETC., ETC.

Through your messenger, the drummer, I accept your demand and exchange for the received ransom, the corporal and three prisoners. Simplicius, the Huntsman, however, as he has formerly served on our side, cannot be released. If I can be of any assistance, your lordship will find in me a willing servant, as I am and remain,

Most obediently,

N. DE S. A.

This letter I did not like at all and yet I had to thank him for giving me the information. I demanded to speak to the commandant, but received the reply that he would send for me as soon as he had finished with the drummer, which would be the next morning; until then I had to be patient.

After waiting the appointed time, the commandant sent for me, just when it was mealtime, so I experienced for the first time the honour of sitting at his table. During the meal he made me drink much, in very friendly manner, but in no way mentioned what his intentions were, and I had no chance to enquire. But as soon as we left the table and I was rather intoxicated he addressed me:

"Dear Huntsman, you understand from my letter under which pretext I keep you here, and I do not intend to behave improperly or do anything against reason or usage of war. You yourself have confessed to me and to the advocate-general that you have served before on our side with the main army. Therefore you will have to make up your mind to accept service in my regiment and with good conduct I will promote you in time to such position as you could never have dared to hope for under the Imperial flag. Otherwise you cannot blame me if I should hand you back to the very same lieutenant-colonel from whom the Dragoons took you."

I answered: "Most honoured colonel, I was never bound by oath to the Crown of Sweden nor their allies and even less obliged to that lieutenant-colonel as I only served as a stable boy and am therefore not bound to accept Swedish service and to break the oath which I have sworn to the Roman Emperor. Therefore I implore my honoured colonel most obediently to relieve me from this demand."

"What!" replied the colonel, "Do you despise the Swedish service? You should know that you are my prisoner and before I let you go back to Soest, I would show you a different treatment or let you perish in a dungeon. Keep that in your mind – once and for ever."

Although I was frightened at these words I did not relent but replied:

"May God preserve me from such contempt of the Swedes and such perjury to the Imperials. For the rest, I would not give up hope that the colonel would treat me as a soldier, according to his well-known discretion."

"Indeed," he said, "I know very well how I could treat you harshly, but think it over that I do not find reason to prove it."

After that I was again taken back to prison. As can be imagined I did not sleep much that night but was afflicted by all kinds of thoughts. The following morning several officers and the cornet came to me under the pretext to pass my time; in fact however to make me believe that the colonel had in mind to prosecute me as a black magician, unless I would give in. By this they wanted to intimidate me and find out what character I really had. Consoled by my good conscience I remained stubborn and did not talk much, as I well realized that the colonel did not want anything else but to keep me out of Soest, where he knew I hoped for promotion and, besides two horses, owned other precious belongings.

The following day he again ordered me to come and asked me whether I had decided one way or the other. I answered:

"This, my colonel, is my decision rather to die than to commit perjury! But if it will please my honoured colonel to set me free and to relieve me from war service, I will promise with heart, mouth and hand not to carry or to use arms, neither against Swedes nor Hessians for six months."

To such proposals the colonel at once agreed; he offered his hand to me and so released me from ransom. He even gave orders to his secretary to draw up an undertaking in duplicate, which we both signed and in which he promised me protection, care and all freedom as long as I remained in the fortress under his command.

I on the other hand promised that during my stay in the fortress I would do nothing to the detriment of the garrison or the commandant, would keep silent if any attempt to the detriment of the fortress would be made, and on the contrary would help the welfare of the garrison according to my ability, and if the place were attacked by an enemy, I would help to defend it.

Hereupon the colonel kept me again at his table and showed me more honour than I ever could have hoped for in all my life with the Imperials. By such means the colonel won my favour to such a degree that I would never have returned to Soest, even if he would have let me go and relieved me of my promise.

What must happen cannot be prevented. It appeared that Fortune had taken me in marriage bonds or was at least so closely associated with me that the most loathsome events would turn out for the best. I was sitting at the commandant's table when I heard that my servant had come from Soest with my two beautiful horses. But I did not know (as I later discovered) that fickle fortune has the character of the sirens, who want to destroy those to whom they show most favour, and lift him the higher, the deeper to cast him down. This servant – I once had taken him prisoner from the Swedes – was faithful to me beyond all measure because I had been his benefactor. Every day he saddled my horses and rode a good distance to meet the drummer, who had to bring me back to Soest, so that I had not to walk so far. He even brought with him my best clothes as he believed I had been looted and he did not want me to return naked or in rags to Soest.

Thus he met the drummer and his exchanged prisoners, and as he did not find me and learnt that I was retained to take service with the enemy, he gave the horses the spur and said: "Farewell, drummer and you corporal! Where my master is, there I want to be!" He broke through and came to me, just as the commandant had set me free and had shown me great honour.

The commandant ordered my horses to be brought to an inn, until I myself was settled in lodgings to my liking. He praised my fortune that I had such a loyal servant and was astonished that I, a common dragoon and so young, owned such excellent horses and was so well mounted. When I took leave to go to the inn, he praised one of the horses especially that I felt he would like to buy it from me. But as he in his modesty did not make an offer, I said to him that if he would give me the honour to keep the horse, it was at his service. He refused emphatically however, perhaps more because I was rather drunk and he did not want to be blamed afterwards for having encouraged a drunken fellow to give up such a fine horse which he might regret perhaps when sober.

The same night I considered how in future I should arrange my life. I decided to remain six months where I was and to spend the winter which was approaching, in peace. I had enough money to see me through, even without touching my treasure in Cologne. During this time, I thought, I will mature fully, reaching my full strength, and in the coming spring go even braver into battle with the Imperial army.

Early in the morning I cut open my saddle which was far better filled with ducats than the one the cornet had got from me. I had my best horse brought before the colonel's quarters and said to him that I was resolved to spend six months quietly here under his protection, my horses would be of no use to me and it would be a pity thus to spoil them. I therefore asked him kindly to accept this old soldier's hack and place it in his own stables as a sign of my gratitude for his favours.

The colonel thanked me most courteously and that very same afternoon sent to me his steward with a fattened live ox, two fat pigs, a barrel of wine, four barrels of beer, and twelve cartloads of firewood. All this was brought to my lodgings, which I had just rented for half a year, with the message: As he could see that I wished to stay with him and not being well provided with food, he had sent me a contribution of wine, meat and fuel. If he could be of further service, he would gladly oblige. I expressed my thanks to the steward most politely, gave him two ducats and asked him to commend me to his master.

When I saw that the colonel honoured me for my generosity, I determined to bring myself into good repute with the common folk also, that they might not consider me a miserly boaster. So, in the presence of my landlord I called my servant and said to him:

"Dear Nicholas, you have shown more loyalty than any master can expect from his servant. But now, having no chance to fight and gain booty with which to reward you as I wished, and as my retired life demands no servant, I will give you my other horse together with saddle, harness and pistols, asking you to be content with this and to look for another master. And if I can be of any help in the future, please do not fail to ask me."

He kissed my hands and could scarcely speak for weeping; he refused to accept the horse saying I should rather sell it for my own support. At last I persuaded him to take it and promised to reinstate him in my service as soon as I needed him.

This farewell moved my landlord so much that he too started to weep, and as my servant praised me among the soldiery, so my landlord esteemed me among the townspeople higher than all those pregnant peasants.

The commandant considered me a resolute fellow and believed firmly in my parole of honour, as I not only had kept my oath to the Emperor but in order to keep my promise to him had bereft myself of my splendid horses, armour and my faithful servant.

17

SIMPLICIUS THE LOVER

I BELIEVE NOT A MAN IN THE WORLD exists who has no trace of foolishness in his heart, since we are all of the same tree and I can well observe from my own pears when others are ripening. Why, boastful fellow, if you are a fool, should you think others are too? One man can hide his folly better than another. We all have foolish trends in our youth and he who lets them out is considered a fool; others keep the fool hidden and others show but half of him.

He who suppresses the fool altogether is but a poor misanthrope; but those who let their fool out to show its ears and get fresh air, I consider the best and most reasonable of them all. I myself let mine out a trifle too much as I was my own master with too much money in my purse, for I took a boy, dressed him as a page in a foppish livery of violet blue with yellow braid because it pleased my fancy. He had to wait upon me as if I were a nobleman, and not a short while ago a dragoon and half a year earlier a poor stableboy.

This was my first folly committed in this town, and although it was rather a serious one, was neither noticed by anyone nor condemned. But what does it matter? The world is so full of follies that no one need laugh or wonder at them, so accustomed are they to such things. That's why I was reputed a clever and brave soldier and not a simpleton scarcely out of his child's shoes.

I arranged full board for me and my page with the landlord and gave as payment on account the meat and fuel which the commandant had given to me. For the drink however I gave the key to my page as I wished to entertain those who came to visit me. And as I was neither townsman nor soldier and had none of my own kind to keep me company, I fraternized with both sides and each day had comrades enough to drink with me.

My best friend was the organist as I loved music and had an excellent voice which I did not wish to neglect. He taught me how to compose, to play the clavichord and also the harp; I had already mastered the lute and I bought myself one, amusing myself with it daily. When I was tired of music I sent for that same furrier who before had instructed me in the use of arms, and we practised together to become more perfect. The commandant allowed me also to study (for which I paid) the art of armoury and some gunnery. Altogether I lived quietly and secluded that people were astonished that I, being accustomed to robbery and bloodshed, sat continuously over my books like a student.

My landlord was the commandant's bloodhound and my warden, for I noticed that all my comings and goings were reported. I played my game accordingly and never spoke of matters of war and pretended, if ever war was mentioned, that I had never been a soldier and cared only for my daily studies.

Although I wished my six months had come to an end, I did not betray in which army I intended to serve later on. Whenever I visited the colonel he kept me at his table and every time he tried to turn the conversation that he might find out my intentions, but I always answered most carefully so that no one knew what was in my mind.

Once he said to me: "Tell me, Huntsman, would you not like to join the Swedes? Yesterday one of my ensigns died."

I replied: "Honourable colonel, is it becoming for a wife to marry immediately after her husband's death? Why should I not wait six months?"

In this way I always extricated myself, yet gained more and more the colonel's favour, so that I was permitted to walk freely inside and outside the fortress. I was even allowed to hunt hares, partridges and other game, not permitted to his own men. I also fished in the Lippe and was so fortunate that it seemed I could charm fish and crayfish out of the water. I ordered a simple hunting costume for myself and roved by night, knowing all pathways, into the plains of Soest where I collected my hidden treasures from their hiding places and brought them to the fortress as if I intended to live with the Swedes for ever.

Once I came across the witch of Soest, who said to me:

"Look here, my son, did I not advise you well, when I told you to conceal your money outside the town of Soest? I assure you now, it was your greatest fortune that you were captured, for if you had returned to Soest, some villains, jealous of your success with the wenches had sworn to murder you and would have slain you while out hunting."

I questioned her: "How could anyone be jealous of me who cares not for women?"

She answered: "Be sure, you will soon change your mind, or else the womenfolk will chase you out of the land with ridicule and shame! You always laughed at me when I prophesied to you; will you refuse again to believe me if I tell you more? Have you not found better friends here than in Soest? I swear to you that they love you dearly and this excessive love will harm you if you are not careful!"

To which I replied that if she really knew as much as she pretended, she should tell me what she knew of my parents and if I would ever meet them in my life again: but she should not prophesy in obscure words but speak clearly in plain German! To that she answered that I should enquire after my parents when I would unexpectedly meet my foster-father leading the daughter of my wet nurse on a rope. And at that, she laughed exuberantly saying that she had voluntarily told me more than to others who had asked for it. When I began to ridicule her, she quickly departed after I had given her several thalers, for I had anyhow far too many silver coins to carry.

In those days I had a pretty hoard of money and many precious rings, for I often bought jewellery from the soldiers for half its value. Such treasure always cried out to be squandered again among the people, and I willingly obeyed – and, as I was somewhat conceited, I boasted with my possessions and let my landlord see them without reserve. He exaggerated my wealth among the folk, who were amazed how I had accumulated so much, as it was well known that the treasure I once had found was in safe custody in Cologne, for the cornet had seen the merchant's receipt when he took me prisoner.

My intention to learn the art of artillery and fencing completely in six months was a good one, and I succeeded. But this was not enough to protect me from idleness – the source of many evils – especially as there was nobody to give me orders. Industriously I studied all sorts of books from which I learnt many interesting facts, but I also came across books which suited me as much as eating grass suits a dog. The incomparable *Arcadia*,* from which I wanted to learn eloquence, was the first bait which distracted me from the study of true history to amorous books and from historical reports to heroic poetry. I collected such books as much as I could and when I got hold of one, I read through it without interruption even if I had to sit over it day and night. Instead of eloquence, these books taught me to chase the maidens. However I did not become affected to such a degree that I fell into a divine rage or serious illness, as Seneca would have called it. Where I loved, I received that for which I asked easily and without much effort, so that I had not reason to lament like so many other lovers and paramours do who are full of fantastic ideas, longings, secret sufferings, crying, hating and being jealous and a hundred more follies and out of impatience wishing for death. I had enough money and was not mean with it. Besides I had a good voice and practised on all sorts of instruments.

Instead of dancing, of which I was never very fond, I displayed my straight body by fencing with the furrier. Besides I had a smooth and pleasant face and adopted a friendly pose so that the wenches without much effort on my part ran after me more than I desired.

It was St Martinmas, when among Germans the time of eating and drinking begins, which lasts till Shrovetide. I was invited to officers and burghers alike to eat the Martin goose and enjoy the acquaintance of young ladies. My lute and my songs made them look at me and I used such enchanting glances and gestures to my new love songs which I composed myself, that many a pretty girl was bewitched and fell in love with me. Not to be taken for a poor beggar, I gave two banquets; one for the officers and another for the more respectable burghers, to gain favour and admission to both circles, and I entertained them splendidly. With all that I only cared for the sweet virgins; and although I did not always find among them what I looked for, since some of them were able to refuse, yet I visited them all, so that these who showed me more favour than is suitable for an honourable virgin, should not come into suspicion, but that everybody should think I visited them only for the sake of conversation. And that I persuaded each single maid to believe, that none was jealous of the other but each believed herself to be the only one who enjoyed my love.

I had exactly six who loved me and whom I loved, but none possessed my heart or me alone: in one I only loved her black eyes, in the other her golden hair, in the third I liked her charming gracefulness and in the rest something else which the others did not have. If I visited others besides I did it because they were strange or new to me and anyhow I despised nothing, for I did not intend to stay here for ever.

My page who was an arch-rascal was busy enough with procuring and carrying love letters here and there. He kept his mouth shut and my loose dealings secret from one to the other so that nobody heard of it. He received many presents from the wenches, which cost me most, as I had to pay for them all and could truly say: what is gained by drumming is lost with the pipes. Yet all the time I kept my affairs so veiled that not one in a hundred would have taken me for a loose lover except the vicar, from whom I borrowed less religious books than formerly!

When fortune wishes to destroy a man, she first lifts him up to the heights, but before each fall God faithfully gives warning. So it happened to me, but I ignored the warning! I fully believed in those days that my position was firmly established and no misfortune could shake it as everybody, especially the commandant, wished me well. I won the favour of those he esteemed through respectfulness, and his servants through presents, and those who were my equals by drinking brotherhood together and swearing eternal loyalty and friendship. The common burghers and soldiers liked me because I spoke to everyone in a friendly way. "What a friendly man the Huntsman is," they often said to each other. "He chats to every child in the street and angers no one."

When I had caught a hare or some partridges, I sent them to the kitchen of those whose friendship I desired and invited myself too, bringing a measure of wine which was expensive here. Indeed I arranged that all the cost fell on me. In conversation I praised others, not myself, and behaved most modestly as though I had never known conceit. As I now had attained everyone's goodwill I believed that misfortune would never cross my way, especially as my purse was still well stuffed.

I often visited the oldest priest in the town, who lent me many books from his library; whenever I brought one back we discussed all sorts of things and became so familiar that we grew fond of each other. When the Martin's geese and the pig-killing feasts were over and the day of Holy Christmas had passed I made him a New Year present of a bottle of Strasburg brandy which he sipped in the Westphalian manner with a piece of sugar-candy.

When I came to see him I found him to my surprise reading *Joseph*, a book which I had written, and which my landlord had lent to him without my knowledge. In horror I turned pale that my writing should have fallen into the hands of such a learned man, the more so because a man is known by what he writes. He asked me to sit down and although he praised my inventiveness he scolded me that I had indulged so long in the love affairs of Potiphar's wife, Suleika.

"Out of the abundance of the heart the mouth speaketh," he quoted. "If you would not know yourself how a lover feels, you would never have been able to describe this woman's passions so well!"

I answered that what I had written was not my own invention, but I had extracted it from other books to exercise myself in writing.

"Indeed," he said, "that I readily believe! But be assured that I know more of you than you imagine."

I became frightened when I heard these words and thought to myself: has the Devil told you this? And seeing that I changed colour he continued:

"You are a young gentleman, handsome and idle, who lives carefree and in affluence; I ask you therefore to consider, in the name of our Lord, what a dangerous position you are in. Beware of the long-haired beast if you wish to preserve your fortune and salvation! Of course," he added, "you may think what concern is it of the priest and why should he give orders." (You are right, I thought.) "Truly," he concluded, "I am a shepherd of the soul, my friend, and your welfare is close to my heart, like that of my benefactor, as if you were my own son. It would be an eternal pity and an irresponsibility before our heavenly Father if you would bury the gifts which He has given to you, and your noble intelligence, which I recognize from these writings, would be wasted. My true and fatherly advice would be: make use of your youth and your wealth, which you now waste here fruitlessly, and study so that one day you may be of service to God and men and to yourself. Leave warfare alone, which I hear you liked so much before you were defeated, or you will find the truth of the proverb proved which says: 'Young soldiers make old beggars.'"

I listened to this sermon with great impatience for I was no longer used to hearing the like; yet I did not show my feelings lest I should lose my reputation of being well-behaved. I even thanked him for his frankness and promised to consider his advice. Within myself I pondered what did it concern the priest how I arranged my life, for just then I had reached the height of my adventures and would not like to miss the pleasures of lovemaking which I had now tasted. So it is with such warnings, when youth has lost the bridle and spurs of virtue and gallops headlong to his destruction.

I was not yet drowned in lust nor so foolish not to consider keeping every man's friendship for as long as I intended to stay in the fortress, that is until winter was over. So I realized in what distress a man may be involved if he encounters the hatred of the clergy, who among all nations, whatever their religion may be, have great power.

Therefore the very next day I went straightaway to the same priest and told him with well-chosen words such a delightful heap of lies that I was resolved to follow him; he was obviously delighted as I observed from his expression.

"Indeed," I said, "until now and already in Soest, nothing have I lacked more than the angelic counsel given to me by Your Honoured Reverence. If only the winter would soon be over and the weather more comfortable that I could travel!"

I asked him to help me further with good advice and to tell me to which University I should go. He answered that he himself had studied in Leyden but would advise me to go to Geneva because according to my pronunciation I spoke High German!

"Jesus Maria!" I exclaimed, "Geneva is farther away from home than Leyden."

"What do I hear," he said with great amazement, "I can hear you are a papist. Oh, my lord, how I have been deceived!"

"Why that, dear parson, must I be a papist because I do not want to go to Geneva?"

"Oh no," said he, "But I know that you are because you call on the name of Mary."

"Should a Christian not be allowed to quote the name of the Mother of his Redeemer?"

"Very well," he said, "But I must warn and beg you earnestly to give honour to God and admit to me to which religion do you belong? Although I have seen you every Sunday in my church I am very doubtful that you believe the Gospels, because last Christmas you attended Holy Communion neither with me nor in the Lutheran church."

I answered: "Your Reverence knows well that I am a Christian: if I were none I would not have attended your sermons so often. But altogether I must confess that I believe neither in Peter nor in Paul, but simply in the contents of the twelve articles on the Holy Christian Faith. And I shall not commit myself to either party till one of them can bring me sufficient proof to believe that they possess the right, true and only redeeming religion."

"Now," he said, "I truly believe that you have the brave heart of a soldier to risk your life since you can live from day to day without religion or worship and sinfully to hazard your eternal salvation. Oh, my God, how can a mortal man who once must be either damned or saved be so defiant! Were you not brought up in Hanau and did you learn there no better Christianity? Tell me why do you not follow in your parents' footsteps in the true religion of Christ? Why don't you accept our faith of which the foundations are clear as the light of the sun on nature, as in the Holy Writ that in all eternity neither Papist nor Lutheran can ever overthrow them?"

"Your Reverence," I replied, "so say all of their own religion; but whom shall I believe? Shall I entrust my soul's salvation to any one party which is reviled and accused to be a false doctrine by the other two? Look with unbiased eyes at the writings which Conrad Vetter and Johannes Nass have published against Luther, and Luther and his followers against the

Pope, and especially what Spangenberg has written against St Francis, who for hundreds of years was considered a holy and blessed man, and all that has been publicly printed. To which party shall I commit myself when each slanders the others and leaves no good hair on it? Does Your Reverence believe that I am wrong if I hold back until my understanding has matured and I know black from white? Shall I plunge like a fly into the hot broth? Oh no, Your Reverence cannot advise me to do that with a good conscience. Without doubt only one religion can be right and the other two false. And should I confess myself to one without much meditation? I could as easily join the wrong one as the right and so repent in all eternity. I would rather stay off the roads altogether than go astray. Besides there are still more religions than these in Europe, for example, those of the Armenians, Abyssinians, Greeks, Georgians, and such like, and which ever I may choose, I must, with all my fellow believers, contradict the others. If now Your Reverence can convince me that your religion is the true one, I will follow you with great thankfulness and join that religion which you confess."

He then replied: "You are in great error but I place my hope in God that He may enlighten you and help you out of the slough. To this end I will prove to you the truth of our confession from the Holy Script so convincingly that it will resist even the Gates of Hell."

I accepted his offer with gratitude, yet I thought to myself: if only he will not reproach me about my love affairs, I will be content with his creed. And so the reader may conclude what a godless, wicked rascal I then was, for I cost the good priest fruitless effort that he might leave me unhindered in my vicious life, thinking that before he were ready to substantiate his theory I might well be far, far away where the pepper grows.

SIMPLICIUS MAKES A SPEEDY MARRIAGE

OPPOSITE MY LODGINGS lived a retired lieutenant-colonel, who had a most beautiful daughter of great dignity. I had long wished to make her acquaintance, although at first I had no intention at all of loving her alone or possessing her for ever. I went out of my way many times to see her and even more cast loving glances at her, but she was so well guarded that I was never able to speak to her as I wished. Moreover I could not intrude on her as I had no acquaintance with her parents, and their house seemed far too highly placed for a fellow of such humble descent as I thought I was.

I came nearest to her when we were entering or leaving church. It was then I took advantage to get close to her and impressed her with my passionate sighs in which I was a master, though all sprang from a false heart. But she received my efforts with such coldness that I had to believe that she was not so easily seduced as any small burgher's daughter, and the more I realized that I was not succeeding in my wooing, the more violent grew my desire for her.

The lucky star which brought me finally to her was the very same which the schoolboys carry about on the feast of the Three Kings. As the Three Kings were led to Bethlehem, so the lucky star – a good omen – led me to her house, for her father himself sent for me.

"Monsieur," he said, "the neutrality which you keep between burghers and soldiers is the reason why I have sent for you to act as an unbiased witness in a case which I have to settle between two parties."

I expected he had some very important business in mind, for paper and pen lay on the table. So I offered him my most willing service to all honest ends, and I would consider it a great honour if I were so fortunate as to do him a service of any kind. Yet it was nothing more than to set up a kingdom, as was the usage in many towns on the Eve of the Feast of the Three Kings. My duty was to see that everything went smoothly and fairly and that the roles were distributed by lot without respect of persons.

During this business, at which the colonel's secretary assisted, the lieutenant-colonel (as supper time was passed) had wine and confectionery

served – for he was a manly drinker. The secretary wrote, I read the
names and the damsel drew the lots, whilst her parents looked on.
But I do not want to go into detail how it happened when I first
made her acquaintance in that home. They complained of the long
winter nights and gave me to understand I should be welcome to
visit them in the evening to pass the time more easily as they had
not much business to occupy them. This was just the thing I had
wished for a long time. From that evening, on which I had but little
chance with the damsel – I began anew to play the lover until both
daughter and parents believed I had swallowed the hook, though I still
had no serious intent. Like the witches do, I dressed myself up only
towards night to visit her, and the day I spent reading erotic books,
from which I concocted love letters to my sweetheart as if I lived a
hundred miles away or would not see her again for many a year. At
last we became quite intimate as the parents did not much interfere
with our lovemaking, and even asked me to teach their daughter to
play the lute. Now I had free entrance by day and at night, so that I
had to change the motto of my tune—

> The bats and I
> By night we fly

into another song, in which I praised my good fortune which after so
many pleasant evenings had granted me so many delightful days when my
eyes could feast on the charm of my beloved and rejoice my heart. And
in the same song I bemoaned my misfortune that made my nights bitter
and did not permit me to spend them like the days in sweet enjoyment. I
sang this to my sweetheart, though it had turned out a little daring, with
enchanting sighs and a beguiling melody, whereby the lute played its part
gallantly as if it too implored the damsel to condescend and make my
nights as happy as my days.

But to all that I got a rather cold refusal as she was highly intelligent and
had a polite answer ready to all the tricks which I so cleverly employed. I
had been careful not to mention matrimony and if the conversation came
to this, I formed my words most cautiously. This was noticed by her married sister who barred all meetings between me and my beloved, so that
we might not be together alone as often as before, for she saw that her
sister was in love with all her heart and that the affair would in the end
do no good to anyone.

There is no need to describe all the follies of my lovemaking in detail, for all books of love are full of such foolishness. It is enough for the reader to know that soon I succeeded in kissing my sweetheart and at last dared to employ other caresses. I pursued such desired advances with all sorts of titillations until one night I was admitted by my beloved and laid myself nicely by her side in bed as if I belonged there. As we all know what usually goes on at such harvest festivals, the reader may easily think I committed something unbecoming. But far from that. All my hopes were frustrated and I found such resistance as I never imagined to meet in any woman. Her intentions were only aimed at honour and marriage and although I promised her this with the most horrifying oaths, she would not allow anything to happen before the conclusion of the marriage ceremony. Yet she allowed me to lay next to her in bed on which I finally gently fell asleep, tired by bad temper. But soon I was violently awakened at four o'clock in the morning. The lieutenant-colonel stood before the bed, a pistol in one hand and a torch in the other.

"Croat!" he shrieked violently at his servant, "Go quickly, Croat go and fetch the priest."

At that I awoke and saw in what danger I lay. Woe, I thought, this will be my last confession before he makes an end of me; everything appeared green and yellow before my eyes and I did not know whether I should open them or not.

"You debauched rogue," he said to me. "Must I find you thus disgracing my house? Should I do wrong to break your neck and that of this harlot who has become your whore? You, brute, why shall I not tear your heart from your belly, chop it to pieces and throw it to the dogs?"

With these words he ground his teeth and rolled his eyes like a demented beast.

I did not know what to do and my bedfellow could do nothing but weep. At last, when I came to my senses a little, I tried to protest our innocence but he told me to keep my mouth shut and started all over again to say that he had trusted my honesty and that I had repaid him with the greatest treachery in the world.

In the mean time, his wife came in too and started another brand-new sermon that I would have preferred to lay in a hedge of thorns, and she would not have stopped, I believe, within two hours had not the Croat returned with the priest. Before he arrived I had tried several times to get out of bed, but the colonel forced me threateningly to lie down. And so I learnt how little courage a fellow can show if he is caught on an evil errand and how a thief must feel in his heart if he has burgled a house and is captured yet having stolen nothing. And I thought of the good old days when, if such a colonel with two such Croats had attacked me, I would have been sure to have chased off all three. But now I had to lay down like a sluggard and did not dare to open my mouth, let alone use my fists.

"Look here, your Reverence," said the colonel, "what a pretty spectacle to which I must invite you as witness of my shame!" And hardly had he started to utter these words in a normal tone than he began again to rage and to mix the hundreds into the thousands, that I could grasp nothing but breaking of necks and washing of hands in blood. His mouth foamed like a wild boar and it seemed that he would lose his senses completely. Thus every moment I thought that he would chase a bullet through my head. The priest did his very best to prevent anything fatal happening which might be repented.

"My colonel," he said, "make use of your reason and remember the proverb that if deeds are done, make the best of them. This handsome young couple, who can hardly be matched in the land, is neither the first, nor will be the last to be vanquished by the invincible powers of love. The fault which the two have committed, if it has to be called a fault, can easily be amended by themselves. I am not really very fond of marrying this way, but the young couple deserve neither gallows nor wheel, nor has the lieutenant-colonel to expect any shame if he only forgives and keeps this fault secret (of which up to now no one is aware), thus giving his consent to their marriage, and having the marriage confirmed through the usual ceremony in church."

"What," the colonel answered, "should I, instead of well-deserved punishment, make them my compliments and pay them honour? I would rather have them tied up together tomorrow and drowned in the Lippe. You must wed them this very moment! For what purpose have I brought you here? Or I will strangle them like chickens."

My thoughts were: what shall I do? Swallow it or die? Here is a maiden of whom I need not be ashamed. Indeed, considering my own lineage, I am hardly worthy to sit where she puts down her foot. Aloud I swore and protested that we had not behaved dishonourably together, but received the answer that we were not to be trusted after behaving like this. So we were married by the parson, sitting up in bed, and as soon as this was over we were compelled to rise and leave the house together. At the threshold the colonel told his daughter and me that we should never set ourselves before his eyes again. But I, having recovered myself and feeling again a sword at my side, answered him jocularly: "Dear father-in-law, I don't know why you arrange everything topsy-turvy; when other young couples are being married their relatives lead them to their bedchamber. But you, after the ceremony throw me not only out of bed but even out of the house. And instead of congratulating me on my marriage, you will not even grant me the happiness of seeing my father-in-law and serving him. Verily, if this custom should come into vogue, little friendship in the world would be brought about through weddings."

The people at my house were all amazed when I brought this young maiden home with me and even more when they saw that she went to bed with me without hesitation. For though this mock play which I had undergone had disturbed my mind, I was not foolish enough to despise my bride. Whilst I held my sweetheart in my arms, a thousand thoughts raced through my head how I should settle this affair. At one moment I thought this had served me right and the next I believed that I had met the greatest degradation in the world, which I could not take in honour without proper revenge. But when I considered that all such revenge must hurt my father-in-law and my innocent and devout sweetheart, all my plots came to nothing. I was so ashamed that I decided to stay indoors and be seen by no one, and then again I realized that that would be to commit the greatest folly.

In the end I decided to win back my father-in-law's friendship and to behave to the others as if nothing wrong had happened to me and as if I had prepared everything for my wedding in the very best way. I told myself that as all this had started in such a strange and unusual fashion I had to bring it to an end in the same fashion. If the people would know that I was tricked against my will to the marriage like a poor spinster to a rich old cripple, I would meet with ridicule. With such thoughts I began the day early, though I had rather stayed longer in bed. First I sent to my brother-in-law, who had married my wife's sister, and told him briefly how closely akin to him I now was. I asked him to allow his wife to come and help me, that I could feed my wedding guests, and if he would be kind enough to calm down my father and mother-in-law on my behalf, whilst I in the mean time would invite such guests who would complete the peace between me and them.

He promised his help, and I went to the governor, to whom I merrily and amusingly recounted in what quaint new fashion my father-in-law and I had concluded a marriage which went so quickly that in one single hour I went through the betrothal, the church ceremony and the wedding. But as my father-in-law had grudged me the morning broth, I was willing to treat some honourable guests to a wedding breakfast to which I begged him to accept an invitation.

The commandant almost burst with laughter at my farcical report and as I saw he looked at the matter intelligently I talked more freely and apologized that I could now hardly be as reasonable as other bride-grooms who lost their senses four weeks before and after their weddings. But whilst they had four weeks' time in which they could let loose their foolishness, matrimony was urged upon me in surprise and I had to get rid of my follies at one fell swoop to start my married life more soberly. He asked me about my wedding settlement and how many good ducats my father-in-law had given me as a dowry, of which the old miser had many. I replied that our marriage settlement contained only one clause which was that his daughter and I should never come before his eyes again! But as neither notary nor witnesses had been present – I hoped the clause might be revoked the more so as all marriages are made for the propagation of friendship and I had never insulted him with intent.

Joking in this way, to which nobody here was accustomed, I obtained the promise that the commandant would attend my wedding feast together with my father-in-law, whom he would try to win over. The commandant forthwith sent a barrel of delicious wine and a stag to my kitchen, and I made my preparations as if I were to entertain princes. I assembled a respectable company who not only made merry with one another but particularly reconciled my father and mother-in-law with me in such a way that they wished us more happiness now than they had cursed us the night before. And in the whole town the rumour was spread that our marriage had intentionally been arranged in such a strange and secret fashion that no evil people should have served a trick on us.

To me this speedy marriage was to my liking, for had I tried to marry in the usual custom, with the banns publicly called from the pulpit, I fear there would have been some maidens who would have made a lot of trouble and confusion, as I had among the burghers' daughters a good half dozen who knew me only too well.

The next day my father-in-law gave a feast to my wedding guests, though not as good as mine for he was a miser. Then he talked to me of what profession I had in mind and how I would arrange my household; and thus I first became aware that I had lost my noble freedom and had to live henceforth in serfdom. But I behaved obediently and asked my dear father-in-law as a gentleman of reason for his trustworthy advice, which I would follow.

The commandant praised my answer and said:

"As he is a smart young soldier, it would be a great folly if in the present state of war he would intend to follow anything but the trade of a soldier. It is far better to put one horse in another man's stable than to feed another man's hack in your own. As far as I am concerned, I will give him a detachment whenever he wishes."

My father-in-law and I thanked him and I did not refuse as I had done before but I showed the commandant the merchant's document who kept my treasure in Cologne in trust.

"This," I said, "I must collect first before I go into Swedish service, for should the Imperials learn that I serve their enemies they will mock me in Cologne and keep my treasure which cannot easily be found by the roadside."

They both agreed and thus we all three concluded that I should go to Cologne in a few days to claim my treasure, return to the fortress and take command of a detachment. A day was also fixed when my father-in-law should take over a company, as well as the commission of a lieutenant-colonel in the regiment of the commandant.

As at this time Count von Götz was stationed in Westphalia with many Imperial troops at his headquarters in Dortmund, my commandant expected a siege in the coming spring and tried therefore to recruit good soldiers. Yet his efforts were in vain, because Count von Götz had to leave Westphalia that same spring (after Johann von Werth had been defeated in the Breisgau) and fight the Duke of Weimar on the Rhine.

19

SIMPLICIUS IN COLOGNE

LIFE PURSUES ITS OWN MANIFOLD WAYS. To one ill-fortune comes by degrees and slowly, to another it falls in a heap. Mine had such sweet and pleasant beginnings that I thought it to be utter bliss. Yet hardly had I spent a week with my dear wife in wedlock when, clad in my huntsman's outfit, my gun on my shoulder, I said farewell to her and to our friends. Luckily knowing all the paths by heart, I strode ahead encountering no danger and unseen by the soldiery, until I reached the tollgates at Deutz, which lay opposite Cologne on this side of the Rhine. I met some country people, in particular a peasant in the province of Berg who reminded me strongly of my dad in the Spessart, and his son resembled the former Simplicius even more.

This peasant boy was herding swine as I was passing and because the sows scented me they began to grunt, and the boy to swear that thunder and hail should shatter them and the Devil take them. The maid, hearing this, called to the boy to stop swearing or she would tell his father. The boy answered she should lick his behind and boil her mother too. Hearing this the peasant ran out of the house with a cudgel and shouted:

"Stop, you thousand times damned rascal. I'll teach you to swear! May hail strike you and the Devil strike into your belly!"

Whereupon he grabbed him by the neck and whipped him like a dancing bear, shouting with every stroke: "You wicked creature. I'll teach you to curse, may the Devil take you! I'll lick *your* arse, I'll teach you to boil *your* mother!"

This sort of education reminded me naturally of my own dad but I was not honest nor religious enough to thank God for delivering me from such darkness and ignorance to a better knowledge and understanding. Why should God continue to bless me with good fortune for ever?

On arrival in Cologne I took up lodgings with Jupiter who was then in a quite reasonable state of mind. When I told him why I had come he said at once that he was afraid I would only be threshing empty straw, as the merchant to whom I had entrusted my wealth had become bankrupt and had absconded. Although my properties had been sealed by the magistrate and the merchant summoned to appear, his return was very doubtful for he had taken with him the best that could be carried, and before the case would be called much water would flow down the Rhine.

One can well understand how I welcomed this message. I cursed worse than a drayman, but what help was that? I had neither my property nor any hope of ever getting it back. I also had not more than ten thaler with me, so that I could not stay long enough for the calling of the case. Apart from that there was some danger in prolonging my stay as I belonged to an enemy garrison and might be denounced and fall into still greater trouble.

But to return with my affairs unsettled, leaving my wealth light-heartedly behind seemed to me even more foolish. So at last I decided to wait in Cologne until the case was heard and to inform my sweetheart of the cause of my absence. I went to an attorney who was also a notary and told him my predicament and asked his help in advice and action, and if he would expedite the case I promised him a good reward in addition to his proper fees. As he hoped to find good fishing in my case, he gladly accepted me and offered me board and lodging as well. Next day he went with me to the magistrate who dealt with bankruptcy and handed a certified copy of the merchant's letter, and showed him the original, upon which we received the answer that we should be patient till the final examination of the case, as some objects mentioned in the document could not be traced.

So I had again a long time of idleness ahead of me in which I could see how life went on in great cities. My host was as I have mentioned a notary and an attorney, and besides that he took in about half a dozen lodgers and always kept eight horses in his stables which he hired out to travellers against payment; a German and a French groom served for driving, riding and tending the horses. With this threefold, or better, three-and-a-half-fold business, he not only made a good living, but also doubtlessly a rich profit, and as no Jews were allowed in the town, the easier he could practise usury in many ways.

During the time I stayed with him I learnt a number of things, especially to recognize human maladies, which is the highest skill of a doctor of medicine; as it is said, if only the illness is diagnosed correctly the patient is already half cured. The understanding of this science I owed to my host, for I began studying him and thereafter examined the complexities of others. I found many a man sick to death who often did not know it himself and who was considered by everybody, indeed even by doctors, to be a healthy man. I found people who were diseased with ill-temper and when this sickness attacked them, their faces changed to those of devils, they roared like lions and scratched like cats, and behaved worse than wild beasts, throwing everything about which their hands could grasp. People say this illness has its origin in the gall, but I believe it derives from a man's vanity. So if ever you hear a man in a rage, especially about some trifle, be sure that man has more conceit than reason. Much misfortune results from this illness, both for the diseased and for others, and the patient in the end suffers paralysis, gout and early death, if not indeed eternal death! And yet with good conscience one can hardly call these men patients, although they are dangerously ill, but patience is what they lack most.

I saw some people stricken with envy, of whom it is said that they eat up their own heart, as they move about so pale and sad. This disease I hold to be the most dangerous as it has its origin in the Devil, and he who can cure a man of envy can praise himself to have converted a lost soul to the Christian faith. The passion of gambling I consider a disease too, as all who are infected with it appear to be poisoned by this addiction. The malady has its origin in idleness and not in greed as some believe, and if you take away lust and idleness the sickness fades away naturally. I also believed that gluttony is a disease and it comes from habit and not from abundance. Poverty is a good remedy against it but it cannot be cured by that alone as I have seen beggars feasting and wealthy misers starving. It carries its own remedy on its back called Want; thus in the end these patients must recover by themselves when either through poverty or sickness they can no longer eat.

Vanity I considered a kind of insanity, having its origin in ignorance, because if a man knows himself and considers from where he came and whither he goes, it is impossible to remain an arrogant fool. And yet I never could find the right remedy against it, because those who are thus affected are without humility and cannot, like all other fools, be cured. No less did I observe that curiosity must be a disease, especially inborn to the female sex. Although it seems of little importance, yet it is truly most dangerous, considering that we all still have to suffer for our first mother's curiosity. The rest such as sloth, revenge, jealousy, cruelty, lechery and other vices I will not mention, it not being my intention to describe these, but I will turn again to my host who was the cause of my pondering over such human frailties for he was possessed by greed to the roots of his hair.

He followed several trades by which he scraped money together. He ate with his lodgers and he could have fed himself and his household sufficiently with the profit they brought him, had the miser made use of it, but he fed us in the Swabian manner and kept us short. At first I ate not with his lodgers but with his children and servants as I had not much money. There were only little scraps which were strange to my stomach accustomed to the rich Westphalian feasts. No good piece of meat came to our table, but only that which had been left over a week before on the student's table, well nibbled and as grey with age as Methuselah, over which our hostess, who had to run the kitchen herself (as he allowed her no help), poured a black sour gravy bedevilled with pepper. Thus we licked the bones so clean that one could have made chess figures out of them. Yet they were utilized still further and put into a pot kept for this purpose, and when our miser had a good quantity, they were chopped and boiled to get the last drop of fat out of them, and I never knew whether the soups or the boots were greased with it.

On fast days, of which there were more than enough and which the miser kept solemnly, we had to content ourselves with stinking herrings, over-salty or foul stockfish and other stale fish, for he purchased it only if it were cheap and he did not mind the trouble of going himself to the fish market and picking up what the fishmongers were just about to throw away. Our bread was usually black and stale, our drink a thin and sour beer which cut into my bowels and yet was called fine old March-brew.

And yet I heard from his German groom it was even worse in summer for then the bread was mouldy, the meat full of maggots and the best food was a few radishes for lunch and a handful of lettuce for supper. I asked why did he remain with the old miser? He told me that as he spent most of his time travelling he had to consider the gratuities from the travellers rather than the musty old Jew who would not even trust his own wife or children in the cellar, who grudged even himself a drop of wine and in short was such a niggard that another such as he would be hard to find. He added that what I had seen so far was nothing and if I could stay a little longer I would realize that he was not ashamed to boil the carcass of a donkey to save a few coppers.

Once the miser brought home six pounds of tripe, which he put in his cellar and, to the good fortune of his children, the window was left open, so they fixed a fork onto a stick and hooked out the lot, which they gulped down half cooked in a great hurry, pretending the cat had done it. But the skin-flint would not believe this, caught the cat, weighed it and found out that with skin, fur and bones the cat was not as heavy as his tripe had been.

As he behaved so niggardly I requested that I should no longer eat at his servants' board but with the students, whatever the cost might be. There it was indeed somewhat better, but helped me little because all the dishes served to us were only half-cooked, bringing our host twofold gain: first he saved firewood and second, we could digest very little. In spite of that he counted every mouthful we swallowed and scratched behind his ears when we had a good appetite. His wine was well watered and not helpful for the digestion, the cheese which was served at the end of each meal was usually stone-hard and the Dutch butter salty to such a degree that no one could eat more than one ounce at a meal. The fruit was served and carried away until at last it became ripe and eatable. And if one or the other complained, he started to scold his wife abominably that we all could hear, though secretly he ordered her to continue playing the same old fiddle.

Once one of his clients gave him a hare as a present, which I saw hanging in the larder, hoping that we for once would have game to eat. But the German groom told me we should hope in vain, as his master had agreed with his lodgers that he need not supply such delicacies, and I should go to the Old Market in the afternoon and look if it were there for sale. Thereupon I cut a little piece out of the hare's ear and as we sat over our midday meal, our host being absent, I told them that our miser had a hare for sale and that I was resolved to cheat him if one of them would help, to the end that we would not only have some merriment but the hare as well. All agreed and were eager to play a prank of which our host would not be able to complain. Thus in the afternoon, we went to the place where the miser was in the habit of standing and watching what the buyer paid in case he might be cheated of a farthing. We saw him there in discussion with some gentlemen. I had hired a fellow who went to the hawker who was to sell the hare and said:

"Neighbour, the hare is mine and I claim it by law as stolen goods. It has been pilfered from my window last night and if you do not surrender it I will take you to court at your risk and expense."

The salesman answered he could do what he liked but there stood the gentleman who had given him the hare to sell, and he certainly had not stolen it. As the two quarrelled, many people gathered round them and when our miser saw that the clock had struck he gave a sign to the hawker to surrender the hare as he feared even greater insult because of his many lodgers. But the fellow, whom I had hired, showed cleverly to the whole crowd the missing piece of the ear, so that everybody adjudged him the ownership of the hare. Meanwhile I came nearer with my companions as if by chance, approached the fellow with the hare and started to bargain, and when we agreed I surrendered the hare to my host, asking him to take it home with him and to have it prepared for our table. The fellow I had hired received instead of payment from me some money for two jugs of beer. So our miser had to treat us to the hare against his will and dared not contradict, which caused us much laughter. Had I stayed longer in his house I would have played more such tricks on him.

PART FOUR

20

SIMPLICIUS BECOMES AN ACTOR

"A KNIFE TOO FINELY SHARPENED may become notched and a bow bent too far will break." The prank I played on my host with the hare was not enough for me and I invented more to punish his unappeasable greed. So I taught my fellow boarders to water the salty butter and to extract the surplus salt, and to grate the hard cheese like the Parmesans and to moisten it with wine, which were nothing but stabs in the heart to the miser. Through my tricks at table I drew the water out of the wine and composed a song in which I compared the miser with a sow which is no good to anyone until the butcher has her killed on his trestle. I ought not to have played such pranks in his house, for by doing this I gave him cause to pay me back handsomely with the following treachery.

Two of our young noblemen received a letter of exchange and the order from their parents to go to France and learn the language, just at the time our host's German groom was elsewhere on his travels.

The French groom, said our host, could not be trusted with the horses in France as he may forget to come back and so cheat him of them. Therefore he asked me to render him a great service and accompany the two noblemen with his horses to Paris, for my case would not be heard within the next four weeks. In the mean time, he would, if I gave him full powers of attorney, faithfully promote my affairs as if I were personally present. The noblemen urged me likewise and my own curiosity to see France without much expense persuaded me too, as I had to waste four weeks in idleness anyway and pay for it as well. So I started the journey as postilion to the two students and nothing remarkable happened on the journey.

When we reached Paris and had taken lodgings at our host's agent, where the noblemen cashed their letter of exchange, I and the horses were the next day legally arrested and a man who pretended my host owed him a sum of money confiscated them with the permission of the district magistrate in lieu of the debt, and sold the horses. God only knows what I said to all this! There I sat, like the foolish Mathias of Dresden, and did not know how to help myself nor to find out how to return by such a long and dangerous road.

The noblemen showed great sympathy and presented me willingly with a good reward and did not want to dismiss me before I had found either a good employer or a good opportunity to return to Germany. They rented some lodgings and I spent a few days looking after one of them who through the long and unaccustomed journey had become indisposed. In gratitude he gave me his clothes, which he discarded as he wished to be dressed in the new fashion. They advised me to stay a couple of years in Paris and learn the language, for what I had to collect in Cologne would not run away. While I still hesitated on what to do, the doctor who attended my nobleman daily by chance heard me play the lute and sing a German song, which pleased him so much that he offered me a good post with free board if I would come to him and teach his two sons. He knew already better than I how my affairs stood and that I would not refuse a good master. So we soon agreed, for both noblemen recommended me warmly, and I took the engagement for not more than a quarter of a year.

The doctor spoke German as well as I, and Italian like his mother tongue, so all the more gladly I pledged myself to him. When I was having a farewell drink with my noblemen, he too was present, and many sad thoughts went through my head, thinking of my newly wedded wife, my promised ensigncy and my treasure in Cologne, all of which I had been persuaded to abandon light-heartedly. And when we came to discuss the greed of our former host it occurred to me to say at table: "Who knows whether perhaps our host had not intentionally pushed me off here that he may claim and take over my property in Cologne?"

The doctor answered that this might well be, especially if he suspected me to be a fellow of humble origin.

"No," said one of the noblemen, "if he was sent here to stay, it was because he had ridiculed him so much on the score of his greed."

The sick man however believed the reason was that the miser had become suspicious of his wife having an affair with me. Then the doctor said:

"Whatever the reasons were, I am sure things have turned out so that you must stay here. But do not worry, I will soon help you back to Germany at the first opportunity. Write only to your host in Cologne to take great care of your treasure or he will be painfully called to account. I have however the suspicion that it is a pre-arranged plot, as the man who gave himself out for the creditor is a very good friend of your host and agent here, and I am convinced that the document by force of which he confiscated and sold the horses was actually brought by you yourself."

Monseigneur Canard (this was the name of my new master) offered me his help in word and deed, that I might not lose my property in Cologne, for he saw well how sad I was. So, as soon as he had taken me to his house he asked me to tell him frankly about my affairs that he might advise me how best to assist me. I knew very well that my esteem would be rather low had I revealed my humble origin and so I gave myself out to be a poor German nobleman having no father nor mother but only a few relatives at present in a fortress occupied by a Swedish garrison. This I told him I had concealed from my host and the two noblemen as they were of the Imperial side so that they might not confiscate my treasure as enemy property. It was my intention to write to the commandant of the fortress in whose regiment I had been promised an ensigncy and to inform him in which way I had been deceived and to ask him to take possession of my property until I could find a chance to return to my regiment.

The good Canard agreed with this plan and promised to forward the letters to their proper destination even should they be addressed to Mexico or China. So I composed letters to my sweetheart, to my father-in-law, and to the Colonel St Andre, commandant in Lippstadt, to whom I addressed the whole envelope and enclosed the two others. The message was that I would return as soon as I could find means to make such a long journey, and I asked both my father-in-law and the colonel to try to recover my property by military means before the grass grew over it, and gave them a detailed list of the amount in gold, silver and jewels. All these letters I made out in duplicate, one of which Monseigneur Canard sent off, and the other I delivered to the post, so that should one get lost the other might arrive.

I thus became light-hearted again and instructed the two sons of my master with ease. They were educated like young princes for their father was very rich, had great vanity and wanted to display his wealth, a disease which he had adopted from the great lords with whom he dealt daily and whom he aped. His house was like the castle of a count in which nothing was amiss; he was called "Your Grace", and his conceit was so great that he would treat a marquis as if he were his equal when he came to visit him. He helped poor people, too, with his skill, and did not take their small fees but rather acquitted them their debts to gain in reputation. I was eager to learn and knew that he liked to show off with my person, when I accompanied him with other servants on visits to his patients, and I helped him in his laboratory in the preparation of his medicines, thus becoming rather intimate with him, especially as he liked to speak the German language.

I once asked him why he did not use the title of the estate which he had recently bought near Paris for 20,000 crowns, and why he wished to make doctors of his sons, forcing them to study so hard. Were it not better to buy them positions, as was the custom of noblemen, and introduce them entirely into the nobility?

"No," he said. "If I visit a prince they say to me 'Herr Doctor, be seated', but to a nobleman they would say 'Wait upon my pleasure'."

I retorted: "Are you aware that a physician has three faces, the first that of an angel, when the patient first sees him; the second that of a god, when he has cured him, and the third that of a devil, when a man is healed and wants to get rid of him. A doctor's honour only lasts as long as the wind plagues a sick man in his belly – but as soon as the fart is out and the rumbling over the honour is at an end, and they say "Doctor, the door is there". So the nobleman gains more honour by his standing than the doctor by sitting because he waits upon his own prince and has the honour never to leave his side. You, Herr Doctor, have recently taken something from a prince in your mouth to examine its taste; I would prefer to stand and wait for ten years before I would taste somebody's excrements, even should they place me on a bed of roses."

He answered: "There was no need for me to do this yet I did it willingly to show the prince my strenuous efforts to discover his condition and to improve my reputation. And why should I not experiment with someone's muck if he pays me a few hundred pistoles for it, whilst he has to swallow quite different stuff from me for which I pay him nothing. You discuss this matter like a German, and were you of another nationality I would say you have talked like a fool!"

With these words I kept quiet for I saw that he might become angry, and in order to bring him again into a good humour I asked him to forgive my simplicity and began to talk of more pleasant things.

Monseigneur Canard had more game to throw away than some had to eat, even including those who had their own game reserves, and more meat was given to him than he and his household could consume. Thus, daily he had many hangers-on so that it looked as if he kept an open house. Once, the King's Master of Ceremonies and other distinguished persons from the Court paid him a visit, to whom he offered princely refreshments, knowing well whom to keep as friends, namely those who were always near the King or had his favour. To show him his most willing devotion, and to entertain them all, he asked me to sing a German song accompanied with my lute. I gladly agreed, being in the right mood, for musicians are mostly temperamental. I was at my very best and pleased the company so much that the Master of Ceremonies said it was a great pity that I could not speak French, for he would gladly recommend me to the King and Queen. But my master, who feared I might be taken from his service, replied that I was a nobleman and did not intend to stay long in France and could hardly be used as a musician. Upon which the Master of Ceremonies said that in all his life he had never found such rare beauty, such a clear voice and such artistic skill on the lute combined in one person. Very soon a comedy was to be performed before the King at the Louvre and if he could make use of my talent he hoped to gain much honour.

This Monseigneur Canard translated to me and I answered him that if they would tell me what to play and what kind of songs to sing I could learn both tune and words by heart and sing them to my lute, even if they were in French. When the Master of Ceremonies saw me so willing, I had to promise him to come to the Louvre the next day to find out whether I was fit for the role.

At the appointed time I arrived. The tunes of the various songs which I had to sing I could play at once perfectly on my instrument as I read from the sheet of notes before me. Then I received the French text of the songs to learn by heart and to pronounce correctly, which was at once translated into German that I might adjust my expressions accordingly. All this did not trouble me much and I mastered it sooner than anyone had expected and to such perfection that only one in a thousand would not have sworn I was a born Frenchman. When we met for the first rehearsal of the comedy, I knew how to act so sorrowfully with my songs, melodies and movements, that everybody believed that I had played the part of Orpheus mourning his Eurydice, whom I had to represent, many times before. In all my life I never enjoyed such a pleasant and delightful day as that when the comedy was played. Monseigneur Canard gave me something to make my voice still clearer, but when he tried to improve my beauty with oleum talci and to powder my curly hair he found that this would only spoil me. So I was merely crowned with a wreath of laurels and dressed in an antique sea-green costume in which all could see my neck, the upper part of my breast, my arms and knees and my legs down to the calves, all bare and naked. I wrapped myself also in a flesh-coloured cloak of taffeta which was more like a pennant. In such apparel I mourned my Eurydice, called on Venus for help in a pretty aria and at last carried my sweetheart away. All through my role I acted perfectly and gazed upon my beloved with sighs and expressive eyes.

And when I had lost my Eurydice, I put on a costume entirely black made in the same fashion as the other, from which my white skin shone out like snow. In this attire I lamented my lost wife and imagined my loss so vividly that in the midst of my tender songs and melodies the tears burst out and my weeping almost overpowered my singing. Yet I continued my part in beautiful style until I came before Pluto and Proserpina in Hell. To them I described in a most touching song their own love for each other and begged them to remember in what great sorrow I and Eurydice were separated and singing to my lute implored them humbly that they would give her back to me. When I had received their assent I thanked them with a joyful song and changed my expression, my gestures and my voice into such gladness that all the spectators were astonished, but on losing my Eurydice unexpectedly again I imagined the greatest danger in which a man could find himself and turned so pale as if I would swoon. I was then alone on the stage and the audience looked at me as I played my role so devotedly, and I earned the honour of having acted the best of all.

In the following scene I sat on a rock and began to deplore the loss of my beloved with pitiful words and a mournful melody, calling on all creatures for compassion. Whereupon all sorts of tame and wild animals, mountains, trees and the like came to me, so that it truly looked as if it were done supernaturally by magic. Nor did I make any mistake, but at the very end, when I renounced the company of all females and had been strangled by the Bacchantes and thrown into the water, it was so arranged that only my head could be seen, whilst the rest of my body was beneath the stage in safety. Now the dragon had to gnaw at me and the fellow who was inside the dragon manoeuvring it could not see my head, so he let the dragon's head nibble close to mine. This appeared to me ridiculous that I could not help making a grimace, which the ladies watching me could well perceive.

This comedy brought me, besides universal appraisal, a considerable reward, and yet another name, for from now on the French would call me "Beau Alman". More such plays and ballets were performed as it was carnival time, and I participated in all of them. But in the end I found I was envied by others because I charmed the spectators and especially captivated the ladies, who cast their eyes upon me. So I gave it up, particularly because I once received many blows when fighting as Hercules with Achelous for Deianira, being almost naked in a lion's skin, and I was maltreated as is not usual in a play.

Through all this I became familiar with high-standing personalities and it seemed as if good fortune would shine on me again, for even service to the King was offered to me which does not happen to every Tom, Dick or Harry.

It happened that a lackey came to Monseigneur Canard and brought a note on my behalf as I sat in the laboratory experimenting. Out of interest in the doctor's work I had already learnt how to resolve, sublimate, coagulate, calcinate, filter and such like alchemistic work with which he prepared his medicines.

"Monsieur Beau Alman," said the doctor, "this letter concerns you. A gentleman of high rank asks you to come to him to find out whether you would agree to teach his son to play the lute. He asks me to persuade you not to refuse this request, with the most courteous promise to reward your efforts with friendly gratitude."

I answered if I could be of service to anyone for the doctor's sake, I would spare no trouble. Thereupon he said I should change my clothes to go with the lackey whilst he would prepare some food for me as I had a somewhat long journey to make and I would hardly reach the place before nightfall. So I dressed myself up and hurriedly swallowed some food, especially a few small delicious sausages which appeared to me to taste rather strongly of the apothecary. Then I went with the lackey making strange detours for a whole hour until we reached, towards evening, a garden gate which had been left on the latch. The lackey pushed it open and as soon as we had entered closed it again, then led me to a pleasure pavilion which stood in a corner of the garden. After we had traversed a long passage he knocked at a door which was opened at once by an elderly noblewoman who welcomed me most politely in German and invited me to enter, while the lackey who did not understand any German took his leave with a deep bow. The old lady took my hand and led me into a room hung with precious tapestries and handsomely furnished. She told me to sit down and rest and hear why I had been brought to this place. I gladly sat down in an armchair which she had moved near to the fire, as it was cold outside, and sitting beside me she said:

"Monsieur, if you know that the power of love conquers the bravest, wisest and strongest of men, you will be less amazed to know it masters even a weak woman. You have not been called here by a gentleman for the sake of your lute, as Monseigneur Canard told you, but by a most exquisite Parisian lady for the sake of your superb beauty. She fears she may die if she cannot soon enjoy the bliss of gazing upon you and delighting in your sublime perfection. This is the reason why she has ordered me to inform you of this as a compatriot of yours, and to ask you more urgently than

Venus her Adonis to visit her tonight and reveal your beauty, which I hope you will not refuse to such a noble lady."

I answered: "Madame, I know not what to think and less what I shall say to all this. I can scarcely believe I am such that a lady of high rank would desire my humble self. Moreover, if the lady who wishes to see me is truly so excellent and noble, she should have sent for me at an earlier hour of the day, and not to this lonely place late in the evening. Why did she not order me to come directly to her? What must I do in this garden? My dear compatriot, forgive me if I as a lonely stranger feel anxious that I may be deceived, especially as I was asked to visit a gentleman which has proved to be false. Should I see that there is treason and malicious tricks against me, I shall know how to use my sword before I die."

"Slowly, slowly, my honourable compatriot, cast these futile ideas out of your mind," she answered. "Women are strange and cautious in their plans that one may not easily understand them at once. If the lady who loves you above all wished that you should know her by name, she would not have troubled you to come here but would have asked you to come straight to her. But there is a hood" – she pointed to the table – "which you must wear when you are led to her, for she does not even wish you to recognize either place or person. I pray and urge you, dear Sir, most urgently to offer this lady what her position and unspeakable love for you deserve, unless you wish to experience the power she has to punish conceit and contempt at any moment. If you will behave becomingly towards her you may be assured that the smallest gesture you make for her sake will be rewarded."

It became slowly dark and all sorts of worries and fearful thoughts plagued me as I sat there like a carven image; imagining that I could not easily escape from this place I thought I must agree to everything demanded of me and said to the old woman: "Now, my dear compatriot, if it is as you have told me, I entrust my person to your inborn German honesty, hoping you will not take part in treachery towards an innocent German. So carry out your orders regarding me and I hope your lady has not the eyes of a basilisk to break my neck."

"Oh, may God prevent it," she cried, "if such a handsome youth, the pride of our whole nation, should die so soon, but you will find more pleasure than you have ever dreamt in all your life."

As soon as I consented she called Jean and Pierre, who entered at once from a door behind the tapestry, each in shining cuirass armed from head to foot with pikes and pistols. I was so frightened that I lost all colour and the old woman seeing this, said smilingly:

"You should not fear when you go to a lady."

She ordered the two men to remove their breast-plates and take a lantern and pistols, and she put the hood which was of black velvet over my head, took my hat under her arm and led me by her hand through strange passages. I was certain that we passed many doors and a paved way, and finally after a good while climbed a small stone staircase, where a door was opened; then I traversed a passage and had to ascend a spiral staircase, and descend a few steps. Six paces further on, a door was opened and when I had entered the old woman removed the hood.

I found myself in a large room which was most attractively decorated; the walls were embellished with beautiful pictures, the sideboard with silverware and the bed with curtains of brocade. In the middle stood a table magnificently laid and near the fire was a bath tub, which although quite pretty, according to my taste spoilt the whole room. The old woman said to me:

"Now, welcome, compatriot. Will you still protest that I deceive you by treachery? Give up your bad humour and behave as you did the other day at the theatre when you received your Eurydice back from Pluto! I assure you that you will find a more beautiful one here than you have lost there."

By these words I already understood that I had been called here not only to be gazed at, but for action too. Therefore I said to my old compatriot:

"It is of little help to a thirsty man to sit by a forbidden well."

But she replied: "In France one is not so grudging as to forbid someone to drink the water, especially where it is in abundance."

"Indeed," I said, "that may be alright, Madame, if I were not already married!"

"Nonsense," answered the godless woman, "Nobody will believe that tonight, for married cavaliers seldom come to France. And if it were true I cannot imagine that you would be so foolish rather to die of thirst than drink from a strange well, especially if it contains more sparkling and fresher water than your own."

This was our conversation, during which a maid looked after the fire and took off my shoes and stockings, which in the dark I had dirtied, for Paris is a very filthy town. Soon afterwards came the command that I should bathe before dining, and the young maiden went back and forth fetching bathing accessories all smelling of musk and perfumed soap. The linen was of the finest quality and edged with precious Dutch lace. I was ashamed at showing myself naked before the old woman, but it was of no use, it had to be, and I had to endure being scrubbed by her whilst the maid absented herself for a while.

After the bath a fine shirt was given to me and I was wrapped in a precious fur gown lined with violet silk and a pair of stockings of the same hue; the night-cap and slippers were embroidered with gold and pearls, so that I sat there in pomp like the King of Hearts. While the old woman dried and combed my hair – for she served me like a prince or a little child – the maid-servant carried in the dishes and when the table was laid, three stately young ladies entered the room, revealing their alabaster white bosoms generously but their faces were completely masked. All three appeared to me extraordinarily lovely, yet one even more beautiful than the others, and quite silently I made a deep bow to them. They acknowledged this with the same ceremony, so that we seemed to be a gathering of mutes. All three sat down simultaneously so that I could not find out who was the most noble among them, even less to which I was called to be of service. Their first question was whether I could speak French, and my compatriot said "No". Another said to her that I should be seated, and when this was done, the third one bade my interpreter be seated too. I was sitting next to the old woman and opposite the three ladies, so that without doubt my youth shone the more next to that old skeleton. All three looked at me most devotedly and I could swear that they allowed many sighs to escape, but I could not see their eyes sparkle because of the masks they wore. The old woman asked me – as nobody else could talk – whom I considered the most beautiful among them? I answered that a choice was impossible whereupon she laughed so heartily that I could see all her four teeth which she still had in her mouth, and then she asked:

"Why is that?"

I answered that I could not see them very well but as far as I could tell, none of the three seemed to be ugly. The ladies wished to know what the old woman had asked and what I had answered; she interpreted it and added the lie that I had said: each mouth is worth a hundred thousand kisses – for I could well see their mouths under the masks, especially that of the lady sitting directly opposite to me. Through that flattery the old woman made me understand that this lady was to be considered the most noble, and I gazed at her the more intensely.

This was the extent of our conversation at table and I pretended that I understood not one word of French, and so as silence prevailed we soon concluded our meeting. The ladies wished me good night and went their way and I was not allowed to accompany them farther than to the door, which the old one at once bolted behind them. When I saw this I asked where I should sleep. She answered I should sleep in this bed. I told her that the bed would be good enough if only one of those three could share it with me.

"Indeed," said the old woman, "tonight you will enjoy none of them."

As we thus talked, a beautiful lady who lay in the bed, pulled back the curtain a little and said to the old woman that she should stop gossiping and go to sleep. Wishing to see who lay in bed I took the candle, but she at once snuffed it and said: "Sir, if you don't want to lose your head, don't do that again. Lie down beside her, but if you try again to see this lady against her will, you will never emerge from this place alive." With that she left the room and locked the door. The maidservant, who had looked after the fire, put it out completely, and left through a hidden door behind the tapestry.

Whereupon the lady in the bed said: "Allez, Monsieur Beau Alman! Gee schlaff, mein Herz, gom rick su mir!" So much the old woman had taught her German. I went to the bed to see what was to be done, and as soon as I reached it she embraced my neck and welcomed me with many kisses and in her passionate lust almost bit off my lower lip. Indeed she started to pull open my fur gown and, almost tearing off my shirt, dragged me to her and revealed such demented love that it was indescribable. She understood no other German but "Rick su mir, mein Herz!" Everything else she indicated by gestures. I thought of my beloved one at home but in vain! Alas I was only human and finding such a well-proportioned creature of such delight I would have had to be a wooden log to escape with chastity.

Thus I spent eight days and as many nights in that place, and I believe that the other three laid with me too because they spoke differently from the first one and behaved less passionately. Although I had spent a whole eight days with these four ladies, I was not allowed to see one of them except through a veil, and only in the dark were their faces uncovered. After eight days had passed they put me blindfolded in a closed coach together with the old woman, who on the way unbound my eyes and brought me to my doctor's house, and the coach was driven quickly away.

As reward I received two hundred pistoles, and when I asked the old woman whether I should not give some pourboire, she said: "Under no circumstances. If you would do that you would insult the ladies; indeed they would assume you imagined that you had been in a brothel, where everything must be paid for."

Following this I found more such clients, who however behaved so coarsely that in the end, out of impotence, I became tired of this foolery.

SIMPLICIUS SELLS QUACK MEDICINES

THROUGH MY NEW PROFESSION I received so many presents in money and in kind that I became apprehensive and was no longer amazed that women go into brothels to make a trade out of this beastly lechery, for it is so profitable. I began to feel remorse, not so much out of piety or the urge of my conscience, but from fear of being caught in the act and punished as I deserved.

Therefore I endeavoured to return to Germany, and all the more so as the commandant of Lippstadt had written to me that he had caught a number of merchants from Cologne, whom he would not let out of his hands before my property was handed over to him; further, that he would keep open for me the promised ensigncy and expected me before the spring, otherwise he would have to fill the post with somebody else. Enclosed also was a letter from my wife, full of affectionate assurances of her great longing for me – had she only known how honestly I had lived she would have enclosed a different greeting.

I well imagined that Monseigneur Canard would hardly give me his consent to depart so I decided to slip away secretly as soon as I found an opportunity, which to my great misfortune soon occurred. I met several officers of the Duke of Weimar's Army to whom I revealed that I was an ensign of the regiment of Colonel St Andreas, that I had been busy on private affairs in Paris, and now being resolved to return to my regiment asked them to accept me as their travelling companion. They advised me the date of their departure and accepted me willingly; I bought myself a horse, prepared for the journey as secretly as I could, packed my money (about five hundred doubloons which I had earned from those godless women) and departed with the officers without the permission of Monseigneur Canard. However I wrote to him on the journey, dating it from Maastricht that he should believe I was on my way to Cologne, taking my leave of him with the excuse that it had become impossible for me to stay longer for I could not digest his aromatic sausages any longer.

The second night out from Paris I felt as if I had St Anthony's fire and my head ached so terribly that I could not get up. And that in a most miserable village, without a doctor, and worse still, no one to look after me. The officers continued their journey towards Alsace early in the morning and left me lying mortally ill as of no concern of theirs. Yet they commended me and my horse to the innkeeper and told the village alderman to keep an eye on me as I was an officer on war service with the King. There I lay several days unconscious and talking incoherently. They fetched the priest who could extract nothing reasonable from me. And as he saw he could not cure my soul he tried to heal my body by letting blood and administering a sudorific drink and putting me in a warm bed to sweat. This did me much good that the very same night I came to myself again and remembered where I was, how I had come there and that I was ill.

Next morning the priest came again and found me quite desperate, not only because all my money had been stolen, but because I was convinced that I had the French disease* (which I deserved more than all the pistoles) for my whole body was covered with spots like a tiger. I could neither walk, stand, sit nor lie, and all my peace of mind was gone. Although I did not believe that the lost money had been given to me by God, I now cursed the Devil for taking it from me. Indeed I behaved so desperately that the good priest had more than enough to do to console me for the shoe pinched in two places.

"My friend," he said, "if you cannot bear your cross like a good Christian, behave like a reasonable man. Do you want to lose your life as well as your money, and what is more, your eternal salvation?"

"I am not worrying about the money," I answered, "if only I had not this accursed horrible disease round my neck and if I were only in a place where I could be cured!"

"You must have patience," said the priest, "what shall the poor little children do of whom fifty are lying ill in this very village?"

As soon as I heard that even children were affected, my courage returned for I could not believe that they would be suffering from this foul disease. I therefore reached for my knapsack and searched for what might still be in it; except for my linen there was nothing of value but a medallion containing a lady's portrait set with rubies, which had been given to me in Paris. I took the miniature out and gave the case to the priest with a request to sell it in the next town, so that I had something to live on. But I received hardly a third of its value and as that did not last long I had to get rid of my horse and with the proceeds I carried on miserably until the pock marks began to dry up and I felt better.

As a man sins, so is he punished. These pock marks ruined my appearance so much that from now on I was left in peace by the women. I had such scars on my face that it looked like a threshing floor on which peas had been threshed. Indeed I became so hideous that my beautiful curly hair which had enchanted many a girl became ashamed of me and vacated its homestead. New hair grew in its place resembling pig's bristles so that I had to wear a wig. Likewise my pleasant voice had vanished, my throat being affected by the pock and my eyes that never formerly lacked the fire of love to inflame, looked now so red and watery as those of an octogenarian hag suffering from cataracts. Added to this I was in a foreign land, knew neither dog nor man whom I could trust, neither did I know the language nor had I any money left.

I began to lament the good opportunities on which I could have built my lasting prosperity and which I so slovenly had wasted. I looked back and realized that my extraordinary good fortune in war and the treasure I had found was nothing more than the cause and preparation for my downfall. I found that those things which I had considered good had been evil and had led me to utter destruction. No longer was there a hermit to give me faithful advice, no Colonel Ramsey to adopt me in my misery, no parson to give me good counsel, in short not a single man to help me. As my money was gone I was told to leave the inn and find quarters elsewhere and like the prodigal son to live with the sows.

I thought of the parson in Lippstadt who had counselled me to employ my means and my youth in study. But it was much too late to trim the wings when the bird had flown away. O swift and fatal transformation! Four weeks ago I was a fellow who moved princes to admiration, charmed the ladies, appeared to the people as a masterpiece of nature, indeed an angel, but was now so despicable that the dogs pissed on me. Thousands of ideas raced through my head as to what I should do now that the innkeeper had thrown me out of the house as I could pay him no longer. Gladly I would have enlisted, but no recruiting officer would accept me as a soldier for I looked like a scabby cuckoo. I could not work being still too weak and not accustomed to any kind of labour. Nothing consoled me more than that summer was approaching and if needs be I could shelter behind a hedge, for no one would allow me to enter a house. I still had my fine clothing which I had ordered for the journey, including my knapsack full of precious linen which no one wanted to buy for fear of getting my disease. So I took the knapsack on my back, my sword in my hand and the road beneath my feet; this led me to a small town which boasted an apothecary. There

I went and had an ointment prepared to remove the pock marks from my face, and as I had no money I gave the apprentice a beautiful, soft shirt, he being not so particular as the other fools who would not accept clothes from me. I had hopes that if I could rid myself of these shameful spots, my misery would vanish. The apothecary consoled me that in a week's time little would be seen except the very deep scars which the pocks had eaten into my face, and this gave me some courage. It happened to be market day in the town and there was a tooth-drawer who gained much money by selling quack medicine to the people. "Fool," I said to myself, "why don't you also start such a trade? Haven't you been long enough with Monseigneur Canard and learnt enough to cheat a credulous peasant and make your living? You must truly be a miserable simpleton!"

At this time I could eat like a thresher, never being able to satisfy my belly. Yet I owned nothing but a single golden ring with a diamond worth about twenty crowns, which I sold for twelve. From this I could clearly calculate that this would soon come to an end if I did not earn, therefore I decided to turn doctor. I bought all the materials to concoct a theriac for use against all sorts of poison, and prepared it. I mixed from herbs, roots, butter and some oils a green ointment for wounds which would have cured a sick horse. Further I made up a tooth-powder from calamus gravel and pumice-stone, and a blue healing water from alkali, copper ammoniac and camphor to cure scurvy, toothache and eye disorders. For all this I purchased a multitude of little boxes of tin, wood, paper and glass in which to put my mixtures. And to give the undertaking a reputation I had a handbill drawn up and printed in French from which one could read for which purpose each medicine was made. Within three days I completed my work, having scarcely expended three crowns, and I then left the town.

Having packed my bundle I intended to walk from village to village as far as Alsace and sell my wares on the way, eventually reaching Strasburg – a neutral town, and by travelling with the traders on the Rhine to Cologne, from there to join my wife. My intentions were good but the plan failed completely.

The first time that I stood with my quackeries in front of a church and tried to sell, my profit was poor for I was much too timid and not used to bragging and quackery. I soon realized that I had to change my manner if I wished to make money. So I went with my trash into the inn and learnt at table from the innkeeper that in the afternoon all sorts of people would come together under the lime tree in front of his house and that I might sell something if my wares were good: there were so many deceivers in the land that the people were most careful in spending their money unless they could see with their own eyes that my wonder drug was really good.

Having learnt how the land lay I procured half a wineglass full of good Strasburg brandy and caught a toad which in spring and summer sit in the dirty puddles and sing; they are golden yellow or almost reddish gold with black spots on the belly, most unpleasant to see. Such a one I put in a tumbler of water and placed it next to my wares on a table under the lime tree. When the people began to gather and stood around me, some expected I would pull out teeth with the tongs which I had borrowed from the hostess. But I spoke: "Messieurs and good friends," for I could speak only very little French, "I am not Crack de Tooth, but I have here good eye lotions which stop water running from red eyes."

"Indeed," called out one, "We can see your eyes – they look like Jack-in-the-Lantern."

"True," I continued, "but had I not the lotion I would be blind. I do not sell the lotion. I sell the theriac, the wonder-drug and the powder for the white teeth and the wound-ointment: the lotion I give away. I am no quack and no deceiver. I sell my wonder-drug which I have tried. If you do not like it, don't buy."

Now I asked one of them who stood around to choose one of the boxes with the wonder-drug, from which I took a piece about the size of a peanut and put it into the brandy which the people believed to be water, dissolved it and picked the toad out of the water with the tongs, saying: "Look here, my good friends, if this poisonous worm can drink my theriac and doesn't die – my drug is good for nothing and you need not buy it." And with that I put the poor toad, which had been born and bred in water and could stand no other element or liquid, into the brandy, and covered the glass with some paper so that it could not leap out. It began to rage and to wriggle furiously as if I had thrown it onto fiery coals for the brandy was strong, and after a while stretching out its four legs, it died miserably.

The peasants opened their mouths and their purses when they saw this unquestionable proof with their own eyes. In their opinion there was no better theriac in the world than mine, and I was kept busy wrapping up the trash in the handbills and collecting the money. Some of them bought three, four, five and six times to be provided for every need with this precious wonder-drug against poison. Indeed they even bought for their kinsfolk and friends who lived elsewhere, so that by the evening although it was not a market-day, I had earned ten crowns and still kept more than half of my goods. The same night I moved on to another village, as I feared one of the peasants might be curious to put a toad into a glass of water to try the strength of my drug, and if it should fail they might thrash my back.

To show the excellence of my antidote in a different way, I made a quicksilver sublimate of flour, saffron and gall apples, and a sublimate of mercury from flour and vitriol. When I came to show the experiment, I had two equal glasses with fresh water ready on the table, of which one was strongly mixed with aqua fortis or sulphuric acid and into this I stirred a little of my drug, and scraped from my two poisons as much as was sufficient into it. The water which contained no theriac and no aqua fortis became as black as ink, while the other because of the aqua fortis remained as it was. "Indeed," the peasants cried, "That is indeed a precious theriac for so little money!" And when again I mixed both glasses, everything became clear. So I carried on my new trade and the good peasants pulled out their purses and bought from me to the benefit not only of my hungry belly but also that I could afford a horse again. I earned much money on my journey and safely reached the German border. Alas, dear peasants, do not so easily trust strange quacks, or you will be cheated by them, for they seek not your health but your money.

As I passed through Lorraine my wares came to an end, and because I had to avoid towns with a garrison I had no opportunity to prepare new ones. So I was forced to invent something new before I could make my wonder drug again. I bought two measures of brandy and coloured it with saffron, filled it in half ounce glasses and sold it to the people as a precious gold water, good against fever, and so my brandy brought me a profit of thirty gulden. When my little glasses were running short, I heard of a glass manufactory in the county of Fleckenstein, and I went there to find new supplies. But through choosing by-ways I was by chance taken prisoner by a patrol of soldiers from Philippsburg stationed in the Castle of Wagelnburg. Thus I lost everything which I had fraudulently extorted from the people on my journey, and because the peasant who accompanied me to show me the way had told the fellows I was a doctor, as a doctor, thanks to the Devil, I was taken to Philippsburg.

There I was examined and I did not hesitate to say who I truly was, but they did not believe it and made more of me than I was, so a doctor I had to be! In the end I had to swear that I belonged to the Imperial dragoons in Soest and that I intended to return to them. "But," they said, "the Emperor needs soldiers in Philippsburg as much as in Soest." They proposed to keep me until a good chance offered itself for me to join my regiment, and if this proposal was not to my taste I should content myself with the prison and be treated as a doctor until my release, for I was taken prisoner as such.

So I came down from a horse to the donkey and had to become a musketeer against my will. This was very bitter for me for there was an empty pantry in the house and the bread ration was frightfully small. I say on purpose "frightfully" as every morning when I received my bread ration which had to last me the whole day I was frightened, for I could have chewed it up in one go. To tell the truth, the musketeer who has to spend his life in a garrison is a miserable creature forced to be content with dry bread and not enough of that too. He is nothing else but a prisoner, who by water and bread wastes his poor life in melancholy. Indeed a prisoner is better off, for he needs neither to watch nor to make the rounds, nor to stand on sentry, but he has his rest and as much hope of getting out of his prison as a musketeer has of getting out of his garrison.

Of course there were some musketeers who could improve their condition and this in different ways, but I liked none of them as a means of earning food. Some in their misery took a wife in marriage, and even a strange whore if need be, for no other reason than to be kept by their women's work, such as sewing, washing, spinning or selling, bartering or even stealing. There was a girl-ensign among the women who got her pay as a corporal, another was a midwife and thus gained many good meals for herself and her husband. Others could wash and starch so they washed shirts, stockings and I know not what else for the officers and unmarried soldiers, from which they got their nick-names. Others again sold tobacco and supplied the fellows with pipes who were in need of them. Others dealt in brandy and it was known that they diluted it with water. To gain my livelihood in such a way was not for me for I had a wife already.

Other fellows gained their living by playing cards, which they understood better than thieves, and they knew how to extort money from their simple comrades with false dice and cards, but such a profession I loathed. Others worked on the ramparts and various places like beasts but for that I was too lazy; some practised a craft but I, poor simpleton, had learnt none. As a musician I might have passed if need had been, but in this land of hunger they put up with drums and pipes. Several went on sentry for others and stayed on duty day and night but I would rather starve than wear my body out like this. Some made a living by going on patrol – I was not even trusted to go outside the gates. Others could go stealing better than any cat but I hated such business like the plague. Altogether wherever I turned I found no way to fill my belly, and what vexed me most was that my comrades jeered at me and said: "You want to be a doctor and know no other art than to starve of hunger."

At last need forced me to charm some handsome carp out of the moat and up the rampart. But as soon as the colonel heard of it, I had to ride the wooden donkey as punishment and was forbidden by pain of the gallows to pursue this art further.

In the end others' misfortune became my good luck. After curing a few sick men of jaundice and fever who must have had a special trust in me, I was allowed to go out of the fortress under the pretext of collecting roots and herbs for my medicines. However I set snares for the hares and was fortunate to catch two the first night. These I brought to the colonel and I not only received one thaler as a present but also permission to go out and trap the hares whenever I was not on duty. As the country was deserted and nobody was there to catch hares which had multiplied splendidly, water came to my mill again so that it seemed as if it snowed hares, or that I could charm them into my snares. When the officers saw that they could trust me I was even allowed to go foraging with the others, and so my life as at Soest, started again, only that I could not lead and command a patrol as before in Westphalia, as for this it was essential to know all the highways and byways around the river Rhine.

I have yet to report a few adventures before I can tell how I was relieved from my musket. One was of great danger to life and limb from which I escaped through God's mercy; the other was of danger to my soul in which danger I stubbornly remained, for I will conceal my vices as little as my virtues in order to make my story complete and also to let my reader know what strange fellows roam the world.

As mentioned I was now allowed to take part in foraging patrols, which honour is not conferred on every slovenly fellow in the garrison but only to honest soldiers. Nineteen of us together went up the Rhine beyond Strasburg to ambush a ship from Basel in which it was reported that some officers and goods belonging to the Duke of Weimar's army were secreted. Above Ottenheim we got hold of a fishing boat in which to cross over and hide on a small island, well placed for forcing all approaching ships to land. Ten of us had safely been ferried over by the fisherman when one of us who normally steered well had to fetch the remaining nine, including me; the boat suddenly capsized and in a flash we were swimming together in the Rhine. I did not care much about the others but thought of myself, and although I used all my strength and all the advantages of being a good swimmer, the river played with me as if with a ball, hurling me now over and now under the waves. I struggled bravely and often came up for breath, but had it been somewhat colder, I could never have held on so long and escaped alive. I tried again and again to reach the bank but the whirls prevented me and flung me from one side to the other so that I despaired of my life. Already I was swept past the village of Goldscheur and was resigned to pass under the Strasburg Rhinebridge dead or alive when I noticed a huge tree whose branches stretched over the water nor far from me. The current was strong and carried me straight towards it. I used all my strength to reach the tree and happily I succeeded so that I found myself sitting on the biggest branch which I had at first thought to be the tree itself. Waves and whirlpools however rocked the branch up and down incessantly and my belly was so much shaken that I wanted to vomit lung and liver. Scarcely could I keep my grip for I felt faint and almost dropped back into the water – but I knew well that I was now not strong enough to sustain even a hundredth part of the strain I had so far endured. So I had to hold on and hope for a doubtful deliverance which God might send if I were to escape alive. My conscience consoled me poorly, recalling how wickedly I had forfeited such merciful help these last few years. And still I hoped and began to pray so devoutly as if I had been brought up in a monastery: I resolved to live more piously in future and made some solemn vows: I renounced the soldier's life and forswore foraging patrols for ever: I threw away my cartridge bags and knapsack as well, and resolved to become a hermit again, atone for my sins and thank God's mercy to the end of my days.

Having spent two or three hours on the branch between fear and hope, the very same ship sailed down the Rhine which I had been ordered to ambush. I lifted my voice miserably and screamed for help for God's and the Last Judgment's sake. And as they had to pass quite close to me and clearly saw my danger and pitiable dilemma, everyone in the ship was moved to pity so that they moored at once and discussed how they could help me. Because of the many whirlpools caused by the roots and branches of the tree, it was neither possible to swim nor to reach me with a large or small boat, so that some time was needed for considering how to rescue me, and it is easy to imagine how I felt in the mean time. At last they sent two men with a boat into the river above me, who let a rope float down to me which I with great effort fastened round my body as well as I could so that I was hauled by it into the boat like a fish on a line, and taken onto the ship. As I had escaped death in this way I should have rightly fallen on my knees to thank God's mercy for my deliverance and started to amend my life as I had vowed and promised in my distress. But far from this! For when they asked me who I was and how I had come into such danger, I began to tell lies that the sky could have turned black because I thought if I tell them that I had intended to plunder them, they would throw me back into the Rhine again. So I gave myself out for a fugitive organist on his way to Strasburg to seek service as a schoolmaster or the like; a party of soldiers had caught me, stripped me and thrown me into the Rhine which had swept me to this tree. And as I embellished my lies convincingly and fortified them with oaths, they believed me and treated me kindly with food and drink to revive me, which I needed mightily.

At the custom house in Strasburg most of those on board went on shore and I with them, thanking them heartily, when I noticed among them a young merchant whose face, gait and gestures revealed to me that I had seen him before, but I could not remember where. At last I realized by his voice that he was the very same cornet who once had taken me prisoner, but I could not imagine how such a brave young soldier, especially being of noble birth, had become a merchant. My curiosity to know whether my eyes and ears deceived me impelled me to go to him and say:

"Monsieur Schonstein, is it you or not?"

But he answered: "I am not von Schonstein, but only a merchant."

To which I replied: "And I am not the Huntsman of Soest but an organist or better, a vagrant beggar!"

"Oh, brother," he replied, "What the devil are you up to and where do you go?"

"Brother," I said, "If heaven has chosen you to save my life, as it now has happened a second time, doubtlessly my fate demands that I should be not far from you."

So we embraced as two faithful friends who have vowed to love each other until death. I had to share his lodgings and tell him everything that had happened to me since I departed from Lippstadt for Cologne to collect my treasure; nor did I conceal how I had laid in ambush with a patrol for their ship and how we failed. But not a word I told him about my escapades in Paris as I feared he might reveal it in Lippstadt and cause ill temper in my wife.

On his part he confided to me that he had been despatched by the Hessian general staff to Duke Bernhard of Weimar in matters of the greatest importance concerning the conduct of the war, to discuss future projects and campaigns. This he had achieved and was now on his return trip disguised as a merchant, as I well could see with my own eyes. He told me further that on his departure my wife was an expectant mother and together with her parents and kinsfolk in good health; and that the colonel still kept the ensigncy open for me. But he jeered at my pock-marked face that neither my wife nor any other woman in Lippstadt would accept me for the Huntsman. Then we arranged that I should stay with him and at the next opportunity return with him to Lippstadt as was my wish. And as I had nothing but rags on me, he lent me some money with which I equipped myself as a merchant's servant.

But what is not to be, will not be. As we sailed down the Rhine and our ship was examined at Rheinhausen, the Philippsburg soldiers recognized me, arrested me and brought me to Philippsburg to carry a musket once more. My good cornet was as angry as I to be separated again, but he could help me little as he had trouble enough himself to get through.

Thus my life had been in grave danger but the danger to my soul was graver still, for it was obvious in carrying my musket again I became a wild fellow who cared neither for God nor his Word. No villainy was too much for me and the grace and kindness which I had ever received from God was completely forgotten. I cared neither for time nor eternity but lived unthinkingly like a beast. No one would have believed that I had been brought up by such a pious hermit; I rarely went to church and never to confession, and the less I cared for my own soul's salvation the more I harassed my fellow men. Wherever I could deceive somebody, I did so, indeed I boasted that nobody escaped me without being insulted. From this I often earned a heavy beating and more often had to ride the donkey as punishment. Indeed they threatened me with birch and gallows, but nothing helped for I continued in my godless ways, so that it seemed I played the desperado running recklessly to hell. And although I did not commit a crime through which to forfeit my life, I was so profligate that except for sorcerers and sodomites, no man more wicked could be found.

All this was noticed by our regiment's chaplain, and, being a true pious fighter for souls, he sent for me at Eastertide to enquire why I had not attended Confession and Holy Communion. But after his many warm-hearted admonitions I treated him in the same way as earlier I had treated the parson in Lippstadt, so that this good man could do nothing with me. Finally, when Christ and baptism seemed to be lost in me, he said:

"O wicked man! I believed you had gone astray through ignorance, but now I know that you continue to sin from pure malignity and on purpose. Who will feel pity for your poor soul in its damnation? I for my part protest before God and the world that I am free of blame for your ruin. I have done and I am still willing to continue to do what is needed to promote your salvation. I fear I can do nothing more for you. Should your poor soul leave your body in such a wicked state I can only have you dragged to the carrion pit among the carcasses of decayed beasts and other godforsaken fellows and desperadoes and refuse to bury you with pious persons."

But this severe warning helped as little as all previous admonitions and for one reason only: that I was ashamed to confess! What a complete fool I was! How often did I brag of my roguish exploits in company and added boastful lies as well. Yet now when I should amend and confess my sins to a single man representing God, to receive absolution, I was stubbornly silent. I say stubborn truly, and stubborn I remained when I answered:

"I serve the Emperor as a soldier, and if I die as a soldier there is no doubt I will like other soldiers who cannot always be buried in sacred ground, be content to rest in the fields, the ditches or in the bellies of wolf and raven outside the churchyard."

And so I parted from the priest who in his holy struggle for souls gained nothing from me. Not even a hare – I once declined to give him one for which he had earnestly begged, under the pretext that the hare since it had hanged itself in a snare and thus taken its own life, as a desperado could not be buried in such a sacred belly.

No amendment of my ways came to pass but I became daily worse and worse. Once the colonel said to me that he would send me off with the knacker since I would do no good. But because I knew too well he was not serious, I replied this could easily be done if he sent his jailer with me as well. And so he let me off again as he could imagine that it would be no punishment but a blessing for me to be dismissed. Thus I was forced to remain a musketeer against my will and suffer hunger until summer.

The closer Count von Götz approached with his army, the nearer came my liberation, because when the Count had his headquarters at Bruchsal, Herzbruder was sent by the general staff to our fortress with several orders and was received with great honour. I stood sentry before the colonel's quarters and although Herzbruder wore a black velvet coat I recognized him at the first glance but could not find the courage to address him at once as I feared he would, as is the way of the world, be ashamed of me and not wish to know me; according to his dress he held a high rank whilst I was nothing but a lousy musketeer. But as soon as I was off duty I asked his servants his name and rank to be quite sure, and yet I still had not the heart to address him but wrote this letter and had it handed to him in the morning by his valet:

MONSIEUR, ETC.,

If it would please my noble lord to deliver one whom he saved before through his gallantry in the Battle of Wittstock from iron and chains, now through fickle fortune thrown into the most miserable state, it would cause him little trouble but would oblige for all eternity his faithful servant, who is now the most miserable and forsaken man—

SIMPLICIUS SIMPLICISSIMUS

As soon as he had read the letter he asked me to come to him and said:

"Fellow countryman, where is that somebody who gave you this note?"

"Sir," I answered, "He is a prisoner in this fortress."

"Well," he replied, "Go to him and tell him that I will liberate him, even if he already has the hangman's rope round his neck!" "Sir," said I, "So much trouble is not needed. I am poor Simplicius himself, thankful to you for delivery at Wittstock and praying you to save me from the musket which I have been forced to carry against my will."

He did not let me finish but by embracing me showed me his willingness to help. In short he did everything which a faithful friend should do for another, and before he even asked me how I came into the fortress and such servitude, he sent his servant to the Jew to buy me a horse and clothes. In the mean time, I told him my adventures since his father had died before Magdeburg, and when he learnt that I was the Huntsman of Soest, he regretted that he had not known this before as he could easily have helped me to command a company.

When the Jew came with a whole load of soldier's clothes he selected the best for me, urged me to dress, and took me to the colonel. To him he said:

"Sir, I have found in your garrison this fellow here to whom I am so much obliged that I cannot leave him in this mean rank even if his qualities deserve nothing better. I therefore beg the colonel to do me the favour either to promote him or to allow me to take him with me to further his career in the army, for which perhaps the colonel here finds no opportunity."

The colonel crossed himself in amazement to hear somebody praise me and replied:

"Honoured Sir, forgive me if I believe that you only wish to test my willingness to serve you as you deserve: if that is true ask anything else which is in my power and through my actions you will understand my wish to oblige. But as to this man – he actually does not belong to me but, as he pretends, to a regiment of dragoons. Besides he is such a villainous fellow that since he came here has given more trouble to my provost than

a whole company, so that I must believe no water will ever drown him."
He ended his speech with a laugh and wished me good luck in the field.

This was not yet enough for Herzbruder for he asked the colonel to invite
me to his table which was granted. He did this for the purpose of telling
the colonel in my presence what he had heard about me in Westphalia from
Count von der Wahl and the commandant in Soest. And he so praised me
that everyone took me for a fine soldier, whilst I for my part behaved so
modestly that the colonel and his men who knew me before believed that
I had changed my character with my clothes. When the colonel enquired
how I had come by the name of doctor, I narrated to him my whole journey
from Paris to Philippsburg and how many peasants I had deceived to gain
my living, which caused much laughter. At last I admitted frankly that it
had been my intention to disturb and trouble the colonel with all sorts of
mischief that he would be forced to get rid of me from the garrison if he
were to live in peace from all the annoyances I caused.

Then the colonel described the many roguish pranks I had played, how
I had boiled peas, poured lard over them and sold the lot as pure lard; and
also sold sacks of sand for salt by covering the top with salt, and teased,
troubled and ridiculed everybody with insults. During the whole meal they
talked only of me. Had I no such influential friend, all my deeds would
have been punished, and so I realized how things go at Court if a villain
gains a prince's favour.

When the meal was over, the Jew had no horse which Herzbruder
considered good enough for me, but as he was esteemed so highly by the
colonel who did not wish to lose his favour, he gave one from his own
stable. On this Herr Simplicius was mounted, and with his Herzbruder
rode merrily out of the fortress. Some comrades shouted: "Good luck,
brother, good luck," whilst others out of envy: "The bigger the rascal,
the greater the luck!"

A PROPHECY COMES TRUE

ON THE WAY, Herzbruder persuaded me to give myself out as his cousin in order to receive more honour. He promised me further another horse and a servant and to take me to the regiment of Neuneck to serve as a volunteer-rider until an officer's place in the army should be vacant to which he could help me.

And so hastily I again became a fellow with the appearance of a brave soldier. Yet this summer I did few heroic deeds except helping to steal here and there a few cows in the Black Forest and to get acquainted with the Breisgau and Alsace. Altogether I had very little luck. My servant and his horse were captured by a Weimar detachment near Kenzingen, so that I had to exert the other the more and finally ride it to death, that in the end I was forced to join the order of the "Brethren of Merode". Herzbruder would gladly have equipped me again but as I had finished the first two horses so quickly, he hesitated and kept me in suspense, that I might learn to be more careful. And I did not press him as I found in my new consorts such pleasant company that until winter quartering I wished for no better trade.

Here I must tell a little of what kind of people these Brethren of Merode are, as without doubt there are many, especially those ignorant of war, who know nothing about them. So far I have never found a writer who included something of their customs, manners, rights and privileges in his writings, in spite of the fact that it is well worthwhile not only for the generals but also for the peasants to know what sort of a guild this is.

Concerning their name, I hope it will not disgrace that brave cavalier in whose service they acquired it. When this Merode once brought a newly conscripted regiment to the army, his soldiers were so weak and rotten that they could not endure the stress of marching and other hardships which soldiers in the field have to suffer. Soon their brigade became so depleted that it could hardly defend its flag. Wherever one met one or more sick or lame soldiers in the market place and in houses, behind fences and hedges and asked: "What regiment?" the answer was commonly: "Of Merode." Hence it came that all soldiers, sick or sound, wounded or well, found straying outside the line of march or their regimental quarters, were called Brethren of Merode.* The same fellows were known before as pig-roasters and honey-thieves, for like the drones which have lost their sting and neither work nor make honey, they do nothing but devour. When a rider loses his horse, or a musketeer his health or has to stay behind because his wife and child have fallen ill, he easily falls into the company of such rabble, a rabble best compared with the gipsies because they straggle wantonly in front, behind, around and in the midst of the army. And like the gipsies they keep their own manners and morals. You can see them in flocks like partridges behind the hedges, in the shade or in the sun, lingering round a fire, smoking tobacco and idling, whilst the honest soldier endures heat and thirst, hunger and frost and other miseries with his colours.

There a pack of them may be looting along in the line of march whilst many a poor soldier is near collapse through exhaustion under the weight of his arms. They ravage everything they can find before, beside and behind the army, and what they cannot use they destroy so that the regiments, when they reach their quarters or camp, often can scarcely find a drink of water. When they are forced to join the baggage train, their numbers swell, bigger than the army itself. Although they march, lodge, camp and plunder in gangs, they have no sergeant-major to give them orders, no sergeant to whip their backs, no corporal to call them to the watch, no drummer to beat the tattoo, in all nobody to lead them into battle like the adjutant or show them their quarters like the quartermaster, but they live like gentlemen of leisure. But whenever free rations are issued to the soldiery, they are the first to claim their undeserved share. However, the provosts and the provost-marshal are their greatest fear for these if their pranks become too violent put iron bracelets round their wrists and ankles, or decorate their necks with hempen collars and hang them by their tender necks.

They do not stand sentry, neither do they work on the ramparts, nor do they go into attack or into battle – yet they feed well. But the havoc they cause to the general, the peasant and even to the whole army when such a rabble lingers around can hardly be described. The most foolish stable boy who does nothing more than forage is of more use to the general than one thousand Merode Brethren, who make a trade of plundering and are otherwise lazy. Often they are captured by the enemy and even beaten by the peasants. And when such a loose rascal has spent the summer, he has to be re-equipped in winter with great expense so that he can lose it all again in the next campaign. They should be tethered together like dogs or chained in the galleys. How many a village have they burnt down in carelessness or malice, how many comrades from their own army have they robbed of their horses, plundered and even murdered. And many spies may be hidden among them, knowing the name of a regiment or a company in the army.

Such an honest brother I was too and I remained in the brotherhood until the day before the Battle of Wittenweier when our headquarters were at Schuttern; as I went that day with my comrades into the district of Geroltzeck to steal some cows or oxen, as it was our habit, I was taken prisoner by a Weimar detachment. They knew very well how to treat us for they gave each a musket to carry and assigned us among the regiments, I being put into the Hattstein regiment.

At that time I was convinced that I was born only to misfortune. About four weeks before the battle I heard some officers of Götz's army discuss the war and one said: "This summer will not pass without a battle! If we beat the enemy we shall conquer Freiburg in the coming winter; if we are beaten we will at least have our winter quarters." Upon this prophecy I built my plans and rejoiced in the coming spring, with good wine from Lake Constance and the Neckar and the enjoyment of all that the Weimar army had won. But I fooled myself for here I was in the Weimar Army itself, predestined to help in the Siege of Breisach,* which began soon after the Battle of Wittenweier.

Like other musketeers I had to stand sentry and dig ditches by day and night and gained nothing except that I learnt how to attack a fortress by trenches to which subject I had paid little attention once before at Magdeburg. Besides, my condition was lousy as I shared the same quarters with two or three soldiers; my purse was empty, and wine, beer and meat a rarity. Apples with a half ration of mouldy bread were my finest savouries. This was painful for me to bear and made me think of the fleshpots of Egypt, I mean Westphalian hams and sausages in Lippstadt. I thought little of my wife, but when half frozen in my tent I remembered and often said to myself: "Ho, Simplicius, do you think it would serve you right if your wife pays you back in your own coin for what you did in Paris?" With such ideas I tormented myself like any other jealous cuckold though I had nothing but honour and virtue to expect from her. At last I became so impatient that I made a frank confession to my captain of how things stood with me, and I also wrote by post to Lippstadt. In the end I succeeded with the help of Colonel St Andreas and my father-in-law (who approached the Duke of Weimar) so that my captain had to issue a pass to me.

A few weeks before Christmas I marched out of the camp with a good musket, down through the Breisgau, hoping to collect twenty thalers at Strasburg which my father-in-law had sent there, and then to proceed down the Rhine by a merchant's ship, for there were many Imperial garrisons in the district. But when I had left Endingen behind and came to a lonely house, a shot was fired at me so that the bullet slashed the rim of my hat, and a strong, square-built fellow leaped from the house towards me shouting at me to lay down my gun. I shouted back: "By God, comrade, not to please you!" and cocked my gun. But he drew out from his leather belt a thing which looked more like an executioner's sword than a rapier and jumped at me. Seeing he was in earnest I pulled the trigger and shot him squarely on his forehead that he staggered and finally fell to the ground. To make best use of this advantage I quickly wrenched his sword out of his fist and tried to thrust it through his belly but it would not pierce it. Suddenly he leaped up again onto his feet and grappled me by my hair and I grabbed his, having thrown away his sword. So we began a serious game together, each showing clearly his embittered strength and yet neither mastered the other. One moment I was on top of him the next he was upon me, in a flash we both jumped to our feet again each craving the other's death. The blood which gushed thickly from my nose and mouth I spat into my opponent's face since he so hotly yearned for it, and that to my advantage, as it hindered him from seeing. Thus for an hour and half we dragged each other around in the snow, exhausting ourselves so much that it seemed neither of us without arms had strength left to kill the other with bare fists.

The art of wrestling which I had often practised in Lippstadt now served me well, otherwise without doubt I would have been lost as my enemy was much stronger than I and moreover proof against bullet and steel. When we had tired each other almost to death he at last cried out:

"Brother, make an end. I surrender."

I answered: "You should have let me pass at the beginning!"

"What use is it for you," he went on, "if I should die?"

"And what profit would you have gained if you had shot me dead, for I have not a heller in my pocket?" said I.

Hereupon he begged my pardon and my heart softened and I allowed him to stand up after he had solemnly sworn not only to keep the peace but to be my faithful friend and servant, though had I known his previous villainous deeds I would neither have believed nor trusted him.

Both now standing on our feet again we shook hands, agreeing that what had happened should all be forgotten, and each was amazed that he had found his master in the other. He believed that I also was covered with a magic skin and invulnerable as himself; I did not contradict him so that should he have his gun again he would not trouble me. My bullet had caused him a big bruise on his forehead and I lost a lot of blood, yet we both groaned most about our necks which were so wrenched that neither of us could keep his head upright.

As evening drew near my opponent told me that as far as the Kintzig there were neither dogs, cats nor humans, but he knew a lonely cottage near the road where a good piece of meat and drink could be found. I was persuaded and went with him and on the way he assured me with many sighs how sorry he was to have injured me.

A courageous soldier who devotes himself to hazarding his life and esteems it little is nothing more than a stupid beast. One would hardly find a man in a thousand with the courage to follow somebody who had just murderously attacked him, as a guest to an unknown place. On the way I asked him to which army he belonged. He answered that at the moment he served no master but made his own war and asked to which camp I belonged. I replied that I had served the Duke of Weimar but had now my discharge and was on my way home. Then he asked my name and when I said Simplicius, he turned round, for I let him walk in front of me not trusting him, and looked squarely into my face.

"Are you not also called Simplicissimus?"

"Indeed," said I, "a knave who denies his name! But who are you?"

"Oh, brother," he cried, "I am Olivier whom you will well remember at Magdeburg."

With that he threw down his gun and fell on his knees to beg my forgiveness for his intentions to do me harm. He assured me that he well knew he could find no better friend in the world than me.

I showed my astonishment over this strange reunion remembering old Herzbruder's prophecy, that I would revenge his death, but he continued:

"This is nothing new; mountain and valley will never meet but old friends do. Strange only is how we both have changed! I here turned from a secretary into a robber and you from a fool into a brave soldier! Be assured, brother, ten thousand like we could relieve Breisach tomorrow and in the end become masters of the whole world!"

With such talk we reached a small and lonely cottage at nightfall, and though I disliked his boastful balderdash I agreed with him, mostly because his villainous character was well known to me. Though I did not trust his good intentions I followed him into the little house, where a peasant was heating the oven. Olivier addressed him:

"Are you cooking something?"

"No," the peasant said, "I still have the leg of veal which I brought from Waldkirch."

"Well, then," answered Olivier, "bring it here and the small barrel of wine as well."

When the peasant had gone I said to Olivier:

"Brother (I called him this to be on the safe side), you have an obliging host."

"The Devil may thank the rascal," he answered, "I feed him and his wife and child included, and he makes good booty for himself as well for I leave him all the clothes which I can plunder."

I asked where he kept his own wife and child and Olivier told me that he had taken them to Freiburg, where he visited them twice a week and from where he supplied himself with food, powder and lead. He told me further that he had practised this freebooting for a long time and he found it more profitable than to serve a prince, nor did he intend to give it up until he had filled his purse respectably.

"Brother," I told him, "You follow a dangerous trade and if you are caught at such robbery, how do you think they will treat you?"

"Oh," he answered, "I can well hear you are still the old Simplicius; but I know well that he who will win must risk and you should know that the judges of Nuremberg will hang no one before they have caught him!"

I argued: "But suppose, brother, that you are not caught, which is improbable, since the pitcher goes to the well until it breaks – such a life as you lead is the most shameful in the world that I cannot believe it is your wish to die in that state."

"What!" he shouted, "The most shameful? My brave Simplicius, I assure you that robbery is the most noble *exercitium* you can find in the world these days. Tell me, how many kingdoms and principalities have not been taken by violence or robbery? Where in the whole world do you blame a king or a prince that he enjoys the proceeds of his lands which his forefathers have commonly stolen by violence? What trade can you call more noble than that I now practise? I can see that you would like to reproach me that many have been broken on the wheel, hanged and decapitated for murder and robbery. I know that well for that is the law, but you will see but poor and humble thieves being hanged, which is only right as they have dared to interfere in this excellent occupation which should be reserved for men of noble courage. Where have you seen a person of high rank punished by justice for having burdened his lands too much? Indeed, no usurer is punished who practises his magnificent art in secret under the cloak of Christian charity? Why should I be punished for following my trade in good old German fashion without hypocrisy and disguise? My dear Simplicius, have you never studied Machiavelli? I have an honest character and pursue this way of life freely in the open and without shame. I fight and risk my life like the heroes of old. And I know that he who does so imperils his life and so it follows without denial that it is right and fair for me to practise this art."

To this I replied: "May robbing and stealing be permitted to you or not, yet I know it is against the law of nature which does not allow that one man should do to another what he would not wish to have done to himself. It sins against the law of this world which demands that thieves be hanged, robbers beheaded and murderers broken on the wheel; lastly and most seriously it is against the laws of God who leaves no sin unpunished."

"You still are, as I said," replied Olivier, "the same old Simplicius who has not yet studied his Machiavelli. And if I could establish a monarchy in this way I would like to see who would preach against me."

We would have argued still longer had not the peasant brought food and drink, so we sat together and filled our bellies of which I stood in great need.

Our meal was white bread and a cold leg of veal. With it went a good drink of wine and a warm room.

"Truly, Simplicius," said Olivier, "it is better here than in the trenches in front of Breisach!"

"Indeed," I answered, "if only one could enjoy such a life in safety and honour."

At this he burst into laughter and replied:

"But are the poor devils in the trenches safer than we, expecting every moment a sortie from the fortress? My dear Simplicius, I can see that you have thrown off your fool's cap but have kept your foolish head which cannot grasp what is good or bad. And if you were not Simplicius who after Herzbruder's prophecy should avenge my death, I would force you to confess that I lead a nobler life than any baron."

Now I began to fear, if I would not find smoother words to calm him, this monster, with the peasant's help, might still finish me off in the end. I therefore said:

"How can an apprentice understand the craft better than his master? Brother, if you really have such a noble and happy life as you say, let me participate in your good fortune since I need some luck urgently."

Olivier answered: "Brother, be assured that I love you as I love myself and that the injury I have done to you hurts me more than the bullet you fired at my forehead. I will refuse you nothing. Stay with me; I will care for you as for myself. Should you not wish to stay with me, I will provide you with money and take you wherever you wish. And to prove to you that my words truly come from my heart, I will tell you the reason why I am so fond of you! You will remember how right the prophecies of our old Herzbruder turned out to be! Look, at Magdeburg, he foretold the following to me, which I kept well in my memory: "Olivier, this Simplicius though he seems to be a fool will once frighten you through his bravery and play the worst prank on you that you ever experienced at a time when you both do not recognize each other. Yet he will spare your life when it is in his hands. After a long time he will come to the place where you will be slain and there will successfully avenge your death." For the sake of this prophecy, dear Simplicius, I am prepared to divide my very heart with you. Already a part of this prophecy has been fulfilled, since I attacked you and you as a brave soldier shot me on the forehead, took my sword from me which nobody has done before, and you spared my life when I lay under you choking in blood. So have no doubts that the rest of the prophecy will be fulfilled also, and that you will avenge my death. And how could you take revenge, dearest brother, if you were not my faithful friend? There you have my heart's resolve – now tell me what you wish to do?"

I thought to myself: may the Devil trust you – I do not! If I take money from you for my journey you may repent of it and slay me – and if I stay with you I fear to be hanged with you. So I intended to hoodwink him and to stay only with him until I found opportunity to get away. Therefore I said that I would like to stay some days with him to see whether I could get accustomed to such a way of life and if I liked it he should find in me a faithful friend and good soldier; if I disliked it we could part at any time in friendship. Upon this he urged me to drink more but I distrusted him and pretended to be drunk to find out if he would attack me when I was unable to defend myself.

In the mean time, lice were tormenting me noxiously since I had brought a good company with me from Breisach; in the warmth they did not want to stay in my rags but came out to make merry. When Olivier observed this he asked me whether I had fleas.

"Yes, truly," I answered, "more than all the ducats I hope to collect in my life."

"Don't talk like that," he replied, "if you will stay with me, you will have more ducats than you have lice now."

I answered: "This is as impossible as that I can get rid of my lice!"

"Oh, yes," he said, "both are possible!" And he ordered the peasant to bring me some clothes which were hidden in a hollow tree not far from the house. These consisted of a grey hat, a cape of elk leather, a pair of scarlet breeches and a grey coat; stockings and shoes he would give me in the morning. Seeing such charity, I trusted him somewhat better than before and fell asleep in good spirit.

By daybreak next morning Olivier called: "Up, Simplicius, let us go out in God's name to seek some booty."

"Oh, God," I thought, "must I go robbing in your holy name?" And I remembered how I once came from my hermit and was horrified when one man said to another: "Come, brother, let's drink in God's name a measure of wine together." for I considered it a double sin to get drunk in God's most holy name.

"Oh, heavenly Father," I prayed, "how I have changed since then! My faithful God, what will become of me if I do not convert myself? O, curb my path that will lead me to hell if I do not repent!"

With such words and thoughts I followed Olivier into a village in which there was no living creature, and to have a better view we went up the church steeple. There he had hidden the stockings and shoes he had promised me the night before as well as two loaves of bread, some joints of dried meat and a barrel half full of wine which would have well lasted him as provisions for a week.

Whilst I dressed myself with what he had given to me, he told me that this was the place where he used to lay in ambush hoping for good booty, and that was the reason he had provisioned himself so well. He had more such hideouts, provided with food and drink so that if he could not find his prey in this place he might snatch it in another. Although I had to praise his prudence I let him know that it was not pleasant to besmirch this sacred place dedicated to God, to such a purpose.

"What!" he shouted, "Besmirch! If the churches could only speak they would have to confess that my deeds committed in them are but a trifle compared with the sins that have been committed here in the past. How many men and how many women do you think have entered this church since it was built, under the pretext of serving God, but indeed only to show their new clothes, their fine bodies and their nobility? Here one comes into church like a peacock and yet places himself before the altar as if he would pray the feet off all the Saints! There another in a corner sighs like the publican in the temple, yet his sighs are merely addressed to his mistress: another comes only to admonish his debtors than to pray, and if he knew these would not be at church would have stayed at home working on his accounts. And don't you believe that many are even buried in church who have deserved sword, gallows, fire and wheel? Many a man could not have completed his lascivious courtships if the church had not helped him. If there is something for sale or to hire, a notice is pinned on the church door. Many an usurer who cannot find time during the week to invent new extortions will sit in church on Sundays to think out fresh rogueries. How many besmirch the churches not only during their lives with their vices but fill them even with their vanity and foolishness after death? Only enter a church and look how they pride themselves on their gravestones and epitaphs who long ago have been eaten by worms. Only look up there and you will see more shields and helmets, swords and banners than in many an armoury; is it surprising that in this war the peasants defended themselves in churches as if they were fortresses? And why should I not be allowed, I a soldier, to follow my trade in church? Why should it be forbidden to me to earn my livelihood through the church when so many other people thrive on it? If I had known that it irks you to lay ambush in a church, I would have found another solution; in the mean time, make the best of it till I persuade you to something better."

I wanted to contradict Olivier that only vile men like he dishonour the churches and that they would find their punishment. But as I did not trust him and did not like to quarrel with him again, I said nothing. He then asked me to tell him my adventures since we had parted at Wittstock, and why I was dressed in the jester's clothes when I arrived in the camp at Magdeburg. But as my bruised neck still gave me pain, I excused myself and asked him instead to tell me his life-story which might contain some amusing adventures. He agreed and began thus the narrative of his villainous life:—

"My father," began Olivier, "was born not far from the city of Aachen of humble parents and he became the servant of a rich merchant who traded in copper wares. With him he progressed so well that his master let him learn to write, read and count, and put him in charge of his whole trade, as Potiphar entrusted Joseph. This was beneficial to both parties, for the merchant grew richer and richer in time through my father's diligence and caution. But my father grew more and more conceited so that he even became ashamed of his parents and spurned them, of which they often lamented in vain.

"When my father was twenty-five years old the merchant died, leaving an old widow and one daughter, who only recently had foolishly borne an illegitimate child – this however soon followed its grandfather to another world. When my father saw that the daughter had lost father and child but not her money, he cared little that she could no longer wear the virgin's crown, but with a thought to her wealth, began wooing her. The mother was well satisfied with all this not only because her daughter would regain her honour but also because my father knew all the tricks of the trade and was well aware how to practise usury. By this marriage my father became suddenly a rich merchant and I his heir whom he brought up in splendour because of his overflowing wealth. My clothes were those of a nobleman, my food that of a lord, my attendance that of a count, for which I had to thank copper and zinc more than silver and gold.

"Before I had completed my seventh year I clearly showed what I was to be, for what will be a nettle will sting early. No rascally trick was too much for me and where I could do some malice I never missed the chance, since neither father nor mother punished me for it. With other young bloods like myself I roamed the streets through thick and thin and soon had the courage to battle with boys stronger than myself. If I happened to get a thrashing, my parents would lament: "How is that, how can such a big churl strike a small child?" But if I got the upper hand, since I scratched, bit or threw stones, my parents would rejoice: "Our little Olivier will turn out a fine fellow!" And so my insolence grew. For saying prayers I was still too childish but if I cursed like a coachman, they claimed I was ignorant of its meaning. And so I steadily grew worse till I was sent to school; and there I carried out what other wicked rascals maliciously had planned, yet did not dare to practise. If I soiled or tore my books, my mother bought me new ones that my niggardly father should not be angered. Much did I torment my schoolmaster for he could not treat me harshly as he was dependent on gifts from my parents, whose foolish love for me he knew well.

"In summer I caught crickets and put them secretly into the school where they entertained us with their delightful singing. In winter I stole sneeze-wort and scattered it in the corner where the lads were whipped, and when a culprit started to struggle my powder would whirl in the air and give me a pleasant pastime as I watched everybody sneezing. Later on I considered myself too superior for ordinary rogueries and aimed at higher levels. I often stole from one and put the stolen thing in the satchel of another boy whom I wanted to have flogged, and in these manipulations I was so artful that hardly ever was I found out. Of the fights we had with myself as leader I scarcely need recount, nor of the blows I got for I always had a scratched face and my head was covered with bruises. You can guess from what I have just told you how I started my youth.

"As my father's wealth increased day by day, more parasites and wheedlers gathered around him who praised my true ability for scholarship, yet kept silent on all my other failings. They knew too well that he who did not do so would lose my parents' favour. Thus my parents found more delight in their son than a hedge sparrow which brings up a cuckoo. They hired a special tutor for me and sent me with him to Liège, more to learn French there than to study, for they did not wish to make a theologian out of me but rather a merchant. My tutor had strict orders not to keep me in severe discipline so that I would not acquire a timid or servile mind. He had to allow me to associate freely with other students that I might not shun mankind and he should consider that I was to be made not a monk but a man of the world, knowing the difference between black and white.

"My tutor needed none of these instructions, being himself inclined to all sorts of villainy. Why should he rebuke me for my small failings when he committed much coarser knaveries himself? He was mostly disposed to lechery and drink but bullying and fighting was more in my nature, and so I roamed the streets at night with him and his fellows and soon learnt more rogueries from him than Latin.

"Concerning my studies, I relied on my good memory and clever wit and was for this reason even more negligent; besides I was immersed in vice, knavery and malice and my conscience had already grown so wide that a big hay wagon could have been driven through it. I cared not if I secretly read Burchiello or Aretino* during the sermon in church, and nothing pleased me more than the final words of the service: '*Ite, missa est*'.

"I dressed like a dandy as well and every day was for me a carnival since I lived as a man of leisure and wasted not only my father's considerable allowance but also my mother's generous pocket money so that loose women lured us (especially my tutor), into their nets. With these creatures I learnt to wench and to gamble; how to brawl and to fight I already knew, nor did my tutor object to these orgies for he enjoyed them even more than I. This splendid life lasted a year and a half before my father heard of it through his agent in Liège, who had orders to shorten my reins, discharge my tutor and curtail my money spending. This angered us both and although the tutor had been chased away, we spent both day and night together. As we could not spend so freely as before, we joined up with a gang which snatched the cloaks off people during the night or even drowned them in the Meuse. What we gained from this dangerous trade, we squandered with our whores and let our studies go to the wind.

"One night when we were prowling about as usual ready to rob students of their cloaks, we were overwhelmed, my tutor stabbed to death and I with five others, these being true thieves, apprehended and thrown into prison. On being questioned next day, my father's agent, a well esteemed citizen, was called and interrogated on my behalf. On his surety I was bailed but had to be under house arrest with him till further notice. In the mean time, my tutor was buried and the other five punished as robbers and murderers. When my father heard of the affair, he came at once to Liège, settled the case with money, preached me a severe sermon and reproached me for the unhappiness I had caused him so that my mother was in utter despair. He also threatened me, if I would not mend my ways, to disinherit me and chase me to the devil. I promised to improve and rode home with him, and so my studies came to an end.

"At home my father discovered that I was thoroughly depraved. I had not become an honest student as he had hoped but a brawler and a boaster who thought he knew everything. I had scarcely warmed myself a little at home when he said to me, 'Listen, Olivier, I can see your donkey ears growing longer and longer. You are a worthless rascal! Too old to learn a trade, too impudent to serve a master, and a good-for-nothing incapable of mastering my business. What have I gained through all the money I have spent on you? I had hoped to find happiness in you and to make a man of you. On the contrary I had to buy you from the hangman's hand. Shame upon you! The best would be to confine you in a treadmill until you repent of your misdeeds.' Such lectures I had to endure daily till at last I tired of it and told my father boldly: I was not altogether guilty but he himself and his fine tutor who had seduced me. If he could find no pleasure in me, it served him right since his own parents found no joy in him when he had left them almost starving in beggary. At this he grasped a cudgel to reward me for my truthful words, swearing high and low he would deliver me to the penitentiary in Amsterdam. So that same night I ran away to his newly acquired farm, took his best stallion which he kept in the stable there, and rode off to Cologne. I sold the horse and attached myself to a band of thieves and robbers such as I had left in Liège. We recognized our kind by cheating at cards which we all understood so well.

Without delay I joined their guild and helped in their nightly burglaries as much as I could. Yet when soon after one of us was caught on the Old Market whilst he tried to snatch a purse from a noble lady and when I saw him standing with an iron collar in the pillory for half a day and saw one of his ears cut off and him flogged with rods I lost my taste for this trade. And so I enlisted as a soldier, for at that time the colonel with whom we served at Magdeburg was trying to reinforce his regiment.

"When my father heard where I was, he instructed his agent to enquire about me – but by then I had already received my recruiting money: my father gave orders to buy me out whatever it might cost, but I feared the penitentiary and refused it. Meanwhile my colonel learnt that I was a rich merchant's son and charged such a high price for my release that my father left me where I was to teach me a lesson for a while, hoping that war would make me change my ways.

"Not long after this it happened that the colonel's clerk died and he took me in his stead, as you well know. I conceived then high ideas and formed my hopes to climb from one rank to another and in the end become a general. I learnt from our secretary how to deport myself and my ambition made me behave as if I were honest and reputable, nor did I consort any more with rogues. I did not get very far however until our secretary died. Now I thought I shall see that I get his place! To this purpose I bribed as much as I could since my mother, having heard I had mended my ways, continued to send me money. But as the young Herzbruder had become the favourite with our colonel and was preferred to me, I aimed to get him out of the way, particularly as I realized that the colonel was willing to give him the secretary's post. So urgently did I wish for this promotion that I had made myself bullet-proof with the help of our provost, as I intended to fight a duel with Herzbruder and kill him by the sword. Yet I could not find a good chance to get at him and our provost warned me of my intent and said: 'Even if you will sacrifice him, it will do you more harm than good since you will have murdered the colonel's most beloved servant.' But he advised me to steal something in Herzbruder's presence and give it to the provost and he would arrange it that Herzbruder should lose the colonel's favour. I followed this course, stole a golden beaker at the christening feast of the colonel's newborn child, and handed it over to the provost. You will remember how he, through his tricks, put the blame on Herzbruder and had him banished in disgrace, and in the same way filled your pockets with puppies in the colonel's big tent."

Green and yellow danced before my eyes when I heard from Olivier's own mouth how treacherously he had tricked my dearest friend and yet I could take no revenge. I had even to suppress my emotion, lest he might notice it, and I asked him therefore what further happened to him after the Battle of Wittstock.

"In this battle," Olivier continued, "I proved myself not as a quill-sharpener sitting on his inkbottle, but as a brave soldier. I was well mounted and bullet-proof like iron and not assigned to a squadron, and so I showed my fearlessness as a man willing to succeed by his sword or die. I galloped round our brigade like a whirlwind to show our men that I was better suited for arms than for the quill. But it was of no avail. The Swedes' good fortune got the upper hand and I had to share the miseries of our men and accept a pardon of surrender which a short time before I would not have given to anybody. With other prisoners I was pushed into a foot-regiment which was sent to Pomerania for replenishment. There were many newly enlisted recruits and since I had shown remarkable courage, I was promoted to corporal. Yet I did not intend to carry the manure there too long but wished to return to the Emperor's forces to which party I had more affection, although without doubt I would have found better advancement with the Swedes.

"My desertion I accomplished in the following way: I was sent out with seven musketeers to remote parts to extort some outstanding war levies and when I had collected more than some eight hundred gulden I showed my men the money and made their eyes greedy for it, so that we bargained to divide it between us and escape. When this was done, I persuaded three of them to help me to shoot the other four dead, and when that was accomplished we divided the money, namely two hundred gulden each, and with that we marched towards Westphalia. On the way I again persuaded one of the three to help me shoot down the remaining two, and when we divided the money for a second time I strangled the last one as well and came safely with the money to Werl where I enlisted and made merry with my wealth.

"When this was almost spent, I still wanted to go on feasting. I had heard much of a young soldier in Soest who had gained great booty and had made himself a big name and I was encouraged to follow his example. They called him the Huntsman because of his green clothes, and so I had such a green costume made for myself, and under his name I stole and looted in his and our own quarters and committed all sorts of villainies so that it was forbidden for both parties to go on foraging patrol. He stayed

at home, but I continued to steal in his name as much as I could so that in
the end the Huntsman challenged me. But the Devil may have fought with
him since I had heard he had the Devil under his skin, and he would soon
have finished me off in spite of my being bulletproof. I succumbed to his
cunning for with the help of a servant he enticed me and my comrade into
a sheep pen and wanted to force me, in the presence of two living devils
whom he had as seconders to fight with him. And because I refused it they
forced me to the most humiliating shame on earth, which my comrade
soon spread among the people. I was so ashamed that I had to run away
to Lippstadt where I took service with the Hessians. Even there I did not
stay long as no one trusted me, but I journeyed on into service with the
Dutch. There I found good military pay but a boring war for my liking,
since we were closed in like monks and had to live chastely like nuns.

"I could show myself neither among the Imperials, the Swedes nor
the Hessians without grave danger as I had deserted from all three, and
since I could no longer stay with the Dutch, having raped a young girl
with violence, I thought now to find refuge with the Spaniards, hoping to
abscond from them homeward and find my parents. But when I started
to put my plan into action, my compass turned mad and I landed all of a
sudden with the Bavarians with whom I marched among the Merodians
from Westphalia to Breisgau, earning my livelihood by gambling and
stealing. When I had some money I loitered by day in the gaming places
and by night among the sutlers. When I had nothing I stole as much as I
could, often two or three horses a day from the grazing places or out of
the stables, sold them and squandered the money at gaming. At night I
dug under the soldiers' tents and stole their best possessions from beneath
their heads. On the march I had my eyes on the purses which hung from
the waists of the women traders, which I cut off and thus made my living
until the Battle of Wittenweier where I was taken prisoner and once again
pushed into a foot-regiment and made one of Weimar's soldiers. But I
disliked the camp at Breisach so I soon deserted and went off to make
my own war as you have seen for yourself. And believe me, brother, since
then I have struck down many a proud fellow and gathered a handsome
hoard of money, and I don't intend to give it up until I see I can get no
more. Now your turn has come to tell me of your life and adventures."

Whilst Olivier delivered his narrative, I could not admire enough God's
miraculous providence. Now I understood how my dear God had protected me like a father from this monster in Westphalia and had made him
frightened of me. Now I could see the trick I had played on him which the

old father Herzbruder had prophesied but which Olivier, luckily for me, had misinterpreted. Had this beast known that I was the Huntsman of Soest he would most certainly have revenged himself for what I had done to him in the sheep-pen. I realized how wisely and obscurely Herzbruder had made his predictions. Yet, though his prophecies usually turned out to be true, I could not think that I should revenge the death of a man who deserved the wheel and the gallows!

What good fortune that I did not tell him my life story first, for thus I would have confessed how I once had humiliated him. Pondering over this, I noticed some scars in Olivier's face which were not there at the time of Magdeburg, and I imagined they were the reminders of Harum-Scarum, when he in the shape of a devil had clawed his face. I therefore asked him from where these marks had come and that he should not conceal from me what may be the best part of his life story.

"Oh, brother," he answered, "if I should tell you all my rogueries and misdeeds, it would take too long, but to prove to you that I will not conceal any of my adventures I will tell the truth even if this turns out to my own mockery. I really believe that from my mother's womb I was predestined to a marked face. Even in my childhood my schoolfellows scratched my face when I brawled with them, and in just the same way one of those devils who helped the Huntsman of Soest, treated me so perniciously that for six weeks I felt his claws in my face, but subsequently the wounds healed. The scars you can still see have another cause. When I lay in quarters with the Swedes in Pomerania, I had a beautiful mistress. I ordered my host out of his bed that we could lie in it, but his cat which was used to sleeping in the same bed came every night and pestered us greatly, as it did not want to lose its wonted place of rest. This vexed my mistress who did not like cats anyway, that she solemnly swore not to make love with me any more until I got rid of the cat. To enjoy her favours further I decided not only to fulfil her wish but also to take revenge on the cat and have some fun as well. So I put the cat in a sack and took my host's two strong peasant dogs with me to a wide meadow to amuse myself. As there was no tree nearby up which the cat could escape, I expected the dogs would chase the cat up and down the meadow like a hare and give me a pleasant entertainment. But by the Devil, it turned out differently. When I opened the sack, the cat, seeing only an open field, and on it two savage enemies and nothing high in which to take refuge, refused to jump to the ground to have its skin torn to pieces. Instead this beast, finding no higher spot, climbed upon my own head. When I tried to push her off, my hat fell down and the more I tried to pull her down the deeper she clutched her claws into my head to keep her hold. From such a fight the dogs could not long withhold but joined the game, jumping with open jaws from behind, in front and from both sides after the cat, which would not leave my head but defended her position by clawing my face and head as well as she could. If the cat missed the dogs, striking out with her thorny gloves, she certainly hit me, and when she hit the dogs on their noses, they jumped into my face. When I tried to pull the cat down with my hands, she bit and scratched me with terrific violence.

"Thus I was attacked by dogs and cat all at once, and was so disfigured and terribly deformed that I scarcely looked any more like a man. The worst was the danger that the dogs, snapping at the cat might catch my nose or an ear and bite it off. My collar and cape were so bloodstained that they looked like a blacksmith's stable on St Stephen's Day when the horses are bloodletting. I could think of nothing to save me from this fearful agony, until at last I threw myself down on the ground that the dogs could seize the cat. They strangled it but I had no such merriment from this as I had hoped but only mockery and such a face as your eyes can see. I was so infuriated that I soon shot both dogs dead and gave my mistress, who was the cause of all this foolery, such a thrashing that she ran away from me, for obviously she could not be in love any longer with such an abominable grimace."

I would have liked to laugh at Olivier's story, yet I had to pretend that I pitied him, and just as I began to tell him my life's history we saw a coach with two outriders approaching in the distance. We therefore came down from the church tower and hid in a house near the road well suited to ambush the travellers. I had to keep my musket loaded in reserve, whilst Olivier with one shot brought down one rider and his horse before they had noticed us. Thereupon the other escaped in a hurry. Whilst I with cocked gun had forced the coachman to halt and descend, Olivier rushed upon him and split his head with his broadsword down to the teeth. He would have also butchered the lady and the children in the coach, who already looked more dead than alive, but I boldly intervened and told him if he wanted to do this he must strangle me first.

"Oh," he said, "you foolish Simplicius, I would never have believed you to be such a hopeless fellow as you now behave."

"Brother," I answered, "what have these innocent children done? If they were men, who could defend themselves, it would be another matter."

241

He replied: "Throw the eggs in the pan and no cockerels will be hatched. I know these young blood-suckers too well. Their father is a major, a dog of an oppressor, and the worst tormenter in the world."

With these words he wanted to go on butchering them, but I prevented him until in the end he relented. They were the major's wife, her maids and three lovely children, whom I pitied with my whole heart. We locked them in a cellar that they might not betray us too soon, and the only food they had was fruit and some white turnips until someone might deliver them. After this we looted the coach and rode off with seven handsome horses into the thickest part of the forest.

When we had tethered them I looked around and saw nearby a fellow stock-still at a tree, and meaning to be on our guard I pointed him out to Olivier.

"Oh, you fool," he said, "that's a Jew I bound up there. The rascal was frozen and dead long ago!"

With that he went up to him and knocked him under the chin with his fist, saying: "Ho, you dog, how many fine ducats have you got there for me?" And as he nudged the chin some doubloons fell out of the Jew's mouth which the poor devil had saved until the hour of death. Thereupon Olivier thrust his hand into the Jew's mouth and grabbed twelve doubloons and a precious ruby, saying:

"I have to thank you, Simplicius, for this loot!" He presented me with the ruby, took the money and went away to fetch his peasant, telling me to stay with the horses and look out that the dead Jew did not bite me, implying that I had not such courage as he.

When he had gone I had fearful ideas, thinking of the dangerous position in which I stood. I thought at first to mount a horse and escape but feared that Olivier might surprise and shoot me down, as I suspected he was nearby watching me and only wanting to prove my loyalty. Then I considered running away on foot but feared if I would escape Olivier I would hardly be able to escape the peasants in the Black Forest who were renowned for giving no quarter to lonely soldiers. But supposing I took all the horses with me, so that Olivier had no means of chasing after me, I might easily be caught by the Weimar troops and as a proven murderer broken on the wheel. In short I could think of no sure way of escaping, particularly as in the wild forest I knew neither road nor path.

Moreover my conscience woke up and tormented me for having ambushed the coach and lent my aid that the coachman had lost his life so lamentably and both the women and innocent children had been locked in the cellar where perhaps they might perish and die like this Jew. I tried to console myself that I was innocent, being forced to it against my will; but again my conscience pricked that long ago I had deserved my proper reward at the hand of justice together with this murderer for our evil deeds. Perhaps it was the providence of God's justice that I should be punished in this way. At last I began to hope and prayed for God's mercy to help me from this predicament and said to myself: "You fool, you are neither imprisoned nor in chains; the whole wide world is open to you. Have you not horses enough to escape, nor quick feet to run away?" While I tormented myself, yet could decide nothing, Olivier came back with the peasant. He guided us with the horses to a farm where we fed the animals and slept a few hours in turn. At midnight we rode on again and reached the Swiss border by noon. Here Olivier was well known and we were splendidly entertained. As we regaled ourselves, our host fetched two Jews who bargained for the horses at half their value. All went smoothly so that little argument was needed. The Jews' main question was whether the horses were Imperial or Swedish, and when they heard they were from the Weimar army, they said: "Then we must ride them not to Basel but into Swabia to the Bavarians." I was amazed at such knowledge and cunning.

We feasted like lords and I enjoyed the good forest trout and delicious crayfish. When evening came we went on our way, loading our peasant like a donkey with roasted joints and other foods. The following day we came to a lonely farmhouse where we were welcomed and remained a few days because of bad weather. After that, through forests and by-paths, we reached the very same cottage where Olivier had first taken me.

While we sat there regaling our bodies and resting, Olivier sent the peasant to buy provisions and powder and shot. As soon as he had gone, Olivier took off his coat and said: "Brother, I do not wish to carry this devil's money alone." With that he untied a few sausage-shaped bags which he carried on his bare body and threw them onto the table, saying: "You must look after these until I give up my trade and we both have enough, for this devilish gold has blistered my body."

I replied: "Brother, if you had as little as I, you would have no blisters."

"What is mine is yours," he interrupted, "and what more we gain we shall share!"

I took both bags and found them very weighty indeed as they were coins of pure gold. I told him they were badly packed and if it would please him I would sew the money in such a way that it would be half as sour to carry. He agreed and we went to a hollow oak tree from where he took scissors, needle and thread, and I made for both of us a pair of shoulder-bags out of a pair of breeches, and many lovely red pennies I stitched into them. These we put under our shirts and it was as if we were clad in golden armour front and back. Then I questioned him why he had no silver coins and got the answer that he had more than a thousand thalers stored in a tree, from which he let the peasant take, without asking an account, as he did not esteem this sheep's dung very highly.

When the gold was well packed we returned to our cottage, cooked our meal and warmed ourselves at the oven over night. At one o'clock in the early morning when we least expected it, six musketeers and a corporal, their muskets at the ready, burst open the door and shouted for us to surrender. Olivier, who like me had his loaded gun by him, answered them with a couple of bullets which brought two to the floor while I finished a third one and wounded a fourth. Then Olivier heaved out his ever-ready sword and slashed the fifth man from shoulder to belly, that his bowels gushed out and he fell down beside them. In the mean time, I had thrashed the sixth soldier on his head with the butt end of my gun so that he died. But Olivier was struck with a similar blow from the seventh, with such violence that his brain was scattered about, and I in return knocked him who had done it, with such vehemence that he joined the rest of the bodies on the floor. When the wounded musketeer saw that I went after him with the butt of my gun, he threw away his musket and ran off as if the Devil chased him. The whole encounter lasted not longer than a Paternoster, and in this short time seven brave soldiers lost their lives.

I remained the only victor in the field and I examined Olivier to see whether he had any living breath in him but found him without life. I thought it foolish to leave so much gold on a corpse who had no need for it, and so I stripped him of his golden fleece which only yesterday I had stitched, and I hung it round my own neck with the other half. As I had broken my gun, I took Olivier's musket and sword in case of need and departed on the path by which I knew our peasant must return. Sitting by the wayside I waited for him and pondered what I should do next.

I had hardly sat there half an hour, lost in my thought, when the peasant approached, panting like a bear and running with all his might. He did not see me until I stood next to him: "Why so fast?" I cried, "What news?"

"Quick," he answered, "run away! A corporal and six musketeers are coming to catch you and Olivier and will take you to Lichteneck dead or alive! They took me prisoner that I should guide them to you but luckily I escaped and came here to warn you!"

"You rascal," I thought. "You have betrayed us to get Olivier's money hidden in the tree." Yet I gave no hint of my thoughts, as I needed him to show me the way, but told him that Olivier and those who tried to catch him were dead. As he did not believe this, I was good enough to go with him that he could see the misery of the seven bodies. I said: "The seventh I allowed to run away and I wish God would grant it that I could bring these to life again."

The peasant was astounded and horrified.

"What shall we do?" he asked.

"What I shall do," I replied, "is already decided. I give you the choice of three things: either lead me at once safely through the forest to Villingen, or show me Olivier's money that is hidden in the tree, or die here and keep company with these dead men! If you take me to Villingen, you may keep Olivier's money for yourself alone. If you show me the tree, I will share the money with you. If you will do neither, I will shoot you dead and go my way."

The peasant would have liked to run away but feared my musket. Therefore he fell down upon his knees and offered to lead me out of the wood. So we hastened off and marched the whole day and the following night – fortunately it was moonlight, without food or drink and little rest until we saw at daybreak the town of Villingen before us: there I dismissed the peasant. On this long march, the peasant was driven by fear of death and I by greed to save myself and my gold. I almost believe that gold will give a man great strength, for though I had a heavy weight to carry, I scarcely felt any fatigue.

I thought it a good omen that the gates were just being opened as I reached Villingen. The officer on watch examined me and I gave myself out to be a volunteer of the regiment in which Herzbruder had put me. I told him that I had escaped from the Weimar Army at Breisach where they had taken me prisoner and I now wished to rejoin my regiment among the Bavarians. He gave me an escort of a musketeer to take me to the commandant. The latter was still asleep, having spent more than half the night awake over his administrative work, so that I had to wait an hour and a half before his quarters. Just then many people came from morning Mass and a big crowd of burghers and soldiers assembled around me who wanted to know how things were at Breisach. This noise awoke the commandant and he ordered me to see him. He began to examine me and my answer was the same as at the gate. Thereafter he asked me of certain details of the siege and other items and I then confessed all: that I had spent about a fortnight with a fellow who also had escaped and with him had attacked and looted a coach with the intention of getting enough booty from the Weimar army to mount us in order to rejoin our regiments again. But only yesterday we had been ambushed by a corporal and six soldiers who wanted to capture us, whereby my comrade and six of the enemy were slain on the spot. The seventh and I had escaped, each to his own party. I did not say a word that my true intention had been to reach my wife at Lippstadt in Westphalia, nor that I had two well stuffed shoulder garments front and back: my conscience did not prick me that I concealed this, for what concern was it to him? He did not even ask me about it, but was greatly amazed and would scarcely believe that Olivier and I had slain six men and chased away a seventh, though my comrade had lost his life. Through this we came to talk about Olivier's sword, which I had by my side and which I praised. It pleased him so much that I, in order to get away from him in good esteem and obtain a pass, presented it to him in exchange for another. In truth it was an excellent and beautiful blade, a whole perpetual calendar was engraved on it and I was inclined to believe that Vulcan himself had forged it in *hora mortis* and imbued it with magic strength.

When the commandant had dismissed me and ordered that a pass be written out for me, I went by the shortest cut to an inn, not knowing whether first to eat or sleep since I needed both. Yet I preferred to quieten my belly first and so ordered food and drink, and pondered how I could succeed in reaching my wife in Lippstadt safely with my money – for I had as little intention to rejoin my regiment as to break my neck. While I thus speculated, a fellow limped into the dining-room with a stick in his hand, a bandage round his head, one arm in a sling and clothes so miserable that none would have given a penny for them. As soon as the ostler saw him he wanted to throw him out, for he stank atrociously and was so covered with lice that the whole Swabian heath could have been populated with them. He begged for God's sake to be allowed to warm himself a little. But in vain, and only when I took pity and pleaded for him was he grudgingly allowed near the oven.

He looked at me with longing eyes and great devotion, often sighing, as I tackled my meal. When the ostler had gone to fetch me a piece of roast, he came to my table holding out an earthen penny-pot so that I could well imagine what he wanted, and before he even asked I took the wine jug and filled up his pot.

"Oh, friend," said he, "for Herzbruder's sake, give me something to eat too."

When he said this it pierced my heart for I knew it was Herzbruder himself. I almost fainted to see him in such misery but controlled myself, embraced him and placed him next to me. Our tears ran freely, mine from compassion and his from joy.

Our unexpected reunion almost prevented us from eating and drinking while one asked the other what had happened since last we were together. But because the innkeeper and ostler went to and fro, we could not speak intimately. Our host was astonished that I tolerated such a lousy fellow, and I replied that this was common usage in war among honest soldiers who were comrades. I learnt from Herzbruder that he had been confined to the poorhouse, had lived from alms and his wounds were badly dressed.

So I rented a separate room at the inn and put Herzbruder to bed, called for the best surgeon as well as for a tailor and a needlewoman to clothe him and release him from the grip of the lice. I still had those doubloons, which Olivier had grabbed from the mouth of the dead Jew, and throwing them on the table I cried to Herzbruder, so that the innkeeper could hear: "Look here, brother, this is my money which I will spend on you and share with you!" After this the innkeeper served us splendidly.

To the surgeon-barber I showed the ruby, which also had belonged to the Jew and was worth about twenty thalers, saying because I had to spend my ready money on food and clothing, I would offer him the ring if he would cure my comrade completely. The barber was well satisfied and applied his cure with his greatest skill.

I nursed Herzbruder like my other self, and had a simple grey cloth suit made for him. I also went to the commandant about my pass and told him that I had met a badly wounded comrade, for whom I wished to wait till he was well as I could not join my regiment without him. The commandant praised my intentions and allowed me to stay as long as I wished, offering that as soon as my friend could travel he would supply both of us with passes.

Returning to Herzbruder I sat at his bedside and asked him to tell me frankly how he had come into such a wretched state. I suspected he might have lost his high dignity through serious reasons or default, thus losing favour and falling into misery. But he told me:

"Brother, you know that I was the right hand and closest friend of Count von Götz, and you know too how unfortunately his last campaign under his command ended, not only losing the Battle of Wittenweier but also failing to relieve Breisach. For this he was criticized from all sides and even summoned to Vienna to vindicate himself. So I live voluntarily in fear and shame in this distress and often wish to die or remain hidden until the Count has proved his innocence, for I believe he was always loyal to the Roman Emperor; his misfortunes this year were due to God's will which grants victories, and not to the Count's neglect. When we tried to relieve Breisach and I saw that our side made no progress, I armed myself and went on the pontoon bridge with such violence as if I wanted to end the battle alone, although it was neither my profession nor duty. I did that as an example for the others, and so I was one of the first to face the enemy on the bridge. It was a fierce struggle and being the first in attack, I was the last in retreat under the vehement onslaught of the French, and thus I fell into enemy hands. I was shot in the right arm and in the leg, so I could neither escape nor use my sword, and as the narrowness of the place allowed no quarter, I suffered a slash on my head that I fell to the ground. Being well dressed, I was stripped in the fury of the battle and thrown for dead into the Rhine.

"In this dire need I cried to God and made several vows; his help came, for I was cast up onto land, where I staunched my wounds with moss. Although half frozen I found with God's grace a miraculous strength to crawl away. Miserably wounded, I reached some Merode brothers' and soldiers' wives, who had pity on me although they did not know me. They already despaired of a possible relief of the fortress which pained me more than my wounds. They refreshed and clothed me by their campfire and before my wounds were scarcely dressed I had to witness our troops preparing for a shameful retreat and the loss of our cause. This gave me grave pain and I resolved therefore to reveal myself to nobody and not to participate in such disgrace. I joined a number of wounded soldiers of our army who had a surgeon with them, to whom I gave a golden cross from round my neck which I had saved, and he bandaged my wounds. In this misery, my dear Simplicius, I have made my way here and am willing to reveal myself to no one until I know how Count von Götz's affairs have turned out. Your kindness and loyalty give me great comfort that our dear God has not forsaken me; this morning when I came from early Mass and saw you standing before the commandant's quarters, I thought that God had sent you instead of an angel to help me in my misery."

I consoled Herzbruder as well as I could and confided to him that I had still more money than the doubloons he had seen, all of which were at his service. I told him how Olivier had perished and how I had avenged his death. All this cheered him in spirit so that his body gained strength and his wounds healed daily.

PART FIVE

23

SIMPLICIUS WITH HERZBRUDER
ON A PILGRIMAGE

WHEN HERZBRUDER WAS RECOVERED and healed of his wounds, he revealed to me that in his deepest need he had vowed to make a pilgrimage to Einsiedeln. As he was so close to Switzerland he was determined to fulfil this now, even if he should go all the way begging. I was glad to hear this and I offered him money and my company; indeed I wished to buy two horses for the journey. It was my desire, rather than piety, to visit the Confederacy as the only country where beloved peace still blossomed. Further I was glad to be of some service to Herzbruder on such a journey as I loved him almost more than myself.

But he refused both my help and my company with the pretext that his pilgrimage must be done on foot and with peas in his boots. My company would not only hinder his meditation but would also annoy me through his own slow and painstaking progress. He said this to discourage me as his conscience troubled him to live from money gained by murder and robbery, when undertaking such a holy journey. Besides, he did not wish to cause me too great expense and told me frankly that I had already done more than I owed to him, or he ever could repay. Upon this we began a friendly quarrel, which was so amiable that I have never heard the like, for we each protested that neither had done for the other what a friend should do; indeed neither had yet repaid the favours he had received.

All this, however, would not persuade him to tolerate me as a companion, until at last I realized that he abhorred Olivier's money and my godless life. So I took refuge in a lie, pretending that my desire to convert myself urged me to Einsiedeln. If he prevented me from this good intention and I should die, a heavy responsibility would rest on him. Thus I persuaded him at last to allow me to go with him to the holy place, especially as I showed great remorse for my evil ways, though all was deceit. I told him that I too would make the pilgrimage on peas as a penance.

This dispute was hardly finished when we began another. Herzbruder was too conscientious and did not allow me to use the commandant's pass, which was issued for my return to the regiment.

"How," said he, "can we proceed to Einsiedeln to amend our lives if we start in the name of God with fraud and obscure men's eyes with falsehood? 'He that denieth me before the world, him will I deny before my heavenly Father,' Christ said. Why should we be timid? If all martyrs and confessors had acted like that there would be few saints in Heaven. Let us go in God's name where our pious intent urges and let God's will be done, for He will lead us where our souls will find peace."

I reproached him that we should not tempt God but adapt ourselves to circumstance. Pilgrimages are strange affairs for soldiery and if our intentions were discovered we would be treated as deserters rather than pilgrims, bringing us in great trouble and danger; as even the holy apostle, Paul, with whom we cannot compare ourselves, adapted himself marvellously to the customs of the world.

So at last he agreed that I should fetch my pass to go to my regiment and with that we left the town just before the gates were closed, pretending to go to Rottweil with a reliable guide. But soon we turned off and by using a side path crossed the Swiss border that same night. Next morning we reached a village where we equipped ourselves with long black cloaks, pilgrims' staves and rosaries, and dismissed our guide with a good reward.

The country appeared to me, compared with other German lands, as strange as if I had come to Brazil or China. I saw the people work and go in peace, the stalls were full of cattle, the farm yards filled with fowls, geese and ducks, the roads alive with peaceful travellers and the inns crowded with people making merry. There was no fear of an enemy, no fright of plundering, no horror of losing goods, life or limb. Everyone lived safely under his own vine and fig tree, and, compared with German lands, in such sheer happiness and joy that I considered this country an earthly paradise although it seemed to be rugged by nature.

All the way I did nothing but gaze around me, whilst Herzbruder prayed with his rosary and he gave me many reproaches as he wished me to pray incessantly too, yet I could not accustom myself to it.

In Zurich he found out my secret tricks and told me the truth as boldly as he could. The night before we had rested in Schaffhausen and my feet ached painfully from the peas; fearing to walk again upon them the following day, I had the peas boiled and put them back into my shoes. Thus I came quite comfortably to Zurich whilst he suffered great pain.

"Brother," he said, "you are blessed with great favour by God that in spite of the peas in your shoes you can march so well!"

"Truly," I replied, "dearest Herzbruder, I have boiled them or I had not been able to walk so far."

"May God have mercy!" he cried. "What have you done? You should better have taken them out of your shoes altogether than to play mockery with them! I fear that God may punish you and me alike. Dear Brother, let me tell you in plain German that I fear if you will not mend your ways before God, your soul's salvation is in greatest danger. I assure you I love no man more than you, yet if you do not reform, my conscience forbids me to continue our friendship."

I was speechless from fear and could hardly recover, but I confessed in the end that I had put the peas into my shoes not out of religion but only to persuade him to take me on his pilgrimage.

"Oh, Brother," he said, "apart from the peas you are still far away from the road to salvation. May God improve your ways, for without this our friendship cannot last."

From this time on I followed him dejectedly like someone on the way to the gallows. My conscience began to pain me, thinking of all the villainous deeds I had done during my life. I lamented my lost innocence which I had brought with me from the forest and thoroughly squandered away in the world. And as Herzbruder did not talk much to me, yet looked at me only with sighs, I truly felt as if he knew of and lamented my damnation.

In this way we came to Einsiedeln and entered the church just when a priest was exorcizing the Devil out of a possessed man. This was to me a new and strange experience that I left Herzbruder to kneel and pray as long as he wished and went in curiosity to watch the spectacle. But hardly had I approached a little nearer when the evil spirit cried out of the poor fellow: "Oho, you villain, has the hailstorm sent you here? I thought to find you with Olivier in hell, and now you are here, you adulterous, murderous whore-hunter – do you hope to escape us? O, you priests, do not accept him! He is a hypocrite and a worse liar than I am; he makes mockery and blasphemes God and religion." The exorcist ordered the spirit to be silent, for no one would believe this arch-liar. Yet the spirit answered back: "Yes, yes, so ask this runaway monk's companion; he will tell you this atheist was not ashamed to boil the peas on which he vowed to make his pilgrimage."

I scarcely knew whether I stood on my head or my heels, hearing this with all the people staring at me, but the priest reproached the spirit and commanded him to silence, yet was unable that day to cast him out. In the mean time, Herzbruder approached when I was looking more dead than alive from horror, and between hope and fear I did not know what to do. He consoled me as best he could and assuring the crowd and especially the clergy that in all my life I had never been a monk but a soldier who easily might have done more evil than good. The Devil was a liar and had made the case with the peas worse than it was; for myself, I was so confused in my mind as if I had already suffered the punishment of hell.

The priests tried hard to comfort me and they admonished me to go to confession and communion, when the spirit again shouted out of the possessed man: "Yes, yes, he will make a fine confession, not even knowing what confession is! What do you want to do with him anyhow, he is a heretic and belongs to us! His parents are more Anabaptists than Calvinists…" But the exorcist again commanded the spirit to silence and said to him: "So it will pain you even more if this poor lost sheep is pulled out of the teeth of hell and rejoined with the fold of Christ." Upon this the spirit began to bellow so gruesomely that it was horrible to hear. Yet this fearful song gave me great consolation for I realized that if I could not gain God's favour any more, the Devil would not have roared so terribly.

Though in these days I was in no way prepared for confession and all my life long I had no intention ever to do so because for shame I had feared it as the Devil detests the Holy Cross – yet at that hour I felt in me such repentance for my sins and such desire to do penance and reform my life that I at once asked for a confessor. Herzbruder rejoiced highly over my sudden conversion since he knew well that so far I had belonged to no religion at all. Now I avowed myself openly to the Catholic Church, went to confession and to Holy Communion after having received my absolution. Thereafter I felt so light and joyous in my heart that I could scarcely express my feeling. The most miraculous fact was that the Devil, who had possessed the man's spirit, left me in peace henceforth, although before my conversion he had blamed me for all the knaveries I had perpetrated. However the assembly had not believed him but trusted my honest pilgrim's clothes.

We remained about a fortnight in this blessed place, where I thanked God for my conversion and admired the miracles which were done. All this roused me to some kind of piety and godliness, which however did not last too long. As my conversion had its origin not from love of God but from fear of damnation, I soon became callous and sluggish again as I slowly forgot the terror with which the Devil had struck me.

After we had sufficiently beheld the relics of the Saints, the treasures and all the other remarkable objects of the Abbey, we travelled on to spend the winter in Baden.

There I rented for us a pleasant chamber and a bedroom such as commonly the visitors who take the waters occupy during the summer. These visitors are mostly rich Swiss citizens who come here more to make merry and to boast than to take cures for illness. I arranged for our full board and when Herzbruder saw how splendidly I did this he admonished me to thrift as we had yet to endure a hard and long winter and he did not think that my money would last as long: I should need my reserve in the spring when we would depart. Much money was easily squandered away if one only spends and earns nothing – like smoke blowing away, never to return. At such loyal advice I could no longer conceal from Herzbruder how rich my treasure was and that it was my intention to spend it on both of us since its origin was so unholy that I did not wish to buy a farm with it. That Herzbruder should benefit from Olivier's money was only right considering the insults he had suffered from him at Magdeburg. And when I found a safe moment I pulled off my two shoulder-bags and cutting the seams brought out the ducats and pistoles, telling Herzbruder he might make use of them as he wished, spending them as he thought most useful for us both.

When he saw my confidence in him and the great amount of money through which I could have become a fairly wealthy man, he said:

"Brother, as long as I have known you, you have shown me nothing but your constant love and loyalty, but how do you think I can ever reward you? I do not mean the money, as this in time might be repaid, but your love and faithfulness and principally your great confidence which is immeasurable. Brother, in one word your deep devotion makes me your slave and what you have done for me is easier to admire than to repay. Oh, my faithful Simplicius, in these godless times when the world abounds in dishonesty, you never suspected for a moment that I in my poverty might run away with your treasure. Brother, this token of true friendship binds me closer to you than if I had been given thousands. But I beg you, remain the guardian of your gold – it is enough for me that you are my friend."

I answered: "If as you say you are my friend then you will care that I do not waste my money." So we argued foolishly, for we were drunk with devotion for each other, and thus Herzbruder became my marshal, treasurer, servant and master.

During this time of leisure he told me of his life and how he met Count von Götz and found promotion with him. I too recounted what had happened to me since his father died, for until now we had never found time to talk. When he heard that I had a young wife in Lippstadt, he rebuked me that I did not go to her rather than to Switzerland, for that would have been my duty. And when I excused myself that I could not forsake my dearest friend in misery, he persuaded me to write to my wife letting her know of my whereabouts with the promise to join her as soon as I could. In my letter I added my apologies for my long absence which was due to all sorts of obstacles, although I had wished to be with her long ago.

Herzbruder in the mean time got news that the affairs of Count von Götz were favourable, that he had been vindicated before his Imperial Majesty, set free and even expected the command of an army, so he wrote to him in Vienna. He also communicated with the Bavarian army with regard to his baggage, and began to hope that his fortune would take a turn for the better. We therefore agreed in the coming spring to part, he to the Count, and I to my wife at Lippstadt.

To avoid being idle during the winter we studied with an engineer how to construct more fortresses on paper than the Kings of Spain and France could ever achieve. Besides I became acquainted with some alchemists who wished to teach me how to make gold at my expense as they scented money behind me. I am sure they would have persuaded me, if Herzbruder had not prevented them saying: "He who knows this art has no need to go about like a beggar nor to ask for money."

Although Herzbruder received a favourable answer and promises from the Count in Vienna, I had not a single word from Lippstadt, in spite of the fact that I wrote in duplicate on different post days. This made me bad humoured and was the reason that in the spring I did not go to Westphalia but asked Herzbruder to take me with him to Vienna to share the good fortune he expected there. Thus we equipped ourselves like two cavaliers from my money, with clothes, horses, servants and arms and went through Constance to Ulm. Here we embarked on the Danube and arrived safely in eight days' time in Vienna. On that route I observed nothing unusual except that the women who stood along the banks answered the travellers who shouted to them not with words but by displaying their female charms to the embarrassment of many a fellow.

24

SIMPLICIUS LEARNS HIS TRUE PARENTAGE

RARE THINGS HAPPEN IN THIS CHANGING WORLD. One used to say: he who knows everything will soon be rich. But I say he who knows the trend of the times can be great and powerful. Many a skinflint may become rich by using his opportunities, though he does not achieve greatness and remains in low esteem. But he who is great and powerful will be followed by wealth. Good Fortune, who distributes might and wealth, looked upon me with favour and stretched out his hand to help me climb the ladder to success. Yet I did not grasp it. Why? I believe because my fate had decided differently and my foolishness led me another way.

Count von der Wahl, under whose command I had made my name in Westphalia, happened to be in Vienna when we arrived. Herzbruder attended a banquet at which several Imperial counsellors of war were assembled as well as the Count von Götz and others. They talked of all sorts of brave soldiers and famous fighters and mentioned too the Huntsman of Soest. Count von der Wahl told of the Huntsman's many exploits admiringly, that the company was astonished at his youth and regretted that the cunning Hessian Colonel St Andreas had caught him out, made him marry and forced him thus to serve under the Swedes... Count von der Wahl had heard of everything which had happened to me at Lippstadt.

Herzbruder, who was nearby and had my wellbeing in mind, asked for permission to speak. He told them all that he knew the Hunstman of Soest better than any man alive, not only as a brave soldier who knows the smell of powder but also as a good horseman, a perfect swordsman, expert in armoury and gunnery, and a skilled engineer as well. He added that the Hunstman had left not only his wife, with whom he had been cheated so treacherously, but all his possessions in Lippstadt, and had joined the Imperial service again. In the last campaign under Count von Götz he was taken prisoner by the Weimar army and trying to return to the Imperials he had massacred a corporal and six musketeers who had tried to recapture him. Now he had come with him to Vienna, wishing again to offer his service against His Roman Imperial Majesty's enemies, if he could obtain suitable terms as he wished no more to fight as a common soldier.

At that hour the illustrious company, excited by much good drinking, expressed their wish to see the Hunstman in person. And so Herzbruder was sent off to fetch me in a coach. On the way back he instructed me how to behave among these people of rank, as my good luck in the future might depend on it. When I arrived, I answered questions so briefly and clearly that all admired me, for I said nothing which did not make a good impression. In short I appeared to everybody a pleasant companion, for Count von der Wahl had already praised me as a good soldier. With that I too got drunk and, as can well be imagined, thereby disclosed my inexperience in Court behaviour.

The result was in the end that a colonel promised me a company of infantry in his regiment, which I accepted at once, thinking that to be a captain is truly no child's play! But the next day, Herzbruder blamed me for my foolishness and said if only I had resisted a little longer I would have risen higher.

So I was presented to a company as their captain, which with me in command was complete in numbers on paper, though there were not more than seven able-bodied soldiers among them. My corporals were for the most part old crocks, which caused me anxiety so that in the next heavy engagement I and my men were routed: Count von Götz lost his life, and Herzbruder his testicles, which were shot off. I got my share in the leg but it was only a minor wound.

We returned to Vienna to be cured and because we had left our possessions there. Although our wounds soon healed, Herzbruder developed a dangerous condition which the doctors at first could not diagnose as he became paralysed at all extremities like a choleric suffering from gall. Finally he was advised to undergo a cure of mineral water, and Griesbach in the Black Forest was recommended.

Fortune changes suddenly. Herzbruder had only recently intended to marry a noble lady and to this end had planned to have both of us raised to the rank of nobility. Now he had to change his mind as he had lost that by which he hoped to propagate a new generation. Further he was threatened by a wearisome illness due to his paralysis in which he needed good friends. So he made his last will and made me his only heir of all his belongings, chiefly because he saw that I threw my good fortune to the winds, relinquishing the command of my company to follow him to the spa and to serve him until he should regain his health.

When Herzbruder was able to ride again, we transferred our common purse by Note of Exchange to Basel, equipped ourselves with mounts and servants and went up the Danube to Ulm and from there to the recommended spa; it was May and a pleasant time for travelling.

In Griesbach we rented some lodgings and I rode on to Strasburg not only to collect my money which was transferred there from Basel, but also to find some experienced doctors who could prescribe for Herzbruder and advise him how to take the waters. They came with me and found that Herzbruder had been poisoned, but as the poison had not been strong enough to kill him outright, it had gone into his limbs and had now to be expelled by antidotes and sweating-baths. This cure would take about eight weeks.

Herzbruder now remembered when and through whom he had been poisoned, namely by those who would have liked to take over his position in the army. And when he learnt from the doctors that his recovery actually needed no watering cure, it was obvious that the field surgeon had been bribed by his enemies to send him so far away. Yet Herzbruder decided to complete his cure here as the spa had not only healthy air but offered pleasant company among the guests.

I did not wish to waste this time because I longed to see my wife again, and as Herzbruder did not need me urgently, I told him that I planned to visit her. He praised my intention and gave me some precious jewellery which I should present to her on his behalf and so ask for her forgiveness as he had been the cause for my long absence from her. So I rode to Strasburg where I collected my money and enquired how I could proceed with my journey in the safest way. Riding alone on horseback was impossible as all roads were unsafe through the many patrols from the numerous garrisons of the two fighting armies. I therefore got hold of a pass for a Strasburg post-rider; wrote several letters to my wife, her sister and parents and acted as if I would send him with them to Lippstadt. Pretending to have changed my mind, I snatched the pass back from the courier and sent my servant and horse back to the spa, disguised myself in a red and white livery and travelled thus by ship to Cologne, which was at that time a neutral city between the two opposing armies.

First I paid a visit to Jupiter, who once had declared me to be his Ganymede, to find out what had happened to the property I had left. But he was at that time again quite out of his mind and infuriated over the human race.

"Oh, Mercury," he addressed me, as soon as he saw me, "what news do you bring from Münster? Do men hope to conclude peace without my

SIMPLICIUS SIMPLICISSIMUS

good will? Nevermore! They once had peace – why did they not keep it? Have they not all indulged in vice, when they forced me to send them war? How have they deserved that I should give them peace again? Have they since atoned? Have they not turned worse and run into war as to a harvest festival? Have they repented through the famine I let loose among them, when thousands had to die of hunger. Has the horrid plague frightened them into amending their ways when millions perished? No, Mercury, no, those who survived, having seen that frightful suffering with their own eyes, have not reformed but have grown worse than they were before. And as they have not changed by so many punishments and tribulations from living their godless lives, what will they do if I should bestow them again with the pleasures of golden peace? I must fear that they, as once the giants, would dare to storm my heaven. But such foolhardiness I will rebuke in good time and will let them meanwhile waste in war."

As I well knew how to catch lice with this god, to bring him to a good humour I said: "Oh, great God, the whole world is sighing for peace and promises great improvement – why will you refuse it longer?"

"Indeed," answered Jupiter, "they sigh – but not for my sake but their own! Not that they may praise God under their own vine and fig tree, but that they may enjoy their fruits in idleness and voluptuousness. Only recently I asked a scabby tailor whether I should grant him peace and he answered that he did not care as he had to struggle with his needle in peace as in war. And the same answer I got from a brazier who told me that if in peacetime he has no church bells to found, he had enough work with guns and mortars during war. And a blacksmith in like manner said if he had no ploughs or carts to mend during wartime, he found enough warhorses and army wagons to keep him busy that he can well be without peace. You see, dear Mercury, why should I then grant them peace? Indeed, there are some who long for peace but only for their belly's sake and their earthly lust; on the other side there are many who wish to keep the war going because it is profitable. Just as masons and carpenters wish for peace to make money by rebuilding the burnt houses, the others who dare not make a living with their trade in peace desire the continuation of war to go on stealing."

Jupiter being in this frame of mind, I could not hope to gain much information from him of my own affairs. Therefore I did not disclose them to him, but went my way through well-known bypaths to Lippstadt. Still disguised as a foreign messenger, I enquired for my father-in-law and heard at once that he and my mother-in-law had died six months ago. My dear wife, who had given birth to a son, had also left this earth soon after childbed, the infant now being with her sister.

Thereupon all the letters I had written I delivered at my brother-in-law's house. He wanted to give me lodgings in order to hear from me (as the messenger) what had happened to Simplicius and what rank he now had. To this end I discussed my other self with him and my sister-in-law, and I told whatever I could think of that was praiseworthy, for the pocks had changed my face so much that nobody recognized me any more, except Herr von Schonstein, who, as my true friend, kept silent.

When I now told in detail how Herr Simplicius possessed many fine horses and servants and was dressed in a coat and hat of black velvet, trimmed with gold, my sister-in-law cried: "Truly I thought he was of no such humble origin as he pretended. The commandant of our town told my parents that my sister, who was indeed a pious virgin, had made a good match, although I myself never believed it would end happily. He started well in our garrison and took over Swedish or rather Hessian service, but when he wanted to collect his property in Cologne he was treacherously tricked to France. My sister, who was hardly married four weeks, and about half a dozen other citizens' daughters here, were left behind pregnant by him, and one after the other gave birth to baby sons, my sister the last of all. As my father and mother died and I and my husband cannot hope for children, we have adopted my sister's child as heir to all our possessions, and with the help of the commandant we have claimed his father's property in Cologne, which amounts to approximately three thousand gulden, so that the boy when he grows up has no reason to consider himself a poor man. I and my husband love the child so much that we would not surrender him to his father, even if he came in person to fetch him. The child is the most lovely among all his half-brothers and so like his father as if he were cut out of his image. I am sure if my brother-in-law would know what a handsome son he has here, he would not hesitate to come hither only to see the dear sweetheart – though his other bastards may prevent him."

With such talk my sister-in-law showed her love for my child, who was running about in his first trousers, and made my heart glad. I took out the jewels which Herzbruder had given to make a present on his behalf to my wife and said that these were given to me by Herr Simplicius as a greeting to his dearest wife and as she had died, I thought it fair to hand them over to his child. My brother and sister-in-law received them with joy and concluded that I must now be well off and a different fellow from that they imagined. I wished to depart and asked to be allowed to kiss the young Simplicius in the name of the older one that I could tell this to his father as a token of love. When this was done with the permission of my sister-in-law, my nose and the child's nose both started to bleed, that I thought my heart might break. Yet I concealed my affection and to give nobody time to ponder over the reasons for this sympathy of blood, I left at once.

After a fortnight of troublesome and dangerous travelling I returned again to the spa – but as a beggar, since I was robbed on the way.

On my return I found Herzbruder's condition rather worse than better in spite of the fact that the doctors and apothecaries had plucked him more than a fat goose. He appeared to me quite childish and he could hardly walk upright. I encouraged him as much as I could, but he was in a bad way. He realized it himself by the loss of strength that he would not last long; his best comfort was that I would be with him when he should close his eyes.

Contrary to him I made merry and looked for pleasure wherever I could find it, yet without neglecting Herzbruder's care. As I was now a widower, my youth and good living seduced me again to lovemaking, in which I indulged thoroughly, as I had fully forgotten the terror I suffered at Einsiedeln. There was at the spa a fine lady pretending to be of noble birth, but I thought she was more of mobility than of nobility, and to this man-trap I paid much courtship, so that in a short time I obtained not only free entrance to her but all the pleasure I could wish for. Yet I soon found repulsion in her wantonness and tried to rid myself of her in good manner, since I believed she was more interested to fleece my purse than to marry me. She harassed me with fiery and seducing glances and other protestations of her burning affection wherever I happened to be, that finally I became ashamed for both her and me.

I lived godlessly like an Epicurean and I enjoyed the spa more the longer I stayed, because guests arrived daily and the manner of life there appeared to me most delightful. I made acquaintance with the merriest people and began to learn courtesies and compliments which I had hardly known before. I was considered to be of nobility as my servants called me "Herr Captain", and no soldier of fortune could easily reach such rank at my age. So the rich dandies sought my company and I theirs, and even friendship. Pleasure, gambling, eating and drinking were my greatest labour and care, and many fine ducats were spent without thought as the purse of Olivier's inheritance was still of considerable weight.

In the mean time, Herzbruder's condition grew worse and worse till at last he had to pay the debt of nature and the doctors and physicians abandoned him, having fleeced him to their hearts' delight. He confirmed again his last will and made me the heir of all that which he had to expect from his father's inheritance. I supplied him with a magnificent funeral and dismissed his servants with their mourning clothes and a handsome reward.

Herzbruder's departure from life grieved me deeply, especially as he had been poisoned; and although I could not change it, yet it changed me! I fled all company and searched solitude to follow my sorrowful thoughts. Often I hid in the woods and pondered over the loss of my friend, such a one whom I would never find again in all my life. I tried to make plans for my future without being able to come to a decision. Sometimes I wanted to go back to war, yet then I thought that the poorest peasants in this land lead a better life than a colonel. Because no foraging patrols came into these mountains the farmyards were as in time of peace in good condition and the stalls full of cattle, whilst in the villages of the plains neither dog nor cat could be seen.

Once I listened to the song of the birds and pondered that the nightingale through her loveliness will cast a spell over all other birds to be silent, when on the opposite bank of the stream a beauty approached, who, although only dressed in the simple costume of a peasant girl, moved me more than any splendid demoiselle. She lifted a basket from her head in which she carried a lump of fresh butter to sell at the spa. She cooled the butter in the water that it might not melt in the great heat, whilst she sat down in the grass, throwing aside veil and peasant hat and wiping the sweat from her face. I could gaze at her at leisure and thought that I had never seen a more beautiful creature in all my life. Her body appeared to be perfect and without fault, arms and hands were snow-white, her face fresh and lovely, her black eyes full of fire and enchantment. When she packed up her butter again, I called to her:

"Dear maiden, your fair hands have cooled the butter, but your bright eyes have kindled a fire in my heart!"

As soon as she saw and heard me, she ran away as if she were chased, without answering a word and left me behind with all the follies which torment a frenzied lover. My desire to be warmed by this sun did not let me rest in my solitude but caused that I cared no more for the song of the nightingale than for the howling of wolves. So I also returned to the spa and sent my boy-servant along to delay the butter-maiden and to bargain with her until I came. He did his best, and so did I after my arrival, but I found a heart of stone, and cold stubbornness such as I would never have expected to find in a country girl. This made me even more ardent, although I should through my experience have known that she was not easily to be seduced.

At this time I should have had either a strong enemy or a good friend. The enemy to concentrate my thought against him and so forget my foolish love – or a friend who could give advice and warn me from the foolery which I planned. But unfortunately I had nothing but my money which confused me, my blind desires which led me astray and my coarse rashness which wrecked me and brought disaster.

I, fool, should have considered it a bad omen that we both wore mourning when we first met – I for Herzbruder and she for her parents; so that our love could find no good end. In a word I was truly entangled in a fool's net and quite blind without sense, as the child Cupid himself. Not having any hope to satisfy my bestial cravings in any other way, I decided to marry her. I thought after all I am only a peasant's son and will never possess a castle. This is a good land to live in, untouched by the gruesome war; besides I have still money enough to buy the best farm in the neighbourhood. Why should I not marry this honest country Gretl and establish myself in a quiet squire's seat among the peasants? Where could I find a more delightful homestead than near this spa, where I can see a new world every six weeks by the ever changing guests and glimpse the passing of the world from one era to another. A thousand of such plans I made until at last I asked my beloved to marry me, and though not without much effort, received her consent.

I made most splendid preparations for the wedding, for our future sky appeared all rosy-pink. I bought the whole farm where my bride was born and began to build a beautiful new mansion as if I intended rather to keep court than to keep house there. Before the wedding was over I had already more than thirty head of cattle: for so many the farm could sustain the year round. In short, I arranged everything for the very best and furnished the household as magnificently as my foolishness could imagine. But soon I discovered that my pipe had fallen into the muck, for hoping to sail with good wind to England, I arrived against all expectations in Holland. Now, but much too late, I found the reason why my bride had been so obstinate in refusing my proposal. It grieved me most that I could not lament my shame to anybody. Although I understood very well that I had to dance to the music but such knowledge neither made me more patient nor more God-fearing. And seeing myself deceived, I began to deceive the traitress myself and went out grazing on other meadows wherever I could.

I spent more of my time at the spa than at home, and for a year at least I let my household care for itself. My wife became just as negligent as I. An oxen which I had slaughtered at the farm, she salted in baskets, and when she had to prepare a sucking-pig for me, she tried to pluck it like a bird. Indeed she tried to roast crayfish on the grill and trout on a spit, from which examples one can imagine how she looked after me. Moreover she was very fond of the beloved wine which she shared freely with other good folk. All this indicated my future perdition.

One day I walked down the valley with some cavaliers to visit a company at the lower bath, when we met an old peasant with a goat on a rope, which he wanted to sell. Thinking I recognized him, I asked him from where he came with his goat? Taking off his hat, he replied:

"Your lordship, this I can truly not tell you!"

To which I queried: "I hope you have not stolen the creature."

"No," he answered, "but I bring her from the small town down in the valley, the name of which I cannot mention in the presence of a nanny-goat."

This moved my company to laughter and because I changed colour they imagined that I was annoyed or ashamed that the peasant gave me such a pert answer. But I had quite different thoughts; by the great wart which the peasant had in the middle of his forehead – like a unicorn, I was at once sure that he was my dad from the Spessart. I wanted to play the soothsayer before revealing myself and delighting him with such a stately son, as my clothes proved me to be, so I addressed him:

"Dear old father, is your home not in the Spessart?"

"Yes, your lordship," he answered.

I continued: "Did not the troopers some eighteen years ago loot and burn your house and farm?"

"Indeed, may God have mercy," the peasant replied, "but it is not quite as long ago!"

I questioned him further: "Did you then not have two children, namely a grown-up daughter and a young boy, who tended your sheep?"

"Your lordship," cried my dad, "The daughter was my child but not the lad. I only reared him as a foster child."

By this I realized at once that I was not the son of this coarse peasant lout, which partly made me glad, but also worried me thinking that I must be a bastard or foundling. I therefore asked my dad how he had got hold of the lad and why he had taken him to bring him up as his own?

"Oh," said he, "that is a strange story: the war gave him to me and the war took him away."

As I now feared some detrimental facts about my birth might come to light, I turned our conversation to the goat again, asking whether he had sold her for the kitchen, which seemed strange to me since the guests at the spa were not used to eating old goat's meat.

"Oh no, your lordship," the peasant answered, "there are enough goats at the inn and they would not pay much. I am bringing the goat for the countess who is taking the waters at the spa. Doctor Knowall has prescribed certain herbs for the goat to eat and with her milk he will then mix medicine for the countess to drink and be cured. Folks say she has trouble with her innards and if the goat can help her, it will have done more good than the doctor and his apothecary together."

In the mean time, I was thinking how I could contrive to speak more intimately with the peasant. I offered him a thaler more for the goat than the doctor or countess wanted to pay. To this he agreed at once, as a small bargain easily persuades, on condition that he might tell the countess and if she would pay the same she should have priority. He promised to tell me in the evening how the bargain went. So my dad went his way and I mine with my company. But I, not caring to stay with them any longer, turned back to find my dad again. He still had his goat as the others did not want to pay as much as I had offered, and I was amazed that such people could be so mean. I took him to my new farm, paid him for the goat and having made him slightly tipsy, I asked from where the lad had come of whom we had spoken earlier.

"Sir," he said, "the Mansfeld war gave him to me and the Battle of Nördlingen took him away."

"That must have been a cheerful story," I said, and asked him to tell it to me to pass the time.

So he began: "When Count Mansfeld had lost the battle at Höchst* his fleeing army scattered far and wide, not knowing where to retreat. Many came to the Spessart to hide in the woods. But whilst they tried to escape death in the plains, they found it among us in the mountains. As both fighting parties marauded and butchered each other on our land, we too knocked them on their heads. No peasant then went out into the forest without a gun, as we could not stay at home with our ploughs.

"Among this tumult in a wild and vast forest yet near my farmstead, I met a beautiful young lady on a fine horse, just when I had heard nearby some gunshots. I thought at first she was a man for she rode like one. But when I saw her lifting up her hands and eyes to Heaven and heard her calling out in mournful tone and foreign tongue to God, I lowered my gun with which I intended to fire at her and uncocked it, as her lament and actions assured me she was a women in sorrow. So we approached each other and seeing me she called: 'If you are an honest Christian I beg you for God and his mercy, indeed for the sake of the Last Judgment, to bring me to some good woman who with God's help will assist me to deliver the burden from my body!'

"These words evoking such holy thoughts, together with her tender voice and in spite of sadness her beautiful and enchanting face, moved me to pity. I led her horse by the bridle through thickets and undergrowth to the densest forest, where I had hidden my wife, child, servants and cattle. Within half an hour she gave birth to the boy of whom we spoke to day."

So my dad ended his story and drank again, for I encouraged him to it. When he had emptied his glass, I asked him: "And what happened then to the lady?"

He replied: "When she was in childbed, she begged me to be Godfather and have the child baptized as soon as possible. She also gave me her name and her husband's name, so that it could be written in the church register. Then she opened her satchel, in which she had precious jewellery and gave to me, to my wife and child, to my maid and another woman so much that we could all be well satisfied. But whilst she was doing this and telling us of her husband, she died before our eyes, commending her child to our care.

"As there was such chaos in the land so that scarcely anyone could stay at home, we had difficulty in finding a priest to conduct the funeral and baptise the child, but when that was finally done, our burgomaster and the vicar ordered me to rear the child until it grew up; for my cost and trouble I should take all the possessions of the lady except a few rosaries, precious stones and jewellery which I should keep for the child. So my wife weaned the baby with goat's milk and gladly looked after him and thought, when he was grown up, to give him our daughter in marriage. But after the Battle of Nördlingen, I lost both boy and girl and everything we possessed."

"You told me," I said to my dad, "a pretty story, yet have forgotten the best of it – you did not mention the names of either the lady, her husband or the child."

"Sir," he replied, "I did not think that you would care to know. The lady's name was Susanna Ramsi, her husband, Captain Sternfels von Fuchsheim, and as my name is Melchior I had the lad christened Melchior Sternfels von Fuchsheim and written in the register."

So I learnt at last that I was the true son of my hermit and of Governor Ramsay's sister – but alas, too late, as both my parents were dead. Of my kinsman Ramsay I could learn nothing except that the people of Hanau had expelled him and his Swedish garrison and that he had gone quite mad from grief and rage.

I regaled my godfather with more wine and the next day had his wife fetched too. When I revealed myself to them, they could not believe me until I showed them a black hairy spot which I had on my breast.

25

SIMPLICIUS VISITS THE CENTRE
OF THE EARTH

SHORTLY AFTERWARDS, I rode with my godfather down into the Spessart to obtain documentary evidence of my origin and legitimate birth. I achieved this without much trouble from the church register and my godfather's witness. I also visited the vicar, who had been in Hanau and taken care of me. He gave me a document stating where my father had died and that I had lived with him until his death, and that I later had spent some time under the name of Simplicius with Governor Ramsay in Hanau. Moreover, I had the whole story according to witnesses drawn up in a statement and certified by a notary, for who knew when I might be in need of it. This journey cost me more than four hundred thalers, for on the way back I was caught by marauders, robbed of my horse and looted so that I and my godfather escaped naked and scarcely alive.

In the mean time, things went badly at home. Since my wife had heard that I was a nobleman, she not only played the great lady but neglected everything in the household too, which I suffered in silence for she was great with child. In addition, bad luck had struck at my cow-sheds so that most of my best cattle perished.

All this would have been endurable but misfortune comes seldom alone. In the hour when my wife gave birth, the maid also was brought to childbed. The child which she bore resembled me completely, but that which my wife bore was the counterfeit of my farmhand. Moreover the other young lady whom I had courted earlier, also had a child which she laid on my doorstep the very same night with a note that I was the father.

Thus I had three children at once and expected that from every corner another one might crawl out, which brought me many grey hairs. But so it happens if a man follows his bestial desires in such a vile and godless life as I led. And now what was to be done? I had to have them baptized and was heavily punished by the magistrate. And as the government at the time was Swedish and I had formerly served the Emperor, my fine was even higher. All this was only the prelude of my approaching complete disaster.

Although I was deeply grieved over these many calamities, my wife on the contrary took it lightly; indeed she plagued me day and night over the pretty gift which had been laid at my door and the heavy penalty by which I was punished. Had she known about my affair with the maid, she would have tormented me even more, but that good maid was so loyal that the same amount of money which I had to pay as penalty, persuaded her to attribute her child to a fop who the year before had paid me visits and was at my wedding, but whom she hardly knew. In spite of that she had to leave the house as my wife suspected me of that which I suspected her with the farmhand. And yet I dared not suggest it, as otherwise I would have to admit that I could not have been both with her and the maid the same night. The idea grieved me deeply that I should bring up the child of a farmhand yet had no heir of my own; but I must be silent and thankful that no one knew of it.

With such thoughts I tormented myself daily whilst my wife delighted in wine at every hour, for she had become used to the wine-jug since our marriage, that it was seldom far away from her mouth, and scarcely a night went by that she did not fall asleep in drunkenness. In that way she drank her child to death and inflamed her own intestines so severely that her own life was soon snuffed out, and so I became a widower again which touched my heart to such a degree that I almost laughed myself sick.

My old freedom was regained but my purse was emptied of money. As my huge household was burdened with farmhands and too many cattle, I took my godfather Melchior and my godmother his wife as father and mother, and accepted my bastard Simplicius, who had been laid on my doorstep, as my heir. I entrusted house, farm and all my property to the old couple except for a few gold coins and some jewellery which I had saved for extreme need. A disgust for living with women and for their company enveloped me and I was determined, having undergone such harm through them, never to marry again.

The old people who in rustic matters could not be equalled changed my household into a different shape at once. They got rid of such servants and cattle that were of no use and replaced them with profitable ones. My former dad and mum gave me good courage and promised if I would let them manage the farm, there would always be a fine horse in the stable for me and so much profit that I could drink my measure of wine with any honest man. I soon noticed what kind of people now managed the farm: my godfather tilled the fields with his labourers, he bargained for cattle, wood and resin more thriftily than any Jew, whilst my godmother began to breed cattle and knew how to save the milk pennies better than ten such wives as I had had before. So in a short time my farmyard was furnished with the necessary implements and livestock that soon it was considered the best in the land, whilst I was able to pursue my walks and follow my contemplations. I realized that my foster mother would never be caught napping when I saw how she gained more profit by her bees alone in wax and honey than my wife had earned from cattle, pigs and all the rest.

I once made a walk round the spa to take the spring waters – I had given up the company of dandies as I had begun to follow the thriftiness of my old couple who advised me not to consort with people who wilfully wasted their own and their parents' possessions – and by chance I met a company of fellows who were just discussing a strange thing, namely the Mummelsee, a lake which they said was bottomless and quite nearby on one of the highest mountains. They had fetched a few old peasants who told us what they had heard of the miraculous lake and I listened with great pleasure to these stories, although I considered them sheer fables, appearing to me as mendacious as some of the tales of Plinius.

One peasant said that if an odd number of peas or stones or something similar were wrapped in a handkerchief and put into the water, their numbers would change into even numbers, and the same would happen vice versa. Almost all of them told and confirmed with examples that if stones were thrown in, a horrible storm with rain, hail and gales would arise, however beautiful the weather had previously been. They further told of strange stories which happened: that miraculous gnomes and water-sprites had been seen and these had spoken to the people. Once, when some herdsmen grazed their cattle near the lake, a brown bull had come out of the water and joined the cattle; a little gnome followed him to drive him back into the lake but the bull would not obey until the mannikin swore that if he did not come back he should suffer all the pains of the human race, and at those words both returned into the lake. Another told how when the lake was frozen, it happened that a peasant crossed the lake without harm together with his oxen and a load of tree-trunks commonly used for floorboards, but when his dog followed him, the ice broke under it and the wretched animal sank never to be seen again. Another declared solemnly that a huntsman, following some game nearby, saw a water-spirit sitting in the lake with his lap full of coined gold as if he were playing with it. When the hunstman aimed his gun at him, the spirit faded into the water and a voice was heard: "If you had only asked me to help you in your poverty, I would have made you and your kin rich for ever."

Such stories appeared to me like fairy tales for the entertainment of children and I laughed at them, for I could not believe that a bottomless lake existed on a high mountain. Among the peasants were old trustworthy men who reported that within living memory high and princely persons had visited the lake; a raft was built and launched onto it by a reigning Duke of Württemberg to measure the depth, and when the measurers had let down the weight with already nine bales of twine – a measure better understood by Black Forest peasant-women than by myself or surveyors – they still failed to find the bottom. Moreover the raft started to sink, contrary to the nature of wood, so that the men had to abandon their task and hurriedly make for land. Even today parts of the raft can be seen on the shore, and a stone stands there carved with the Württemberg coat of arms as a memento of this event. Others again proved through witnesses that an Arch-Duke of Austria intended to drain the lake but many people dissuaded him and through the peasants' petitions the plan was abandoned, for they feared the whole land might be submerged and all drowned. Further, some high princes had ordered barrels of live trout to be emptied into the lake, but within an hour they had all died in front of their eyes and drifted to the outflow, although the stream into which the lake flows is by nature full of trout.

These last stories made me almost believe in the earlier ones and they aroused my curiosity that I made up my mind to see this miraculous lake. I thought that the German name "Mummelsee" suggested clearly that a kind of mummery was connected with its character so that it was impossible to fathom its nature and depth. I made my way to the same place where only a year ago I had first met my departed wife and tasted the sweet poison of love. I lay down in the shade on the green grass but no longer noticed how the nightingale sang, being deep in contemplation of how my life had changed since then. I visualized that here I had turned from a free fellow into a slave of love, that from an officer I had become a peasant, from a rich farmer, a poor nobleman, from a Simplicius, a Melchior, from a widower, a husband and from a husband, a cuckold, and from a cuckold a widower again. In short I had changed from a son of a peasant into the son of a noble soldier and back again to be the son of my old dad. I recalled how fate bereaved me of Herzbruder and in his stead gave to me an old married couple; I pondered over the godly life and death of my father and the pitiful death of my mother and the many changes I had experienced in my life, and I could not hold back my tears. As I was lamenting, remembering how much good money I had owned and wasted, a pair of old tippling topers whom the cholic had lamed in the limbs sat down beside me, for it was a pleasant place to rest. Believing they were alone they began to complain of their miseries. One said to the other:

"My doctor has sent me here as he despaired of my health. Would that I had never seen him in all my life, or else that he had recommended these waters before, because then I would be richer and healthier since this spa is doing me good."

"Indeed," replied the other, "God is to be thanked that He has given me little wealth, for if my doctor had expected more from me he would never have sent me to this spa; he would have shared it all between himself and his apothecaries until I died. These misers do not advise such healthy places until they know there is nothing more to pluck, in truth whilst they know you have money they keep you sick."

The two fellows had still more complaints about their doctors which I will not report lest the medical profession become my enemies and give me a purge to expel soul from body. I recount this only because the latter patient's gratitude to God for not bestowing wealth on him consoled me so that all my doubt and depression regarding my lack of money disappeared. I resolved neither to aim for honour, gold nor for any other thing that the world commonly loves, and intended to devote my life to contemplation and godliness, to repent my sins and like my beloved father reach the highest degree of virtue.

My craving to see the Mummelsee grew when I learnt from my foster father that he had been there and knew the way to it. But when he heard of my intent, he said:

"What will you gain even if you go there? You will see nothing but the image of a pond in the middle of a great forest, and reap only regret and tired feet, as it is impossible to ride there, and all you will know is the way there and the way back. I would never have gone there myself had I not been forced to flee when doctor Daniel (he meant the Duc d'Anguin), with his soldiers swept through the land down to Philippsburg."

My rashness took no heed of his warning and I engaged a man to guide me there. When my dad saw my serious intent he offered to go with me himself as the oats were sown and on the farm there was neither hoeing nor reaping to be done. He loved me so much that he did not like to let me out of sight and as everyone in the country believed me to be his real son, he was proud of me and behaved as any humble man might do whose son has become through good fortune a fine gentleman.

So we climbed over hill and dale and reached the Mummelsee in less than six hours, for my godfather was as energetic as a beetle and as nimble on his feet as a young man. There we ate and drank what we had brought with us, for the long walk to the top of the mountain had made us hungry and tired. After refreshing ourselves, I examined the lake and found several cut timbers in it which I believed to be the remnants of the Württemberg raft. With the aid of geometry I measured the length and breadth of the water for it was too tiresome to walk round and measure it by paces and feet. I wrote the results in reduced scale in my notebook and when this was done I tried to find out what truth there was in the legend that a storm would arise if a stone were thrown into the lake, especially as the sky was bright and the air still and calm. I had already proved by tasting the mineral contents of the water that according to the legend no trout could live in the lake.

To begin this experiment I walked to the left side of the lake to a place where the water, which otherwise was as clear as crystal, was as black as coal because of its horrifying depth and here it appeared so frightening that the sheer look of it was terrifying. There I started to throw in stones, as huge as I could lift and carry. My godfather refused to help but warned and begged me with all his strength to desist. But I persisted in my labours and those stones which I could not lift because of their size and weight, I rolled along until I had pitched more than thirty into the lake.

Now black clouds began to cover the sky from where a gruesome thunder could be heard. My godfather, standing on the other side of the lake at the outlet and lamenting my labour, shouted to me to save myself from rain and fearful storm or even greater disaster. But contrariwise, I answered:

"Dad, I will stay and see the end of it, may it rain battleaxes!"

"Aye, indeed," he answered, "you act like all reckless rascals who do not care if the whole world is destroyed."

While I listened to his scolding I gazed incessantly into the depth of the lake expecting to see the rising of some bubbles which usually happens when stones are thrown into still or running water. I could see nothing like this but very deep down in the abyss I saw some creatures flapping about, whose shape reminded me of frogs swishing around like small rockets. The closer they came towards me the greater they grew, and to my amazement they looked more and more like humans; when they finally were quite close to me I was seized with horror and fear.

"Oh," I cried in terror and wonder, loud enough for my dad to hear beyond the lake, through the crashing thunder, "How great are God's miracles in the bowels of the earth and the depth of the waters."

As soon as I had uttered these words, one of the water sprites appeared above the water and answered:

"You say that before you have seen anything! What would you say if you were truly in the centre of the earth and beheld our homes which you have so wantonly disturbed?"

Meanwhile more such water creatures came up like little ducks from everywhere, all looking at me and carrying up the stones I had thrown in, at which I was much astonished. The first and most noble among them, whose robes shimmered with pure gold and silver, threw a shining stone to me, big as a pigeon's egg, green and translucent like an emerald, calling:

"Take this jewel as a memento of us and our lake."

Scarcely had I taken it into my possession than it was as if the air would suffocate or drown me; no longer could I stand upright but spun round like a spindle and finally tumbled into the lake. As soon as I was in the water I recovered and could breathe as well as in the air through the power of the stone. And like the water spirits I was able to swim about without difficulty and dived with them into the abyss in large circles just like a flock of birds descends from the heights to alight on the earth.

When my godfather saw this miracle, at least what happened above the water, and my sudden disappearance, he rushed away from the lake towards home, as if his head were burning. There he told the whole story, especially that in a thunderstorm the water-creatures had brought up again the stones I had thrown down, putting them in their former place, and instead had taken me down with them. Some believed him but most thought it was a fable. Others had the opinion that I had drowned myself like Empedocles from Agrigento who threw himself into the crater of Mount Etna to achieve an immortal name, for they had noted my melancholic despair. Indeed some would have assumed, had they not known my bodily strength, that my foster father had murdered me to live as a greedy old man alone as master of my estate. Thus at the spa and in the country, people gossiped of nothing else but of the Mummelsee, of my dad and me and of my disappearance.

Plinius writes in his second book on geometry that it is 42,000 stadia to the centre of the earth. The prince of the Mummelsee who was my guide assured me that it was 900 German miles, whether it was measured from Germany or from the Antipodes. They had to make such journeys through similar lakes of which there were as many inside the earth as there were days in the year, and their beginnings and endings all met in the King's palace. This vast distance we traversed in less than one hour so that we kept up almost with the speed of the moon yet without enduring stress or fatigue and in this gentle downward gliding I was able to converse with the prince. Noticing his friendliness I asked him why he was taking me on such a long, dangerous and, for humans, unattainable journey? Modestly he answered that the way was not long nor dangerous, as I was in his company and I had the stone with me, but it was not surprising that I found it miraculous. He had fetched me on his King's orders, who wished to speak to me and show me the wonders of nature inside the earth and in the waters, which I had admired from the ground before I ever had glimpsed a shadow of it.

I asked him further to explain why God had created so many miraculous lakes since they were of no use to mankind but could bring danger. He answered:

"Rightly you ask about what you do not know or understand. These lakes are created for three reasons. Firstly, through them all seas and especially the great oceans, whatever names they may have, are fixed to the earth as if with nails. Secondly through these lakes all waters are driven from the abyss of the oceans as if through pipes and hoses into all the wells of the earths, feeding all the fountains in the whole world, moistening the soil, refreshing the plants and quenching the thirst of man and beast. Thirdly we live in these lakes as reasonable creatures of God, fulfil our tasks and praise God, the creator, for His great works of wonder. This is the reason for the existence of the lakes and ourselves, and will be until the last Day of Judgment. If we did not fulfil what God and nature has destined, the waters would disappear and the earth through the heat of the sun would ignite and finally perish through fire and be regenerated. But such is not for us to know, only God; we can but guess and your chemists with all their knowledge can merely grope."

When I heard him talking thus and quoting the Holy Scriptures, I asked him if they were mortal creatures who after the present world expected eternal life, or if they were spirits, who whilst the world existed only performed their assigned tasks? To which he answered:

"We are no spirits but mortal people, having reason and soul, which however will die and perish with our body. From others of God's creatures we differ in this way. The holy angels are spirits made in God's image, intelligent, free, pure, beautiful, swift and immortal, created to praise and honour God. Since however innumerable angels have fallen through pride, God created your first parents in his image with an intelligent and immortal soul and equipped with a body to propagate so that their offspring may surpass the hosts of fallen angels. God gave mankind the world with all the creatures to live on it, to praise God and find their livelihood. The difference between man and angel was that man was burdened with a mortal body, not knowing what was good or evil. We water spirits consider ourselves as a link between you and all other living creatures in the world, since we too have reasoning souls, which however will disappear when we die. I talk and understand nothing of eternity, being unable to enjoy it, but our gracious Creator has bestowed on us in this world, sound reason, knowledge of the will of God, healthy bodies, long life, noble freedom and sufficient science and understanding of nature: finally, the most important, we cannot sin and are therefore not subject to punishment nor the wrath of God, nor do we suffer bodily disease."

I answered: "I do not understand, if you cannot commit a crime and are subject to no punishment, why then do you need a King? How can you boast of freedom if you are subject to a monarch? And how can you be born or die, if you know neither pain nor disease?"

To that my little prince replied: "We have not our King that he may administer justice nor that we may serve him, but that he may, like the queen of the bees, direct our affairs. Just as our womenfolk find no pleasure *in coitu*, they suffer no birth pangs which I could compare with cats which conceive in pain and give birth in pleasure. We die not in pain nor from fragile old age, even less from illness but we are extinguished like a candle which has burnt its time and our souls vanish with our bodies. Our freedom is greater than that of the mightiest monarch among mortals, as we cannot be killed by you nor any other creature, nor forced against our wish nor imprisoned, for we can pass through fire, water, air and earth without strain or stress."

"If it is so," I said, "your race is more highly blessed and gifted by the Creator than ours."

"Oh, no!" the prince replied, "You sin if you believe this and blame God's grace. You are more blessed than we, as you are created to behold the face of God in eternity and you will enjoy in one moment more joy and bliss than our whole race can enjoy from the creation to the Last Judgment."

"But what use is that to the damned?" I asked.

He answered with a counter question: "How can you blame God's grace if one of you forgets himself and indulges in evil lust, gives way to his low desires and thus lowers himself to the status of the beast and through disobedience to God likens himself to the hellish rather than to the godly spirits? The lament of those who willingly plunge into damnation does not deprive your race of nobility, since they could have reached eternal bliss if only they had followed the way."

As I would hardly have the chance on the earth's surface to enquire, I made use of the opportunity to ask the prince to tell me the cause why such great thunderstorms arose when stones were thrown into the lake. He answered: "Because everything of weight will fall towards the centre of the earth and as these lakes are all connected with each other and bottomless, the stones will naturally fall upon our homes and remain there if we would not carry them back again to the place from where they came. We carry them back with a rage to frighten and check the audacity of the stone-throwers. Through this task of our race you will understand the necessity of our existence, for if we would permit it and the stones would not again be removed, in the end the canals through which the wells on earth are supplied, would be blocked and great damage, indeed the end of the world, could occur."

I thanked him for this explanation and asked further why the waters, although they all came from the abyss of the great oceans, were of different smell, taste, power and effect. Some wells contain a lovely sour water of healing property, others have a bad taste and are detrimental to drink, indeed poisonous and deadly, some are lukewarm, others boiling hot and some ice cold.

The prince answered: "All these facts have their natural causes: if the water runs through stones, it will remain cold and sweet, but if it passes on its way through metals it adopts their taste, smell, character and power, so that it becomes healing or detrimental to mankind. The great belly of the earth is in each place of different structure; there is gold, silver, copper, tin, lead and mercury and minerals like sulphur and salt with all its varieties as sal gemmae, sal radicum, sal nitrum, sal armoniacum, sal petrae; there are white, red, yellow and green colours such as vitriol, bismuth, lapis lazuli, alumen, arsenicum, and from these the waters are affected."

Finally I asked the prince whether it would be possible to bring me back through some other lake than the Mummelsee to the surface of the world.

"Indeed," he answered, "why not – if it is God's will! In this way our great grandparents have guided some Caanites to America, after having escaped Joshua's sword and after having thrown themselves in despair into a lake. Still today their descendants point out the lake from which their parents once originated."

Seeing that he was surprised at my astonishment – as if his story were not worthy to be wondered at – I asked him whether they were never amazed to see something strange and rare among us humans. To this he answered:

"We are not amazed any more about you – but – that you, created to participate in eternal life and heavenly bliss, are led astray through earthly desires that you lose your claim to Heaven and the sight of the most holy face of God and that you throw yourselves to the fallen angels into eternal damnation! Alas, if only our race could be in your place, how everybody would make the greatest effort to pass that trial of your fleeting earthly life better than you do. For the life that you live is not your life, and that which you call life is only a short moment which God has granted that you may discover Him and approach Him so that He may take you to Him."

This was the end of our conversation as we came near to the seat of the King to whom I was brought without ceremony or loss of time. I had much cause to marvel about His Majesty, for I saw no courtiers nor stately pomp, neither a chancellor nor secret counsellors nor interpreters, lackeys nor bodyguards, indeed not even a jester, kitchen master, servants, pages, favourites nor flatterers. But around him floated the princes of all the lakes which are in the world, each dressed in the costume of the country to which their lake leads from the centre of the earth. So I saw assembled the images of Chinese, Africans, Tartars and Mexicans, Samoyeds and Moluccans which offered indeed a remarkable spectacle. As in a book of costume, I discovered the shapes of Persians, Japanese, Muscovites, Finns and Lapps, and all the nations of the world. He who was in charge of the Lake Pilatus carried a broad honest beard and a pair of wide breeches like a respectable Swiss citizen.

I did not need to make many compliments, as the King himself began at once to talk to me in good German. His first question was: "Why did you dare to throw so many stones wantonly into our realm?"

To which I answered briefly: "Because in my country everybody is allowed to knock at a closed door."

"And what," he replied, "if you will receive the punishment for your impertinent importunity?"

I answered: "I cannot be punished with more than death, but since I have seen and experienced so many wonders which among millions no other man was fortunate to see, I consider my death as no punishment at all."

"Oh, miserable blindness!" said the King, lifting his eyes towards Heaven in astonishment. "You humans can only die once, and if you are Christian you should not wish to die before you have ascertained through faith and love to God the infallible hope that your soul will behold the face of our Lord as soon as your dying body closes its eyes. But now I have to talk to you about different matters.

"I have been told," he continued, "that the humans, especially the Christians, expect the last day to approach soon, not only because all prophecies of the Sibyls have been fulfilled but also because every creature on earth is so terribly addicted to depravity that Almighty God will no longer hesitate to make an end of the world. As then our race too must perish with the world and wither in fire (for we can only live in water) we are horrified about the advent of such terrible times. Therefore we have fetched you here to learn whether we should foster fear or hope. Although we can find no evidence from the stars nor from the earth itself indicating the coming disaster, we have to ask those to whom the Saviour has given signs of his return. So we ask you in all urgency to confess if the true faith still reigns on earth, or will the approaching heavenly Judge find it there no more?"

I answered the King that he enquired about matters too high for me to answer, in particular, to predict the future and the arrival of our Saviour which was only known to God himself.

"Well, then," he replied, "tell me how the people of the world behave in their various professions that I may draw my conclusions from that as to whether the world and my race are doomed to perish, or whether I and my people may hope for a long life and a blissful reign. And afterwards I will show you what few have seen and reward you with such a precious gift to give you pleasure all your life, if only you will confess the truth."

As I remained silent and pondered, the King continued and said:

"Come, come, start with the highest and finish with the lowest! It has to be done if you wish to return to the surface of the earth."

So I answered: "If I have to begin with the highest I will rightly start with the clergy: all of them, whatever religion they profess, are just as Eusebius has described them in his sermon – contemptuous of leisure, evading all lusts, eager in their obligations, patient when in contempt, poor in goods and gold but rich in their conscience, modest to their merits but forceful against their faults. Eagerly they serve God and lead their fellow men more through their good example than words to God's empire. The theologians are like St Hieronimus, the cardinals like St Borromaeus and the monks must be compared with hermits in the desert of Thebes! The temporal heads and administrators have only in mind to serve our beloved justice which they administer without regard for rank, to poor and rich alike!

Our merchants trade not from greed or for the sake of profit but to serve their fellow men with goods, which they bring from foreign lands. The innkeepers do not want to become rich but keep their houses to refresh the hungry, the thirsty and tired travellers as an act of charity! Physicians and apothecaries do not seek their own advantage but only the health of their patients! The craftsmen know nothing of cheating, lies or defrauding, but are anxious to supply their customers with lasting and honest work! Our tailors are pained by the sight of stolen cloth and the weavers in their honesty remain so poor that no mouse can find enough food in their houses! We know of no usury but the rich will help the needy quite willingly in Christian charity and if a poor man cannot pay without detriment to his livelihood, the rich man will voluntarily renounce his debt!

"We know no haughtiness, for everybody realizes and remembers that he is mortal! There is no envy, for everyone knows and recognizes his neighbour as the image of God, beloved by his Creator! None is angry with the other, as they know that Christ has suffered and died for all of them! We hear of no unchastity or disorderly fleshly lust among us – what takes place is done from the desire and love to bring up children! No drunkards can be found – one man may honour the other with a drink but then they will be satisfied with a small degree of Christian tipsiness! There is no slackness in the service of God, everyone shows great eagerness in serving our Lord, and at present we have for this very reason such bloody wars on earth as one part of us believes that the other does not serve God well enough! There are no more misers among us but only thrifty men, no money wasters only generous people; no marauders who rob and murder but only soldiers who protect their fatherland; no lazy beggars but men with contempt for wealth and love for voluntary poverty; no Jews usuring in grain and wine but men with foresight who preserve abundant provisions against future famine for the sake of the population!"

I paused a little considering what else I could bring forward but the King said he had already heard as much as he needed to know. If I wished his people would return me at once to the place from whence they had taken me, but if I preferred – 'for I well see that you are somewhat curious," he said – to look at this or that in his empire, I would be safely guided under his jurisdiction wherever I wished to go. And afterwards he would release me with a gift which would well satisfy me.

As I appeared undecided and was unable to find an answer, he turned to some of his people who were just going into the depths of the Mare Del Zur to fetch provisions as if to a garden or hunting expedition. To them he said: "Take him with you and return with him soon that he may today be put back on the surface of the earth." To me he said I should in the mean time consider something of eternal memory which if it were in his power he would give me as a memento to take back to the earth.

So I glided with the water creatures through a grotto several miles wide until we reached the ground of the mentioned Pacific Ocean. There stood coral rocks, large as oak trees, from which the creatures picked pieces of coral not yet hardened and coloured, which they ate as we eat the antlers of young stags. We saw shells of snails high as a bastion and wide as a barn gate; also pearls thick as a fist which they ate instead of eggs, and many other still more strange miracles of the sea. The ground was covered everywhere with emeralds, turquoise, rubies, diamonds and sapphires and other precious stones, mostly of the size of pebbles such as lie in our streams.

Here and there we saw gigantic rocks reaching upwards for many miles jutting high above the water supporting enchanting islands. All round they were adorned with delightful and marvellous vegetation of maritime plants and inhabited by all sorts of strange crawling, standing and walking creatures as the earth is by men and beasts. The fishes, of which we saw small and big ones in an unaccountable multitude floating through the waters above, reminded me exactly of our birds, which in spring and autumn amuse themselves in the air. As it was full moon and a bright period, the Antipodes having night and the Europeans day, I could see the moon through the water and the stars, including the Antarctic pole, which astonished me greatly. But my guide explained that if it were daytime, it would be more miraculous still as we would see that at the bottom of the ocean there were mountains and valleys more ravishing yet than the most beautiful landscapes of the earth.

When our expedition had gathered sufficient provisions, we returned again through a different grotto back to the centre of the earth. On the way I told some of our company that I had believed the centre of the earth was hollow and in this cavity the pygmies ran around as in a treadmill, turning the earth around that it may be shone upon everywhere by the sun – which according to Aristarch and Copernicus stands motionless in the middle of the sky. They laughed heartily over my simplicity and said I should abandon the theory of those scientists and my own imagination as sheer dreams, and should rather consider what gift to ask from the King so that I may not return to earth with empty hands. I answered that the wonders I had seen had confused me so much that I could think of nothing and asked them to advise me what I should desire from the King.

Since the King ruled over all the wells in the whole world I concluded that I would beg of him a health-giving fountain to rise on my farmland; nothing would I covet more than to bring a rare spring back to my countrymen on earth, for their blessing and to the honour of the King of the Waters and to my eternal memory.

The prince replied that if I desired such a gift he would speak a good word on my behalf, although it was a matter of indifference to the King whether he was honoured or shamed on earth. And so we came again to the centre of the earth and to the King, just as he and his princes were about to dine. They had neither wine nor strong drinks but drank pearls instead which were not yet hardened, being similar to raw or soft-boiled eggs. Then I observed that the sun shone upon one lake after the other and its rays penetrated through them into this tremendous abyss, so that the water sprites lacked no light. I saw sunlight in these depths shining as pleasantly as on earth and even shadows were cast. Thus the lakes served these creatures as windows through which they received light and warmth, and where some lakes and cavities were curved the brilliance was transported everywhere through reflection into all the corners by natural rocks covered with crystal, diamonds and garnets.

The time had come for me to go home again and the King commanded me to tell him what favour he should grant me. I answered that he could bestow no greater benefice upon me than to create a good medicinal spring on my land.

"Only that!" the King said, "I believed you would have wished to take with you some large emeralds from the American ocean, but now I see there is no greed among you Christians!"

With that he gave me a stone of rare and lustrous colours saying: "Take this with you. Wherever you put it upon the soil it will begin to seek the centre of the earth again and pass through the appropriate layers of mineral until it returns to us, sending back to you on our behalf a splendid mineral spring for your health and blessing which your revelation of the truth deserves."

Thereupon the prince of the Mummelsee took me again under his guidance and we traversed together the way through the lakes by which we had come. The journey back appeared to me far longer than the way there – I estimated it to be about two-and-a-half thousand well-measured German miles – but the reason that the time appeared so long was certainly because my companion hardly spoke with me except to say that his kind could live to an age of three, four or even five hundred years and for this time without disease. Altogether my mind was richly occupied with my spring and where I should place it and how I should use it to my profit. I already planned splendid buildings for the comfort of the spa guests and to gain good money by treating them. I intended to persuade the doctors with bribes to praise my miraculous medicinal well above all others and to send me heaps of rich clients. Already I moved whole hills in my imagination so that the travellers should not complain about the hazards of the road. I hired cunning ostlers, thrifty cooks, careful chambermaids, observant grooms, clean attendants for the bath and spring. I planned a pleasure garden levelled out of the wilderness for the guests and their wives to enjoy, where the patients could be refreshed and the healthy amused with games. I would urge the physicians with a fee to write a splendid treatise about the magnificent qualities of my spring, which I would print embellished with a beautiful copper engraving, so that any patient by reading it would almost regain his health through hope. I fancied to fetch all my children from Lippstadt that they might learn something suitable to assist at my new spa. But none should become a barber as I intended to suck my guest's money but not their blood!

With such thoughts of wealth and fortunate speculation I reached the air again, the water prince putting me out of his Mummelsee to land with my clothes dry! At once I had to return the magic jewel which he had given to me when he fetched me or else I had been drowned in the air or must put my head under water to breathe – such was the power of this talisman. When the prince had taken back the stone we blessed each other as people who would never see one another again. Then he dived with his attendants and went down into the depths, and I departed with the stone which the King had given to me, full of happiness as if I had gained the golden fleece from Colchis.

But alas! My joy did not last long, for hardly had I left that miraculous lake when I began to lose my way in the frightening forest as I had given no attention to the way when my dad had brought me to the lake. I had covered a good distance before I was aware of my error, so that I strayed farther and farther away from the place which I most eagerly wished to reach – and, worse still, I did not notice this before the sun went down and I was hopelessly lost. There I stood in the middle of the wilderness, without food and arms which I might need during the approaching night, but I was consoled by the stone which I had brought from the innermost bowels of the earth. "Be patient!" I said to myself. "My stone will reward me for all my torment; good things take time and splendid achievements need toil and labour, or else every fool would hope without effort to produce such a noble spring as I carry in my pocket."

With such comfort I found new strength and I walked along more bravely although night had engulfed me. The full moon shone well, but the tall fir trees dimmed its light just as the deep ocean had done the day before, yet I walked on until at midnight I perceived a distant fire and I made my way there.

From a distance I could see that there were some forest peasants who were collecting resin: although one cannot always trust such fellows, my need forced and my courage persuaded me to approach them.

I sneaked up to them unnoticed, saying:

"Good night or good morning or good evening, gentlemen! Tell me what is the hour before I can greet you accordingly!"

There they sat or stood, all six of them, trembling with fear not knowing what to answer. I was the tallest of them all and as I wore black in mourning for my wife and was carrying a terrifying cudgel on which I leant like a wild man of the woods, I appeared to them horrifying.

"How," I said, "will no one answer me?"

But still they remained silent in astonishment until one recovered and asked: "Who be that gintleman?"

By the accent I heard they must be Swabian peasants who generally but wrongly are considered simpletons. Therefore I said:

"I am a travelling scholar just come from the Venusberg where I have learnt a lot of miraculous arts."

"Oh," answered the oldest peasant, "thank heaven – now I believe we may five in peace again as the wandering scholars start to travel once more."

Thus we began our conversation and I enjoyed so much courtesy from them that they bade me sit down at their fire and offered me a chunk of black bread and dry cheese which I accepted gratefully. Finally they became quite intimate and begged me as a travelling scholar to tell their fortunes. As I understood something of physiognomy and chiromancy I began to talk big to one after the other intending to make them happy for I did not want to lose credit among this uncomfortable rabble of wild woodmen. They were anxious to learn all sorts of strange arts from me but I put them off until the morrow and begged them to grant me some rest.

Having played the gypsy, I lay down close by, more to listen and find out what was in their minds than to sleep, although I had a great desire to doze. The more I appeared to snore, the busier they became; they put their heads together and argued and guessed who I might be – I could not be a soldier because I wore black garments, nor could I be a townsman as I wandered at such an uncommon hour far from habitation through the Mückenloch, as this wood was apparently called. At last they agreed I must be a Latin artisan who had lost his way, or as I had told them a travelling scholar as I knew so well how to tell fortunes.

But one of them protested: "He did not know everything. Perhaps he is a wicked soldier in disguise to spy upon our cattle and our hide-outs in the forest. If only we knew how, we should put him to sleep so that he would forever forget how to stand up again."

Another contradicted him whilst I lay there pricking up my ears, thinking that if these rogues attacked me, two or three of them would bite the dust before they could butcher me.

As they argued together and I worried myself with fear, I suddenly felt as if somebody had pissed into my bed since I found myself lying in water. O, shame, now Troy was lost and all my splendid projects had gone! At the smell I could recognize that it was a mineral spring which was created prematurely for the magic stone had slipped out of my pocket. In rage and disappointment I fell into such a fury that I almost went for all six peasants. I jumped about with my terrible cudgel and shouted:

"You godless rascals, this medicinal well which springs out from my resting place will show you who I am! You should not be surprised if I punish you all that the Devil may fetch you, as you had such wicked ideas in your mind." With these words I made such threatening and terrifying gestures that all were frightened of me.

But soon I regained my balance of mind and realized what folly I had done. No, thought I, it is better to lose the spring than my life which I might easily squander if I scuffled with these bumpkins. So I spoke again kindly words before they had a change of mind: "Stand up and taste this wonderful well, which you all – resin and timber men, will henceforth enjoy through my favour in this wilderness!"

They could not grasp my meaning but looked at each other like living stockfish until they saw that quite soberly I took the first draught (using my hat). One after the other stood up from the fire, inspected the miracle and tasted the water. But instead of being grateful to me they started to curse and to shout that I should move myself with my spring to another place, for if the lord of the manor would hear of it the whole district of Dornstetten would have to do forced labour and build roads to the place, which would bring great burdens upon them.

"On the contrary," I replied, "you will all have advantage from it, for you will sell your fowls, eggs, butter and cattle for better money."

But they said: "No, no, his lordship will install an innkeeper who alone will grow rich whilst we will be his fools to keep the roads and bridges in order, thereby getting no thanks!"

In the end they quarrelled among themselves: two of them wished to keep the spring whilst four demanded me to remove the well, which, had it only been in my power, I would gladly have done without their wish whether they liked it or not.

As now the day began to break and I had nothing more to do and I feared we would come to blows I said to them: "If you do not wish that all the cows in the whole valley of Baiersbronn will give red milk as long as the spring flows, show me at once the way to Seebach!"

To this they agreed and gave me two men as escort, for one alone was frightened to accompany me. I departed in this way and although the whole district was barren and bore nothing but pine cones, I would gladly have cursed it to even greater misery for here I had lost all my hopes. Silently I marched on with my guides until we reached the top of the mountain where I could find my whereabouts again. There I said to them: "My good men, you could have fine profit from the new spring if you will inform the landlord of its origin and you will get a good reward, as the prince will improve it to the glory and advantage of the whole country and will proclaim it for his own interest to the world."

"Indeed," they replied, "we would truly be fools to cut a rod for our own behinds. Rather may the Devil fetch you and your spring. Haven't you heard already enough why we don't like it?"

"You hopeless blockheads!" I answered them. "Should I not call you perjuring villains abandoning the loyalty of your pious forefathers, who were so faithful to their prince that he could lay his head in the lap of any of his subjects and there rest in safety? And you, thieving rats, are so dishonest for fear of a little labour, which in time would repay you and reward you and your offspring, that you refuse the blessing of this healing spring to your noble prince and to many sick people. What harm would it do to you if you toiled a few days to that purpose?"

"What!" they said, "We would rather slay you to keep the spring secret!"

"There should be more of you gallows-birds for that!" I cried, and swung my cudgel and chased them away in the name of the Devil. With much labour and effort I reached my farm towards sunset and found what my dad had predicted was true – that I had gained nothing from this pilgrimage but tired legs, and the way there as well as the way back.

26

SIMPLICIUS REJOINS THE SWEDISH ARMY,
TRAVELS TO MOSCOW, AND FINALLY
RETURNS TO HIS BOOKS

AFTER MY RETURN, I lived in retirement; my greatest joy and pleasure was to sit over my books, of which I had collected many, especially those which needed meditation, but very soon I loathed all that grammatists and pedantic scholars must achieve in knowledge, and tired soon of arithmetic too. Music I had also begun to hate some time ago like the plague so that I shattered my lute into a thousand pieces. Mathematics and geometry still enjoyed my favour but when I came to study astronomy I dismissed these too and indulged in the latter as well as in astrology, where for a while I found great delight. But finally they too appeared false and uncertain to me that I did not pursue them so that in the end I embraced the art of Raimundus Lullus, the alchemist,* but found there only noise and little sense and discharged it as a deceit to find refuge in the Cabbala of the Hebrews and the hieroglyphs of the Egyptians. In the end I discovered that of all the sciences and arts, nothing was better than theology, if with its help one loves and serves God.

With the guidance of theology I constructed a theory for men to live their lives, which however was more suited for angels than humans – that is, if a society of men and women could be assembled, who following the example of the Anabaptists, would combine their efforts to gain their livelihood through their hands' labour and devote the rest of their time to the praise and service of God and their souls' salvation.

I had seen such a way of living among the Anabaptists in Hungary and I would have voluntarily joined them and considered their way of life the happiest in the whole world, if they had not observed some heretical ideas, for their work and life was as Josephus and other Jewish Essenes have described. They had great possessions and abundance of food and wasted nothing. There was no cursing, no discontent and no impatience among them, indeed no futile word was heard. Craftsmen worked in their workshops as if they were paid piecework; the schoolmaster instructed the youth as if they were his own children. Nowhere did I discover men and women together but each sex fulfilled the appropriate work at a special place. I found rooms occupied only with expectant mothers who together with their children were nursed by their sisters. Other specific rooms contained nothing but cradles and their newly-born babes, fed and cleaned by special attendants so that their mothers had nothing to do but to offer them their breasts three times daily. Further I saw women engaged with spinning only, more than a hundred spinning wheels in one room. Each occupation was orderly distributed among the women, and the same applied to the trades of men and youths. If one fell ill he had his own male or female nurse, doctor and apothecary, although because of the excellent diet and healthy regulations sickness was rare. I saw many fine old men of sound and peaceful age, scarcely to be found elsewhere. They had their special hours for eating and for sleeping, but no single minute for games or walks, except the youths, who for health reasons walked with their teacher after meals when they prayed and sang spiritual songs.

There was no rage, no jealousy, no revenge, no enmity, no worries for material matters, no pride and no regret! In short everything went in most pleasant harmony with one aim only: to propagate the human race and God's empire in all honesty. No man saw his wife except at certain times to share her bedchamber in which was nothing but a bed, a chamber pot, a water jug and white towel so that he could go to bed with clean hands and arise the next day ready for work. They called each other brothers and sisters and in this familiarity there was no trace of unchastity.

Such a blissful life as these heretic Anabaptists lead, I would have loved to lead as well, for I thought it even surpassed life in a monastery, and if I were to succeed in such honest Christian work I might become a new St Dominic or St Francis. On the other hand I said to myself:

"Fool, what concern are other people to you? Join the order of the Capuchin monks, as you have anyway taken a dislike to all wenches!"

Yet soon again I considered that tomorrow is not today and who knows what strength I might need to follow the road of Christ. Today I might be inclined to chastity but tomorrow I might regret it. With such and like thoughts I pondered for a long time. Gladly would I have given my estate and all my property to such a Christian community only to be one of them, but my dad predicted at once that I would never find such a community.

During that autumn, French, Swedish and Hessian troops arrived to recoup in our district and at the same time to blockade our neighbouring Free City, Offenburg, named after an English King.* All the peasants therefore, with their cattle and most precious possessions, fled to the forests in the mountains. I did what my neighbours did and left my house almost empty in which a Swedish colonel took lodgings. He found in my cabinet some books which in my haste I could not remove, and among them were some mathematical and geometrical drawings and sketches of fortifications which are usually designed by engineers. He at once concluded that his quarters could not belong to an ordinary peasant and made enquiries after me, wishing to make my acquaintance, and in the end succeeded by courteous offers intermixed with threats, that I went to see him on my own farm. Here he treated me most politely and instructed his soldiers not to cause unnecessary harm to my property. With such friendliness he won my confidence so that I told him all my personal circumstances, especially about my family and descent. He was amazed that in the midst of war I lived among peasants, tolerating that a strange man tethered his horse at my fence whereas with more merit I could have tethered my own horse to the fence of any man alive. He said I should take up my sword again and not let the gifts which God had given to me rot behind the oven and the plough, and if I would accept Swedish service, my ability and knowledge of the science of war would soon bring me to high rank.

I remained disinterested and told him that advancement would be far away if a man had no friends to help him. However he replied that my qualities would soon secure me both friends and advancement and he had no doubts that I would find kinsmen of high rank in the Swedish army as many Scottish noblemen served there. He himself had been promised a regiment from von Torstenson, and if this promise were kept he would make me at once his lieutenant-colonel. With such and similar words he made my mouth water, and since there was little hope for peace and I only had to expect further troops to be billeted on my farm, which meant complete ruin, I decided at last to soldier again and promised the colonel to go with him if he would keep his word and confer on me the post of lieutenant-colonel in his future regiment.

Thus the die was cast. I sent for my dad and godfather, who was still with my cattle at Baiersbronn, and transferred my farm to him and his wife as their property, on condition that after his death my bastard son, Simplicius, who was laid upon my doorstep, should inherit everything, as no legitimate heirs existed. Then I fetched my horse and all that I possessed in gold and jewels, having arranged my affairs and the education of my son. Suddenly the blockade of Offenburg was lifted, so that without delay we had to depart and march to join the main army. I acted as the colonel's

marshal and maintained his household and all his horses and men by stealing and robbing, which is called foraging in the language of the soldier.

The Torstenson's promises, of which he had boasted so at my farm,
were far less important than he had pretended, indeed he seemed to be
rather looked down upon.

"Oh," he said, "what villainous dog has slandered me at Headquarters;
I can't stay much longer here!"

As he now suspected I would have no more patience with him, he pretended to have received orders from Livonia, where his home was, to recruit
a fresh regiment, and persuaded me to embark in Wismar for Livonia. There
too was nothing, for not only had he no regiment to raise but altogether
he was a very poor nobleman, and what he had all came from his wife.

Although I had been deceived the second time and had been abducted
so far away, I was persuaded even for the third time. He showed me letters from Moscow in which, as he pretended, high war commands were
offered to him, at least this is how he translated the letters to me, and he
boasted highly of good and generous pay. And seeing him departing at
once with wife and children, I was sure that he went there not to chase
geese. Therefore I went with him in good hope as I could see no chance
and means anyhow to return to Germany.

When we had crossed the Russian border we met several disbanded
German soldiers, especially officers, so that I began to feel dismayed and
said to my colonel:

"Why the devil are we here? We leave a country where there is war – and
where there is peace and the soldiers out of favour and sacked, there we go!"

Yet he still lulled me with consoling words and said that I should let
him worry as he knew better what to do than those fellows who were
good-for-nothings.

As soon as we had safely arrived in Moscow I realized at once that it
was all a blunder. My colonel conferred daily with the magnates, but more
with the officials of the church than with the nobility, which caused me
great concern and doubt, not knowing what was his purpose. At last he
revealed to me that there was no hope for a war but that his conscience
urged him to embrace the Greek Orthodox religion. His most trustworthy
advice was that I should do the same since he was unable to help me as
promised. His Majesty the Tsar had already received good reports of my
person and my great abilities and was graciously willing to endow me as
a nobleman with a magnificent estate with many serfs, if I would submit
to his conditions. This benign offer I should not refuse, as it was more

advisable to have such a powerful monarch as a gracious lord than as an affronted prince.

This made me quite bewildered that I did not know what to answer; if I had been with the colonel in another country I would have answered him rather with my fists than with words. But so I had to change my tune and conform to the place, where I was like so to say a prisoner and I therefore remained silent until I could think of an answer. At last I said to him that I had come with the intent to serve the Tsar's Majesty as a soldier, to which the colonel had encouraged me; and if my services in war were not needed, I would not blame His Majesty for my having made such a long journey in vain as he had not written to me to come. However I wanted to praise His Majesty's graciousness before the world but I could at the moment not resolve myself to change my religion, but only wished to return to my farm in the Black Forest and trouble no one with my affairs.

To which he replied that I should do what pleased me most but I should consider that when God and good fortune smiled at me, I should be grateful to both, and if I refused all help to live like a prince, I should at least acknowledge that he had done his best for me! Thereupon he made a deep bow and left me sitting there not even allowing me to see him to the door.

As I sat in all perplexity and pondered over my predicament, I heard two Russian coaches before my lodging, and, looking through the window, I saw my good colonel entering one of these with his sons while his wife and daughters got into the other. They were the Tsar's carriages and lackeys and, moreover, several clergymen, who displayed reverence and goodwill to this couple.

From now on I was watched – not openly but secretly – by some Strelitz guards. My colonel and his family I never saw again and I knew not what had become of him, which caused me many worries and grey hair. I made the acquaintance of Germans who lived in Moscow as merchants and artisans, and told them how dangerously I had been deceived. They gave me comfort and advice of how with good opportunity I could return to Germany. But as soon as they got wind that the Tsar was determined to keep me in his country by force, they all became silent, indeed they shunned me. It was even difficult to find quarters for myself – my horse including saddle and bridle I had already sold for my livelihood.

Every day I ripped another of my ducats out of my clothes, into which I had wisely stitched them. In the end I began to change my rings and jewels into silver, hoping to keep myself until a good opportunity came to make my way back to Germany. So a quarter of a year passed; the colonel and all his family had changed their religion and had been bestowed with a considerable nobleman's estate and many serfs.

At this time a Government mandate under pain of heavy punishment was issued that, among natives and foreigners alike, idlers would no longer be tolerated, for these eat the bread from the mouths of the workers. All strangers who would not work had to leave the country within a month and the town within twenty-four hours! So about fifty of us joined company, trying to find our way together through Podolia to Germany. Hardly two hours from Moscow we were overtaken by several Russian troopers with the pretext that His Majesty the Tsar had found great displeasure in that we wickedly had dared to band together in such numbers and cross his country wantonly without a pass, adding that His Majesty was entitled to send us to Siberia for this insolent behaviour.

On the way back I learnt how matters stood, for the commander of the troop assured me that the Tsar would never let me out of the country. His own friendly advice was to submit to His Majesty's most gracious will, to embrace his religion and like the colonel not disregard a pleasant estate, adding that if I would refuse to live among them as a nobleman, I would be forced to serve them as a serf. Nor could His Majesty the Tsar be blamed for not permitting such an experienced man (as the colonel had described me) to leave the country.

Then I belittled myself and said that the colonel probably had attributed to me more arts, virtues and knowledge than I possessed. I had come to this country to serve His Majesty and the praiseworthy Russian nation against their enemies even with the offer of my blood; yet I could not resolve to change my religion, but would do my utmost everywhere to serve His Majesty without burdening my conscience.

I was separated from the others and lodged with a merchant, where I was from now on publicly watched but supplied daily with splendid food and precious drinks from the Court. Every day people came to visit and persuade and occasionally asked me to be their guest. There was especially one man, to whom I doubtlessly was recommended, a cunning fellow, with whom I had daily friendly conversations as I could already speak Russian quite fluently. He spoke mostly about all sorts of mechanical arts, of machines of war, of fortifications and artillery and the like. In the end after much beating about the bush and having assured himself that under no circumstances I would adopt the Russian religion, he prayed I should at least to the honour of the great Tsar reveal to their nation some of my knowledge, which would be acknowledged with great Imperial favours.

To this I answered that it had always been my desire most obediently to serve His Majesty the Tsar, to which purpose I had come to his country; my intentions were still the same, although I saw that I was kept like a prisoner.

"Not at all, Sir," he answered. "You are not a prisoner but His Majesty the Tsar only loves you so much that he does not wish to lose you."

"Why then," I asked, "am I guarded?"

"Because," he answered, "His Majesty fears some harm may come to you."

As he now understood my proposals, he said that the Tsar graciously wished to dig for saltpetre in his own land and to produce gunpowder, but as there was nobody among them able to do it, I would do him a welcome service if I would undertake the work. I should be sufficiently supplied with men and material and he personally advised me in the friendliest manner not to refuse this most gracious demand as they were already fully informed that I was well experienced in these matters.

I replied: "Sir, I repeat that I am willing to serve His Majesty the Tsar in everything and if only he will graciously let me adhere to my religion, I assure him of my greatest effort."

With that the Russian, who belonged to the highest nobility, was delighted, so that he drank with me more than any German.

The next day the Tsar sent two noblemen and an interpreter to make a final agreement with me and presented me with a precious Russian robe. A few days later I began to search for saltpetre in the ground and to teach the Russians who were attached to me how to separate the saltpetre from the earth and refine it. I designed a plan for a powder-mill and instructed others to burn charcoal, so in a very short time we manufactured a considerable amount of best musket powder and coarse powder for the guns, for I had men enough in addition to my own servants who had to wait on me (or better, to spy and watch over me).

As I made such a good beginning, my colonel came to me in Russian robes in a stately procession and with many servants. Without doubt he wished to persuade me through this splendour to change my religion. But I knew too well that his clothes were only borrowed from the Tsar's wardrobe to impress me, as is customary at the Court of the Tsar.

That the reader may understand how these things are done, I will tell one of my own adventures: Once I was busy in the powder-mill, which I had built on the river outside Moscow, giving orders to my men as to the work they should do during the next few days, when suddenly an alarm was given that the Tartars, numbering about 100,000 horses, were plundering the land only four miles away, and advancing steadily. I and my men had to proceed at once to the Court, where we were newly equipped from the Tsar's armoury and stables. Instead of a cuirass I was dressed in an armour of quilted silk which stopped every arrow, but would hardly protect against a bullet. I received boots, spurs and a princely headdress with a bush of heron plumes including a sharp sabre inlaid with pure gold and pearls and precious stones, and from the Tsar's stables a horse the like of which I had never seen nor ridden in my life before. I had a battleaxe of steel hanging at my side, glittering like a mirror, well shaped and so heavy that I could easily kill a man with one blow. Even the Tsar could not have ridden about better equipped.

A white banner with a double eagle followed me, to which from all sides soldiers gathered, so that before two hours had passed we were 40,000, and after four hours about 60,000 horses strong, with which we advanced against the Tartars. Every quarter of an hour I received a new order from the grand Duke with always the same content, namely: Today I should confirm myself as the soldier I professed to be, that His Majesty might acknowledge and recognize me as such.

Every moment our troops multiplied with small and big detachments yet in all haste I saw nobody who would command the whole army and give orders for battle. I will not give all details as my story depends little on this skirmish, but I will say that suddenly we encountered the Tartars in a valley, when they with tired horses and laden with much booty least expected our attack. We assaulted from all sides with such fury that we dispersed them at the first charge. In the first attack I called to those who followed in Russian:

"Forward, everybody shall do what I do!"

And this they all cried to each other, whilst I stormed with loose reins towards the enemy and crushed the first man's head, a prince, that his brain dripped from my battleaxe.

The Russians followed my brave example, so that the Tartars could not withstand their onslaught and turned in general flight. I fought like a madman or better like someone seeking death from desperation, which he cannot find. I crushed everything that came under my hand, be it Tartar or Russian, and my men followed me eagerly, that my back was always guarded. The air was full with arrows as if bees were swarming and one pierced my arm as I had turned up my sleeves, the better to fight and kill. Before the arrow had struck, my heart rejoiced over such bloodshed, but when I saw my own blood running, the laughter turned into demented rage.

After the cruel enemy had retreated in a rout, some noblemen brought me the Tsar's order to report to their emperor how the Tartars had been vanquished. So I rode back, followed by about a hundred horseman. I proceeded through the town to the Tsar's palace, greeted by all the folk with rejoicing and congratulation. But as soon as I had made my report of the battle – although the Tsar had already been informed of all that had happened – I had to give up my princely robes. These went back into the Tsar's wardrobe, although they and the horse's harness were soiled all over with blood and spoilt almost completely. I had expected, since I had fought so well in this battle, the robes together with the horse should have been left to me as a recompense. From this I could imagine how the Russian splendour in robes was handled, of which my colonel boasted; these are all borrowed clothes, which like everything else belongs to the Tsar alone.

As long as my wound was healing I was treated like a prince in every way, and although my wound was neither deadly nor dangerous I walked about dressed in a nightgown of golden brocade lined with sables. Never in my life have I eaten such rich cake as in Moscow, but this was all the reward I received for my labours, except the praise which the Tsar granted me, though this was impaired by the envy of some noblemen.

When I was fully recovered they sent me in a ship down the Volga to Astrakhan to install there a powder mill as in Moscow, for it was impossible to supply these fortresses at the frontier steadily from Moscow with fresh and effective gunpowder, which had to travel such a long way on the water through great hazards. I agreed willingly as I had the promise that after the completion of the work the Tsar would send me back to Holland with a considerable payment of money according to my merits.

But alas! When we think our hopes are nearest to their fulfilment, soon a wind may blow the whole flimsy edifice to pieces on which we have laboured such a long time. The governor of Astrakhan treated me like the Tsar himself and in a short while I put everything in good order. His old ammunition, which had become rotten and useless, I recast as a tinker casts new spoons out of old ones, which was an unheard of novelty among the Russians. For this and other ingenuities, they considered me to be a sorcerer, a new saint, or even a prophet.

But being hard at work and attending a powder-mill outside the fortress over night, I was treacherously captured by a horde of Tartars and with others carried off far into their Asiatic country. They bartered me away for some Chinese goods to the Tartars of Niuchi, who again gave me as a special present to the King of Korea, with whom they had just concluded an armistice. There I was kept in high honour as no one knew the art of fencing as I did, and I taught the King to hit the bull's eye with his rifle on his shoulder and his back towards the target. Therefore at my humble request he granted me freedom and sent me over Japonia to Macao to the Portuguese, who took but little notice of me so that I wandered among them like a lost sheep strayed from his flock.

Finally I was miraculously taken prisoner by some Turkish or Mohammedan pirates who carried me along with them for a whole year at sea among strange tribes in the East Indies and bartered me in the end to some merchants at Alexandria in Egypt. These again took me with their merchandise to Constantinople, and as the Sultan was just then equipping some galleys against the Venetians, he needed rowers, and many Turkish merchants had to sell their Christian slaves for high payments, and being a strong young fellow, I was among them. So I had to learn to row, but this heavy slavery lasted not more than two months.

Our galley was gallantly overwhelmed by the Venetians and I with all my companions freed from the Turkish violence. When the galley was taken with rich booty and several noble Turkish prisoners to Venice, I was given my liberty as I wished to make a pilgrimage to Rome and Loretto to see these places and thank God for my deliverance. To such purpose I easily obtained a pass and from some honest people, especially Germans, a considerable support in money so that I could equip myself with a long pilgrim's garb to begin my journey.

So I walked by the shortest way to Rome, which I managed quite well, since I begged much alms from rich and poor alike. After staying there about six weeks, I continued my pilgrimage with other pilgrims, Germans and Swiss, to Loretto. From there I went over the St Gotthard Pass through Switzerland again into the Black Forest, and to my dad who had taken care of my farm; I brought home nothing else but a beard which had grown in foreign lands. I had been away three years and some months. In this time I had traversed many seas and seen many people, among which I altogether experienced more evil than good. In the mean time, the Westphalian peace treaty had been concluded, so that I could live in safe tranquillity with my dad. I let him care and keep my house, whilst I sat down with my books in which I found my occupation and delight.

27

SIMPLICIUS TURNS AWAY FROM
THE WORLD

I ONCE READ how the oracle of Apollo answered the Roman ambassadors when they questioned how to govern their subjects peacefully: "*Nosce te ipsum!*" which means "Know thyself". Being idle at the time, I brooded over this and decided to render an account to myself of my past life.

I thought: my life has been no life but rather death; my days a black shadow; my years a heavy dream; my lusts wicked sins; my youth a fantasy; my well-being an alchemist's treasure which vanishes up the chimney and leaves you before you are aware! I have followed the war through many a danger and gained much good and much ill fortune. Sometimes I have been high, sometimes cast low, sometimes great, sometimes small, sometimes rich, sometimes poor, sometimes gay, sometimes sad, sometimes beloved, sometimes hated, sometimes honoured and sometimes despised. But now you, oh my poor soul, what have you gained from this long journey? This you have won: I am poor in worldly goods, my heart is burdened with sorrows, to all good deeds I am lazy, idle and corrupt, but the greatest misery which frightens and weighs my conscience down is my soul laden with many sins and horribly polluted. My body is weary, my mind confused, innocence is gone, my prime is wasted, precious time is lost, nothing gladdens me, and above all I am mine own enemy! After my blessed father's death, when I came into this world, then I was simple and pure, sincere and honest, truthful, humble, modest, temperate, chaste, and shy, pious, devout. But soon I became wicked, false, lying, vain, restless and thoroughly godless, and I have learnt all these vices without a master. I cared for my honour not for its own sake but for the sake of my own exaltation. I spent my time not to further my salvation but to please my body. Often I brought my life into danger yet I never tried to better it so that I might die blessed and in peace. I only looked to the present and my timely profit, and not once did I think of the future, much less that I have to give account of my deeds in God's presence.

Daily I tortured myself with such ideas, and just then there came into my hands several writings by Guevara* of which I quote some words as they were so powerful that they made me dislike the world entirely. They were:—

Farewell, oh World, for you are not to be trusted nor do you give hope. In your house the past has gone already, the present disappears under your hands, and the future has never begun. The most permanent tumbles, the most powerful crumbles and the eternal comes to an end. So man is dead among the dead and in a hundred years you do not let us live one hour!

Farewell, oh World, for you imprison us and never release us again. You bind but do not loosen; you sadden but do not console; you rob but do not repay; you accuse yet you have no cause; you condemn yet hear no witness, so that you kill without judging and bury us before we die! With you there is no gladness without grief; no peace without feud; no love without suspicion; no tranquillity without fear; no plenty without want; no honour without blemish; no worldly goods without bad conscience; no class without complaint and no friendship without falsehood.

Farewell, oh World, for in your palace man promises without intent to give; man serves without reward; man caresses in order to kill; man elevates to overthrow; man helps in order to cut down; man honours to defame; man borrows never to repay; man punishes without forgiving!

God be with you, oh World, for in your house the mighty are deposed, the infamous are preferred; traitors are treated with grace, and the faithful are put aside; the wicked are released and the innocent condemned; the wise and capable are dismissed and the fools get high rewards; the treacherous are believed, and sincere and honest men find no trust; each does as he wills and none as he should!

Farewell, oh World, for you call none by his right name! The foolhardy you call brave and the coward cautious; the blustering you call industrious and the lazy one peaceful; a waster you call magnificent and a miser modest; a treacherous gossip you call eloquent and the silent man you call a fool. An adulterer and a raper of virgins you call a lover, and a lewd fellow you call a courtier; a revengeful man you call a zealot and a warm-hearted man you call an oddity. So that you sell us good for bad and bad for good!

Farewell, oh World, for you seduce every man! You promise honour to the ambitious; variety to the disquieted, princely grace to the haughty, a sinecure to the slothful, many treasures to the miser, lust and pleasure to the gluttons and unchaste, revenge to the enemy, secrecy to thieves, long life to the young ones, and continuous princely favour to the flatterers.

Farewell, oh World, for in your palace neither truth nor faithfulness finds a home. He who trusts you is deceived; he who follows you is misled; he who fears you is maltreated; he who loves you is badly rewarded, and he who relies on you entirely is entirely destroyed. With you no gift will help, no service done, no charming words, no faithfulness, no friendship shown to you, but you deceive, depose, defame, soil, threaten, engulf and forget every man! Therefore every man cries, sighs, wails, laments and perishes, and so each finds his end. With you, man hears and learns nothing but to hate each other to destruction, to trade, to theft, and to sin until death.

God be with you, oh World, for whilst we follow you time passes in oblivion, youth is spent in running, jumping over fence and stile, road and path, over hill and vale, through wood and wilderness, over lakes and waters, in rain and snow, in heat and cold, in wind and storm! Manhood is wasted in hewing ore and smelting, in hewing stone and cutting, in chopping and timbering, planting and building; in planning and counselling, in sorrow and complaints, in buying and selling, in feuds and quarrels, in wars, lies and deceit. Old age passes in lamentation and misery, the mind weakens, breath stinking, the face shrivelled, body bent and darkened eyes, limbs tremble, nose drips, the head becomes bald, the hearing fades, the power of smell and taste disappear. Man sighs and wails, is lazy and weak, and he has altogether nothing but work and toil until his death.

Farewell, oh World, for none will be honest in you. Daily murderers are executed; traitors are quartered; thieves are hanged; highwaymen, freebooters and killers are beheaded; witches are burned, perjurors punished and rebels exiled.

Farewell, oh World, for your servants have no other work but idleness, to cheat each other, to court maidens, to attend fair ladies, and to flirt with them; to play cards and dice, and to deal with procurers; to wrangle with neighbours, tell the latest gossip, indulge in new tricks and usury, create new clothes, produce new intrigues and new vices.

Farewell, oh World, for nobody is content with you! If he is poor, he hankers after gain; if he is rich he expects glory; if he is despised he wants esteem; and if he is insulted he wants revenge.

Farewell, oh World, for with you is no constancy. The high towers are shattered by thunderbolt; the mills are washed away by the waters; the wood is eaten up by worms; the corn by mice; the fruit by caterpillars, and cloth by moths; cattle perish with age and poor men with disease! One has scabs, the other cancer, a third has ulcers, the fourth the French disease, the fifth gout, the sixth arthritis, the seventh dropsy, the eighth stones, the ninth grit in the bladder, the tenth consumption, the eleventh fever, the twelfth leprosy, the thirteenth epilepsy and the fourteenth is mad!

In you, oh World, not one is doing what the other does, for if one is crying the other laughs; if one is sighing the other is gay; if one is fasting the other drinks; if one feasts the other hungers; if one rides the other walks; if one talks the other is silent; one plays, another works and if one is born another dies!

Behold not one lives as the other, for one rules and the other serves; one tends men, the other tends pigs; one follows the court, another the plough; one travels on the seas, another over land to the markets; one works in fire, another in the earth; one fishes in the water and another catches birds in the air; one toils with great effort and another steals and robs the land.

Oh, World, God be with you, for in your house, man leads no holy life nor finds an easy death; one dies in the cradle, the other in his youth on his bed, the third on the rope, the fourth by the sword, the fifth on the wheel, the sixth at the stake, the seventh in the wineglass, the eighth in a river of water, the ninth suffocates in his bowl of food, the tenth chokes with poison, the eleventh dies suddenly by a stroke, the twelfth in a battle, the thirteenth through witchcraft and the fourteenth drowns his poor soul in the inkpot.

God be with you, oh World! I am tired of your company! The life you are giving us is a miserable pilgrimage, an inconstant, uncertain, hard, rough, fleeting, unclean life, full of poverty and error, which should rather be called death than life, and in which we die every moment through many illnesses and many ways of death. You give from the golden chalice which you hold in your hands bitterness and falsehood and make the poor man blind, deaf, mad and senseless! Oh, blessed are those who refuse your company, who forgo your fleeting pleasures and do not perish with such a treacherous impostor. For you turn us into a dark abyss, into a miserable piece of earth, a child of rage, a stinking carrion, an unclean vessel in the dung, a vessel of decay full of stench and horror! For when you have tortured us long enough with flattery, caresses, threats, beatings, torments, so you allow the exhausted body into the grave and leave the soul in uncertainty. For though nothing is more certain than death, man is unaware how, when and where he will die, and what is most miserable how his soul will fare and what its fate will be! Woe, then, the poor soul which has served and obeyed you, oh World, and followed your lusts and extravagances! For if such a sinful and unconverted poor soul has left the miserable body suddenly, the soul will not be surrounded as the body was with servants and friends, but it will be led by a host of most horrible enemies to Christ's seat of judgment!

Therefore, oh World, God be with you, for I know that you will forsake me when my poor soul will appear in the presence of the stern Judge and when the most frightful judgment will be pronounced: "depart, ye condemned into the eternal fire!"

Farewell, oh World, oh base and evil World! Oh stinking, miserable flesh! Because of you and because one has followed and served you, the godless unrepentant is sentenced to eternal damnation; in which for all eternity nothing else is to be expected but instead of past pleasures, misery without consolation; instead of carousing, thirst unquenchable; instead of feasting, hunger without relief; instead of glory and magnificence, darkness without light; instead of pleasure, pains without deliverance; instead of exultation and triumph, howling, whining and lament without cessation; heat without cooling, fire without quenching, coldness immeasurable and distress without end.

God be with you, oh World, for instead of your promised pleasures, the evil spirits will get hold of the unrepentant damned soul and pull it down into the abyss of hell! Thence it will hear and see nothing but horrifying shapes of devils and condemned souls, sheer darkness and vapours, fire without glow, screaming, howling, gnashing of teeth and blasphemy!

God be with you, oh World, for although the body will stay for a while in this earth and decay, on the Last Day it will rise again and will after the Last Judgment be together with the soul in the eternal fire of hell! Then, the poor soul will say: "Cursed be with you, O World, for through your temptation I have forgotten God and myself and I followed you in all your voluptuousness, wickedness, sin and shame, all the days of my life. Cursed be the hour in which God created me! Cursed be the day on which I was born in you, oh evil, wicked World! Oh, ye mountains, hills and rocks fall upon me and hide me from the stern anger of the Lamb and from the face of Him who is sitting on the throne and judging the living and the dead." Oh woe, and woe again, in eternity!

Oh World! You unclean World! Therefore, I exorcize you, I pray you, I implore you, admonish and protest against you. From now on you shall have no part of me and I want nothing more from you. You know what I intend: *posui finem curis; spes et fortuna valete!*

On all these words I pondered thoroughly and they moved me so deeply that I left the world and became again an hermit. I would have liked to live near my health-giving well in the Mückenloch, but the peasants in the neighbourhood would not endure it, although for me it was a pleasant wilderness: they feared I would betray the well and urge their authorities to force them to build roads to it, as peace was now established. Therefore I went into another wilderness and started my life again as I led it in the Spessart.

Whether I shall stay there to my end, as my blessed father had done before me, I do not know. May God give us all his grace so that we may receive from him that which is most precious to us—

A BLESSED

END

NOTES

p. 11, *Nova Zembla*: Novaya Zemlya, an archipelago in the northern part of Russia.

p. 32, *Johann von Werth… St Andreas*: Generals and leaders in the Thirty Years War, risen from humble origin.

p. 33, *Battle of Nördlingen*: A crushing victory of the Imperial Army over the Swedes. It took place on 6th September 1634.

p. 40, *General Mansfeld*: Peter Ernst, Count of Mansfeld (*c*.1580–1626).

p. 42, *Ramsay*: Jacob von Ramsay (1589–1639), governor in Hanau, commanding the Swedish and Hessian troops.

p. 85, *Duke Bernhard of Weimar*: Bernhard of Saxe-Weimar (1604–39), supreme commander of the Swedish army after the death of King Gustav Adolph in November 1632.

p. 87, *mill fleas*: Lice.

p. 87, *Melander, the Hessian general*: Greek version of the name "Eppelmann", the original family name of Peter, Count of Holzappel (1589–1648), Imperial field-marshal.

p. 94, *Magdeburg*: This reference is to the second siege of 1636. The first fall of Magdeburg was in 1631 under Tilly, when the town was completely destroyed.

p. 106, *the Battle of Wittstock*: The battle, a Swedish victory under Johann Banér (1596–1641) as Commander-in-Chief, took place on 4th October 1636.

p. 108, *von Hatzfeldt*: Melchior von Hatzfeldt (1593–1658), general of the Imperial forces besieging Magdeburg.

p. 108, *von Wallenstein, Duke of Friedland*: Albrecht von Wallenstein (1583–1634), supreme commander of the Imperial army, murdered at Eger in February 1634.

p. 109, *Havelberg and Perleberg… our troops*: Havelberg surrendered in August 1636, and Perleberg fell at the end of September the same year.

p. 119, *ohmen*: An old measure for wine, equal to approximately two buckets.

p. 133, *great god*: A reference to a large silver Crucifix in the church of St Patroclus at Soest.

p. 143, *Schlaraffenland*: In German folklore, a fairyland with abundance of food and pleasure without toil and care – a Land of Cockaigne.

p. 150, *Count von der Wahl*: Johann Joachim, Graf von Wahl (1590–1644). He moved into Westphalia with the Imperial corps in 1637.

p. 159, *a Count Palatine*: An Imperial official empowered to grant titles.

p. 178, *Arcadia*: *The Countess of Pembroke's Arcadia*, a pastoral romance by Sir Philip Sidney (1554–86).

p. 211, *French disease*: Syphilis.

p. 225, *Brethren of Merode*: Grimmelshausen's explanation of the word is mistaken: it is not derived from the name of the French general Merode, but from the French word "maraud", i.e. "scamp", "good-for-nothing".

p. 226, *Siege of Breisach*: Besieged by Bernhard von Weiman, Breisach finally fell on 18th December 1638.

p. 235, *Burchiello or Aretino*: Domenico di Giovanni (better known as "Il Burchiello", 1404–49) was a famous writer of eccentric satirical sonnets; Pietro Aretino (1492–1556) was the main satirist of his age, and is remembered for his burlesque and salacious writings.

p. 266, *When Count Mansfeld had lost the battle at Höchst*: Mansfeld was defeated by Tilly at Höchst in June 1622.

p. 288, *Raimundus Lullus, the alchemist*: The famous Catalan philosopher and theologian Ramon Llull (*c.*1232–*c.*1315). In Grimmelshausen's time, he was regarded by some as an alchemist, because a large body of alchemical works had been falsely attributed to Llull.

p. 289, *Offenburg, named after an English King*: According to a German legend, Offenburg was founded by the King Offa of Mercia (d. 796 AD).

p. 299, *Guevara*: Antonio de Guevara (1480-1545), a Spanish bishop and moralist writer who was appointed royal chronicler to of Charles V.

EVERGREENS SERIES

Beautifully produced classics, affordably priced

Alma Classics is committed to making available a wide range of literature from around the globe. Most of the titles are enriched by an extensive critical apparatus, notes and extra reading material, as well as a selection of photographs. The texts are based on the most authoritative editions and edited using a fresh, accessible editorial approach. With an emphasis on production, editorial and typographical values, Alma Classics aspires to revitalize the whole experience of reading classics.

For our complete list and latest offers

visit

almabooks.com/evergreens

ALMA CLASSICS

ALMA CLASSICS aims to publish mainstream and lesser-known European classics in an innovative and striking way, while employing the highest editorial and production standards. By way of a unique approach the range offers much more, both visually and textually, than readers have come to expect from contemporary classics publishing.

LATEST TITLES PUBLISHED BY ALMA CLASSICS

www.almaclassics.com